The Command

THE COMMAND

Christopher Nicole

C

CENTURY

LONDON SYDNEY AUCKLAND JOHANNESBURG

First published in Great Britain in 1989
by Century Hutchinson Ltd
Brookmount House, 62–65 Chandos Place
London WC2N 4NW

Century Hutchinson South Africa Ltd
PO Box 337, Bergvlei 2012
South Africa

Century Hutchinson Australia Pty Ltd
89–91 Albion Street, Surry Hills
NSW 2010 Australia

Century Hutchinson New Zealand Ltd
PO Box 40–086, Glenfield 10
Auckland, New Zealand

British Library Cataloguing in Publication Data

Nicole, Christopher, *1930–*
The command.
I. Title.
823′.914 [F]

ISBN 0–7126–2570–4

Filmset by Deltatype, Ellesmere Port
Printed and bound in Great Britain by
Mackays of Chatham PLC, Chatham, Kent

This is a novel. The characters, except where they can be identified historically, are invented and are not intended to depict real persons, living or dead. Similarly, there is no such regiment as the Royal Western Dragoon Guards, and the campaign against the Mahsuds in 1929 is invented, although based upon previous campaigns in Waziristan.

The wars and other battles depicted in the book are however based on fact, and are recounted as accurately as the story will allow.

Contents

Prologue – 1984 1

Part One   The Colonel

Chapter 1   England, 1914 11
Chapter 2   France, 1915 30
Chapter 3   Mesopotamia, 1916 58
Chapter 4   Mesopotamia, 1916–17 87
Chapter 5   France, 1917–18 112

Part Two   The General

Chapter 6   England, 1918–23 139
Chapter 7   Germany, 1924 165
Chapter 8   India, 1924 188
Chapter 9   The North West Frontier, 1925–29 219
Chapter 10   The North West Frontier, 1929 249

Part Three   The Veteran

Chapter 11   England, 1929–33 289
Chapter 12   England, 1933–38 317
Chapter 13   Holland, 1939–40 345
Chapter 14   Holland, 1940 372
Chapter 15   Dunkirk, 1940 400

Prologue
May 1984

'Good evening, sir,' greeted the doorman at the Savoy Hotel, London, holding the door of the taxi to allow the young man to step down. 'Regimental dinner, is it?' He regarded the sky-blue shell jacket, the burnished helmet carried under the arm, the dark blue breeches with the yellow stripe, the highly polished black boots, lacking spurs, and the cavalry sword hanging at the new arrival's side. If the guest appeared as a relic from a long-forgotten imperial past, he was not the first such to enter the hotel this evening.

One of the under-managers was waiting for him. 'It's down the stairs and on the left, sir,' he explained confidentially.

'Thank you.' The Second-Lieutenant crossed the floor, heels clicking, trying to ignore the curious stares of the people in the lobby, and descended the stairs, breathing a sigh of relief as he saw the Sergeant-Major, also wearing full dress uniform, standing before the door to one of the banqueting rooms. 'Lieutenant Manly-Smith,' he murmured diffidently.

The Sergeant-Major came to attention. 'Lieutenant Manly-Smith, sir,' he repeated, as if he did not already know the newcomer by sight. 'The Colonel hasn't arrived yet, sir. You're in good time.' He knew how nervous the boy was. 'Why don't you go in, sir?'

'Ah. Yes.' Lieutenant Manly-Smith stepped through the doorway, pausing again as he did so. The large room was festooned with bunting, dominated by the huge light blue regimental flag, but surrounded by others, ensigns and standards representing the battle honours won by the Royal Western Dragoon Guards during their remarkable history.

Sedgmoor – the regiment had been raised by Sir William Lord of Taunton in 1683 just to oppose Monmouth's Rebellion – and Blenheim, Minden and Busaco, Salamanca and Vittoria, Waterloo and Chillianwallah, Kabul and the Modder River, Le Cateau and Amiens, Dunkirk and El Alamein, the list seemed endless. Beneath the flags the long tables sagged under the weight of the regimental silver; there were four tables, a top and three arms stretching away from it, with the centre arm slightly longer than the others. Along the near wall had been placed another long table, on which the helmets of those diners who had already arrived were arranged.

The room was filled with officers, past and present, from youthful second-lieutants only just senior to Manly-Smith himself to active captains and retired majors, all wearing the unique sky-blue jacket – a reminder of the Peninsular War, when, the original red tunics having worn out and no replacements being available, the then lieutenant-colonel had obtained permission from the Duke of Wellington to clothe his men out of his own pocket. Sky-blue had been the only colour of material available in sufficient quantity. Already known as 'Lord's Own', from the name of their founder, the nickname had promptly been changed to 'Heaven's Own' by the rest of the army, and had been worn with distinction and pride ever since.

'Manly-Smith! Bright and early.'

'Wilson! Thank God!' Manly-Smith greeted his fellow junior, just a year his elder.

'Scared, are we?' Wilson grinned.

'Weren't you, last year?'

'It pays to be keyed up. Now, you have it all memorized, I hope?'

'I think so.'

'You'd better, boy, or it'll be civvy street for you tomorrow. Come along.' He murmured apologies to senior officers as he escorted Manly-Smith through their ranks to stand behind the centre of the top table. Most of them, recognizing that one of the pair had to be the junior lieutenant and was therefore about to undergo the greatest ordeal of his life, gave way readily enough.

'Now,' Wilson said, indicating the huge framed painting hanging on the wall. 'Tell me all about that picture. The Mackinders will expect you to do that for them.'

Manly-Smith licked his lips. He was looking at the most famous episode in the entire history of the Royal Western Dragoons. The painting depicted an enormous number of turbaned warriors, some on horseback, most on foot, milling about a sunbaked Pakistani plain beneath a brilliantly blue sky, and being charged by about four hundred horsemen armed with swords and wearing sky-blue jackets, weapons pointed in front of them as they followed their commander into what seemed certain death.

'Come on, come on,' Wilson said. 'They'll be here any moment now.'

Manly-Smith licked his lips again. 'That was April 1843,' he said. 'Just after the battle of Hyderabad, when Sir George Napier was completing the conquest of Sind. Two squadrons of the Royal Westerns were detailed to carry out a reconnaissance towards the Baluchi position. Their commanding officer was Major Ian Mackinder, a Scot who had only recently been seconded to the regiment, but was in acting command owing to the illness of the lieutenant-colonel. The regiment was led into a trap by its guides, and found itself surrounded by fifteen thousand Baluchis, who summoned Major Mackinder to surrender.'

'And did he?' Wilson asked. And grinned. 'If he had, we wouldn't be here tonight.'

'Major Mackinder refused to surrender,' Manly-Smith said. 'Instead, he led his men in prayer, and then drew his sword and gave the order to charge. The Baluchis broke and fled, and Major Mackinder led his men to safety, with the loss of but thirty lives.'

'And you know that prayer off by heart, do you?' Wilson asked.

Manly-Smith drew a long breath. 'May the great . . .'

'Save it,' Wilson said. 'Just remember it, when the time comes. They're here.'

The two young officers hurried to the end of the table and stood to attention, as did everyone else in the room. The

3

Sergeant-Major had opened the doors wide, and several men were framed there as they entered. Easily recognizable was the current commanding officer of the regiment, Lieutenant-Colonel Ian Mackinder the Third, a tall, powerfully built man with clipped features and piercing blue eyes. With him were two other men wearing sky-blue mess kit, and remarkably like him in appearance, save that these were much older. One was his uncle who, like him, had in his day commanded the regiment and was now in his seventies.

But like everyone else in the room, Manly-Smith had eyes only for the third man. Because if the Major Ian Mackinder of so long ago had been the founder of a legend, this man, his great-grandson, was the most famous soldier ever to wear the sky-blue jacket of the regiment. It was not merely his exalted rank, Lieutenant-General (retired) Sir Murdoch Mackinder, VC, KCMG, DSO and Bar, Légion d'honneur, followed by a host of other honours and decorations which were all tonight displayed upon his breast, which made him memorable, or even the fact that he was still alive, at the age of one hundred and three – and still stood erect, and moved firmly, if slowly, smiling a greeting here, nodding another there, clearly remembering many of the faces – which made him seem an immortal. That was based on the legend of his life, and the manner in which he had gained all of those decorations. And now, having handed over his helmet to a waiting orderly to be placed beside the others on the table along the wall, he was coming closer. Manly-Smith tightened his shoulders, both to keep himself from shaking with apprehension and to give himself the courage to speak.

Lieutenant-Colonel Ian Mackinder beamed at him. 'May I present Second-Lieutenant Manly-Smith, sir. Just joined.'

Manly-Smith gazed at a tall, very spare man, clean shaven and not, at the moment anyway, wearing glasses – nor was it easy to suppose that the cool blue eyes ever needed them. His features had the somewhat clipped regularity of his family, which tended again to create an

4

impression of coolness, perhaps even aloofness, but they were smiling as he extended his hand. 'Manly-Smith,' he remarked. 'I knew your father.'

'My grandfather, sir.'

Ian Mackinder frowned at the contradiction, but the General smiled with his mouth as well, now. 'Why, yes, of course. He would have had to be.'

'You recommended him for his Victoria Cross, sir,' Manly-Smith said eagerly.

'So I did,' Murdoch Mackinder agreed. 'No man ever deserved one more. This is your big night, Manly-Smith. Are you nervous?'

'I . . . yes, sir.'

The general nodded. 'We were all nervous the first time we had to utter the prayer.' The smile broadened. 'Even the first Ian Mackinder, who composed it, I would suppose.'

'Were you nervous, sir?' Manly-Smith was incredulous.

'My dear boy, I was shivering like a kitten. No nerves, no performance.' He turned to his grandson. 'Well, Colonel Mackinder, shall we begin? Late nights are bad for me nowadays, I'm told.'

'Of course, sir. Take your place, Manly-Smith,' Colonel Mackinder said, and escorted his uncle and grandfather to their seats at the head of the table, where the old gentleman was seated exactly beneath the picture of the first Ian Mackinder's charge. The other officers took their places, and the Sergeant-Major stood to attention beside Manly-Smith at the foot of the longer centre arm, facing both Murdoch Mackinder and the picture, and carrying the regimental standard in his right hand, haft resting on the floor, flag itself furled against his shoulder.

'Gentlemen, the regimental prayer.'

Every officer stood to attention, and then, with a single movement, drew his sword and pointed it at the ceiling. There were some seventy men present, and it was possible to suppose, looking at the upheld swords, that this was what the Baluchis had seen on that hot and dusty plain, a hundred and forty-one years before, when Ian Mackinder and his men had accepted the simple choice: victory or death.

5

'Mr Manly-Smith, sir.' The Sergeant-Major's voice was quiet, as the room was now absolutely still.

Manly-Smith hesitated for a moment, then spoke in a strong, clear voice. 'May the great God of battle, who has guided the fate of this famous regiment on many a hard-fought field, and never failed to lead it to distinction, grant that on this day, faced as we are with a host of enemies of our Queen and our Country, every man will do his duty, so that should we fail in our ordained task, it will yet be said of us, they were the Royal Western Dragoon Guards, who fought and died according to the ancient valour of their regiment and their blood.'

He paused for a moment, and then added, 'Gentlemen, there is your enemy.'

There was a burst of applause as the swords were sheathed with a scintillating rasp, and the orderlies moved forward to relieve the diners and stack the weapons against the wall. The assembly then sat down, but Murdoch Mackinder remained standing.

'That was well said, Mr Manly-Smith. Well said. The regiment is proud of you.'

There was another ripple of applause while the old gentleman took his seat, and the waiters immediately began serving the soup.

'Carries me back,' muttered Major-General Fergus Mackinder. 'Every year. Carries me back.'

'Yes,' his father the great Murdoch agreed. Back, back, back. To Bath and the night he himself had spoken the prayer. To South Africa, where he had won the Victoria Cross and been all but cashiered for falling in love with a Boer girl. To the Modder River, where he had first understood the horror of modern war. To Somaliland, and the Mad Mullah. To the tragedy of the Curragh Mutiny.

And then France, and Le Cateau.

And Ralph Manly-Smith. And Chand Bibi. God, would he ever forget her?

'Where did they hold the dinner the year young Manly-Smith's grandfather said the prayer, Grandad?' asked Ian Mackinder.

6

Murdoch Mackinder's smile was grim. 'There was no regimental dinner the year Ralph Manly-Smith joined us, Ian. It was 1914. We were too busy killing. And being killed.'

PART ONE

THE COLONEL

1
England, 1914

When the rumble awoke Murdoch Mackinder he threw back the covers to stand at the window and look out at the flashes in the sky.

'Only thunder,' Lee said. And when her husband didn't immediately turn, she asked, 'Is it so like gunfire?'

'Yes. I suppose it is.' He returned to the bed and sat beside her. 'I didn't mean to wake you.'

She put her arms round him, holding him close. 'I was awake anyway. I guess I'm counting the hours.'

'So am I, dearest. So am I.'

'Because you want to get back. And I'd like you to stay.'

He kissed her. 'I have to get back.'

'Oh, sure.' She held herself away and smiled at him. 'Not yet thirty-four, and colonel of the regiment. There's something.'

'Too much, for poor Martin Walters.'

'So it'll be too much for you, too, when you get yourself shot again. Oh, Murdoch . . .' She allowed her fingertips to trace down his back, feeling the scar tissue. There was more scar tissue on his leg. His body, hard and tough and lean, had been scoured by a dozen wounds. He was a real-life, genuine hero, and he had the medals to prove it. She had known all of that when she had set her cap at him almost ten years ago – but had not really been aware of what would be involved.

Murdoch Mackinder VC had been a hero to her before she even met him. It started because her brother Harry had been sent from New York to cover the Boer War, and had there elected to build his stories around the exploits of a young lieutenant who had the knack of attracting trouble and surviving it. When she had first seen her future husband in

11

hospital in 1905, Murdoch had been recovering, not from a war wound, but from being rolled on by his horse during an army manoeuvre gone wrong. He had been badly hurt, with several bones broken, but was already on the mend. And surely that would be the last injury. For Europe was at peace, and that meant the world was at peace. Indeed the pundits proclaimed that war between two civilized nations was now impossible. To an American that had to seem true, on every count.

But there was no such thing as peace for a British army officer, and even before they married, Murdoch had been wounded again. His dragoon regiment had been sent to Somaliland to combat a religious leader known quaintly as the Mad Mullah. There Murdoch won more fame, and once again had been wounded almost to death. To what purpose? The Mad Mullah was still at large, causing havoc.

But even that turmoil paled into insignificance last summer, when all of Europe had gone mad. The Royal Western Dragoons was one of the first regiments to land in France, had earned distinction by covering the retreat from Mons and Le Cateau, and in doing so had lost both their colonel and their adjutant. Colonel Walters had died from his wounds. Major Mackinder had survived and been promoted. He was even to be awarded another medal. But, once that was done, the regiment, and the war, wanted him back – to tear at again. And one day the tear would prove fatal.

One day soon, because now he was fully recovered. The doctor had said so, yesterday.

Murdoch kissed her again. 'Just about dawn. May as well get dressed.'

She watched him go to his dressing room, then she lay down again. Marylee Mackinder, she thought. She was fond of repeating that to herself. Indeed she was a much envied woman: she was young, she was pretty, she was healthy; she possessed by right of marriage this magnificent house set in the rolling Somerset countryside. She had dogs and horses, and in-laws with whom she was close friends. She had three healthy children – and a famous husband. Could she ask more?

12

She touched her flat stomach. The family was soon to grow. She knew it, even if she had only missed one period. Murdoch might have been badly wounded, but he remained a strong and vigorous man, and he had recovered splendidly. But she had not told him yet. That was nothing to tell a man who was about to go to war. It could wait till he came back the next time.

If he came back the next time.

'Glad to be up and doing, I'll bet, sir.' Corporal Reynolds fussed over his master, removing an imagined speck of dust from the sleeve of the dark brown tunic, frowning at the silver insignia of crown and star on his shoulder straps to make sure they were as bright as they should be, peering down at the khaki breeches to check that the crease was a knife-edge, at the brown boots in which he could see his face reflected.

'Yes,' Murdoch said. He gazed at himself in the shaving mirror. It was a lean, handsome face. No doubt he was fortunate in that, for all the scars his body carried, none had occurred above the shoulder. It was also a youthful face, and the hair above was still black. Only the eyes were old. Far older than thirty-three years. He remembered how, when he had returned from South Africa and gone down to the Isle of Wight to visit his father's friend Lord Roberts, the great old man had told him that one could always identify a soldier used to combat by his eyes.

Murdoch's eyes were now ageless – and were about to become more so.

It was not a life-role he had ever questioned. He did not question it now. His name was Murdoch Mackinder, and he was the only son of Colonel Fergus Mackinder, who had died in India while commanding the Royal Western Dragoon Guards. Fergus Mackinder's father, also named Murdoch, had also commanded the Royal Westerns, as had his father, Ian Mackinder, the man who had led the famous charge. Mackinders joined the army. More, they joined the Royal Western Dragoon Guards. More yet, they rose to command the regiment. When he went up to London today, for the first time wearing the badges of a lieutenant-colonel, and on his way to take up that command, he was but obeying the family tradition, fulfilling the family's requirements. That on the way he had become the first Mackinder to achieve the Victoria Cross, for saving his commanding officer's life in South Africa, and to this had added the Distinguished Service Order for his accomplishments in Somaliland, was a personal satisfaction.

He would not have had it any differently. Yet he knew that it *was* different, for him. Not that he had married, and fathered a family. This too was a family requirement. He loved Lee, and he loved his children. He loved Broad Acres, and his dogs and horses. This was as it should be. If he was perhaps more torn between this domestic bliss and the requirements of his profession than were his ancestors, this was no doubt because general human attitudes were changing as the twentieth century sped on its ebullient, horrifying way.

But there were other aspects of his life about which very few people were aware. George Reynolds, his batman during all his service life, was one of those few. George knew all about that mad adventure with Margriet Voorlandt which had all but cost his master his career. There were officers in the army who knew of that, too. But only George knew how they had together returned to the Transvaal in search of the girl, only to find her married – and a mother.

Had Margriet waited, who could tell what might have happened to Murdoch's famous career? Marylee Caspar from Baltimore, Maryland, had been no more than an acquaintance at that time.

And thus George also knew, as did no one else in the world, that when Colonel Paul von Reger had struck down Major Murdoch Mackinder in the cavalry mêlée outside Le Cateau, there had been more than national rivalry involved.

'The lads will be glad to see you, sir,' Reynolds said, noting his colonel's pensiveness.

'Yes,' Murdoch said again.

★

Breakfast was a quiet affair. Even the children were subdued.

Philippa tried to be her usual jolly self. 'Do you think you'll be home for Christmas?' she asked. Two years older than Murdoch, she had never married, and never would now, he supposed. On the whole she preferred horses to humans.

'I doubt it.' He grinned at his sister. 'I've had my leave for the year.'

'I thought this war was going to be over by Christmas,' Florence Mackinder complained. Mother was going to be sixty next year, and had survived the loss of her husband by twenty years.

'That could happen,' Murdoch agreed. 'Well . . .' He wiped his lips with his napkin and stood up.

'Do write,' his mother said, 'whenever you have the time.'

'I will do that.' Murdoch stood above the children, who gazed at their father in awe; to them he remained a somewhat distant figure. Ian was five, Fergus four, and Helen only two. An entire generation of Mackinders, he thought, waiting to take their places. Helen would undoubtedly marry a soldier; his oldest sister, Rosemary, was married to a Guards officer.

He kissed them in turn. 'Be good.'

'Bring us back a German, Daddy,' Ian piped.

'Whatever would you do with him?' Murdoch chuckled.

Lee waited by the door. She alone of the family would accompany him to London. She looked exquisite, as always, in her green and white horizontally-striped gown with its double tunic and its peg-top skirt revealing just a trace of white-stockinged ankle rising out of her black patent-leather shoes, her dark green velvet jacket, her green velvet hat with its black and white plume, her leather handbag and black umbrella. But clothes did no more than show off her own very real beauty: the cropped fair hair, the piquant features, the strong healthy body. She was a woman to come back to – which made her that much more difficult a woman to leave.

15

As they stepped outside they were surrounded by barking labradors, both black and yellow.

'Good lads,' Murdoch said. 'Good lads.'

The dogs followed him to the stables where he said farewell to Buccaneer: the faithful stallion that had carried him for nine years, and had survived the set-to at Le Cateau, but only just, and was clearly too old now for active service.

'I wonder who they'll have for me this time, old fellow,' Murdoch asked the sad old eyes.

The chauffeur had the Rolls purring, and Reynolds had already strapped the kitbags in place. Now he joined the chauffeur in the front, separated by a glass partition from the rear seats where Lee and Murdoch sat together. As the car moved down the drive, they waved at Florence and the children, gathered on the porch.

'Your mother is a very brave woman,' Lee observed.

'A very experienced one at saying goodbye. When I come back, I think we should change cars. This is terribly old-fashioned.'

'Mm. Did I tell you I've learned to drive?'

'You?' He turned his head in surprise.

'Mm,' she said again, and looked out the window as they passed the croquet lawn and tennis court. 'Doesn't it ever strike you as unutterably futile that you should own all this, and so seldom be here to enjoy it?'

'I'll enjoy it in my old age,' he promised.

'Oh, yes,' she breathed. 'Do hurry up and reach retirement, Murdoch.'

King George V was a short man, but looked very military in his uniform. Murdoch knew, of course, that he had actually served in the navy, but this was an army occasion.

'I see you have one of these already, Colonel Mackinder,' he observed, pinning the cross with the blue and red ribbon of the Distinguished Service Order on his breast, amidst the other decorations he wore, and eyeing the crimson ribbon which stood out beyond them all. 'I congratulate you.'

'Thank you, sir.' Murdoch stepped back and saluted,

16

then shook hands with Queen Mary while Lee was doing her curtseying. Lee had been with him before, as his fiancée, when he had received his first DSO from King Edward VII.

They emerged into the pale autumn sunshine, posed for the cameras, chatted for a moment with other recipients of honours, then they were by the car. 'Well . . .' she said. 'I guess you have a lot to do.'

They had enjoyed one last night together at the Savoy Hotel.

'I'm afraid so,' he said. 'I have to report to the War Office, and I have to make sure all our replacements have turned up – there's a new lieutenant due, as well. And, believe it or not, Churchill wants to see me before I return to the front.'

Lee giggled. 'Maybe he wants you to transfer to the navy.' Winston Churchill was First Lord of the Admiralty in the Liberal Government of Henry Asquith.

'Wouldn't work. I get seasick,' he laughed.

'So did Nelson . . . Murdoch, supposing you see Harry, give him my love.' She knew her brother was somewhere in France, covering the war for his New York newspaper.

Murdoch remembered how Harry Caspar had originally appeared to oversee the battle of Le Cateau. 'I've an idea he'll find me as soon as I get back,' he said pensively.

The she was serious again, clinging to his arm. 'Oh, Murdoch . . . *do come back.* Soon,' she added quickly, although her original meaning was clear.

'Soon,' he promised. 'But we still have time for lunch before your train.'

Murdoch was always astonished at how young the First Lord of the Admiralty appeared. Churchill was actually only seven years his senior, but he did not think they looked even that far apart. They had met several times previously, not least because they both had the distinction of having escaped from the Boers in South Africa. But they had never been more than acquaintances, and he was now intrigued

17

by the First Lord's invitation. So, apparently, were the various clerks and secretaries, who gazed at the unfamiliar khaki uniform with disapproval.

'Mackinder.' The First Lord shook his hand. 'Another decoration. I read all about it. And now colonel of the regiment. You must be one of our most distinguished soldiers.'

'Thank you, sir,' Murdoch said.

'Now, let's get out of here before Fisher finds out about it. Sir John is a dear old boy, but he regards the army as a nuisance. You have an hour to spare?'

'Why, yes,' Murdoch agreed, seeing no option as Churchill was already hurrying along the corridor and down the stairs. 'May I ask where we're going?'

'For a ride in the country.'

As they sat in the back of the official Daimler, alone except for the marine driver, Churchill turned to smile at him. 'I imagine you'll be glad to get back to France.'

'To the regiment, yes.'

'Things aren't going so well, eh?'

'We're holding them. And the Marne was a victory. No one can argue against that.'

'A victory of defence, Colonel. We stopped the Hun from taking Paris. We have not driven him back into Germany, forced him to his knees. Now he is entrenched across most of Belgium and the most valuable part of France. We can hardly regard that as a victorious situation for the Allies.'

They were soon being whisked across the Thames and through south London, heading generally south-west.

'We shall have to mount an offensive of our own,' Murdoch suggested.

'That's being done at the moment. We are trying to cut him off from the sea – and we are not succeeding. The casualty lists are horrifying. One simply cannot launch flesh and blood against machine-guns and barbed wire.'

Murdoch refused to join the First Lord's pessimistic mood. 'Then we shall have to find a way round the obstacle.'

'Now there's a tall order, with one enemy flank resting on

the Swiss border and the other on the North Sea. Mind you, Mackinder, you are absolutely right. We shall only beat the Germans by rolling up their flanks. The alternative is to starve them into surrender. That is the province of the navy, and I can tell you that we are prepared to carry out the task. But it may take a very long time. And, meanwhile, our men are dying at the rate of more than a hundred a day. Nor will they cease doing so. Even were we to discover a flank that can be turned, their armies will still have to be fixed by frontal attacks. I'm told you are a go-ahead soldier who is not afraid of the future.'

The abrupt change of subject took Murdoch by surprise. 'I like to think I am.'

'Good. I have something to show you. I'd like your opinion.'

They had left the houses behind by now and were approaching a village which was surrounded by several small farms.

'If you think it's worth having,' Murdoch murmured.

'If I didn't, I wouldn't have brought you here. Ever met Ernest Swinton?'

'Swinton. Ah . . . yes, in South Africa.'

'Royal Engineers. Brilliant mind.' The car turned into one of the farmyards, which was devoid of animals although there were two tractors in the sheds. 'This is a confidential visit, Mackinder. Captain Swinton is actually carrying out some research, using naval funds. He cannot obtain any support from the War Office. I would prefer no one to know that you have been here.' He gave Murdoch a searching look. '*No one.*'

Murdoch understood that he was referring to Field Marshal Lord Kitchener, who was Minister of War, and therefore the supreme soldier in Britain, especially since the death of Field Marshal Lord Roberts only a fortnight previously. Murdoch knew that Churchill and Kitchener saw eye to eye on very little. But he also knew that Churchill was aware that Kitchener and Murdoch himself were not the best of friends either. They had clashed in South Africa, and if Kitchener had been the man to save him from a

19

court-martial, he had done it not out of regard but because he did not see how the army could award a man the Victoria Cross on one day and cashier him on the next without being made to appear very foolish. Since then he had regarded Murdoch Mackinder as a confounded nuisance – nor was their relationship improved by Kitchener's awareness that Murdoch was a protégé of Sir John French, Commander-in-Chief of the British Army in France.

'It shall be confidential,' he promised.

'We are not trying to pull the wool over anyone's eyes,' Churchill assured him as the driver opened the door for them. 'Should our hopes be justified, then the whole business will be handed over to the army. It is merely that the powers that be are so confoundedly conservative that anything new has to be displayed to them and proved to be successful before they'll even think about it. The support of experienced officers will be very useful when the time comes.'

Murdoch was pleasantly interested. He was about to be shown a secret weapon, but could not imagine what it was.

It was certainly well guarded: there was an armed sentry on the door and more soldiers within. Swinton was waiting to greet them, and Murdoch was introduced to him.

'My pleasure, sir.' Swinton shook hands, and Murdoch felt somewhat embarrassed: Swinton, clearly much the older man, still held only the rank of captain, while he was already a lieutenant-colonel – that was the difference between serving in the Engineers, an essential part of the army but one in which there was little glory to be had, and serving in the cavalry.

'Has the First Lord discussed the problem?' Swinton inquired as he escorted them into an inner room.

'In a general way.' Murdoch looked at the large sand-table on which had been created a representation of a portion of the western front. The little villages and the roads, the lines of poplars and the canals, were very familiar. But the green of the earth had been scarred by a series of trenches cut into it, each several inches from the others – representing perhaps a hundred yards, he supposed. The trenches were filled with lead soldiers wearing German uniforms, and before each trench were extensive areas of miniature barbed wire.

'I know it didn't look like this at Le Cateau,' Swinton hastened to say, 'but I'm afraid that is how it is starting to look all over northern France and Belgium nowadays. The Germans have dug in. So have we, of course. But unless we intend to spend the rest of our lives just facing them, we have to devise some means of turfing them out. The High Command still feels that this can be done by frontal assault, but they are not succeeding.'

'And our people are being massacred,' Churchill growled.

'The problem is simply this,' Swinton said. He signalled an orderly, who immediately took out a box and began placing khaki-clad lead soldiers on the far edge of the table. 'Our artillery bombards the enemy lines, and when it ceases, our men assult. All very classic. Unfortunately the damage done by the bombardment bears no proportion to the amount of shells delivered; the enemy merely retires into its dugouts until the guns stop.'

'And I can tell you that right now we are using up shells faster than we can make them,' Churchill put in.

'The bombardment also has the drawback of advising the enemy that something is going to happen,' Swinton went on. 'They can afford to wait. It takes our men several minutes to cross a couple of hundred yards of open ground, especially where they have to cut their way through barbed wire; and long before they can reach the German trenches they are being cut to pieces by the enemy machine-guns. You see how they're sited . . .' He indicated with his swagger-stick the toy machine-gun nests, placed not to look straight ahead, but obliquely to each side. 'You have a constant enfilading fire. Now, although it seems incredible, our chaps, and the French, have on occasion survived that and gained the first line of trenches. But then they are faced with another line, and then another. It is simply not possible for them to go on. And the moment they stop, they are counter-attacked by the Germans and thrown out again.'

21

'Couldn't the cavalry be loosed the moment the first line is taken?' Murdoch asked.

'They'd be cut to ribbons by the machine-guns behind,' Churchill pointed out. 'No, the answer is an old one, which has been somewhat neglected these last centuries. Armour!'

Murdoch stared at him, half in amusement, half in dismay. 'You'd have us back in armour? And the horses? But armour won't keep out a bullet.'

'Of course it won't, Swinton agreed. 'Not any armour a man or horse could wear and still stand up. But the question we face, Colonel, is not how an individual can be sent against a machine-gun, but how a group of men can be delivered to the enemy lines, protected all the way.'

'Of course,' Murdoch said. 'Armoured cars. They not only keep out bullets; they carry a machine-gun. We're already using those.'

'Certainly,' Swinton agreed. 'But not very successfully. They're badly designed. They're too angular. Their armour may keep out most bullets, but not all. And they are very vulnerable to shell fire. But those things are irrelevant. They can be corrected by some streamlining and extra protection. The big problem with the armoured car is that it can only operate on a road or a smooth surface. Take it into a field and it bogs down. The only true answer to the problem of entrenchments lies in tracked vehicles.'

He gave another signal, and the orderly reached beneath the table, brought out the model of a tractor, wound it up, and set it on the sand. The clockwork shirred, and the toy moved forward.

Murdoch peered at it with interest. Although it had caterpillar wheels with endless tracks, it was more than just a tractor. It was longer and lower, shaped somewhat like an elongated matchbox with a frame on top, and out of that top there protruded what was obviously intended to be a machine-gun.

'The armour would of course have to be thick enough to stop a bullet,' Swinton said. 'And this would mean it would not travel very fast – perhaps two or three miles an hour. But it would be unstoppable.'

'Watch,' Churchill said.

The armoured tractor had simply rolled across the barbed wire. Now it reached the first trench, paused for a moment on the outer lip, appeared to dip, then made contact with the inner lip and continued on its way; the German soldiers were scattered.

'How many men?' Murdoch asked.

'Only a couple inside the tank. But if your first line consisted of them, the infantry could follow on behind in comparative safety. Even the cavalry could do so.'

'Tanks?' Murdoch asked. 'You call them tanks?'

'I call it a tank. It makes me think of a tank on a tractor.'

Murdoch gazed at the 'tank'. It was still moving, having crossed the area between the first and second trenches, and then crossed the second trench. There its clockwork gave out and it stopped. He scratched his head.

'It's an old idea, of course,' Swinton said modestly. 'A Captain Bretherton dreamed it up more than half a century ago. But no one was interested then. Besides, he had to use steam power, which was hopelessly inefficient on a small scale like this. The petrol engine has changed all that.' He grinned. 'Although nobody, except Mr Churchill, is interested now, either.'

'They will be,' Churchill promised him. 'They will be.'

'What did you think?' he asked as they drove back to London in the dusk.

'It could work,' Murdoch said. 'You'd need a lot of them.'

'We shall have a lot of them, eventually. Will you endorse the idea, if you're asked?'

Murdoch thought for a moment. It *could* work. And if the tanks could indeed knock down the other fellow's barbed wire and make a nonsense of his trenches, it could bring war back to the days of true manoeuvrability, as in South Africa, in which cavalry would have a full part to play . . .

'Yes, Mr Churchill,' he said. 'I'll endorse the idea, if asked.'

'Good man. How'd you like to drive one?'

'Me? I can't even drive an automobile.' Although my wife can, he thought. 'I'm a horseman, not a mechanic.'

23

'I think you should learn, Colonel. I can foresee a time when you chaps will have abandoned your horses entirely for tanks.'

'After my time, First Lord.' He grinned. 'Besides, it'd be a bit tricky saying the regimental prayer before a charge, with all those engines roaring.'

Churchill grinned back. 'I'm sure we'll find a way, Mackinder.'

'Another medal, eh?' grunted Field Marshal Lord Kitchener, glaring at Murdoch from between huge eyebrows and his famous moustache. 'I suppose you wish to be congratulated, Mackinder.'

'I've had enough congratulations, sir,' Murdoch replied.

'Harrumph. So. Back to France tomorrow, eh? Looking forward to that?'

'To rejoining the regiment, yes, sir.'

'And in command. You're young to be a lieutenant-colonel. Dead men's shoes. There'll be a lot of those in this war.'

Murdoch waited for the great man to say something relevant.

'The situation,' Kitchener announced. 'You'll know Antwerp has fallen. It was never defensible. Sending marines there was a waste of bloody time – and men. Churchill's idea.' He brooded for a few seconds. 'We have to push them back, Mackinder. We have to *drive* them back. The next offensive will be launched December fourteenth. Just give you time to settle in, eh? All our armies, French and British, will move forward together, and throw the buggers back into their own country. Once we've got them going, we'll keep them going. That'll be your job, the job of the cavalry, eh?'

'Yes, sir, supposing we can break through his defensive system.'

Kitchener glared at him. 'We will. We must. We cannot fight a long war. There are shortages already. Shells. There aren't enough shells. And men. I need more men. If we do not crack them now . . .' his shoulders slumped, 'we may

24

not do it at all. Good luck, Mackinder. We will do it. *You* will do it.'

Murdoch saluted and went to the door.

'What I have said is confidential,' Kitchener growled.

'Well, sir,' Corporal Reynolds said. 'Last night in Blighty until Christmas at the least. On the town, sir?'

'Not on the town, George,' Murdoch said. 'I've a call to make. Get us some tickets down to Sevenoaks for this afternoon.'

'Sevenoaks?' Reynolds raised his eyebrows and then frowned. 'You're not going calling on that Jerry bugger again, sir? Seems to me he's no friend of yours.'

'He did save my life once, George,' Murdoch said.

'And then tried to cut you down when your back was turned at Le Cateau,' Reynolds pointed out.

'An act of war. You get the tickets,' Murdoch said.

But he wondered why he was doing this. If he and Paul von Reger had been friends once, that seemed a very long time ago now – since last August, a million light years away. Their friendship had not survived Paul's marriage to Margriet. It was because she, as a bride, had confessed her sins to her husband, and been beaten for those sins. At least, she had claimed so when last they had met. But it was difficult to determine when Margriet was telling the truth and when she was living in some fantasy world of her own.

Yet the man had once saved his life, when Murdoch had been captured by a Boer commando, infuriated at the destruction of their farms – on Kitchener's orders – and ready to lynch the first British officer to fall into their hands. That Paul had struck at him from behind outside Le Cateau had undoubtedly been a reflex action.

Murdoch straightened his tie as the military doctor escorted him along the corridor of the prison hospital. 'You'll find Colonel von Reger almost fully recovered,' he said. 'He'll leave here in another week.'

'And go to a prison camp?'

'I have no idea, Colonel Mackinder. I presume so,

25

although he is a prominent man in Germany.' He opened the door. 'Lieutenant-Colonel Mackinder to see you, Colonel.'

Paul von Reger stood up. Even in a dressing gown and pyjamas he managed to look military – and Prussian. His yellow hair had been allowed to grow by the hospital staff, but his back was as straight as ever Murdoch recalled it, his manner as precise, his big features as stiff. 'You are returning to service,' he remarked.

'Tomorrow.'

'I also, hopefully,' Reger said.

Murdoch raised his eyebrows.

'I am to be exchanged. I have been told this.'

'Then I congratulate you, assuming you wish to return to the front.'

Reger stiffened even more. 'Do you suppose I am a coward?'

'I never supposed that, Paul. But you are nearly forty. This war is young man's work.'

'Your work, you mean.' Reger glanced at Murdoch's tunic. 'A bar to the DSO. You are a much decorated man.'

'Thank you.'

'Always leading heroic charges, eh? One day your luck will change.'

'Everyone's luck changes eventually,' Murdoch said. 'When you return to Germany, will you give my regards to Margriet, and young Paul?'

'To Margriet, and young Paul. Yes, I will do that.'

'Thank you.' Murdoch hesitated, then held out his hand. When last he had seen Reger, in this very room, after he had been able to leave his hospital bed, his offered hand had been refused. He realized it was going to be refused again now, and let it fall back to his side.

'I wish you to know,' Reger said, 'that I have no regrets at having tried to kill you at Le Cateau.'

'I do not expect you to. I was trying to kill *you*.'

'And the next time we meet, I shall succeed,' Reger told him.

'We'll both be trying then, too,' Murdoch agreed. 'If

there is a next time. But when the war is over, I would hope we can be friends again, Paul.'

Reger stared at him. 'When the war is over, Murdoch, Great Britain will have been defeated. She will have been humbled. *You* will have been humbled. Yes, perhaps then we can be friends.'

'I'll look forward to that,' Murdoch said, and left the room.

'As unpleasant as ever, I'd reckon,' Reynolds remarked as the train chugged them back to London.

'As ever,' Murdoch said. 'He's a frightened man, George. Maybe all the enemy are. They've started something they're no longer sure they can finish. And if they can't . . .'

'No one is going to weep for the Kaiser, Mr Murdoch.'

'Or any of his people,' Murdoch agreed. 'That's what's frightening them.' And me, he thought.

'Troop, atten-tion!'

The recruits brought their heels together and straightened their backs. There were thirty-seven of them, most of whom Murdoch had met already when he had visited regimental headquarters in Bath a week previously. Presumably other drafts had been sent off while he had been in hospital; he knew the regiment had suffered more than thirty-seven casualties during the fight at Le Cateau alone.

'Lieutenant Ralph Manly-Smith, sir!' The young man, wearing an obviously brand-new uniform, stood in front of his colonel and saluted. He was the officer Murdoch had been warned would be accompanying him to France, straight out of Sandhurst, but who had not been at the depot. He was somewhat small, and dark and intense, and surely could not have been more than eighteen.

Murdoch returned the salute, then held out his hand. 'Welcome, Mr Manly-Smith.'

Manly-Smith's grasp was eager and his eyes were shining; he was shaking hands with a legend. 'Troop is ready for inspection, sir.'

27

'Thank you.' Murdoch walked in front of the second-lieutenant, spurs jingling in the crisp November air, heels thudding on the courtyard of the depot. 'Which of you didn't I meet in Bath?' he asked the troop.

There was a moment's hesitation, then someone said, 'Me, sir.'

Murdoch glanced along the rank, and felt his jaw dropping. 'Johnnie?' he asked in amazement.

'Trooper Morton, sir,' the man replied.

Murdoch gazed at him in astonishment. Johnnie Morton had been the senior lieutenant when he had joined the regiment in Bath, fifteen years ago. An instant mutual dislike had grown into a very real friendship beneath the African sun and the bullets of the Boer sharpshooters. Then Johnnie had gone with the main part of the regiment to India, while Murdoch had been sent to Somaliland with his squadron. There he had gained fame and fortune, while in India Johnnie had contracted syphilis and been invalided out, under a cloud.

But he had been retired with the rank of major.

'*Trooper* Morton?' Murdoch asked softly.

'Yes, sir. A man must fight, sir.'

Murdoch gazed at the moustached face, the square shoulders, and remembered a great deal.

'I am fit again now, sir,' Morton said.

'Thank God for that,' Murdoch said. There were a million questions scouring his tongue, but not one he could ask. He was the regiment's commanding officer, and Morton, for whatever reason, was now a trooper. Revelations would have to wait. He completed his inspection of the men and their kit, and returned to where the lieutenant waited, like everyone else intrigued by the exchange. 'Very good, Mr Manly-Smith,' he said. 'Fall the men in. The train is waiting.'

Manly-Smith gave the orders, and the troop mounted and walked their horses out of the yard, the two officers at their head. 'Morton is an old soldier, is he, sir?' Manly-Smith could restrain his curiosity no longer.

'Yes,' Murdoch said.

'He looks a little old to be a trooper.'

'He is,' Murdoch agreed. 'But, as he said, a man must fight. Let us go and do that, Mr Manly-Smith.'

2

France, 1915

'Good morning, sir. Cold today.' Reynolds had not had to change his greeting for weeks.

Murdoch scratched his head, got out of bed, shuddered. The farmhouse, situated a dozen miles north-east of St Omer, was like an icebox. But at least he had a farmhouse. He stood at the window, rubbed a clear spot in the condensation, looked out at the tents of the regiment; some of the more enterprising troopers had even built small huts, scattered over the rolling green countryside. Beyond the camp, the horses were tethered in straight lines. Healthy horses; they had had little to do all winter save exercise.

Another day. A quiet day; there was hardly more than the odd 'burrp' in the distance which meant a shot – the front line was only a few miles away. But it might have been a million miles, as far as the cavalry were concerned. Even during the offensive, which had lasted from just before Christmas right up to Easter, when the guns had boomed day and night and the stream of casualties brought back from the line had been no less continuous, he and his men, the entire cavalry division, had sat on their horses and waited for the gap to be created into which they would gallop, but it never had. And a fortnight ago the battle had ground to a halt, mainly because the artillery had run out of shells, with hardly a yard of ground gained to show for all the effort. But with a quarter of a million British casualties. The French losses were unthinkable.

This was warfare on an unbelievable scale, for most people. Only one or two men, in farmhouses like this one but situated in the English countryside, were trying to think about it, seriously. The rest were going through the motions, and dying.

And Mother had expected him home for Christmas. Now she and Philippa and Lee and the children were in the firing line too. Well, perhaps not quite, down in Somerset. But he could remember the wave of anger which had swept through the British ranks in January when news had been received of a zeppelin bombing raid on England. No soldier had really believed the tales of German 'frightfulness' perpetrated by the newspapers during the invasion of Belgium last summer – but bombing civilians was a newly horrible aspect of war.

Reynolds had Murdoch's hot water for shaving and his cup of coffee waiting, and downstairs Madame Bosnet had his breakfast, bread and butter, honey and more coffee. If Monsieur Bosnet was away, fighting the Boches, Madame and her teenage son – daily expecting his call-up papers – were happy to minister to the English Colonel.

And his senior officers. Breakfast was as much a social gathering as a review of the coming day's activity. Major Billy Prendergast, the adjutant, hurried in; he had already been out on inspection. With him were the three captains, Peter Ramage, John Lowndes and Tommy Hunter; with a steady stream of replacements the regiment was just about at full strength, three squadrons of two troops each, each troop a hundred men. Nowadays each troop also had a Lewis gun section, and of course, as dragoons, his men were equipped with carbines as well as swords – sabres and lances were for the other chaps. While waiting behind the lines, indeed, Murdoch had attempted to train his command as he had trained his squadron as a captain back in the days of peace, dismounting from a gallop and taking up firing positions in the least possible time; and even more, in the vain hope that they would one day be loosed against the enemy, in firing their rifles from the shoulder while at the canter, as in pictures he had seen of American Indians. He did not suppose they would ever attain any accuracy at such a novel practice, but it might have a certain surprise value. With farriers and cooks and the newfangled wireless operators added, he was now responsible for about seven hundred men.

31

Prendergast sat down with a sigh. 'You'd better tell him,' he suggested gloomily.

'I have seven men on sick parade,' Ramage said.

'I have eleven,' Lowndes said.

'I have eight,' Hunter added.

Murdoch raised his eyebrows. 'Sudden. Flu?'

'Ah, no.' Prendergast glanced at Madame, fussing over her range. 'Do you think she understands English, Murdoch?' he asked in a hoarse whisper.

'Not a word.'

'Ah. Well, the fact is, Trooper Clarke has a boil which requires lancing, and ah . . . ' He checked again.

'Somewhere awkward?'

'The other twenty-five have, well . . . RSM Yeald says it's gonorrhoea.'

'Yeald should know,' Ramage muttered.

Murdoch put down his coffee cup. 'Twenty-five of my men have contracted VD? In one night?'

'Well . . . apparently it takes a couple of weeks to come out. Yeald says,' Prendergast added hurriedly. 'And just over a fortnight ago we were pulled back from the line and were able to give our chaps a night in St Omer. There is, apparently, a . . . ah, house there.'

'And how many men have been there since?' Murdoch asked in a steely voice.

'Well, as we are officially enjoying rest and recuperation, I've been giving a couple of dozen passes every night. Well, I mean, the poor devils deserved it.'

'You mean you have given roughly half the regiment VD. With the other half waiting eagerly to get it.'

Prendergast drank some coffee noisily. He and Murdoch were old friends. Together they had lived through the trauma of the Curragh Mutiny and together they had charged the enemy at Le Cateau; hastily promoted to major when Colonel Walters had been killed and Murdoch wounded, Billy had commanded the regiment until their new lieutenant-colonel had returned to duty. 'Yeald says it takes only a couple of weeks to clear up, with treatment. I've sent a report over to Doc Sansom.'

32

'That doesn't alter the fact that we are going to have one hell of a proportion of our ration strength out of action for the foreseeable future. Have you spoken to Dai?'

'Well, no, not yet. I felt it was more a matter for Doc Sansom than the padre, right now.'

'He'll have to be told. Reynolds, have my horse saddled.' Murdoch stood up. 'You . . . no, you'd better stay here, Billy. To explain things to Doc Sansom,' He frowned. 'Let me see the names of the affected men.'

The three captains held out the pieces of paper. But Prendergast knew what was in Murdoch's mind. 'Johnnie Morton isn't amongst them.'

'Thank God for that. I'll take him with me.'

'Where are you going?' Prendergast was alarmed.

'Into St Omer.'

'But . . . I say, Murdoch. And taking Morton . . . anyway, the house doesn't open until the afternoon. Seems the girls have to sleep, some time. I mean, sleep.'

'I've had my sleep,' Murdoch assured him. 'I propose to sort this madame out. You go and get directions from one of those clapped rascals.'

The horses' hooves clipped on the cobbles and flicked away slivers of ice as the two men walked their mounts down the road towards the town of St Omer. Murdoch rode Jupiter, Buccaneer's replacement, a black gelding who was as responsive a mount as he had ever had.

It was mid-morning and the sun was high in a cloudless sky. The ice was beginning to melt and it was going to be a perfect April day. It was not credible that only a few miles to the north three huge armies faced each other, waiting to kill on an unimaginable scale. Just as it was hardly credible that only a few miles to the west was Calais, and the English Channel, and home, where the horror that was northern France was only a nightmare.

Murdoch glanced at his old friend. They had hardly spoken in the four months since their arrival from England. Commanding officers did not seek private chats with their enlisted men, and Morton had not sought an interview with

33

his commanding officer. Now he rode with his gaze straight ahead.

'How's it going?' Murdoch asked.

'I enjoy the service, sir. I always did.'

Murdoch allowed another couple of seconds to elapse before he spoke again. 'Didn't you try for a commission?'

'No, sir.'

'Why not? You have to be one of the most experienced cavalry officers in all England. You have five years' more service than me, for God's sake.'

'Too many other officers know me, sir. Know of me.'

'But you rejoined the regiment. Don't you think the officers know who you are?'

'Yourself, sir. Major Prendergast. Captain Ramage. Captain Llewellyn. No one else.'

'And the men?'

'They're all seven-year men.' Morton's tone was faintly contemptuous.

'Yeald isn't. He's re-enlisted twice. He was with us in South Africa, remember?'

'Mr Yeald treats me as any other soldier, sir.'

'Suppose I recommend you for a commission?'

Morton's head turned for the first time. 'I would prefer you not to, sir. And I would decline.'

'Johnnie . . . haven't you got a wife, or a family?'

'No, sir.' Morton's head was straight again. 'I left nothing behind, sir.'

Murdoch had from time to time heard rumours of how Morton had fallen on hard times, had been earning a living as a used car salesman. He sighed, and also looked ahead. St Omer itself might have been a hundred miles from the line. A few of the more well-to-do people had opted to remove themselves from any danger of encountering a Uhlan patrol; their houses were shuttered. But for the ordinary citizen life went on much as usual. Greetings were called to the English officers, even if sly glances were also exchanged as people observed the street they were taking.

'I presume you know where we're going?' Murdoch asked.

34

'Yes, sir.'

'Any comment?'

'No, sir.'

'I'm looking for advice, Johnie. Men need women.'

'Yes, sir.'

'But I can't have half my command not up to scratch. What would you do?'

'Regulate the house, sir.'

'Regulate . . . you mean take it over?'

'In a sense, sir. Make the tarts have regular examinations, bar any who's found clapped.'

'Will they allow that?'

'If you put it to them so they don't have a choice, sir.'

'Yes,' Murdoch said thoughtfully. 'Thanks.'

'The brass won't like it, sir,' Morton observed.

'Why not? I should think they'd be pleased.'

'Condoning, sir. Looks bad in the newspapers.'

'Ah. Well, I'll cross that bridge when I come to it. From here on you're a witness. Understood?'

'Yes, sir.'

The house was curtained and quiet, set back from the road. Morton dismounted and opened the iron gate, and they rode in. 'Close the gate,' Murdoch said.

He walked his horse up the path between somewhat neglected flowerbeds, dismounted. Before he could knock a man's voice spoke in French. 'Go away,' it said. 'You are too early. Come back at two o'clock.'

'I wish to speak with Madame Leboeuf,' Murdoch said.

'She is asleep. Go away.'

'If you do not open this door and call Madame Leboeuf,' Murdoch said, 'I will break it down.'

Morton, at his shoulder, gave a slight cough. Murdoch wasn't sure whether he was apprehensive of the threat or embarrassed by his superior's French – he had no doubt the private was far more fluent in the language.

There was a scraping of bolts and the door swung inwards. The man had a white moustache and was clearly past the age of military service. Even in the house he wore a cap. 'Madame will not be pleased,' he grumbled.

'Neither am I pleased,' Murdoch told him. He opened the door on his right, and entered a sitting room. It smelt of cheap perfume, cheap wine, and humanity. 'Nothing like Kitty's in Bath back in ninety-nine,' he remarked.

'No, sir,' Morton agreed. And added, 'You never went there, sir.'

'That is absolutely true,' Murdoch acknowledged. 'But I can't believe it was quite as tawdry as this.'

'It wasn't, sir.'

Murdoch faced the woman who stood in the hall doorway. 'Madame?'

He was taken aback. Madame Leboeuf, presuming that was her real name, which it almost certainly was not, was about half the age he had expected – perhaps twenty-five instead of fifty. She was small, and pretty, with reddish-brown hair and a good figure, easily ascertainable since the nightdress under her open dressing gown was sheer. He glanced at Morton, but the private was standing rigidly to attention.

'Monsieur. Monsieur le Colonel,' she observed, studying his shoulder straps. And changed to English. 'I am flattered, Colonel,' she said. 'When Jules awoke me, I was angry. My establishment does not open before two. But now, I am flattered.'

'Thank you, madame,' Murdoch said. 'But this is a business call.'

Madame Leboeuf smiled. 'I was certain of it.' She sat down and crossed her knees. The dressing gown fell still further away.

Murdoch sat down as well, opposite her, determined to be neither embarrassed nor distracted. 'I meant, I am here as colonel in command of the Royal Western Dragoon Guards. I believe you have entertained some of my men.'

Madame Leboeuf's eyes became watchful. 'They come 'ere often. Every night.'

'Beginning just over a fortnight ago.'

Madame shrugged.

'Those first men, madame, I must tell you, have venereal disease.'

36

Madame's eyes flashed. 'You come 'ere to insult me?'

'I have come here to tell you something of which you should be aware. How many girls have you?'

Madame glared at him, but realized that she could not dominate him either by her sex or by her personality. Her eyes drooped. 'I 'ave ten, when soldiers are expected.'

'You mean some of them are amateurs.'

'They are women, monsieur. Girls. They are 'appy to entertain the brave British soldiers.'

'Do their parents know what they are doing? Or that they have contracted gonorrhoea?'

Another flash from the eyes. 'If they 'ave, it is your men who 'ave given it to them. Your men are beasts. Beasts, monsieur.'

'Madame,' Murdoch said quietly. 'That is not true, and you know it. There was no case of venereal disease in my regiment until we were cantoned here. If you wish to quarrel with me, then I will close your house down.'

'Close my 'ouse down? 'Ow will you do that?'

'Wait and see,' Murdoch suggested.

She glared at him for several seconds, then her shoulders drooped. 'You wish to make me starve? And my girls? What do we do? We make men 'appy. Your soldiers are far from their loved ones. They need to be 'appy. A man must 'ave his . . . 'ow do you say in English?'

'I agree with you, madame. But not if it renders him unfit for duty. I do not wish to have to close you down. But if you wish to remain open, and service my men, then you must cooperate with me.'

'Cooperate?' She frowned at him. ' 'Ow?'

'I wish all of your girls examines by one of my doctors. Every girl who is found to have VD will have to rest until she is cured. And all of them, from now on, will have to be examined every week.'

'You will ruin me, monsieur.'

'The doctors will not cost you anything,' Murdoch promised. 'You will have to accept some slight diminution of business while your girls recover. But it will be best for you in the long run.'

37

'Ha,' she remarked. 'And will your soldiers also be examined by this doctor?'

'Certainly.'

She gazed at him for a few seconds, then smiled. 'Very well. I accept.'

'That is very sensible of you,' Murdoch said, and stood up. 'My doctor will be over this afternoon. Until he has been, I am placing this house out of bounds to my men.'

Madame Leboeuf made a moue, and then smiled. 'You do not 'ave to 'urry away, Colonel. Stay and take breakfast with me.' Her eyes drifted to Morton. 'And your friend. I 'ave no disease, I promise you.'

'Thanks very much, madame, but I'm afraid we have duties to attend to. You'll excuse us.'

They walked their horses out of town in silence. The camp was in sight before Morton spoke. 'With respect, sir.'

'Continue.'

'I know you are happily married to a most lovely woman, sir. But don't you ever have the urge?'

'Often,' Murdoch told him. 'But unlike yourself, I am cursed with being an officer and a gentleman. And now I am a senior officer. I have to endeavour to find a woman who will, at least so far as anyone knows, share her bed for free. They are thin on the ground.'

'Brass,' muttered Reynolds. He was in the middle of serving lunch in the farmhouse garden. The weather was steadily warming up.

'Remarkable how they always turn up at lunchtime,' Peter Ramage remarked. As the senior captain in the regiment, and another old friend, he often came up to the farm for lunch with Murdoch and Prendergast. Today the padre, Dai Llewellyn, was with them.

'You'd better nip out and see if you can bag another rabbit, George,' Murdoch suggested, and stood up, walking away from the table towards the gate where the open tourer was pulling to a halt. 'Good afternoon, gentlemen.'

There were four men in the car: the driver, an obvious ADC and two generals. One was Brigadier-General Gough,

Murdoch's immediate commanding officer, and the other was Major-General Allenby, commander of the cavalry division. Both were men Murdoch had known since South Africa.

'And a good afternoon it is, Murdoch,' Allenby agreed. And sniffed. 'Smells like rabbit stew.'

'It is. I'm afraid we've eaten most of it.'

Allenby grinned. 'We've lunched. I wouldn't say no to a glass of wine.'

'That we have in abundance,' Murdoch promised, escorting them to the table. 'You know Major Prendergast, Captain Ramage, Captain Llewellyn.'

'Of course.' The generals shook hands, and sat down. Reynolds poured wine.

'Is this a social call?' Murdoch asked, knowing well, as Morton had warned him, that it wasn't.

Allenby and Gough exchanged glances. 'No,' the Major-General said. 'There are rumblings at headquarters.'

'This brothel business,' Gough put in. 'You'll forgive me, Llewellyn. But Sir John French wants to know just what you are doing.'

'I would have assumed it was obvious, sir,' Murdoch said. 'I found half my men down with VD. I have taken steps to correct the situation.'

'By taking over the brothel,' Allenby suggested.

'No, sir. By making sure that the girls are healthy.'

'They are examined by a regimental doctor, free of charge,' Gough pointed out. 'That virtually means at the expense of the British taxpayer.'

'It saves my men from gonorrhoea,' Murdoch argued.

'Soldiers always have VD. They always have had VD,' Gough grumbled.

'Then maybe all brothels should be regulated, sir.'

Gough looked at Llewellyn.

'Colonel Mackinder has my full support, sir,' the padre said.

'I'm sure you're both right,' Allenby said soothingly. 'The trouble is, Sir John is, equally rightly, worried about what the press will make of it. We live, alas, in a prurient society. And here we have a British colonel regulating the affairs of a brothel . . . I mean, the people back home, the wives and sweethearts, prefer not to know these things exist. Or certainly that their loved ones are using them.'

'But their loved ones *are* using them, sir. And are going to go on using them. My aim is to stop them infecting those wives and sweethearts when they go home. And right now we are talking about gonorrhoea. Unchecked, it could be syphilis in a couple of months.'

'Yes. Hm. I'll put these points to Sir John, of course. I know he appreciates your points of view, as a rule.'

'Maybe we could keep it out of the press,' Gough suggested.

'God, if we could keep anything out of the press . . .' Allenby finished his wine, accepted a refill. 'Actually, that wasn't the main reason we came over, Murdoch. There's to be another offensive.'

Murdoch raised his eyebrows. 'So soon?'

'Well, they've managed to get hold of some shells. And a whole batch of replacements. The rawest recruits you ever did see. Kitchener's Army they call themselves. I suppose Sir John wants to employ them before they also get VD.' He gave a brief grin. 'It's Joffre's idea, actually. He is sure we can beat Jerry this time.'

'So we mount up and wait,' Murdoch remarked.

'Ah . . . no. The Royal Westerns do not.'

Murdoch looked at him, and then at the brigadier. To whom Allenby also looked.

'There needs to be a massive regrouping,' Gough explained. 'But while this is going on, the line must be manned, of course. Fortunately Jerry doesn't have any idea that we're going on the offensive again so soon, as you said, Murdoch. We wish him to continue in that state of ignorance – or even better, to feel that we have definitely exhausted ourselves for the foreseeable future. What we would like you to do is take over a portion of the line until things are ready. It'll only be for a week. And your area will be next to two veteran French divisions, so you'll have plenty of support in case of trouble. But there shouldn't be any trouble. You are specifically ordered to undertake no offensive action, just to sit tight until things are ready, and then you'll be replaced the night before the offensive starts.'

'And if any of my men are taken prisoner, Jerry will say, "Mein Gott, cavalrymen in the line; the stinkers are scraping the bottom of the barrel." '

'I know it's an imposition, Murdoch,' Allenby said. 'But it has to be done. And . . .' another faint grin. 'It'll solve the VD problem for a few days.'

'In favour of trench feet. When do we move up?'

'Ah . . . you'll leave one troop here with your horses . . . and move up tonight.' Allenby handed over a sheet of paper. 'Here are your instructions. Memorize them.' He held out his hand. 'I know you'll make a good job of it.'

The regiment were simply told they were moving out that night, but temporarily; their main gear was to be left behind. There was a great rustle and a bustle, and Murdoch said goodbye to Madame Bosnet. 'Only a week, madame,' he assured her. 'You'll just have time to change the sheets.'

She wept, and kissed him on both cheeks.

Reynolds had packed up all the kit he reckoned his colonel would need; there was not a great deal, as there would be little chance of changing one's clothes in the trenches. Then it was dusk, and Murdoch assembled his officers.

'Right ho,' he said. 'I'm taking A Squadron, B Squadron, and half of C Squadron. One troop of C Squadron will remain here. Lieutenant Destry, you'll command.'

'Me, sir?' The lieutenant was aggrieved.

'Somebody has to. Just make sure there are hot baths all around when we come out. Now, the rest of you, go amongst your men and inform them that we will be leaving the horses and walking. Spurs will obviously be left in camp.'

'Walking, sir?' Only Prendergast and Ramage knew where they were actually going.

'That's right, Captain Lowndes. Never forget that we are dragoons. We began as mounted infantry, and the powers that be are still inclined to consider us as mounted infantry, when they have to. We're for a spot of trench duty.'

'Trench duty! My God!'

'Quite. Destry, you are also responsible for all the horses. Padre, I'd like you to remain as well.'

'I'm sure I will be of more use in the line, Colonel Mackinder.'

'It's only for a week. We're not supposed to do any fighing, and there won't be an opportunity for divine service. This is an unpleasant duty we just have to get over as quickly as possible. Very good, gentlemen.' He looked at his watch. 'We move out at eight fifteen pip emma. You have one hour.'

The officers moved off into the darkness, Prendergast filled his dispatch case with the papers he thought he might need, and they both raised their heads to look at the dimmed headlights bumping along the road. 'A change of plan?' the adjutant wondered.

'We're not that lucky.' Murdoch walked to the gate, peered at the man getting down from the car. 'Harry. For God's sake.'

'Murdoch.' Harry Caspar shook hands with his brother-in-law. 'Hi, Billy. You guys moving out, right?'

'Now how did you know that?' Murdoch hadn't seen Harry since Christmas night, when the two of them had shared four bottles of champagne in St Omer itself.

'I have little birds, who whisper. Say, is that wine in that bottle?'

'The dregs. Help yourself. I suppose Jerry knows all about it too.'

'Wouldn't surprise me.' Harry, only slightly larger than his sister and with somewhat puckered features, drank the last of the wine. 'You're for the line.'

'Great God Almighty! Is nothing secret in this army? When I find out the name of your little bird, I'm going to have him shot.'

'Or her,' Prendergast suggested.

'Okay, you guys. So I found out. Nobody else knows, believe me. But as I'm here . . .'

'We can lock you up for a start. Billy, get Destry. I want this character locked up for the next week.'

'I hope you're kidding,' Harry said. 'Listen, why do you think I'm here?'

'I'd prefer not to know.'

'I want to come with you.'

'Are you out of your mind?'

'Listen! Nobody knows for sure what it's like in the line. Only the guys who have been there. No correspondents. If I can get up there, Murdoch, think of the story I could write. Listen! The folks back home want to know what it's like over here. They really do.'

'And you'll make yourself famous all over again.'

'Sure. I'll make you famous all over again too.'

'That I can do without. And what do I tell Lee when you get your head shot off?'

'I intend to stick closer to the ground than a crocodile's prick. Come on, Murdoch. Give a guy a break.'

Murdoch looked at Prendergast, who looked back and shrugged.

'One haversack,' Murdoch said.

'You got it.'

The regiment was still uncertain exactly what it was doing, and there was considerable grumbling at having to walk, but their officers had them well in hand and they moved off, along a good road to begin with. Murdoch took the lead with Harry and Regimental Sergeant-Major Yeald; Murdoch and Yeald had served together since South Africa, when they had both been boys, and Yeald had been with him in Somaliland. He had never undertaken an action without Yeald at his shoulder. Prendergast brought up the rear to make sure there were no stragglers, and the three captains marched at the heads of their dismounted squadrons. It seemed odd to be on the march, even on foot, without an advance guard, a rearguard and flankers, but he was obeying his instructions. At the crossroads they were met by their guides – two military policemen, a sergeant and a private – and proceeded into the night. All smoking was forbidden and they tramped wearily on, each trooper aware only of the man immediately in front of him. They followed the road for over an hour before out of the darkness to either side there loomed the shattered remnants of houses, and they realized they were marching through a deserted village. A single starving dog barked and then slunk away.

Now the road turned to mud, and walking became more difficult. And now too their nostrils were assailed by a slowly increasing stench which seemed a mixture of every offensive smell any of them had ever inhaled.

'What the hell is that stink?' Harry Caspar muttered.

'You name it, sir,' said the MP sergeant. 'There ain't no latrines out here. And no graves, either.'

'Christ!' Harry muttered.

'It was your idea to come along,' Murdoch reminded him.

'You get used to it,' the sergeant said.

A star shell burst in the sky in front of them, and every man froze.

'Just Jerry keeping himself awake,' the sergeant said. 'He don't know we're here or he'd have opened up.'

At last even the muddy lane ended, and they were on duckboards laid across the churned-up countryside. Men slipped off them and cursed, were dragged back into line by their comrades. They came upon the first trenches unexpectedly, and Murdoch nearly tumbled in.

'Who the hell is that?' someone asked.

'Royal Western Dragoons.'

'Horses, by Christ! That's all we need.'

'No horses,' Murdoch assured him, climbing out the other side.

'Real quiet now, sir,' the sergeant recommended. 'Jerry ain't that far away.'

'Pass the word back,' Murdoch told Prendergast. 'I'll have the balls of any man who speaks.'

Their feet dragging through the mud seemed to make as much noise as a herd of elephants, and when a shot rang out Murdoch had to exercise all his self-control not to hurl himself to the ground.

'Long way away, sir,' the sergeant said, no doubt enjoying playing nursemaid to a famous holder of the Victoria Cross, as well as DSO and bar.

A few minutes later they descended into another trench and this time remained below ground, following connecting passages until they arrived at their sector. Here Murdoch was greeted by the colonel of the infantry battalion they were relieving.

'Quiet as the grave around here,' he said. 'Couldn't be a better place for a first time. Look out for raids, though. Keep your men up to scratch.' He showed Murdoch into the headquarters dugout, one line of trenches back from the front, where a lantern gleamed. 'It's not much, but it's home. Enjoy it.' He saluted. 'Lincolnshires moving out.'

Murdoch saluted in turn. Prendergast came in. 'Holy Jesus Christ!' he remarked. 'We have to spend a week in here?'

Murdoch grinned. 'At least it's not raining.'

Next day it rained, a steady, chilling drizzle. The rain limited visibility to fifty yards, and the German trenches, they had been told, were about a hundred and fifty yards away. They could have been a thousand, and the dragoons the only human beings left on earth. Even when the rain cleared in the afternoon they looked at an absolutely desolate vista, with hardly a tree standing, not a soul to be seen across the muddy plain before them, and just a continuous roll of barbed wire to separate them from the presumed enemy position. Suitably keyed up, the troopers spent all day on the alert, expecting to see grey figures emerging out of the murk at any moment. Several times they opened fire at some suspected movement. On these occasions the Germans invariably fired back, but the dragoons never actually saw any of their enemies and they soon settled down into such routine as was possible in the very nearly impossible conditions under which they were forced to exist. The stench did actually become familiar within twenty-four hours. Less easy to accept was the necessity of using the trenches themselves as latrines, and of being unable to wash, so that hands handling food grew steadily filthier, while it was difficult to conceive what their bodies were like under their uniforms or inside their boots – the itches which increased with every day were evidence that they had a good deal of company in there. Externally things were bad enough; Reynolds was in despair as he watched Murdoch's uniform turn into a soggy, odorous mess.

Worst of all were the rats, huge, bloated monsters which scurried across the mud and in and out of the trenches. Everyone knew that their food supply was dead bodies, but killing them only increased the stench which surrounded them.

And above all there was the boredom. Behind the lines it had at least been possible to exercise the men daily, and there had been the horses to care for, however much the troopers might have grumbled at the constant curry-combing. In the trenches there was simply nothing to do, twenty-four hours a day, but wait and watch; Murdoch and Harry and Prendergast played cards and reminisced, which presumably was what most of their men were doing when not actually on sentry duty, but they got to the stage of praying for an enemy attack, just to relieve the monotony.

The dragoons remained remarkably cheerful in all this – but they knew they were only there for a week. What it must be like to have a fortnight of this, and be pulled out, only to know there was another fortnight of hell waiting, Murdoch could not imagine.

Even Harry Caspar was shocked out of his usual insouciance by his surroundings. 'When we get out of here, Murdoch,' he said. 'We are going to get drunk.'

'That might be an idea.'

'I don't see why they need us at all,' Prendergast grumbled. 'We've been here nearly our week and hardly fired a shot. Our sentries loosed off this morning and didn't even get a reply. Jerry could have pulled out and gone home for all we know.'

'Only he hasn't,' Ramage reminded him. 'He's a hundred and fifty yards away. Waiting for us to start something serious.'

'And as we're not going to, let's hope he stays there,' Murdoch commented.

Their neighbours were also concerned at the lack of activity. The two regiments next to them were composed of French colonial troops, cheerful black men who were used to the heat of North Africa and found the cold and wet of a French spring particularly irksome. 'It is not usually like this,' explained the French major who acted as liaison officer, and spent a good deal of time in the British trenches – he was fond of tea. 'The Boches are up to something. I wonder if we should not mount a raid.'

'Not on your life,' Murdoch told him. 'Because we are also up to something – right, monsieur? – and we don't want to stir it until our chaps are ready.'

'Of course,' the Frenchman agreed. 'But still . . . it is odd.'

'What do you think?' Murdoch asked Prendergast after their guest had departed and they stood together on the firing step, cautiously peering out at their barbed wire. It was quite a good afternoon, and they could see the German lines. They could even hear someone singing over there.

'Well, sir, I think we should obey orders, and just sit tight. We only have until tomorrow night to go. And we haven't lost a single man.'

It was the oddest warfare Murdoch had ever engaged in. He had of course sat opposite Boer armies in South Africa, but that had been in open country, with the opposing forces separated by picquets or perhaps a river or a fortified position – never within a few yards of each other. And never exchanging more than an occasional shot.

'I shall be damned glad to get back to the farm,' he confided to Reynolds that night.

'You can say that again, sir,' the corporal agreed.

'Champagne,' mused Harry, leaning back and staring at the roof of the dugout. 'Bottles and bottles of champagne.'

'So what are you going to write about?' Murdoch asked. 'We're due to be relieved in another twenty-four hours.'

'I'll think of something.'

Murdoch slept heavily. Tomorrow night they would be

47

pulling out, and the infantry would be coming in – to launch the offensive which might just end the war. He wished he could believe that.

'I beg your pardon, sir,' said Ralph Manly-Smith.

Murdoch sat up. So did both Prendergast and Harry. 'What time is it?' the American asked.

'Three seventeen ack emma, sir.'

'For God's sake . . .'

'I think there's something happening out there, sir.'

Murdoch threw off the blanket, buttoned his jacket, and went outside. Reynolds was there to press his steel helmet into his hand before he followed Manly-Smith along the communicating trench to the line.

He found that nearly the entire regiment was awake and standing to arms, listening. The night was shrouded with mist, and they could hardly see as far as their own wire. But from beyond the mist curtain there was certainly sound. 'What the hell is it?' he whispered.

'A kind of slithering,' Ramage suggested.

'There's been some clanking as well, sir,' Manly-Smith said.

'Definitely Jerry is moving some kind of machinery out there,' Murdoch said.

'Artillery, do you think?' Harry wondered.

'Not right up behind the line. I wonder . . .' He checked the words, because he was sworn to secrecy. But could it be possible the Germans were also working on some kind of machine to force its way across trenches? Yet there had been no sound of engines. 'We'll just have to wait and see,' he said. 'Double your sentries, Peter.' He and Harry and Prendergast returned to the dugout, where Reynolds had tea on the go. 'We'll stay awake,' Murdoch decided.

'They must've heard you were due to leave tonight,' Harry said. 'And are planning a celebration.'

'So maybe that was all cases of champagne.' Murdoch looked at his watch. Four o'clock. If anything was going to happen, it would be soon. And it would begin with an artillery barrage. Which the experts said was all noise and little effect. But there had been no bombardment. He looked at his watch again and again as it reached five and the darkness started to fade.

'False alarm,' Prendergast said thankfully.

'Or Jerry's running late,' Harry suggested.

Suddenly there was noise. A huge amount of noise, from over to the right. But not gunfire. Men screaming, shrieking in fear and agony.

'What the hell. . . ?' Murdoch led the rush back to the line, where his troopers were staring into the gloom, hands wrapped around their rifles.

'Those are the French,' Ramage said.

'Listen,' Harry said. 'That sounds a lot like "sauve qui peut".'

'Save yourself if you can,' Prendergast muttered.

'There!' Harry said. He had mounted the firing step, but was looking back. In the steadily growing light they could see the Senegalese streaming away from their trenches, many of them having thrown away their rifles. And now the machine-guns started to chatter, and the exposed men fell left and right. 'What in the name of God . . .' He sniffed, stared at Murdoch in horror.

Several of the troopers were also sniffing, and one was choking.

'My God, sir,' shouted RSM Yeald. 'It's some kind of gas.'

The main body of gas hadn't reached them yet. The wind was blowing along the trench from the direction of the French position, and now Murdoch could see what looked like a yellow cloud lying on the ground, twisting and seeping towards them.

'What are we to do?' Prendergast gasped.

Murdoch's mind seemed to be turning handsprings. The French on their right had pulled out, and there would be a huge gap in the line over there. Into which the Germans would undoubtedly be pouring. If he maintained his position his men would not only be gassed to death, they would be surrounded. 'We fall back,' he said. 'But slowly. No running away. Get on the telephone to brigade and inform them of the situation. Tell them the French have given way. But remember, I want a fighting retreat.'

The orders were given and the men prepared to pull out. But the gas had drifted closer, and Murdoch saw one man crumple and fall to his knees, choking and gasping, while his own eyes were smarting so that he could hardly see, and his nose was burning. He had to do something, because they were not going to get away in time, unless they turned and ran like the French. While the Germans, clearly advancing behind the gas, had opened fire on them as well now.

'Handkerchiefs,' he shouted. 'Anything cloth. Wrap them over your noses and mouths. Wet them. Quickly now.'

'Wet them?' Prendergast gazed at him, handkerchief in hand. 'Is there enough water?'

'Use your bottles. Come on. If there isn't any, well pee on the God damned things.' He tied his own kerchief over his nose and mouth, and breathing, if not easier, was no longer suggestive of immediate choking. Then he started waving his men down the communications trench.

'Aren't you coming?' Harry gasped.

'With the rearguard. You get out.'

Harry hesitated, then stumbled down the trench. Prendergast had already taken command of the retreat, and Ramage, Manly-Smith, Yeald, Murdoch and one troop, but with two Lewis guns, were alone in the forward trench. Now they were entirely surrounded by the pungent yellow fumes, but they could see beyond them, too, into clear air . . . and advancing Germans. 'Open fire,' Murdoch snapped.

The machine-guns began to chatter, and the rest of the troop used their rifles. Several Germans fell and the rest went to ground; they still had not crossed the British wire.

'Withdraw,' Murdoch said.

The Lewis guns were taken down and the men hurried along the communications trench. It meant re-entering the swirling chlorine, but they could not stay where they were. Murdoch was last to leave the trench, with Ramage, and by the time they had reached the second line the Germans were

50

coming again. Now the officers had to use their revolvers while the machine-guns were set up again, but at least a real breeze had sprung up and the gas was starting to clear.

'Talk about Huns,' Ramage said, pulling off his handkerchief and taking great gulps of air.

'I imagine we have something nasty up our sleeves,' Murdoch said. But he kept thinking of those crumpled figures in the trench. What a way to die.

The Germans were now flooding into the abandoned trench and coming along the communications.

'Get those guns working,' Murdoch shouted, and realized the gunner was Johnnie Morton. RSM Yeald himself was feeding the belt as the Lewis gun resumed its chatter. Several of the grey-clad enemy returned fire, and one hurled a stick grenade before falling. With the greatest of calm Yeald picked it up and threw it out of the trench before it exploded.

There was a gasp from beside Murdoch, and he saw Manly-Smith on one knee. He grasped the boy's arm and pulled him back to his feet but several more men had fallen from the close-range firing, even if the Germans had now gone to ground. 'Pull back,' Murdoch snapped, his voice hoarse. 'Pull back.'

They had to cross open ground to regain the next line, but only a couple of men were hit as the Germans had temporarily run out of steam. Here too the gas had drifted through, and Murdoch saw an entire stretcher team crumpled on the ground, suffocated by the swirling chlorine.

'Orders from brigade, sir,' Prendergast gasped. 'We're to fall back to support. It's on its way.'

'So let's do that,' Murdoch agreed, and realized he was still half carrying Manly-Smith. The boy had been shot in the thigh and was groaning horribly, and weeping as the shock wore off and the pain began, but he was unlikely to die. Murdoch handed him over to two troopers and organized the retreat. The regiment pulled back several hundred yards before they encountered masses of infantry coming up in support, and now too the artillery opened up in an attempt to blast the Germans back.

The Royal Westerns were returned to their cantonment. It was like entering heaven, to breathe clean air, to sink into vast tubs of boiling, disinfected water and watch the dirt and lice floating to the surface, to consign uniforms to more vats of boiling disinfectant, to eat clean food. Harry went into St Omer and got his champagne, but no one really felt like getting drunk. Some hundred men – one in five of the ration strength – had not returned, and of those who had, over a hundred had not got their faces covered in time and had to be sent to field hospital, still choking and gasping; their lungs would clearly be affected for a very long time. They, together with the wounded such as Manly-Smith, eventually were taken to the rear and then England. 'Lucky buggers,' RSM Yeald told them. 'You won't be back for months.'

Sir John French himself came over to inspect the survivors; he was their Colonel-in-Chief. 'Brave lads,' he said. 'Always in the thick of it, eh? I am proud of you. Proud of you all.' He returned to the farmhouse with Murdoch. 'And you . . . you kept your men in hand. As always.'

'I have good men, sir,' Murdoch reminded him.

'I wish we could all say that. What a frightful business. I mean, gas! It's not civilized.'

'Neither is war, Sir John. I hope we're going to produce some gas of our own.'

'It's on its way. With some kind of mask as well. But really, Murdoch, it simply isn't civilized.' He gazed at Harry. 'I hope you're going to give this good coverage in your American newspapers, Caspar.'

The two men had met in South Africa. Harry nodded. 'You bet your life, General. You bet your life.'

The bitter fighting lasted a week, although the dragoons had been pulled out of the line after the first day, and at last the enemy were checked. Actually the defeat was less

52

calamitous than it might have been, because the Germans had apparently underestimated the effect the gas was going to have, and had not moved up sufficient reserves to exploit their breakthrough. Thus the line was soon re-established. Yet the consequences were serious enough. The French colonials would need a complete regrouping and, even more important, the Allied offensive had been forestalled. It still went ahead, but with less impetus as officers and men feared an encounter with the deadly gas, and lasted little more than a month. Blunted from the beginning, it never had a chance and accomplished little more than to regain the lost salient. By the end of May the front was quiet again, although by now the British and French were also equipped with gas canisters, and every man went into the line with a breathing apparatus on his hip. These would separate the gas fumes from clear air and ensure survival, but they also made every movement twice as tiring.

The cavalry could recover, as there was nothing for them to do. The casualties were replaced by fresh drafts. Murdoch could watch his three companies being brought back to strength, until he commanded nearly his full six hundred effectives. Manly-Smith returned with a scar but otherwise as fit as before. The regiment was awarded six Military Medals and a Military Cross for its part in stemming the German breakthrough. Murdoch gave the cross to Peter Ramage, one of the medals to RSM Yeald, and another to Trooper Morton. Morton protested that he had done no more than his duty.

'Duty is what it's all about, Johnnie,' Murdoch reminded him, and was then embarrassed to be summoned to headquarters to receive the Légion d'honneur from the hands of Marshal Joffre himself.

'I think the frogs are a little embarrassed by what happened,' Sir John French explained. 'But it's all good for the entente, eh?'

There was even time, that summer, for leave to England. Murdoch rotated his men carefully, but did not feel he could go himself, with so many replacements to be trained. Because once again an offensive was in the air, as the hundreds of thousands of recruits raised by Kitchener's determination were flooding into France, and as shell production was at last stepped up. Marshal Joffre was still determined to throw the Germans out of France by frontal assault, and before Christmas 1915. And, as usual, the cavalry were required to hold themselves in readiness to charge through whatever gap was created and complete the victory.

Murdoch's decision was a bitter blow to Lee, who had to tell him by letter that she was expecting a baby. 'It would be so nice to have you home,' she wrote. 'At least for the birth.'

But the delivery was not due until August, and by then all leave had been cancelled as the huge armies were preparing to attack.

The battle did not begin until 25 September, and by then Murdoch had learned that he was the father of another son, whom Lee proposed to call Harry after her brother. Harry Caspar drove over to celebrate the event, and to complain that he was not being allowed to accompany the assault force when it went over the top.

'I never knew a man so damned determined to get himself killed,' Murdoch remarked. 'Why don't you go home and join your own army?'

'I would, if there was anyone except Mexican bandits to fight,' Harry agreed.

'We could use a few of your people over here.'

'No chance of that. If not even the *Lusitania* business could bring us in, nothing else is likely to. So, when you guys get turned loose, do I get to ride along?'

'If we get turned loose,' Murdoch reminded him.

The cavalry were not turned loose. The British offensive, like the French, ground to a halt in the mud and the autumnal rain with only a few yards to show for the usual horrific casualty list. The attack was called off on 14 October, and the armies went into winter quarters; even Marshal Joffre had learned from the previous year's experiences that attempting to advance in snow and ice was not practical.

It was a month later that Sir John French visited the regiment. It was already bitterly cold, and Murdoch escorted the Field Marshal into the farm's kitchen, where there was a blazing fire.

'You'll pardon us, madame,' Murdoch said to Madame Bosnet. Sir John had already indicated that he wanted a private chat.

Madame smiled happily and hurried off. She understood no English; and it was unlikely that Sir John would converse in French, of which he had learned very little.

'Soon be Christmas,' French observed. 'A second bloody Christmas. Who'd have thought it possible? Do you know that we have suffered damn near half a million casualties, Murdoch, since August 1914? Do you know the strength of the BEF which I brought over then?'

'A hundred and fifty thousand, approximately,' Murdoch said.

'So we have lost three times our original strength. That has got to be unique in military history. The Frogs and the Jerries have lost a lot more. That doesn't make all that much difference to our situation. And there's no end in sight. If the Dardanelles had worked . . .' he sighed.

Murdoch was inclined to sigh too. Not only because of the wastage in men and ships which that abortive campaign had cost, but because it had also forced the resignation of, in his opinion, the most military-minded member of the entire Cabinet – Winston Churchill, whose brainchild the Dardanelles offensive had been. With Churchill gone from the Admiralty, Murdoch wondered if Ernest Swinton's so important experiments were still being funded.

'Lord Kitchener believes the only decision can be reached here on the western front,' he remarked.

'And so do I. But the more we can distract the enemy the more chance we have of breaking through. Now . . . God knows.'

'Perhaps someone will come up with an idea,' Murdoch suggested, wishing he could mention the tanks.

'Oh, they're always suggesting newfangled ideas,' French observed. 'But at the end of the day it's leadership that counts. I have failed as a leader.'

55

'For God's sake, Sir John,' Murdoch protested. 'Your men would follow you to hell and back.'

'And that's just about where I've led them. Anyway, I was not expressing a personal opinion, Murdoch. I'm to be relieved.'

Murdoch stared at him in consternation.

'This is strictly confidential,' French said. 'It won't be announced for another month. But the decision has been taken.'

'But who. . . ?'

'Douglas Haig. He's a good officer. A cavalryman, like us.'

Murdoch knew Haig, of course; they had served together in South Africa. He knew him to be a man of great determination, as well as considerable panache – he was known as the best-dressed officer in the army. But he, and Haig, had fought under French for so long, first as part of the cavalry division against the Boers, then when he had been Chief of the Imperial General Staff, and then these last eighteen months in France, that it seemed impossible the Field Marshal would not be there for ever.

'I'm to take command of the Home Forces,' French said with a bitter smile. 'Ah, well, it'll give me something to do.'

'I imagine the decision was Kitchener's,' Murdoch said no less bitterly.

'Oh, undoubtedly. Although you know he's been relieved as CIGS by Robertson? But he's still Minister of War. Something you want to remember, young man. But I've got something going for you, too.'

'Sir?'

'Well, you can have a brigade if you wish.'

'A brigade!' Murdoch frowned. 'I'd hate to leave the lads.'

'You will have to, eventually, Murdoch. However, as I thought that might be your attitude, I have to inform you that the regiment is being taken out of France. On my recommendation.'

'Sir?' Murdoch was horrified.

'We need you elsewhere, Murdoch. Townshend has got

himself into a mess in Mesopotamia. Do you know anything about that?'

'Not a lot. The idea was to take Baghdad, was it not?'

'The idea. The whole operation was a botched one. Oh, Townshend is a fine fighting soldier. He's proved that in India. But he was taking orders from both the War Office and the India Office at the same time, and neither of them seem to have been in close touch with the other. Anyway, to cut a long story short, he advanced up the Tigris all right, won a couple of victories, was told to press on to Baghdad, and has run right out of steam. So he's managed to lose a battle, and has retired to a place called Kut, awaiting reinforcements. Naturally the Turks have closed in on him. So what was supposed to be a brief campaign is likely to turn into another Dardanelles if we're not careful. Anyway, Stanley Maude has been given overall command, with orders to relieve Townshend and resume the advance as soon as possible. Do you know Stanley?'

'Of course.' General Sir Stanley Maude was another South African veteran.

'Well, he wants cavalry. Cavalry with experience of desert and mountain fighting. Your chaps are veterans of both the North West Frontier and Somaliland. So he's getting the regiment. So, a brigade, or a spot of sunburn, Murdoch. Take your choice.'

'I think a spot of sunburn, sir,' Murdoch said.

French grinned. 'There'll be home leave first, of course. But Maude is in a hurry.'

3

Mesopotamia, 1916

'He looks just like you,' Lee said.

Murdoch cradled the baby in his arms. 'Poor fellow. But he has your eyes.'

'Do you really think so? They'll have changed by the time you see him again.'

'Um.' Murdoch handed Harry to the waiting nurse, and went down the stairs holding Lee's hand. 'Shouldn't take us all that long to beat the Turks.'

'Everyone said that about the Germans, last year. And the Turks . . .' She gave a little shiver. 'Are they as barbaric as people say?'

'Well, they don't have a Christian point of view, I suppose simply because they're not Christians. A beaten man is a beaten man, not suddenly a friend with whom you share a cigarette.' He squeezed her fingers. 'But I've fought barbarians before. And not been beat.'

'The Somalis. You had an awful wound.'

'And recovered. And married you.' He kissed her on the nose. 'So all turns out well in the end. What do you think of my latest accumulation?'

She peered at the crimson ribbon of the Légion d'honneur. 'It rather rounds things off, doesn't it?'

Murdoch peered at himself in the hall mirror. 'Why, I suppose it does.' The row of ribbons stretched in a kaleidoscope of colour from the crimson of the Victoria Cross, through the Distinguished Service Order, with the silver rosette of the second award, the South African Medal, King Edward VII's Coronation Medal, King George V's Coronation Medal, the 1914 Star, and was neatly completed by the crimson of the Légion d'honneur. 'I shall have to make sure I don't get any more.'

'I hope you don't get any more,' she said. 'Not if every time means you're trying to get yourself killed. Oh, Murdoch . . . when is it going to end?'

'If I knew that, my dearest, I'd be commander-in-chief. Or Prime Minister. But it will end. With us on top.'

'Because the British always win in the end. Do you reckon that's an eternal law?'

'It's my business to see that it is,' he told her. 'And the business of millions of others like me.'

She was pensive. 'Will there be brothels in Mesopotamia?'

'There are brothels everywhere. Especially where there are a lot of soldiers.'

'Will you have to regulate them again, as you did in St Omer?'

Because it had, after all, got into the newspapers.

'If I have to, yes.'

'Murdoch . . . do you ever go to brothels?'

'Would you like me to tell you if I did?'

'No. Please. It's just that . . . if you did . . . feel that you had to, I would understand. I mean, you have my permission.'

'Let me tell you a little secret,' he said. 'Commanding officers don't go to brothels. It simply isn't done.' He kissed her again. 'Merry Christmas.'

Much as he loved Lee, and Broad Acre, and the children, much as he had enjoyed Christmas with the family, the utter civilization of being so far removed from the war, he was still glad to rejoin the regiment for embarkation at Plymouth. If there was a war to be fought, he wanted to think of nothing else. Awareness of wife and family was a weakening factor. He could only be grateful that thanks to the careful investments of his father and grandfather, Lee would be a wealthy widow, as well as a beautiful one, should he fall foul of some Turk. He wondered, would she marry again? But that also was not a thought to be taking off to war several thousand miles from England.

The regiment was in high spirits as they set sail, even if

they had the threat of a submarine attack to think of. They had all been reunited with their families for a brief week – but it had been Christmas week – they had shed the muddy horror that was northern France, and now they were shedding the snowbound misery of England for sunny climes; they had not been told where they were going, but the fact that they had been issued with tropical kit told them that.

They were also travelling in some luxury, as an entire erstwhile liner had been requisitioned as their carrier; the size was necessary as in addition to the seven-hundred-odd men there were around nine hundred horses. 'Takes you back,' Peter Ramage remarked. 'Like setting off for Somaliland.'

'Or South Africa,' Murdoch agreed. 'Tell you what, though, Peter. . . we're heading for cavalry country, at last.' He looked down at the well deck and spotted Johnnie Morton, also staring back at the mist-shrouded Devon hills. Murdoch wondered where, and how, Morton had spent his Christmas. What a sad travesty of a career which should by now have had him at least a brigadier-general. And now he was being returned to the climes in which he had earned his disgrace. No doubt he had a lot to think about.

The voyage was incident free. There was bad weather off the Portuguese coast, and then the usual delightful run across the Mediterranean. Here again there were supposed to be enemy submarines, but they never saw one. As the weather hotted up there were the usual ailments amongst both men and horses, and after they had passed through the Suez Canal and were making their way down the Red Sea the animals began to die. Although Murdoch had made this journey before and had known what to expect, he still found it sadly depressing as the carcasses were flung over the side, and reflected thankfully that they had only a short way to go.

The trouble with a long sea voyage was that it gave a man too much time to remember. Murdoch found himself thinking about Reger, who had indeed been exchanged, and was no doubt again commanding a German regiment –

or was perhaps even on the staff. And thoughts of Reger reminded him about Margriet, and young Paul. Young Paul hadn't seemed particularly important before; as he had been born in 1901 he was still only fourteen. But the war was showing no sign of ending. If it didn't, soon, he might find himself fighting his own son. His eldest son.

But was Paul his son? How that thought haunted him. The boy had been born in one of Lord Kitchener's 'concentration camps', where the Boer women and children had been herded after their farms had been burned in an effort to make the commandos come to terms. It had eventually succeeded, but it had been a ghastly way to make war, as barbaric as anything practised by the Mad Mullah, as malnutrition and disease had swept through the ranks of the miserable captives.

Margriet had been imprisoned there after she had helped him to escape from her own people – and after they had become lovers. Unknown to him, she had been pregnant. But there might have been another man: that would indeed explain her decision to aid him and flee her people – a decision which had turned out to be a disaster, for she had been sent back to them.

Lee knew of her, and Paul, of course. As neither Lee nor Murdoch had been a virgin, they had confessed their peccadilloes on their honeymoon. Lee's erstwhile lover had already been dead. She had been utterly sympathetic towards both Margriet and the boy, had wanted to befriend them. He had with difficulty persuaded her that it might not work. And Lee did not know that they had met again, and again disastrously, in Ireland in 1914. Presumably she would have condoned that as well, in view of her remarks about the brothel. Dear, dear Lee. She was far too good for him.

But how he wished this damnable voyage would end and they could get back to some action, to concentrate his mind on his job.

After rounding Aden it yet took them several more days to make their way up the Persian Gulf, uncharted waters for any member of the regiment. The land which came into sight as they closed the Mesopotamian coast was flat and featureless, seeming to stretch for ever in swampy profusion, but as they steamed up the Shatt al Arab they saw evidence of a great deal of fertility, with date palm plantations predominating.

Basra itself was surprisingly large, situated on the west bank of the Shatt and only just downstream of the huge Hawr al Hammar lake, where the Tigris and the Euphrates merged to form the great swamp which was their delta. It was a fairly typical Muslim community, in its mosques and minarets, its veiled women, its flies and dogs and ragged little boys, and its curiosity; vast crowds gathered to watch the regiment disembarking and listen to the band playing the march from *Aïda*.

It was also very hot.

Liaison officers were waiting for the dragoons, and they walked their horses off behind the band to their allotted quarters just outside the town. Murdoch left Billy Prendergast in command while he was hurried straightaway to the office of Sir Stanley Maude, who had himself just arrived, it turned out.

Maude was a bold-featured man who still wore a massive Victorian moustache. There could be no doubting his ability or his powers of decision, however. 'Mackinder!' he said, shaking hands. 'Thank God you've arrived. Now, if only some of these other troops they've promised me were to turn up . . . everything happens with such damned slowness. At least we know Townshend is all right for the time being.'

'Are we in contact with him, sir?'

'At the moment, no. But George Nixon, whom I've replaced, made a sortie up the Tigris last month with such troops as he had. He didn't get very close to Kut and took a bit of a beating, in fact, but he seems to have managed to exchange heliograph signals with the Kut garrison, on the basis of which he assured me, before leaving, that Townsend can hold out for another six months.'

Murdoch pulled his nose.

'Oh, quite,' Maude agreed. 'Six months is a hell of a long

time, and Nixon is a confounded optimist. But what the devil can I do? Nixon estimates there are some sixty thousand Turks around Kut, and even more between Kut and Baghdad. And they are officered by Germans. Townshend has perhaps nine thousand British and Indian. I have two under-strength Indian divisions, and now your dragoons. Say twenty thousand men. We are not going to relieve Townshend by getting ourselves chopped up by a vastly superior Turkish force. He has just got to hold out until the rest of the troops I have asked for are received.'

'Yes, sir,' Murdoch agreed. 'My orders?'

'Get your men fighting fit, first. Then you can commence probing up the river.' He pointed. 'None of your heroics, Colonel Mackinder. I want information, nothing more. I want to open communication with Townshend, if that is possible, by any means. If you can get close enough to use your heliograph, do so; I don't think Townshend has radio, or if he does, it's not working for some reason. I want accurate information as to Turkish strength and morale.' He grinned. 'And I want to remind the Turks, and the Arabs, of our presence.'

Murdoch had both men and horses hard at work training the following morning. The long sea journey had made them soft, and of course it was necessary to get them acclimatized to the heat as rapidly as possible – and to the increased hygiene necessary for survival in the tropical Middle East. Heat stroke caused a wave of sickness, and despite the most stringent regulations the drinking of unboiled water produced an equal number of dysentery cases. Fortunately most occurrences of both of these illnesses were minor, and a lesson once learned was not forgotten – it was too unpleasant to risk again. There was also the problem of persuading the men only to visit the bazaars in groups of at least half a dozen, as there was undoubtedly much pro-Turkish feeling amongst the Arabs – unlike farther west, where reports indicated that the Arabs of the Saudi Peninsula might well fight alongside the British if encouraged sufficiently. And equally, as usual, he had to attempt to control the incidence of VD amongst the troopers.

Murdoch spent much time with General George Gorringe, who was also working hard to restore his two Indian divisions to a capable fighting force – with which, presumably, the dragoons would be operating when the British were able to take the offensive. The previous month the Indians had been led by their then commander, General Aylmer, in a frontal assault against the Turkish positions. That had been before General Maude had replaced Nixon as overall Commander-in-Chief. The assault, apparently based on a total contempt for the fighting ability of the Turks, had been resoundingly repulsed. Now they were licking their wounds and awaiting replacements, which dribbled in with every ship from Bombay. The new arrivals were eager enough but too many of them were raw recruits; and unlike the British, they accepted such misfortunes as dysentery, and even its more severe cousin cholera, as a fact of life. It became apparent to Murdoch that, even without governmental dilatoriness, the march to the relief of Kut-al-Amara was going to be long delayed.

'Our business,' he told his officers, 'is reconnaissance in force until the advance is ready, and if possible, communication with the besieged army. It is not our business to engage the enemy at this time except in pursuance of such objectives. We are the only cavalry this army possesses, and therefore we must preserve our strength. So, no heroics. We march at dawn.'

Next morning the guides arrived, three Arabs who, he was assured, were utterly faithful to the British cause. Their head was named Mulai. Immediately the regiment moved out. Murdoch followed a simple plan of having one troop, accompanied by one guide, two miles in front of the regiment, with orders to retire if meeting any serious opposition. Another troop, with the second guide, flank-marched a similar distance away to the east; their left flank was covered by the Tigris itself. Keeping Mulai with the main body was a means of ensuring the 'utter faithfulness' of the Arabs.

The men were in their usual high spirits as they formed a long column of twos, winding their way north. Murdoch limited them to fifteen miles a day, and it was eight days before they arrived at Amara, which they found to be a sizeable town, and held by a brigade of Indians. 'Not much activity out there,' said the brigadier-general. 'The Turks fight better on the defensive, and are happy to let our chaps do the pushing. Not that we have anything to push with.'

His pessimism was typical of the whole Mesopotamian army, which undoubtedly felt itself a forgotten force.

'Reinforcements are on their way,' Murdoch assured him. 'Any word from Kut?'

'A messenger got through last week. Spent four days in the river, poor devil. Says things are getting a bit tight.'

'I can imagine.' Six months, he thought. Too long.

The regiment moved on next day. They were now within seventy miles of the beleaguered town, and had encountered no opposition, but that afternoon the advance guard was fired upon by a Turkish patrol. Murdoch immediately divided the regiment into squadrons, and himself led B Squadron, Captain Lowndes', in a frontal assault upon the patrol, while Ramage took A Squadron by the river and Hunter led C Squadron in a sweep through the desert. Murdoch's objective was prisoners, but the Turks had disappeared.

Next day he probed again, and this time encountered real opposition in the form of a fortified position supported by machine-guns. Several men were hit, one badly. He hastily drew his own men back out of range and encamped them in the best defensive position he could find, with the river forming a barrier to the west, and some low hills to the north and east. He mounted his machine-guns and sat out the night, ready to ride out should he be counter-attacked by a superior force. But no enemy was seen or heard.

Next morning he and Prendergast surveyed the desert in front of them through their glasses. Because it was just desert, except close to the river, which, brown and sluggish, wound its way through the occasional date plantation. There were people by the river, Arabs who

65

came up to gaze at the British soldiers. Murdoch enticed some of them into the camp, told the guides to find out what they could.

'Many soldiers to the north, effendi,' said Mulai.

'How many is many?'

More conversation.

'As many as the sands of the desert,' Mulai said.

'Which could mean anything,' Prendergast remarked.

'Ask him about Kut,' Murdoch said.

'Kut is entirely surrounded, effendi,' Mulai said.

'Is there any chance of us getting close enough to use the heliograph?'

'These men do not think so, effendi.'

'At least the garrison is still holding out,' Prendergast said.

'But we don't know for how long. I wonder if Nixon did get any messages through. According to the brigadier in Amara things aren't going so well.' Murdoch scratched his head. 'I'm damned if I can see what we are going to do.'

He opted to remain encamped for a day or two longer, sending a troop on patrol well into the eastern desert to see if there was a way round, although Mulai assured him that the only way an army, even a regiment, could move in this country was along the line of the rivers. That made sense. It also reduced warfare to a very straightforward affair. Not that Murdoch believed it need be quite as simple as that, given resolute command.

But it was not his business to anticipate General Maude's dispositions and in any event the patrol returned in three days to say that they had again encountered Turkish entrenchments; the way to Kut was very definitely barred. Certainly the town was not going to be relieved without a very much larger army than was at present available – as Maude had recognized. After three further days of sending patrols north to shoot up any Turks they might encounter, in the hopes of enticing the enemy to move against his position and thus yield some prisoners and perhaps some more information, he gave the orders to break camp on the following day and return towards Amara and Basra. He had sent out the usual patrol, and that afternoon, as he had a cup of tea with Prendergast and Llewellyn, it returned. Its commander, Lieutenant Colin Destry, hurried up to them. 'There are people over there, sir.'

'People?' Murdoch put down his tea cup. 'You mean Turks?'

'Well, I don't think so, exactly, sir. Not soldiers. My guide says it's a caravan. I would say he's right. A lot of wagons. With camels.'

'Going where?'

'Well, sir, I didn't approach them. They were travelling from north to south.'

Murdoch looked at Prendergast. 'A bloody caravan, ambling along as if there was no war on?'

'And coming from the north,' Prendergast said.

'We'll have to have a chat with these chaps. Summon Captain Lowndes, Mr Destry. I want B Squadron to move out, arrest the caravan, and bring it in this direction.'

'Yes, sir.' Like all the regiment, Destry was desperate to see some action.

'But no bloodshed, unless resistance is offered,' Murdoch said.

'Yes, sir,' Destry repeated, and hurried off to find his superior.

'You don't think it could be some kind of a trap?' the padre wondered.

'I don't propose to chance that. Sound assembly.'

The regiment alerted, Murdoch himself took command of A Squadron, and with Ramage rode out to the north. Prendergast was left in command of the camp with all six machine-guns. There was a pleasant sense of imminent action at last as A Squadron cantered to the north for several miles, without seeing a soul other than the occasional Arab, and then swung back to the east. 'If it is a trap,' Murdoch remarked to Ramage, 'then it's a damned deep one.'

They topped a shallow rise and looked down on the caravan, surrounded by Lowndes' B Squadron, making its way west to the river. 'Those people just have to have information.'

They returned to camp, arriving at the same time as the caravan, which Lowndes was making pitch their tents and tether their goats and camels outside the military perimeter. 'Give my compliments to Captain Lowndes, Mr Manly-Smith,' Murdoch said. 'And inform him I would like to interview the head person, or people, of that lot as soon as possible.'

'Yes, sir.' Manly-Smith trotted off.

Murdoch returned to his tent, had a bath in Reynolds' tin tub – being camped next to the river meant they could use all the water they wished – and then changed into a fresh uniform; he knew the value of impressing either Arab or Turk. Prendergast had also changed, and together, in all the glory of their polished brown boots, gleaming spurs, dark brown jackets and khaki breeches, Sam Browne belts, revolvers and swords, medal ribbons and smart topees, they awaited the arrival of the caravan master . . . and saw, moving sedately towards them on the backs of several camels, a retinue of veiled women.

Murdoch stood up, and Prendergast did likewise. The women were escorted by Captain Lowndes and Lieutenant Destry, who were on foot, and were accompanied, also on foot, by Arab grooms.

'What the devil is all this?' Murdoch barked.

Lowndes looked embarrassed. 'You asked to see . . . well, the caravan boss, sir.'

'A bunch of women?'

'A woman, sir. A princess.'

'Oh, for God's sake,' Murdoch snapped. 'Every bloody tart in Mesopotamia claims she's a princess.'

The lead camel dropped to its knees, and the woman who had been riding it stepped down with a swirl of white *haik* which allowed a glimpse of her sandals and exquisitely formed pale brown feet. 'But I am not a bloody tart, Colonel,' she said.

Murdoch was entirely taken aback, both by her English, which was perfect, and by the realization that she was by no means old. He could see nothing of her save her hands and her forehead, as her yashmak entirely concealed her face – but there were no wrinkles to be seen, and the hands were young and strong. As had been her feet and her movements.

He was uncomfortably aware that a considerable number of his men had gathered to oversee the arrival of the women, and that most of them had heard the exchange.

'You'll forgive me, madam,' he said. 'I did not know you spoke English.'

'Of course I speak English,' she said, advancing towards him. 'I am the Princess Chand Bibi ibn Shere ibn Ali ibn Muhammad.'

'Ah,' Murdoch said, none the wiser, except that she seemed to have an impressive lineage. But Prendergast was waggling his eyebrows; he had served with the regiment in India.

'And you?' she inquired, standing in front of him.

He inhaled a subtle perfume, gazed into magnificent black eyes, and became acutely aware that it was a very long time since he had held any woman save his wife in his arms – and that it was several weeks since he had held Lee. 'Lieutenant-Colonel Murdoch Mackinder, Commanding Officer, the Royal Western Dragoon Guards,' he replied.

'The Royal Western . . .' The yashmak fluttered, to suggest that she might have smiled. 'I thought your pennons were familiar. And Mackinder! How quaint.' She held out a heavily ringed hand. 'I am pleased to make your acquaintance, Colonel Mackinder.'

'The pleasure is mine, madam.' Murdoch took the fingers, trying not to evaluate the rubies and sapphires that glittered on them, indicated the camp chairs. 'Will you take tea?'

'Thank you.' The princess spoke to her ladies in Arabic, and they, having also stepped down, formed a little group. The Arab grooms who had followed them hobbled the camels.

Murdoch looked at Lowndes and Destry. 'Dismissed, with thanks, gentlemen. And Captain Lowndes, do find something for those fellows to do.'

Lowndes saluted and hurried off to disperse the gawking troopers.

'Shall I stay?' Prendergast whispered.

'Do you know the lady?'

'No. But I knew her father. Or at least, of him. Tough old bird. Had a habit of mutilating his prisoners.'

'Do you suppose I need chaperoning?'

'Could be. I wonder what she's like beneath all that clobber?'

'Well, I am not about to find out. I'll chat her up. Don't go too far.'

'Yes, sir,' Prendergast said, somewhat enviously, and hurried off.

Murdoch sat in the other camp chair, acutely aware that he was being watched by at least six hundred pairs of eyes. Reynolds poured tea.

'Your men have been without women for too long,' Chand Bibi remarked.

'I'm afraid that's true. I'm sorry they have been staring.'

'You also have been without a woman for a long time.'

Once again Murdoch looked into those black eyes. 'Perhaps I am more used to it. Now, madam, may I ask what is the purpose of your caravan?'

'No, Colonel,' she said. 'You may not ask. Not until you have told me by what right you have arrested me and my people.'

Her effrontery was beginning to irritate him. 'By the right of conquest,' he told her.

'Conquest?' Her contempt was evident.

'We are in the process of conquering this land, madam,' he said. 'I should have thought that would have been obvious. And you are traversing it, from our enemies' position to our own, without permission. I am therefore entirely in my rights to arrest you. How severe that arrest will be depends on how much you are prepared to cooperate with me.'

The black eyes flashed at him. 'You are very bold, Colonel Mackinder, when it comes to browbeating women.' Then her gaze drifted to the medal ribbons on his jacket. 'But then, perhaps you are just very bold,' she added in a softer tone. 'I have never met a holder of the Victoria

70

Cross before. But I have nothing to do with you and the Turks and your wars. I am the Princess Chand Bibi ibn Shere ibn Ali ibn Muhammad. My father is Shere Khan, Sheikh of the Mahsuds in the valley of the Kurram. Perhaps you have heard of him.'

'Ah,' Murdoch said. 'The North West Frontier of India. That is how you knew of my regiment.'

'My father has fought against the Royal Western Dragoons, Colonel. But not, perhaps, these men.'

It was half a question. 'I shouldn't think so. The regiment hasn't been in India for ten years.'

'And your soldiers only enlist for seven.' She seemed to know a great deal about the British army. 'But do they never re-enlist?'

'Indeed they do. But I still doubt any of them were in India ten years ago.' Save for Prendergast, of course. Ramage had been with him in Somaliland, as had Yeald, and all the other Indian officers were now dead or retired . . . except Morton! But he wasn't going to introduce either Billy or Morton into this conversation.

'Still,' Chand Bibi remarked, 'it is a famous regiment, in the valley of the Kurram. I think my father may once have fought against your father.'

'A long time ago.'

'And now the Mahsuds are at peace with the English,' she agreed. 'So you have no cause to arrest me.'

'You were coming from Baghdad,' he pointed out.

'Baghdad has been my home,' Chand Bibi said. 'My father gave me in marriage to a Turkish emir. Six months ago I became a widow.'

'You have my sympathy.'

The shoulders beneath the *haik* gave a slight shrug. 'It was a political marriage. The emir spoke of Turkish support for the Mahsuds.' Once again the yashmak fluttered as she smiled. 'Against the British. But he was overtaken by events. Now I seek to return home. I cannot cross the Hindu Kush. It is too arduous and my people have too many enemies. I wish to take ship from Basra to Bombay. My husband's family said I could not do this.

71

They said the British would arrest me and kill me. I laughed at them, because I know the British are honourable people, who do not wage war upon women. But it seems that they were right and I was wrong.'

'Some more tea, Reynolds,' Murdoch said. He could not remember having so consistently been kept on the wrong foot by anyone before. 'If I have arrested you, madam,' he said, 'it was simply to find out what was your purpose. You must understand that in time of war civilians cannot travel as they please. Now that I understand your purpose, I will provide you with an escort. Indeed, I am withdrawing my regiment tomorrow. You may accompany us.'

'You are very kind, Colonel Mackinder.' This time he caught a glimpse of chin as she raised her yashmak to drink; he hadn't been looking closely enough, before. 'I apologize for my anger. But . . . you are withdrawing your army?'

'I do not have an army. Just my regiment. We are carrying out a reconnaissance.'

'I see. The Turks suppose you are the advance guard of the army marching to the relief of your people shut up in Kut-al-Amara.'

'We will do so, eventually,' Murdoch said. 'But we are not yet ready. As I have said, I am but a reconnaissance. This is where you can help me.'

'I?'

'You wish the British to help you return home. You would find us more helpful were you to give us whatever information you can about the Turks.'

'You are asking me to betray my husband's people.'

'You have just claimed that you did not love your husband. Do you, then, love his people?'

The black eyes gazed at him. 'You are a hard man, Colonel Mackinder,' she said. 'But I have heard this. And of your father. And his father before him. Your name is well known in northern India.'

'Well hated, perhaps?'

The yashmak fluttered. 'You have said, it was all a long time ago. Now India is at peace. There are Mahsuds serving in the British army. Tell me what you wish to know.'

72

'You must have come down the river by way of Kut.'

'Indeed. I have property there.'

'Did you enter the city?'

'Alas, no. General von der Goltz did not think it wise. He tried to dissuade me from continuing my journey at all, but I was admant.'

'General von der Goltz is the German officer commanding the Turks?'

'That is correct.'

'Tell me of him.'

'I know nothing of him, save that he is very old, and that he is not very well.'

'But he has many German officers under him?'

'Not many that I saw.'

'Are there any German troops?'

'I did not see any.'

'But there are a great many Turkish trrops?'

'A large number.'

'How many?'

Another dainty shrug. 'Many thousands. But their men too are unwell. There is cholera in the Turkish army.'

'Are you sure of this?'

'My people had to take precautions.'

'Hm. Will they attack Kut?'

'I do not think they can do that. Kut is very well defended. And the Turks are afraid of General Townshend.'

'He has also fought in India,' Murdoch remarked.

'I know this. He is a famous soldier. The Turks wait for him to run out of food.'

'And will he do this?'

'They do not think so. The town is well stocked with food.'

'Well, that is very good news, madam. I thank you.'

'Now tell me,' she said. 'When will you retake the town?'

Murdoch frowned at her.

'I have property there,' she repeated. 'I must know what will happen to it.'

'We will assault the town as soon as General Maude is ready.'

'You mean as soon as he has accumulated sufficient troops. But he has not yet done so.'

'I mean, as soon as he is ready.'

She gazed at him, then gave one of her quick smiles. 'You do not trust me. That is entirely correct. But I am in your power now. Colonel Mackinder, I will return to my caravan. But I would be greatly honoured if you would dine with me tonight.'

'Is the invitation extended to my officers?'

She appeared to hesitate. 'Of course,' she said. 'How many will you bring?'

'There will be six of us.'

Chand Bibi inclined her head, then rose and extended her hand. 'My people will be honoured to entertain your officers, Colonel. As I will be, to entertain yourself.' She looked around, and her grooms hastily prepared her camel. With the greatest of ease she took her seat, and the animal was allowed to rise. Her ladies also seated themselves. She looked down at Murdoch. 'Shall we say, eight o'clock, Colonel?'

'Now, that is a bit more of what war should be like,' John Lowndes said.

'You don't suppose she's another Mulein type, sir?' Peter Ramage asked, remembering the Somali girl who had attempted to lead them into a trap ten years before.

'No,' Murdoch said. 'She's a Pathan, in broad terms, not an African. She and her people have Greek blood in their veins as well as Mughal. Anyway, she's going our way; there's no chance of a trap. She's given me useful information, and all she wants is an escort to Basra and a ship from there to Bombay. But I'm afraid I want a captain left in charge of the camp, so you fellows will have to draw lots. I am also only taking one lieutenant, so they'll have to draw lots as well. I want the dinner party assembled here at a quarter to eight. I know we don't have any mess kit with us, but I want everyone as properly dressed as he can manage. Understood?'

They saluted, and withdrew. Murdoch went into his tent

74

to shave. He felt pleasantly exhilarated. It was a long time since he had dined with what he suspected might be an extraordinarily handsome woman – judging by her forehead and eyes, hands and feet – who was not also his wife. The last time indeed had been that terrible evening with Paul and Margriet von Reger in Dublin. But this would have none of the guilt of that occasion, or the embarrassment.

He frowned at his chin, removed a fraction more stubble. She knew of Dad, and Dad's exploits. And of Grandfather, as well. It was the oddest chance that of all the Mackinders, he alone had never served in India. When the regiment had last been stationed there, ten years ago, he and his squadron had been seconded to Somaliland, and he had been too badly wounded fighting against the Mad Mullah to continue to Peshawar. He did not know if he ever would now.

She was also sufficiently educated to have recognized his medal ribbons. She was an altogether fascinating young lady.

'Begging your pardon, sir.' Reynolds hovered in the tent doorway. 'Trooper Morton requests a word.'

'Morton? Tell him to come in.'

Morton entered the tent, stood to attention.

'At ease.' Murdoch wiped his chin. 'What's on your mind?'

'Permission to speak in confidence, sir.'

'All right, corporal, thank you.' Murdoch waited until Reynolds had stepped outside. 'I imagine you saw the princess.'

'Yes, sir.'

'Do you suppose she was telling the truth?'

'I don't know what she told you, sir. But I would say it was the truth, as far as it suited her to use it.'

Murdoch frowned at him. 'You have something on your mind, Johnnie.'

'This so-called princess, sir. She is the daughter of Shere Khan.'

'She told me that.'

'Shere Khan is a Mahsud sheikh, sir.'

75

'She has told me that also, Johnnie.'

'He is an implacable enemy of the British. So are all of his family.'

'She told me that too. But now the North West Frontier is at peace. Even implacable enemies can learn to live together, surely.'

'Not that lot, sir. They are only awaiting their opportunity to avenge themselves for past defeats. They are devils, Murdoch. And that woman is the worst of the lot.'

Murdoch's frown was back. 'You know her?'

'I do.'

'But . . . ten years ago?'

'Ten years ago she was about sixteen. That's full grown for an Indian woman.'

'And you met her then?'

'No. I saw her, Murdoch. I saw her assisting in the murder of some of our lads.'

Murdoch sat down on his camp cot. 'You *saw* Chand Bibi, murdering British soldiers?'

'Yes. You know how they do it?'

'I had some, in Somaliland. But I'm afraid I just cannot believe it, Johnnie. Not of that young woman. Tell me how it happened.'

'I was leading a patrol, and we were surrounded. We tried to ride our way out of it, but they caught some of the lads. My horse was thrown, but I was dead lucky; I fell into a gully and they had no idea I was there. The rest of the party got away. But two of my men were taken. There was nothing I could do, save commit suicide myself. There must have been a hundred of the Mahsuds. And a dozen or so of their women. Shere Khan was there, and two of his daughters. Chand Bibi was one of them.'

'How can you know that? You haven't seen her face.'

'I saw it then. It is the face of a devil. And I heard her name spoken. Her father addressed her by name, and she laughed. While castrating one of my men. Then she laughed again while her menfolk flayed him. He was still living, Murdoch. I shall carry his screams to my dying day. And her laugh. She is a cold-blooded murderess. She must be hanged.'

Murdoch stared at him. He too would carry the screams of one of his men being mutilated to his dying day. The difference between him and Johnnie Morton, he realized, was that he had charged to kill the man himself, risking his life to do so, while Johnnie had lain concealed until he could get away. Which implied nothing, he supposed, save that Murdoch was a fool who had been born lucky.

But what Johnnie had said about Chand Bibi . . . he still could hardly believe it. Because he did not want to believe it. And yet at the same time some perverse streak in his character did want to believe it, did want to feel that he was about to cross swords with a female devil.

'Did you report the incident when you regained the regiment?'

'I did.'

'Billy Prendergast knows nothing of it.'

'With respect, Murdoch, ten years ago Billy Prendergast was a green young second-lieutenant. It was Martin Walters' decision to keep the report secret. He felt it might be bad for morale.'

He wanted to see her face. If he arrested her, he would have that right. He would have more rights than that, perhaps. Christ, what was he thinking! He was the colonel of a regiment, and he had been nearly outwitted by a woman. Nearly?

'Would she be working for the Turks, do you think?' he asked.

'Almost certainly,' Morton said. 'You didn't give her any information, I hope?'

'God, yes, I did. She told me the Turks were in some agitation because they presumed we were the advance guard of a relieving force. I told her we weren't.'

'Then, if I may suggest, sir, you should put a guard right round the lady's caravan and forbid anyone to leave. She will certainly endeavour to get a message back to the Turks tonight.'

'Yes. Thanks a lot, Johnnie.'

'You are going to arrest her, Murdoch?'

'Oh, indeed. But no lynchings, Johnnie, no matter how

77

strongly you feel. We will take her back to Basra and hand her over to the military police there. You will have to give evidence against her, of course.'

'It will be a pleasure.'

'And even then, I'm not sure that she can be condemned. Presumably she will claim that what she did was during a war, which is now over.'

'She is still a war criminal, and must be punished.'

Murdoch nodded. 'Leave it with me. And thanks again. Oh, Johnnie, when you said she had the face of a devil . . .'

Morton smiled. 'A very beautiful devil, Murdoch. Look out for it.'

His officers were disappointed that there was not to be, after all, a dinner party with female company. Instead he assembled a squad of eight men commanded by Sergeant Matheson, another of his Somaliland veterans, and gave orders that as soon as they left camp, three of the Lewis guns were to be turned on the caravan, while a troop was to circle round to the north and east of the Arabs to make sure no one left. Then he led his men across the sand, stones crunching beneath their boots.

They were greeted by bowing grooms, and then by bowing women, as they were escorted to the largest and most elaborate of the tents. The flap was opened, and Murdoch led his men inside. Here there waited another six women, in their midst the unmistakable figure of Chand Bibi. Tonight her *haik* was deep blue trimmed with gold, her yashmak a paler blue.

She stepped forward. 'Welcome to my tent, Colonel Mackinder.' Then her eyes flickered to left and right. 'These are your officers?'

'No, madam,' Murdoch said. 'These are my troopers, who have come to place you under arrest.'

Her head rose sharply, her chin pointing at him through the yashmak. 'I had supposed you had already done so.'

'There are varying forms of arrest. I have now to inform you that you have been accused of murdering British soldiers during the campaign against the Mahsuds in 1906.

Murdering them in a peculiarly horrible manner. Have you anything to say against this charge?'

Her eyes glowed at him. 'Only that it is a pack of lies.'

'I'm sorry, madam. But there was, after all, a member of my regiment who had served in India. He has recognized you.'

'Indeed? How could he do this, if I made a habit of murdering British prisoners?'

'He was one that got away. I am not a policeman, madam, and I do not know the correct legal procedures. But I strongly recommend that you say nothing more on the matter until we reach Basra. There you will be handed over to the proper authorities. Until then, I must warn you that your caravan is also under close arrest, and no one will be allowed to leave it.'

The eyes glared, and she looked past him again. 'You come here with less than a dozen men, to arrest me?'

'If you would care to step outside, princess, you will observe that my entire command is ready to wipe this caravan from the face of the earth.'

Chand Bibi continued to stare at him for several seconds, then the yashmak fluttered. 'Why should we quarrel, Colonel Mackinder? One of your men has seen fit to accuse me of a crime. I know that I am innocent. You have your duty to perform. I must be patient and await my opportunity to defend myself in a court of law. I am not afraid of that. I know my innocence, and I have the utmost faith in British justice. I also recall a British saying, the basis of that justice, that every man is innocent until he is proven guilty. Surely that applies to women as well?'

Once again Murdoch realized that he was being verbally outflanked. And yet every word she was saying was absolutely true.

'Therefore,' Chandi Bibi went on, 'cannot we be friends, or at least behave in a civilized manner to each other, until I am proven guilty?' She gestured at the carpet behind her. 'My servants have killed a kid and prepared a fine meal, for your officers and yourself. If they have not come, will you at least not eat with me?'

79

Murdoch stared into her eyes. But he knew he was going to say yes. That devilish fascination with the mind, the whole personality, of a woman who could appear so refined and yet be a murdering savage, was irresistible. And as she had said, she had not yet been found guilty in a court of law. Johnnie Morton had had many strange adventures in India, culminating in that dose of syphilis. He could have been suffering from fever when he saw what he thought he had seen.

And he wanted to see her face.

'I should warn you, madam, that as I am not an Arab the fact that I have eaten with you will not prevent my treating you as an enemy, should the need arise.'

Another fascinating flutter of the linen. 'I should enjoy being treated as an enemy by you, Colonel. But I think I shall enjoy being treated as a friend more. Your men will be fed outside.'

'Thank you, Sergeant,' Murdoch said.

Matheson looked doubtful.

'The lady is aware that if we do not return in one hour, Sergeant, Major Prendergast has orders to wipe this caravan from the face of the earth.' Billy did not have any such orders, but there was no harm in letting Chand Bibi know his men were prepared.

'Yes, sir,' Matheson said, and led his troopers outside.

'Will you not sit down?' Chand Bibi invited, and did so herself, crossing her legs beneath her *haik*. As it was not possible to sit cross-legged while wearing spurs, Murdoch stretched his legs out in front of him. He placed his topee on the carpet beside him, but left his belts in place, heavy as they were with revolver and sword.

'Are you sure you are comfortable?' Chand Bibi asked.

'I'll manage.'

She smiled at him, and signalled her women, who immediately presented the bowl of couscous. It was given to Chand Bibi first, and she scooped some of the meat and semolina up with her fingers, placing it in her mouth with no more than a flutter of her yashmak. Then she took some more, and held it out to him. 'I do promise you that it is not poisoned.'

80

Murdoch hesitated, then leaned forward, and her fingers entered his mouth with the food. Almost he thought he could taste her flesh. Could she really have castrated a living man with those fingers? It was not possible. Or was he being incredibly naive? His problem was that he had always been a romantic. If he had not seen life in those terms he would not have collected the medals and the reputation he had. He sought adventure, and had done all his life. To attempt to change now would be to negate everything he was.

The fingers were back, offering more food to his mouth, and he sucked them. Now the princess laughed, a low gurgle in her throat. And he waited for the next mouthful. Neither of them spoke while they ate. But at last she rinsed her hands in a little dish of scented water.

'There are sweetmeats,' she said. 'But shall we digest a little, first? Here is lemonade.' She filled the gilt goblets herself, held one to his lips. 'It is a long time since I have played the handmaiden to so renowned a soldier,' she remarked.

Murdoch for the first time realized that the other women had left the tent, and they were alone.

'How long will it take us to reach Basra?' she asked.

'Oh . . . a week, perhaps.'

'Then we will have the time to get to know each other.'

'It won't work, princess.'

'What will not work, Colonel?'

'I meant, you will not get me to change my mind about placing you under arrest.'

'But you have already placed me under arrest. I would not expect you to change your mind now. Is it criminal for me to enjoy the company of an attractive man?'

'Nor will I be able to help you in any way, once you have been handed to the authorities.'

'I am not thinking of the future, Colonel. I am enjoying the present. Can you not do the same? Just for an hour?'

Murdoch hesitated, then smiled. 'I am being a little stiff, I suppose. You have been accused of something quite horrible.'

81

'We should not discuss that either, as I can only protest my innocence. Do you really suppose I look like a woman who would do something like that?'

Murdoch drew a long breath. 'I do not know what you look like, princess.'

Chand Bibi regarded him thoughtfully for a few seconds. Then she reached up and released one side of her yashmak. It fell down to her left shoulder, and Murdoch gazed at perhaps the most flawless face he had ever seen. The high forehead and wide-set black eyes had already entranced him. Now he looked at a straight, slightly long nose, but without any kind of hook, a wide, smiling mouth, and a pointed chin, the whole encased in that pale brown skin which he had noted on her feet.

Chand Bibi gave another of her throaty laughs at his obvious admiration, and then shrugged the *haik* from her head, to reveal the long, straight black hair. She continued to gaze at him, and her tongue came out, for just an instant, pink and healthy, before retreating again. 'I think you are handsome, too,' she said.

'Yes. Well . . .' he was sweating with desire – for a cold-blooded murderess? But he did not know that. Well, then, with a traditional enemy of his race? But that surely did not have to be. What did have to be was a rapid escape from this tent. 'I must be getting back to my men.'

'You have not yet had your dessert.'

'I must return in an hour.'

'There is yet time,' Chand Bibi said. 'Are you afraid of me?'

'Perhaps.'

She smiled. It was a beautiful smile. 'Suppose I give you my word that I will never harm you, Colonel Mackinder?'

'Then I should be reassured. But I must still leave.' He stood up.

She rose also. 'I am sorry. I would like to be your friend. I would like to be your lover.'

'My . . . my dear young lady, you shouldn't say things like that.'

'Why not?' she asked. 'You will not take advantage of it.

82

You are an officer and a gentleman.' She gave a little sigh. 'That is an awful waste.'

Murdoch held out his hand. 'It has been a great pleasure.'

She squeezed his fingers. 'And you will remember me, eh? But not enough. Suppose, just suppose, there is no justice in the British courts, and I am condemned for murder. What will happen to me?'

'Oh. Ah . . . I'm afraid they will probably hang you.'

She released him, and her hands went up to clasp her neck. 'That would be horrible. Will you come to watch me die?'

'Good lord, no. And it is unlikely to happen. If, as you say, you are innocent.'

'Of course.' She gave another throaty laugh. 'I hope we may meet again one day, Colonel Mackinder. I should enjoy that.' She stood against him and kissed him on the mouth, took his right hand and placed it on her breast. He realized she wore nothing beneath the *haik*, and the breast was the most heavenly he might ever have touched. Before he could stop himself his other arm had gone round her, and he was crushing her against him. All manner of thoughts raced through his mind, but principally that Lee had given him permission . . . to sleep with a cold-blooded murderess?

He let her go and stepped back, turned and left the tent. Behind him he heard a low, husky laugh.

Murdoch realized he had all but been vamped. But that made him the more determined to keep her under wraps until they reached Basra. He called in Sergeant Matheson, had him place a sentry inside the tent.

Chand Bibi raised no objection. 'He can amuse himself with my ladies,' she said, and retired to the inner chamber.

Murdoch had two more sentries placed outside the tent as well, to patrol all night. 'Operate in two-hour spells,' he told Matheson. 'You'll be relieved at dawn.'

He returned to camp to face a very inquisitive Prendergast. 'All I can say is, if she did cut up any of our men, they probably died happy,' Murdoch grunted. And then saw the expression on Billy's face. 'Sorry, macabre joke. But it's damn near impossible to feel she's guilty. Although I intend her to stand trial.'

Prendergast was reassured, but Murdoch himself hardly slept. The princess's image floated before his eyes, the feel of her lips on his, her scent, her fingers in his mouth, her laugh. . . He could not ever remember having wanted a woman so badly before. That was the heat and the desert and the separation from Lee, he knew. But it was also the princess's beauty and allure. He must make sure not to allow himself to be alone with her again.

He was awakened almost the moment he fell asleep, by a huge noise from the caravan. He leapt out of bed, dragged on his clothes. 'Sound the alarm,' he snapped at Reynolds and ran outside, revolver in his hand.

The regiment was already turning out to the notes of the bugle, but no shots had as yet been fired – the troopers were all veterans and trained not to shoot except at a target. Murdoch gathered several of them and made his way across to the caravan, where there was still a great deal of noise, women screaming, men shouting, English voices protesting.

'What the hell is going on?' Murdoch demanded of Matheson.

Who looked extremely embarrassed. 'Trooper Clarke . . . well sir. . .'

Murdoch looked at Clarke, whose clothes were disarranged and who looked even more embarrassed. Behind him were several of the princess's women, shouting and gesticulating. One of them had lost her yashmak and her *haik* and like her mistress wore absolutely nothing underneath.

'For God's sake . . . Mulai,' he snapped. 'What the hell are these women complaining about? And why is that girl undressed?'

Mulai shouted at the women, and they somewhat calmed down. Then the guide turned back to Murdoch. 'They accuse this soldier of rape, effendi.'

'Rape? Clarke?'

'I never laid a finger on her,' Clarke protested. 'I swear, sir.'

84

Murdoch looked at the girl again. 'Get some clothes on her,' he snapped. 'So how did she get undressed?'

'Well . . .' Clarke hung his head. 'I was on duty inside the tent, sir. And . . . I must have nodded off. Just for a second, sir. Next thing I knew this bint was in my arms, naked as the day she was born, sir, cuddling and squirming and pulling at my clothing. But the moment I woke up she started screaming fit to wake the dead.'

'Yes. All right. You are on a charge for falling asleep. From now on, Matheson, you'll have two men inside the tent. All right, get back to your duties.

'I suppose it was my fault for only putting one man at a time in there. Seems Chand Bibi's ladies are about as amoral as their mistress,' he said to Prendergast, who had appeared.

'It's a wonder all the hubbub didn't wake her up,' Prendergast remarked.

'Oh, Holy Jesus Christ!' Murdoch turned back, pulled open the tent flap, gazed inside. The outer chamber was empty, the women having all left it during the excitement. 'Come with me,' he told Prendergast, and opened the inner silken doorway. He gazed at a pile of cushions on a thick carpet, and inhaled Chand Bibi's scent. But of the princess there was no sign. And there was a slit in the back wall of the canvas.

Murdoch dashed outside, looked left and right. 'Find her,' he snapped. 'She can't have gone far.'

His men swarmed over the encampment, while the Arabs stared at them in wonder. But there was no sign of her. He sent a rider out to alert Manly-Smith's troop, and then they began a systematic scouring of the ground outside the encampment. But again there was no sign of her.

'A woman, alone,' Prendergast grumbled.

'This area is so broken up with wadis and pits she could be anywhere,' Ramage said. 'Maybe at dawn . . .'

'By dawn she'll be miles away,' Murdoch said. 'She was brought up on the North West Frontier. God damn.'

'Maybe she'll die in the desert,' Lowndes suggested.

'She won't do that, either,' Murdoch said. 'She's too close to the river. Well, we aren't doing any good right now. If Manly-Smith's men don't get her, she's made it.'

They went back to the encampment.

'Maybe it's all for the good,' Prendergast said. 'It'd have been a shame for her to hang.'

Murdoch did not feel like meeting Morton's eye, next morning, when he finally called off the hunt.

General Maude agreed with Prendergast. 'Frankly, I'm rather glad you didn't bring her in, Mackinder. We would have had to put her on trial, and God knows what would have happened. Right now we need the support of all India, including people like the Mahsuds. It wouldn't have helped us to put one of their young princesses on trial for murder, even if she deserved it.'

'It's not just that, sir,' Murdoch said. 'It was the feeling that she hoodwinked me . . .'

'Happens to us all, from time to time.'

'And that she was also a spy, all the time. Who now knows we're a long way from ready to march on Kut.'

'The Turks would have found that out anyway, soon enough. For God's sake stop worrying about it. One little Indian girl isn't worth a damn in this situation.'

Murdoch knew he was right. He knew that the real trouble was that kiss, and those few magic moments when all things had been possible. 'I would like to make love to you,' she had said. And he had been up like a ramrod. God, he should have known better. Now it was doubly important to forget her.

But it was difficult to do that. Only a month later, news arrived that Kut had surrendered.

4

Mesopotamia 1916–17

'Well, that at least ends the need for haste,' Maude told his officers. 'When we move, we shall move in strength, and we shall beat those fellows out of sight. Our duty now is vengeance.'

He was of course bitterly disappointed, and chagrined that Townshend could not have held out just a little while longer. Townshend's military reputation had rested to a large extent on the magnificent defence he had made of Chitral on the North West Frontier in 1895, against overwhelming odds. No one had doubted that he would defend Kut to the last possible moment, and his decision was a stunning blow. His action was to a certain extent explained when news came down the river of cholera amongst both the British and Turkish forces – General van der Goltz had even died of it, and been succeeded by a Turkish emir, Halil Pasha. But none of this altered the fact that British arms had suffered a defeat of the first magnitude.

It was a grim year on every count. In France the Germans had already launched an all-out attack upon the fortress of Verdun, which the French were defending with frenzied determination. But at least they were holding. In June, just a month after Townshend's surrender, three tremendous blows were struck at British morale throughout the world. First news was received that the long-awaited clash between the Grand Fleet of Admiral Jellicoe and the German High Seas Fleet of Admiral Scheer had at last taken place, in the North Sea. And the Royal Navy had failed to win. Some even said they had lost, because they had suffered twice as many casualties, in ships and men, as the Germans. The mere fact that the force which Nelson had made the greatest in the world had been unable to annihilate their enemy was distressing enough.

Hardly had this been digested when word came that Lord Kitchener was dead, drowned at sea when the cruiser *Hampshire*, on which he had been travelling to Murmansk to confer with the Russians, had struck a mine. From a personal point of view, Murdoch learned of this tragedy with mixed feelings. He and Kitchener had never got on. But that it was another blow for the country could not be doubted.

Then at the end of the month the British launched an offensive on the Somme, to take some of the pressure off their French comrades at Verdun. It was the greatest British assault of the war, and it was a disastrous failure, with some sixty thousand casualties on the very first day – nineteen thousand of them dead. This brought about the fall of the Government and its replacement with a coalition led by Lloyd George, while Murdoch and his officers gazed at each other in horror when they read the figures. But now distress was tempered by guilt. They should have been there, fighting and suffering with their old comrades; General Allenby, their erstwhile commander, had actually led one of the British armies into the battle. Instead of which the dragoons were lolling about Basra, trying to keep fit, carrying out futile reconnaissance raids which accomplished nothing: the Turks were well satisfied with their great victory at Kut, and had no desire to advance on Basra.

For Murdoch it was a doubly difficult year as he brooded on Chand Bibi. If he told himself over and over again that her escape should have had no effect on Townshend's objective decision to surrender, given his circumstances, the knowledge that the British would not be launching a rescue operation for some time could not have helped but discourage the defenders.

But there was more than that. He did not know whether she had escaped simply because she was a Turkish spy – in which case she would surely have done better to have gone to Basra and seen the British situation for herself, relying on being able to get a message back up the river to her employers – or if she had been forced to escape because she had known that once in Basra she would be hanged. He had not let himself entirely believe Johnnie Morton, had been content to leave that to the courts. But if Johnnie had been right . . . he had held in his arms and kissed a demon from the pit of hell. A woman who had murdered men of his own regiment.

No one in the world knew of that kiss, save only Chand Bibi herself. Or of the temptation which had accompanied it. But he would remember it for the rest of his life.

His letters to Lee were more than usually loving. To her joy, judging by the replies he received. But it was something she should never know, just as she did not know the truth about Margriet von Reger and the Somali girl, Mulein. Because Mulein's face also kept cropping up in front of him. Mulein had also been a devil from hell . . . and he had plunged his sword through her heart. Chand Bibi he had kissed and held in his arms.

The desire for action burning inside him was so intense he had to use all his self-control to stop himself leading the regiment right into the Turkish lines on their own, to slash and cut and thrust and expiate some of the guilt which obsessed him. Close friends like Peter Ramage and Billy Prendergast, no less than George Reynolds, were deeply concerned, and not knowing the truth of the matter, worried that he was suffering from the heat or some lurking illness. Johnnie Morton perhaps suspected more than most, but as a trooper kept his own council. He steadfastly refused all offers of promotion, however, even to corporal. No doubt he looked forward to settling with Chand Bibi in his own way, one day.

And still the year dragged on, while more and more troops, most of them Indian but a good proportion of British and Australian as well, landed at Basra and helped to swell the huge encampment outside the town. The presence of so many soldiers complicated both the health and social problems, but Maude was determined to make it, as he put it, a once and for all victory, and he was not prepared to begin his advance until he was sure nothing would stop him short of Baghdad.

The final straw, for Murdoch, was a letter he received at the beginning of December, via Bombay, but mailed in Peshawar:

Dear Colonel Mackinder,

You may be distressed to learn that I have safely regained the house of my father. It has taken me a long time, and some of the journeying was uncomfortable, but never so uncomfortable as that night I spent on the banks of the Tigris, huddled in a hole, while your dragoons trampled all about me, and even on me, more than once, without suspecting my presence. My discomfort was intense, as I suffered from both hunger and thirst, apart from heat, until you had taken your men away. But I survived.

You may obviously feel that my escape was a form of confession, that I am indeed guilty of the deeds of which your soldier accused me. I, on the other hand, cannot regard anything I have ever done as a crime. When I was a little girl my father made me swear eternal hatred for the British. Your soldiers, led sometimes by your own father, have time and again invaded my homeland, spreading death and destruction. My people, and I, have fought back as best we are able. But we are few, and ill-armed. You are many, and strong. We can but fight, and make those of our enemies who fall into our hands suffer for their crimes against us.

I would not be truthful were I to pretend that to have a white-skinned man at my mercy is not a source of pleasure to me. To hear one of your soldiers beg and scream, to watch the horror in his eyes as he realizes what I and my women are about to do to him, is a thrill I can never overcome. To have you, naked and bound, at my feet, my Mackinder, would be the greatest experience of my life. Do you not suppose you will one day be sent to India?

But I have promised never to harm you. Do you know, when I said that, I was serious. As I was serious when I invited you to my bed. That too I regret. It would have made it doubly pleasurable to slice away your manhood afterwards.

Go fight and win your war, Mackinder. Having lived with the Turks I do not doubt you will. And then return to your green and pleasant England, and your wife and family, and dream of me. Because you will, my Mackinder. I am a woman of whom men dream, throughout eternity.

The letter was unsigned, presumably so that it could never be used in evidence against her. But he would not have used it in evidence anyway. He crumpled it into a ball and then set a match to it. Reynolds, coming into his room while the little fire was still burning, gave him an old-fashioned look but said nothing.

Murdoch watched the paper dissolve into ashes. Sleep tight, my bloodthirsty princess, he thought. I will come to India, one of these days. And I will seek you out. And yes, now I have decided: I will attend your hanging.

The next day, the orders came to move out. The advance on Baghdad would begin.

General Maude now mustered a combat strength of one hundred and sixty-six thousand men, of whom two thirds were Indians. Every preparation had been made, and the advance was to be on both sides of the Tigris, with the main force following the east bank. Communication between the two parts of the army was maintained by a flotilla of gunboats which cruised slowly up the river. There was a brigade of armoured cars, but insufficient cavalry was the only weakness. A regiment of Indian lancers led the march on the west bank, the dragoons followed the familiar road on the east.

The army moved slowly, not more than five miles a day, the general being careful to protect his men from the heat of the midday sun; he wanted a fully effective force when he encountered the Turks. Christmas came and went, and the new year arrived. 'The year of victory,' Maude told his officers. He was totally confident. And for a while it seemed as if the Turks were not going to fight at all. Murdoch's dragoons, ranging in front of the main force, came across abandoned cantonments north of Amara, and north too of where they had camped when they had encountered Chand Bibi's caravan. But this sham warfare came to an end when they sighted the minarets of Kut, and were fired upon. An extensive reconnaissance indicated that the Turks were dug in before the town in considerable force, concentrated on the east bank of the river, which some miles below Kut made a right-angled bend to the west.

'Very good, gentlemen,' Maude said, surveying the maps spread out on the table before his tent and around which his senior officers were gathered. 'The enemy anticipates a frontal assault or an assault on his left flank. He is relying on the river to prevent any turning movement on his right. Well, he is going to get everything he asked for. General Maitland, you will take your division and the Royal Western Dragoons, and perform a flank march to the north. You will approach Kut via the Hawr al Suwavqivah lake, and then advance to the south-west with every evidence of assaulting the town from the rear. You will do enough to force the enemy to commit troops to oppose you, but you will proceed with caution, and once fully engaged, retreat to a previously chosen position. Understood?'

The Major-General nodded.

'General Lake,' Maude continued, 'once the Turks turn their attention to the east, you will launch your division in a frontal assault on the town itself. Your attack, with the second and third divisions, will be pushed home sufficiently to fix the Turkish defence. Once this has been done, I and the main body will cross the river and join our forces on the other side, and bypass the town altogether. Our objective is Baghdad. Halil Pasha will have to be besieged in Kut or leave the city to its fate and pull out. Understood?'

The officers nodded.

'Very good. The first division and the cavalry will move off at dawn. I expect your attack to commence at dawn four days from now. It will mean some forced marching, but now we must make haste. Understood?'

'Understood, sir,' Maitland acknowledged.

'Action at last,' Peter Ramage said. 'Thank God for that.'

General Maitland called a conference to let everyone know his plans. 'We don't have too much time, so we are going to travel light,' he announced. 'No baggage train on the march. We sleep rough. And we take rations for five days only. The train will follow and we will fall back on it after engaging the enemy. If necessary. I know this is a feint,' he said, 'but it has to be a realistic one. And . . . ' He winked at his officers. 'One never knows when a feint can become the real thing. Colonel Mackinder, you'll form a cavalry screen. I have no doubt the Turks will be keeping an eye on us, but we shall let them do that. Chase them off if they approach too closely, or show signs of concentrating. Otherwise, we just march to our position, and see what we find there. Thank you, gentlemen.'

Assembly was blown at three, and the men mounted up. The dragoons rode out first, followed by the infantry and the two batteries of field artillery, drawn by mules. The operation reminded Murdoch of many he had carried out in South Africa. He did not doubt the ultimate result. He was only sorry Chand Bibi was safely away in Kashmir.

It was February, and bitterly cold at night to be sleeping in the open, but equally, hot as soon as the day had warmed up. They covered five miles the first day, and the same the second. On this second day Turkish horsemen were observed away to the north by the advance guard, keeping them under surveillance, but, as instructed, the dragoons ignored them and they melted away. On the third day the order of march was switched to the west; Kut was now actually south-west of them. Murdoch put out a right and left flank guard as well as an advance guard, but still Turkish patrols merely kept them in sight. However, they could not doubt that their movements were being reported to the enemy command.

The land was flat, but uneven, a hundred wadis to the mile. It was also surprisingly fertile, and they passed many plantations, the men being strictly forbidden to loot as the Arabs came out to gawk at them. Equally was it largely lacking in natural defensive features, until riders returned from Destry's troop, this day acting as an advance guard a mile in front of the main body, to say that they had encountered the remains of an old canal, mostly dry but presenting a reasonable natural obstacle, and had been fired upon from the west bank. Murdoch rode forward with Prendergast, and inspected the situation through binoculars. There was no doubt that a Turkish force was dug in on the far side, and with reason – the minarets of Kut were once again visible in the distance, more than ten miles away, but shimmering in the afternoon heat.

The canal itself was a useful obstacle, the first they had encountered. It was surprisingly deep, some eight feet, and about thirty yards wide, while the sides were steep too. there was also water in the bottom. Not a great deal, but enough to make it slushy. And when the sun glinted off their glasses there was considerable firing, from both rifles and machine-guns.

'Dismount your men and keep the enemy under observation, Mr Destry,' Murdoch ordered. 'Billy, see if your radio people can raise division with their machine.'

Radio was the latest concept in warfare: that two commands should be able to talk to each other at a distance of several miles without having to lay telephone wires.

They returned to the regiment, where Reynolds was waiting with a cup of tea, dismounted, and the wireless telegraphers got to work. There was an enormous amount of static, but General Maitland was informed of the situation, and requested Murdoch to show himself to the enemy but not to engage until the rest of the force came up. Murdoch had his troopers mount and move forward again, to within a mile of the canal, when again shots were exchanged. He placed his six Lewis guns and began a long-range duel, keeping his men well out of sight as far as possible. So far the dragoons had not suffered a casualty.

There was no means of telling how many Turks were on the other side of the canal, but from the amount of fire power they commanded there seemed little doubt that there was at least a regiment, strongly emplaced, and if they were resolutely led a frontal assault would be costly. Murdoch dispatched Manly-Smith and B Troop of A Squadron, first of all back the way they had come until they were out of sight of any Turkish observation, and then north to find the canal again and discover how far the defences stretched. Then it was a matter of sitting out the night, watching for any enemy movements, and waiting for the division to arrive.

They began straggling in at dawn, Maitland having kept them on the march all night. He himself rode up to stand beside Murdoch and survey the gradually lightening scene in front of him.

'Desultory fire,' Murdoch told him. 'No attempt to drive us away.'

'Because they're damned sure we are a feint,' Maitland said. 'We will have to disillusion them about that.'

'I have a troop reconnoitring the canal,' Murdoch said.

'Good man. We'll have our people rest up today, and be ready to commence action on schedule tomorrow morning.'

Manly-Smith returned in the middle of the morning to say that the canal appeared to go all the way back to Baghdad, and was held further north only by patrols.

'We are going to have to winkle these fellows out,' Maitland decided. 'All right, General Thorpe, I want you to take your brigade north-west, following the line of the canal, but at a safe distance from it. I'm afraid you will have to move out right away and make a forced march of it; your men have had a couple of hours' rest. At first light tomorrow I wish you to cross the canal. If you meet any strong opposition I will march to your aid; if you do not, I wish your people to be in position on the west bank by eight ack emma, and to commence your march south-west as soon as possible. Either way we'll fix those fellows over there, and have them calling for support. Should you, however, be attacked by a vastly superior force after crossing the canal but before linking up with the division, you are to go on the defensive until you receive further orders from me. This may mean recrossing the canal in order to establish a perimeter. Now, Colonel Mackinder, your dragoons will accompany General Thorpe's brigade. You will proceed in advance to the north, and when the canal is crossed, you will screen to the west and north. Your objective is to prevent the brigade becoming so involved with superior forces it is unable to withdraw. At dawn tomorrow morning I will begin active demonstrations here with an artillery barrage. I shall make every attempt to force the canal, aided by your flank attack. If the enemy are reinforced and counter-attack, we shall withdraw to this bank and hold them. If they are not reinforced, well . . . '

He gave one of his characteristic winks. 'We shall move on and see how far we can get. Good hunting, gentlemen.'

Murdoch and Thorpe marched their men out immediately, the dragoons pushing on ahead. Mulai was still their guide – Murdoch had adopted him permanently – and they walked their horses north-east for a mile before turning back to the north-west. They actually covered the ten miles before dusk, and Murdoch was able to call a halt at a water hole in a wadi and allow the men to water the tired horses and brew up some tea and have dinner in reasonable comfort. They were seething with excitement at the prospect of real action for the first time in very nearly two years. There was no sign of any enemy.

Within an hour or two after the meal, however, many of them had fallen asleep. Murdoch paced up and down, watching the moon rise to turn the night almost bright, looking at his watch . . . this was not his first independent command, as he had been virtually on his own during the battle with the Somalis, but then he had known exactly what he was facing. Here he had no idea what Turkish forces might have been withdrawn from the town to face the threat from the east.

Eventually he turned in himself, but was awakened at first light when the sky to the south lit up as the batteries opened fire, and a moment later the reverberations reached him. He had already forbidden bugle calls, but the officers and NCOs of each squadron were standing by to alert their men, and the regiment was ready in minutes. Murdoch had kept in radio contact with Thorpe's brigade, and the weary Indians were now in position three miles behind him and also ready to cross. He was able to tell them that there were no enemy forces visible to their north – at least as yet. Now it was light enough to see quite clearly; the canal was a further half mile away. Murdoch raised his arm and A Troop of C Squadron moved out as previously instructed, cantering towards the dip. The five hundred remaining Royal Western Dragoon troopers stood by their horses and waited.

Lieutenant Collier, in command of the advance guard, behaved perfectly, trotting his men up to the banks of the canal, surveying it as though encountering it for the first time, and then signalling his men to cross. Crouching on the side of the wadi, Murdoch and Prendergast watched him through their field glasses, and saw a spurt of dust to the right. A moment later two horsemen could be seen galloping away, one to south and the other north. But no shots had been fired.

'Regiment will mount,' Murdoch commanded.

Harnesses jingled as the troopers swung into the saddle.

'Move out.' Murdoch pointed at the canal, and the dragoons surged forward in three lines, in and out of the knee-deep water. Not a shot had been fired, and they were across the canal. Collier was waiting for them. 'Good work, Mr Collier,' Murdoch told him. 'You'll proceed down the west bank, one mile in advance of the main body. Captain Hunter, take C Squadron and form a flank guard one mile to the west. Captain Ramage, Captain Lowndes, column of twos.'

'What about those two scouts?' Prendergast asked.

'Everything will depend on how close their main body is. We'll have to play this one by ear, Billy.' He raised his arm. 'Forward.'

By now the firing from south of them had become general, the artillery booming in the distance, the cracks of rifles and the chatter of machine-guns closer at hand looming across the morning and suggesting that Thorpe's brigade had encountered resistance. They could see the clouds of smoke above the further battlefield. The regiment had covered two miles in a few minutes when they came in sight of the Indian brigade, also across the canal, and advancing south-west; there was a good deal of firing, and clearly the Turkish force opposing them was slowly retreating. Which was according to plan, save for the possibility of a flank attack from an as yet unseen body of the enemy summoned by the two Turkish scouts. Murdoch called a halt to try to raise Thorpe on the wireless. Before he had done so, a rider came in from Hunter's squadron.

'Captain Hunter wishes to inform you, sir, that there is

97

a large body of Turkish cavalry moving up from the south-west.'

'Just what the doctor ordered. Can't you raise brigade, Corporal?'

'I think I have them, sir.'

'Well, give them that information.'

'Yes, sir.' Corporal Denning was soon shouting away. 'Brigade replies, will return to the east bank and hold. Distract the enemy to cover my withdrawal, then join me. Sir,' he repeated.

Murdoch nodded. 'Very good. Signal the Brigadier that his message is understood.' He faced his officers, Hunter having also come in by now. 'We'll need a show of strength, or they won't follow us. Captain Ramage, take your squadron out to within sight of the enemy, and then withdraw towards the regiment.'

'Yes, sir.' Peter Ramage hurried for his horse.

'We will prepare a defensive perimeter here,' Murdoch told Lowndes, Hunter and Prendergast. 'But remember, our business is not to be overrun, only to distract. No heroics.' He grinned at them; they all knew his reputation, and that he was in reality talking to himself.

The Lewis guns were emplaced, and two troops dug in as riflemen on the western bank of the canal. The remainder of the regiment stood by the horses in the canal itself. Murdoch mounted and rode off with Prendergast to see what was happening, but before leaving he dispatched Lieutenant Rostron with B Troop of Lowndes' Squadron to return along the canal and ensure their retreat was not impeded.

The sounds of battle were louder than ever from south of them, but there was still no activity from Kut itself, so far as he could make out; General Maude was making absolutely sure the Turks had committed the maximum number of men to defending their left flank before commencing the second part of his attack.

Murdoch and Billy topped a low rise and looked both south and west. Far south the smoke clouds were billowing skywards, but they were still too far away to distinguish any actual fighting; nearer at hand the Indian brigade had ceased its advance and appeared to be regrouping, but this was obviously part of Thorpe's withdrawal plan; the firing was desultory. West they could make out Ramage's squadron walking their horses in and out of the wadis and low hills, appearing and then disappearing again.

'There!' Prendergast pointed, and Murdoch swung his glasses and saw the dust. 'That's a fair number of men.' He gave a low whistle. 'Several thousand.'

Murdoch was watching Ramage. But there were advance riders out, and now these could be seen returning in haste. 'Let's get back,' he said.

They cantered back to the regiment, and listened to a burst of firing from the south-west, accompanied by a deep roar, the Turkish battle cry. The men needed no reminder to stand by; everyone was keyed up. Soon they could see Ramage's squadron, galloping back towards the canal; there were a couple of riderless horses with them. They charged past the rest of the regiment, ignoring them to conceal their position, and only then did Ramage signal his men to slow up; their horses were quite blown.

The Turkish cavalry could now be seen, small ponies carrying small, grey-clad men with brown fezzes, swords waving, the whole still shouting and cheering as they chased what they assumed to be a British patrol.

'Open fire,' Murdoch commanded.

The machine-guns sprang into life, and the riflemen joined them. The surprise was complete. Horses reared and riders were thrown. Blood flew as the bullets scythed into the Turkish brigade. The pursuers abruptly swung to their left to avoid the ambush and galloped out of range.

'Cease firing. Any casualties?'

Prendergast was back in a moment. 'Not one, sir.'

'Very good. Prepare to move out. Captain Lowndes, A Troop of your squadron will cover the retreat with two Lewis guns. They are not to be overrun. Understood?'

'Yes, sir.'

Murdoch mounted, and the remaining troops followed him. The Turks had dismounted some distance away, and now some probing fire was sent in the Royal Western's direction, but at extreme range. Murdoch deliberately led his men out of the canal and on to the higher ground so the Turks could see them, and was rewarded with a huge hullaballoo. Then the mass of men mounted and surged forward again. Murdoch gave the order to canter, and they moved up to join Ramage's squadron, which had halted while the horses recovered their wind.

The Turkish cavalry were once more advancing rapidly, but again they were checked by the burst of machine-gun fire from the canal, which threw them into angry confusion.

'We'd better not get taken, after this caper,' Prendergast muttered. 'They'll lynch us all.'

Murdoch was watching the canal. 'Come on, A Troop,' he said. 'Come on.'

A moment later he saw them, trotting their horses along the canal itself, bending in the saddle to keep out of sight of the enemy.

'Well done, Lieutenant Bryan,' he said. 'Now let's link up with Manly-Smith before those fellows come to their senses again. Regiment will canter.'

'Looks like Manly-Smith is linking up with us,' Prendergast said, and they saw a rider galloping along the canal bank, horse a lather of sweat.

Murdoch rode out to meet him.

'Compliments from Lieutenant Manly-Smith, sir,' he said. 'But there is a large Turkish force, both infantry and cavalry, moving down the east bank of the canal.'

'Better and better,' Murdoch said. 'He's committing some of the Baghdad force as well. Major Prendergast, send a dispatch rider to tell Mr Manley-Smith to recross the canal and join us on the east bank.' He looked back at the Turkish cavalry. They were regrouping, and were obviously preparing another advance, but on the part of the canal from which the British firing had come. However, Murdoch calculated they would have dealt with that problem in a few minutes. 'We need to move,' he told Prendergast. 'Captain Ramage, you'll cover us.'

Ramage dismounted his men and unlimbered the Lewis

guns. Murdoch led the remainder of the regiment down the bank of the canal and across, splashing through the shallow water and scrambling up the farther side. From their south there came a chorus of yells as the Turks charged the abandoned position of half an hour before.

'Signal recall, Bugler,' Murdoch commanded, and the notes played across the morning. The sun was high by now, and it was extremely hot. But so far the game had been played entirely according to their rules, and they were way ahead on points. As Ramage brought his men back across to the east side, Murdoch saw Manly-Smith leading his troop towards them, already on the east bank.

'We'll check them here, and then withdraw to brigade,' Murdoch said. 'But slowly. We want to keep those chaps occupied until General Thorpe has re-established his position. Peter, how many casualties?'

'Four.'

'All dead?'

'I don't know.' Ramage's face was grim.

'Those are regulars,' Prendergast said. 'They'll obey the rules.'

'Let's hope so.' Murdoch inspected the Turkish cavalry through his glasses. They had halted again, perhaps a mile away and on the west bank, a large mass of horsemen, presently confused by the hit-and-run tactics of the British cavalry.

'Very good, gentlemen,' he said. 'Dismount your men. Horses back to that wadi. Lieutenant Collier, your troop will stand rear guard. The rest of us will give them something to worry about here.'

Cursing and sweating, the Lewis gunners set their machines up again, supervised by RSM Yeald, marching up and down and looking very fierce. The other five hundred odd settled down with their rifles, save for a patrol of ten men under Lieutenant Destry, whom Murdoch sent north to report on the whereabouts of the force reported by Manly-Smith.

'They're not going to try it,' Prendergast grumbled, watching the enemy cavalry through his glass.

'They're waiting for the other fellows,' Murdoch agreed. 'Well, we'll have to pull out. We're not here to fight the whole God damned Turkish army. Withdraw in troops. Quietly now.'

Prendergast crawled away to give the necessary orders, and the grumbling gunners began to dismantle their weapons again. Half the regiment had returned to the wadi and was mounted in concealment when Destry and his men came back. 'The enemy force is three miles away, sir,' he said. 'All foot. I could see no sign of any mounted men.'

Murdoch frowned. Manly-Smith had already taken his troop back to the wadi, so it could not be checked, but he had certainly reported cavalry.

'All right, let's get the hell out of here,' he snapped.

The last troop crawled back to the horses, and mounted. 'Ride for brigade,' Murdoch ordered, and they cantered out of the wadi in column of twos. The Turks on the far bank of the canal gave a great shout as they were spotted, and opened fire, but at such extreme range no one was hit; the enemy however made no attempt to cross the canal to come to closer quarters, preferring to keep pace with the British with the water separating them.

'They probably suspect we have another hidden position somewhere,' Prendergast suggested.

Murdoch didn't reply. He was unhappy about the disappearance of the other Turkish cavalry.

Now they were close to where the brigade was engaged. The Indians were withdrawing across the canal, with great steadiness, firing volleys at a large mass of Turkish infantry which had come up to oppose them. About one third were actually across, Murdoch estimated, digging in as fast as they could. From the south there was now continuous fire; the frontal assault on Kut had commenced. Therefore they had carried out their orders, and now need only beat a fighting retreat to Maitland's division.

'Holy Jesus Christ!' Prendergast muttered.

Murdoch raised his glasses to peer in the same direction and felt his stomach muscles tightening. Advancing from the east was a very large force of mounted men. From the east! The cavalry that Manly-Smith had spotted! They had made a detour, and were now preparing to place themselves between Thorpe's brigade and the rest of the division – and Thorpe's brigade was still in the act of withdrawing across the canal.

'We must break up those fellows until Thorpe's troops have regrouped,' he said.

'How many do you think they are?'

'A brigade. Over two thousand men, certainly.'

Prendergast licked his lips. 'Those aren't Somali brigands, Murdoch.'

'I know,' Murdoch said. 'But we don't have any choice. If they get established south of us we'll be surrounded and overrun. Dispatch a rider to General Thorpe to tell him what we are doing; there's no time to mess about with that damned wireless set. Send back the Lewis guns and their operators as well. Oh, you can go as well, Mulai.' The Arab was looking distinctly uncomfortable. 'Regiment will canter.'

He led his men forward, still in column of twos, Ramage's squadron, then Lowndes', then Hunter's. They passed the rear of the Indian position, where they were cheered by the sepoys, and then on towards the Turkish cavalry. These had now identified them, and had come to a halt, a huge grey-brown mass of men.

The two bodies of horse were about a mile and a half apart. The ground between looked level enough, although there would undoubtedly be the occasional wadi. It was now just after noon, and the sun hung immediately above their heads; it was very hot, and the dragoons' tunics were stained with sweat.

'Long odds,' Billy Prendergast muttered.

'Which we can shorten, a little,' Murdoch said thoughtfully. He raised his voice. 'Captain Ramage.'

'Sir.' Peter Ramage rode forward.

'Now is the time to put some theory into practice, Peter. We are going to charge those fellows.'

Ramage pulled his nose. But he had been at Murdoch's side on that famous occasion in Somaliland.

'However, we may be able to soften them up a little,' Murdoch told him. 'As we rehearsed in France, remember? Your squadron will be the first rank. When we are within a quarter of a mile, I will raise my arm, your men will sheath swords, deliver a volley, and then draw swords again. Understood?'

'Yes, sir,' Ramage said.

Murdoch grinned at him. 'Just remember, Billy and I will be out in front.'

'Yes, sir,' Ramage said again.

'So alert your men, quietly.'

Ramage saluted and returned to his squadron.

'If we attacked in line,' Prendergast said. 'We could use all our rifles.'

'But we wouldn't have any momentum in the charge. We have to drive those fellows away, not just check them. Bugler, sound the prepare to charge.'

The notes rang out, and the columns swung into three lines.

'Sergeant-Major, check the dressing,' Murdoch said. 'I want fifty yards between each line.'

'Sir!' Yeald rode off.

'Stay at my right shoulder, Billy,' Murdoch said. 'Remember, we must disperse these fellows, at least until the brigade is fully withdrawn.' He studied the Turks, who were advancing again, confident of being able to sweep aside the small British force opposing them. and as he watched, he saw the enemy cavalry also forming lines; theirs were six deep, and extended far wider than his own. The enemy horsemen also carried carbines in their saddle holsters, but Murdoch was certain they would not have been trained to shoot at the canter – at least, accurately.

'By God, they mean to charge *us*!' Billy exclaimed indignantly.

'As you said, they're regulars.'

Yeald was back. 'Regiment ready for action, sir.'

Murdoch took out his handkerchief and patted sweat from his eyes, then dried his hands as well. He was aware of no single emotion, or sensation, or expectation. He had charged at the head of his men before. But then he had commanded but a single squadron, and it had very definitely been a case of charge or die. Here he was taking his entire regiment into the jaws of death, as an act of tactical duty. Nothing else really mattered, no memories, of anyone, no expectations, of anyone. His entire life was concentrated in the coming ten minutes.

He drew a long breath, and raised his voice. 'Regiment will draw swords,' he shouted.

There was a gigantic rasp from behind him.

Murdoch pointed his sword at the sky. 'May the great God of battle,' he called, 'who has guided the fate of this famous regiment on many a hard-fought field, and never failed to lead it to distinction, grant that on this day, faced as we are with a host of enemies of our King and our Country, every man will do his duty, so that should we fail in our ordained task, it will yet be said of us, they were the Royal Western Dragoon Guards, who fought and died according to the ancient valour of their regiment and their blood.'

When he paused, the rumble of sound continued for a second, and he realized that every man of his command had also been uttering the prayer. He lowered his sword to point it at the Turkish horse, which had checked again to watch what the British were doing. 'Gentlemen, there is your enemy. Regiment will advance.'

He raised his sword to the upright, his fist resting on his thigh, and walked his horse forward. He was aware of Prendergast at his right shoulder, Yeald at his left, the bugler between, and behind him, Reynolds. Behind them there came the huge jingle of harnesses as the dragoons followed their commanding officer. The Turks continued to study them for a moment, clearly amazed that they should be challenged at such odds, then they resumed their own advance.

'Regiment will trot.'

The jingling increased, half smothered now by the drumming of hooves. The distance was perhaps half a mile.

'Regiment will canter.'

His horse was now bounding forward over surprisingly

level ground, and he could make out the moustached faces of the Turks. He raised his sword to the sky. For what seemed an eternity there was no response, then he seemed to be shrouded in a very hot wind. At a range of no more than four hundred yards Ramage's squadron had delivered a volley, perhaps not truly aimed, but with smashing effect when opposed to so close-packed a target. Horses fell and men went with them, and the centre of the Turkish force seemed to crumple and split.

'Bugler, sound the charge!' Murdoch lowered his sword and rode at the disconcerted men in front of him. Dimly he heard the rattle from behind him as Ramage's men hastily holstered their carbines and drew their swords again. Then he was up to the Turks, who were beginning to rally. But they had lost momentum after the volley, and many of their horses were standing still. Murdoch thudded into the first of them, sword arm held rigid, wrist twisted, thumb locked in its socket on top of the hilt. The man ducked but was bowled over by Jupiter's impetus and went flying into the man behind him, dismounting him as well. Jupiter leapt over them with such power that he almost unseated Murdoch, landed on all four legs together in front of another Turk, who received Murdoch's sword in the face. The flesh seemed to split and blood flew. Again the horses cannoned as the Turk went down, and Murdoch felt a searing pain across his back. But now was no time to look round. There were still three Turks ahead of him, hundreds of others milling to either side, shrieking and yelling. He swung his sword from left to right, dismounting two more men, received a glancing blow on the head which removed his helmet, and then was through the other side. He let Jupiter, gasping and spitting, run on for another fifty yards before attempting to draw rein. He was breathless himself, and he could feel blood trickling down his back inside his tunic, but how badly wounded he was he had no idea. He wheeled the horse, and watched his men thundering up beside him. He spotted Prendergast, and Bugler McCoy, and RSM Yeald . . . and Ramage and Manly-Smith and Lowndes and

106

Collier and Hunter and Destry – the dragoons seemed to have suffered few casualties.

'Reform,' he bellowed. 'Reform.'

Prendergast pointed. There was not going to be another charge. The Turks were streaming away to the north, their morale shattered. Behind them were a good three hundred crumpled figures on the stony earth.

But there were also khaki-clad figures. Murdoch sent out a patrol to make sure the Turks weren't coming back immediately, and led his men back to the scene of the action. Those of the enemy who could walk were pulled up and marched off towards the brigade. Of the English casualties, twelve had been killed outright, twenty-one were wounded in varying degrees of seriousness, and three were alive, but clearly dying.

'Over here, sir,' Lieutenant Manly-Smith said.

Murdoch dismounted and stood above Johnnie Morton. He had received a sword thrust through the stomach and his intestines were spilling on to the sand.

Murdoch knelt. 'There'll be a stretcher along in a moment, Johnnie.'

'Waste of time,' Morton muttered. 'Waste of time.' He touched Murdoch's tunic. 'You're bleeding to death, Murdoch.'

'It's only a scratch,' Murdoch said. 'But Johnnie . . . I'm sorry about Chand Bibi.'

'She could've fooled me too,' Morton said. 'But you'll get her, Murdoch. Promise me that.'

'I'll get her,' Murdoch promised.

'I can see her hanging,' Morton said, and died.

'Mr Murdoch, sir,' Reynolds remonstrated, having ridden up. 'You're all bloody.'

'Another tunic gone,' Murdoch said, and fainted.

'Exceptional show,' General Maude said, standing beside the camp cot on which Murdoch was resting. 'Thorpe says it was the most brilliant cavalry charge he has ever seen. I suppose you forgot that your orders were not to become seriously engaged with a superior force?'

'I was trying to prevent that happening to the brigade, sir.'

'And you accomplished that.' He regarded Murdoch's chest, which was entirely shrouded in bandages. 'They tell me you've got a cut across the back.'

'Nothing serious, sir. I just lost a bit of blood.'

'Well, you'll want to get it back. Prendergast will command the regiment.'

'With respect, sir . . . '

'You are out of action for the next couple of weeks, at least,' Maude pointed out. 'And you'll want to be fit again when we enter Baghdad.'

Murdoch raised his head. 'Then the battle was a victory?'

'Oh, indeed. It was, if I may say so, perfectly executed. By everybody. The enemy drew off men both from Kut and down from Baghdad to block Maitland's feint, then he committed all his reserves to the defence of Kut. When he realised that I was across the river with the main force he hastily pulled out. We're chasing him with everything we've got. Obviously he will make another stand for Baghdad, but his morale has suffered. None more than his cavalry. Get yourself well, Murdoch. I intend to be in Baghdad in a fortnight.'

General Maude was nearly as good as his word. The British forces entered Baghdad on 11 March, eighteen days after the second Battle of Kut. By then Murdoch was just strong enough to sit his horse and lead the dragoons in the victory parade through the streets of the ancient city; they had the post of honour, immediately behind the General himself.

The Turkish troops had withdrawn in great haste, and the inhabitants of the city did not seem especially hostile. The dragoons stared in wonderment at the many spendid buildings, the huge mosques, the towering minarets, and the veiled women who looked down on them from the flat roofs which lined the streets.

'The lads would like a jolly,' Prendergast muttered. He had been intensely relieved to have Murdoch back, and

Murdoch was coming to accept what he had known for some time, that Billy, although a fine fellow and the senior officer in the regiment after himself, was not really command material. There was a looming problem.

One which cropped up sooner than he had expected. General Maude spent the summer consolidating his position around Baghdad, which suited Murdoch, as he was enabled to recover from his wound. It had been a back-handed sabre cut, neither very deep nor affecting any vital part of his body, although his spinal column had certainly received a jolt. But in the heat and lack of proper sanitation of Mesopotamia any wound was potentially dangerous, and healing was a slow and laborious process. The effort of riding into Baghdad at the head of his men brought on a fever which rapidly developed, and he was back in bed for several weeks. But he was well cared for, and if there were no English nurses available he was in the hands of veiled Turkish ladies who fussed over him, resenting the close supervision of Reynolds, who, as on previous occasions, moved into the hospital to make sure nothing went wrong with his Mr Murdoch.

The halt gave time for letters to catch up with him, and there were the usual congratulatory comments from Sir John French and from Sir Edward Allenby who was now commanding the British army in Palestine, really only a desert away, and who commented that he wished he had the Royal Western Dragoons to play with over there. Lee was not quite so complimentary, wondering whether he was going to be held together with string when next she saw him, and why he had not come home like any reasonable wounded officer.

Either Prendergast or Ramage came in every day to keep him up to date on the activities of the regiment, whose duties once more consisted mainly of reconnaissance, and whose problems were the age-old ones of venereal disease and boredom – the situation of the troops as a whole was complicated by a growing number of outbreaks of cholera, mainly amongst the Indian contingents, but none the less worrying.

The victory as a whole had raised the morale of the army immensely, and this was important because the news from overseas was again uniformly bad – in every way but one. Marshal Joffre had suffered the fate of Sir John French for having failed to beat the Germans, and had been replaced as French commander-in-chief by General Nivelle, but his offensive in the spring had been as disastrous as all the others and the French army had actually mutinied when again ordered to advance, although this was a closely guarded military secret. The British, still under Douglas Haig – now a field marshal – had also suffered heavy casualties, but it was exciting for Murdoch to read that Winston Churchill's enthusiasm and Ernest Swinton's imaginative genius had at last borne fruit, and that tanks had been in action, both on the Somme and in the latest battles. They had caused consternation among the Germans, but it had been the same old story. The High Command had not expected the tanks to have any such effect, had sent them into action piecemeal and without adequate reserves, and had squandered their potential. But that tanks were the land weapon of the future could not be doubted.

On the encouraging side, and an event which sent Lee into raptures of joy, was the decision of the United States to enter the war following the resumption of unrestricted submarine warfare by the Germans. This happened in April, and it seemed likely to be just in time, as the submarines were now claiming an impossibly large number of British ships every month – the island was under intensive rationing. 'But with our navy alongside yours, not to mention the doughboys in France, we have just got to win,' Lee wrote enthusiastically. 'Harry has at last got into uniform. He's on General Pershing's staff. Oh, boy, is he over the moon.'

There was another reason for welcoming American intervention. That spring and summer there came disconcerting news from immediately north of the army in Baghdad, that the Russian front had collapsed in revolution. All manner of rumours about what was going to happen filtered through, but the only certain fact was that the Tsar had been forced to abdicate and that Russia, no matter what the provisional government of Mr Kerensky managed to achieve, was never going to be the same again.

General Maude therefore determined to move north as soon as the hot weather ended, and strike for the oilfields of Mosul, in effect securing all of Mesopotamia for the British before any possibly hostile Russian intervention could take effect. Murdoch was now officially healed, and was exercising Jupiter daily in an effort to regain full fitness in time for the coming campaign. He was therefore taken aback to be summoned to Maude's headquarters and told to nominate a replacement brevet lieutenant-colonel for the regiment.

'Sir?' he asked.

'You are being relieved of your command, Murdoch. Orders from England. As of this moment you are a brigadier-general. There is a cavalry brigade awaiting you in France.'

5
France, 1917–18

'You are brevetted lieutenant-colonel, Billy,' Murdoch told Prendergast. 'The rank will be confirmed in due course.' But would it? He had had no choice, in his report to Maude, but to write that while Major William Prendergast was a fine officer, and the most senior in the regiment, he had time and again revealed a tendency to indecision and uncertainty when under pressure. He knew how the army worked. They would not promote Peter Ramage, a far more suitable choice, over Billy; they would bring in an outsider as lieutenant-colonel, until they could shunt Billy aside as painlessly as possible, and then Ramage would eventually succeed to the position. It had happened during his own youthful years in the dragoons . . . to ease his own way past an insufficient officer.

But on the other hand, with a war on . . . things might be different.

'Gosh,' Billy said. 'I really hadn't expected this, well, not so soon. But you . . . congratulations, Murdoch. Oh, best congratulations.'

'I wish to God it hadn't happened,' Murdoch said, truthfully enough. 'To leave you chaps . . . '

'But the fighting's just about done, out here,' Billy said hopefully.

'Don't you believe it.' Murdoch knew Maude's plans for an advance on Mosul in the near future. And he was going back to the mud and filth and futility that was France. As a brigadier-general he might expect to avoid some of the first two – but the last would be even greater after the free-riding campaign in the desert.

His men seemed as sorry as himself to be parting. Only two of them, Corporal Reynolds and RSM Yeald, had

112

served as long as he, and with the regiment. Reynolds, of course, would be accompanying him; Yeald would remain. 'Maybe one day we'll be part of your command again, sir,' the sergeant-major said.

'If I can possibly manage it, Yeald, you will be.' Murdoch felt close to tears. For eighteen years this regiment had been his entire life.

'Good hunting.' Peter Ramage squeezed his hand. 'May your next charge be right up the Unter den Linden.'

Men like Manly-Smith, Collier, Destry and Bryan, who had known no other commanding officer, looked as distressed as he felt.

Then it was the comfortable, boring ride back down the river to Basra in one of the gunboats, with only Reynolds for company; Jupiter and Reynolds' horse, Chinaman, were coralled on the foredeck.

'Mrs Mackinder will be glad to have you back, sir,' Reynolds reminded him as Murdoch brooded at the desert drifting by.

'Yes,' Murdoch said, and attempted to square his shoulders; it was still a painful business. 'And I will be glad to be back.' It was a case of reminding himself of that.

'Oh, Murdoch!' Lee turned him round to look at his back the moment they were alone in their bedroom. 'Oh, my God!'

'It's not really very deep. Just nasty-looking,' Murdoch assured her.

'Yes,' she said. 'It is nasty-looking. How on earth did you get that?'

'You mean the charge wasn't reported?'

'Not that I saw. There's so much going on . . .'

'Well, I'll be damned,' he commented. Then took her in his arms. 'First time I've ever been small beer. But then, I suppose Mesopotamia is small beer compared with what is going on in France.'

'It earned you promotion. Brigadier general, at thirty-six.' She touched the crossed sword and baton on his shoulder strap. 'Oh, Murdoch, I am so proud of you.' She clung to him. 'How long have you got?'

'Four days.'

'Four days? Oh, hell . . .'

He kissed her on the mouth. 'And four nights, my dearest girl.'

Chand Bibi might have been out of a different existence. As she was. The passions aroused by the heat of the desert had no place amongst the passions to be aroused in the warmth of an English bedroom. Now at last she could be forgotten.

'You will command what in effect is the Light Brigade, General Mackinder.' General Sir William Robertson was a tall, spare man of fifty-seven, with a thin moustache and a grim expression. Murdoch had been acquainted with him for a long time – he had been quartermaster-general of the original BEF in 1914 – and was well aware that he had risen from the ranks to his present exalted position as Chief of the Imperial General Staff, in effect, overall supremo of the British army, a post he had taken over from Kitchener even before the latter's death. His career was therefore unique, and had been a difficult one, both socially and in service. He was not a man who made friends easily, or who forgave fools, either.

But now he allowed himself a brief smile. 'With your penchant for leading desperate charges, you would seem to be the right man for the job. So you will have a regiment of lancers, a regiment of hussars, and a regiment of light dragoons under your command. You will be attached to the Cavalry Corps, Lieutenant-General Kavanagh. Have you served with him before?'

'Yes, sir. I was with him in South Africa.'

'Then you'll know him to be a most determined officer. There is every possibility that, with the arrival of more and more American troops, things will begin to turn our way in the near future. Of course the Americans are very raw, and very stubborn . . . they are quite refusing to amalgamate their forces with any of our armies or the French, seem determined to fight on their own, but their very numbers must make a difference. Equally, however, there is a good

114

deal of hard fighting ahead. The Bolsheviks seem to have definitely ousted Kerensky and are suing for a separate peace, which means the Germans will be able to release a considerable number of men for service on the western front. Still, things are coming along. I have every hope that you will discover further opportunities for distinction, Mackinder. But I would strongly advise that you exercise patience and self-control wherever possible. You are one of our youngest brigadiers.' He paused reflectively, as if wondering whether or not Murdoch might be too young for such responsibility, then added, 'Good day to you and good fortune.'

Mr Churchill also wanted to see him again. Churchill had served in France for a spell in 1916 as a colonel, but had been recalled following the reshuffle of the Government to be Minister of Munitions, and apply his enormous energy to ensuring that at last the British army had all the shells and bullets it required. But he wanted to talk about tanks, after the usual brief congratulations.

'I heard about them on the Somme, last year,' Murdoch said. 'Without any endorsement from me.'

'Wasn't necessary, as it turned out.'

'Pity there weren't more of them.'

'They were used prematurely,' Churchill growled. 'That's the trouble with the army. Show them something worthwhile and they immediately ruin it. The fact was that the top brass didn't believe in them, and were only too happy to point up their shortcomings. We always knew they were slow, and short-ranged, and liable to mechanical failure. Tanks have to be used in massed, sharp attacks, then regrouped and repaired, and thrust forward again. Well,' he grinned. 'They are beginning to see the light. They have ordered quite a few of them, and have even had some officers training in how to get the best use out of them. I'll tell you this, Mackinder: I am half American, just like your kids, and I am proud of it. I can't wait to see a full American army on French soil. But it is the tank which is going to win this war for us . . . not all the

115

doughboys in the world. Bear that in mind. Good luck with your command.'

Churchill was proved right sooner than Murdoch had expected. Or perhaps the minister had advance knowledge of British plans. Murdoch's return had been delayed by the necessity of waiting for a ship in Basra, and then he had been allowed a brief leave, so that it was mid-November 1917 before he got back to France, a time when campaigning might have been expected to be over for a few months. He had barely joined Lieutenant-General Sir Charles Kavanagh's corps, however, when the Third Army, commanded by General Sir Julian Byng, launched a unique attack upon the German position in front of Cambrai. It was unique because there was no preliminary bombardment, and because the assault was led, in complete surprise, by two hundred tanks. The Germans were devastated, and a five-mile-deep gap was torn in their line. Then the old story reasserted itself; the tanks began to fail, the infantry were not in close enough support to consolidate, and there were insufficient reserves to follow up. The Germans recovered their nerves and the gap was plugged.

'But it's a sign of what can be done,' General Kavanagh told him. 'Of what will be done, Mackinder. And then our fellows can be let loose.'

Murdoch was inclined to take that with a pinch of salt; apparently two cavalry divisions had been waiting to utilize the breakthrough at Cambrai, but the gap had been closed too quickly. And conditions in France were as he remembered them, only worse. The Cavalry Corps was spread out behind the line of four British armies holding the front north-west of Paris. Of these, Sir Henry Rawlinson's Fourth Army lay just north of the Somme River, within indeed a very few miles of the coast; where Murdoch and Harry Caspar had ridden into St Omer for a French meal, now it was necessary to visit Abbeville.

General Plumer's Second Army was on their left, holding Ypres and the area between the Lys and the Yser; General Byng's Third Army, still flushed with their Cambrai success, however disappointed they were at the eventual outcome, lay on the right, and beyond that was General Hubert Gough's Fifth Army. Both Byng and Gough were cavalrymen under whom Murdoch had served previously. His new commander, Kavanagh, was, like Gough, an Irishman, and like Murdoch and every other cavalryman, feeling extremely frustrated. 'If only they'd give us a chance,' he grumbled.

Murdoch didn't see what they were going to do even with a chance. He took the first opportunity he could to go up to the line and see for himself the tangled, shell-cratered, muddy wilderness that extended for several miles to the north and east. Presumably if they could cross that they would find open, rolling country, the country across which Wellington and Marlborough had manoeuvred their armies in the past. But they had to cross the slough first, and having watched the horsemen under his command slithering and sliding, their mounts whinnying in discomfort, some having to be shot after breaking legs in unsuspected potholes, he for the first time began to feel pessimistic about the future.

The quality of both men and horses was, however, high. His three lieutenants-colonel, Moore of the Lancers, Cawdray of the Hussars, and Bright of the Dragoons, were experienced soldiers, as was Major John Proud, his adjutant. He had met all four of them before the war, on the Curragh, but had never actually been brigaded with them, much less been in command of them. For their part, they, and their men, were delighted to have been given such a famous cavalryman as their commander, and undoubtedly looked forward to achieving great things under his leadership. They were somewhat dashed when he immediately inaugurated his vigorous training methods, having the men learning to shoot at the canter, and performing all other manner of intricate exercises in the winter snow. 'Preparation is what wins battles,' he kept telling them. 'Being in the best shape to take advantage of whatever situation crops up.'

They couldn't argue with his experience, but they

groaned with each new exercise he devised, and the more so when he talked the local tank corps commander – for the tanks were refitting behind the lines – into joint exercises, so that at least the horses would cease to be terrified of the huge, smelly, noisy creatures.

He himself was aware for the first time of being lonely. His staff were the best of fellows, and Proud soon became a friend, but it was not the same thing as being part of the huge family which was the regiment. There were no personal problems to be listened to – and, hopefully, solved – no quarrels to be settled, no health or kit problems to be tackled, merely the business of planning and training men who were in every way strangers – it was quite impossible to know the name of every man in a brigade. He was also disturbed by the news which arrived from Mesopotamia, which was where his heart really lay. General Maude had duly launched his advance to the north in September, had won another battle over the Turks at Ramadi, and had continued to force his way up the Euphrates towards Mosul. And then had died, on 18 November, of cholera. This ghastly disease was making its presence felt throughout the Middle Eastern army, and Murdoch could only wonder, and worry, about the state of his beloved Westerns. More encouraging was the news from Palestine where General Allenby was steadily forging ahead, and at Christmas word was received that he had taken Jerusalem.

With the new year, the Americans began to make themselves felt. Not only by arriving in France in increasing numbers, but on the diplomatic front as well, and it was in January that President Wilson put forward his Fourteen Points on the basis of which he felt a just and honourable peace could be achieved. The points were the sole topic of conversation in the various messes, and the actual war suddenly seemed less important, especially with the wintry snow lying on the ground and the armies quiescent. The British officers also had a new topic of conversation in the sudden replacement of General Robertson as CIGS by General Sir Henry Wilson. Another Irishman, Wilson was regarded with mixed feelings by the normal serving officer, in that he had spent most of his senior career either as commandant of the Staff College or, more recently, as chief liaison officer between the British and French armies – he spoke French fluently. Murdoch surmised that this was the principal reason for his appointment, as relations between Field Marshal Haig and the new French commander-in-chief, Pétain, had grown somewhat strained over the past year as offensive after offensive had gone astray. And there could be no doubt of Wilson's efficiency; he had been responsible for the transshipment of the BEF to France in 1914, and had carried out his mission without losing a man or a horse.

All these changes and considerations became irrelevancies, however, on the morning of 21 March. There was little wind, and by dawn when Reynolds awoke Murdoch with his usual cup of tea, a dense fog lay right across the river valleys. But Murdoch had hardly taken a sip when he heard the rumble of gunfire to the east.

'Something's up,' Reynolds remarked.

'Can't be our chaps,' Murdoch mused. He had not been apprised of any looming offensive.

He shaved and dressed, met Proud in the room they were using as an office in the Chateau they were occupying, and went over the morning's reports, looking at each other from time to time as the roar of the guns seemed to grow louder and louder. 'There's something big going on around Cambrai,' Murdoch said. 'I wonder if the buggers have gone and launched another tank attack without this time letting the cavalry even know about it. What have we got on today, John?'

'The usual exercise,' Proud said.

Murdoch grinned at him. 'Well, I tell you what we'll do, Johnnie. We'll give the lads a rest today, and ride over to Byng's HQ and find out what's going on.'

'Now, that's a splendid idea,' Proud agreed.

They were in the middle of breakfast when the wireless telegrapher appeared in the doorway. 'Urgent dispatches, sir,' he said.

Murdoch glanced at the typewritten sheets of paper. 'Bloody hell!' he commented, and handed them to Proud. 'Those are German guns. They've smashed right through Gough's and Byng's outer defences.' He ran outside, stared to the east. The noise was tremendous, and he was sure he could see planes wheeling over the lines; the Germans were attacking with everything they had. 'Brigade is to concentrate immediately on Amiens. Reynolds, where the hell is Jupiter?'

By the time they reached the cantonment assembly was already sounding and the men were falling in. 'Orders, sir?' Moore asked.

'The Cavalry Corps is to concentrate on Amiens. We'll get our orders there,' Murdoch snapped.

They clattered along the main road, watched by alarmed French villagers. Even before they reached Amiens they were passing convoys of wounded British soldiers being driven to the coast.

'It's like all hell has broken loose over there,' one of their officers said. He was a colonel, hardly older than Murdoch, and had lost his left hand. His face was pale with loss of blood, and he was sedated against the pain of the wound and the tourniquet which was keeping him alive. 'There must be millions of the bastards.'

Kavanagh was waiting for his divisional commanders in the city, and the orders were very rapidly filtered through to the brigades. The Germans had broken through on a massive forty-two-mile front by the use of novel tactics rather than novel weapons. They had concentrated a huge number of men opposite the weakest of the four British armies, that commanded by Gough, and then had launched an all-out attack with only a limited preliminary bombardment. The secret of their rapid advance had been their refusal to become bogged down before British strongpoints. Wherever one of these was encountered the attacking force had simply flowed around it, effectively ignoring what had hitherto been a required tenet of warfare; isolated and surrounded, the strongpoints were being cleaned up by second- and third-wave attackers. It was so incredibly

120

simple a method of continuing an advance it was amazing no one had thought of it before.

That Gough and his army had been taken by surprise was evident. Perhaps his arrangements had not been of the best. His units were scattered and unable to cooperate quickly enough. Byng's army, on his left, was better equipped to withstand the sudden onslaught, but the almost complete collapse of the Fifth left them, and the French on Gough's right, with exposed flanks, and there was no option but to fall back. Every man was needed to plug the gap, regardless of rank or station. Murdoch found his brigade dismounted and manning newly dug trenches about ten miles north-east of Montdidier, a long way behind the original front line, while troops with crushed morale filed silently past them, heads hanging.

The difficulty was in discovering exactly what was happening. The brigade was in position by nightfall, and listening to the bangs and crashes from in front of them. Next morning various rumours arrived from time to time, but none of these were confirmed until the arrival of Douglas Haig himself, in the course of a rapid tour of the battlefronts. Murdoch had known Haig well in South Africa and before the war, but he had not met him since 1914; Murdoch had served with Plumer's army when first in France and had been posted to Mesopotamia before Haig took over as commander-in-chief. Now it brought back memories to see that sturdy, moustached figure, as flawlessly dressed as ever, leaving his car and striding towards him.

'Murdoch!' Haig shook hands. 'Good to see you again. Can your people hold here?'

'As long as we have ammunition, sir. But . . . we have no enemies at the moment.'

'They'll be here. There's bugger all between you and them at the moment. The French are pulling out to the east.'

'But . . . that'll increase the gap in the line,' Murdoch protested.

'Of course it will. It's that man Pétain. He has informed

me that the preservation of Paris is more important than the preservation of the British army, and is concentrating all his force to that effect.'

'So much for the entente cordiale,' Murdoch remarked.

'Yes. Well, I've been on to Wilson and he's promised to do something about it. Not all the French generals are as narrow-minded as Pétain, thank God. Now tell me, have you seen Gough?'

'No, sir. I imagine he's up front trying to steady his people.'

'Yes.' Haig's face was grim. 'I want to get hold of him. Tell him that if he comes this way.'

'Yes, sir.'

'And hold, Murdoch. Hold. If there's any man in this bloody army who can do it, it should be you.'

'Yes, sir. Thank you, sir.'

'Just do it.' The Field Marshal returned to his car and drove away.

The sound of gunfire was much closer, and Murdoch toured the brigade positions. They were dug in over a mile, and he had fifteen hundred men. In old-fashioned terms that was fairly good coverage, almost a man to a yard. In terms of modern fire power he had no idea; the last time he had manned a trench had been in 1915 and it had been a different situation then. For one thing, they were now subjected to assault from the air. In the middle of the morning a swarm of black-crossed biplanes raced above them, spotted them, and turned to swoop down behind the chatter of their machine-guns. The trenches were useless against this sort of attack, as the planes could fly up and down them, strafing. The cavalrymen blazed away with their rifles, and one or two even manhandled the Lewis guns into an upright position to shoot at their tormentors, but they never seemed to hit any, while suffering over a hundred casualties themselves. More important was the damage to morale, as the troopers felt absolutely helpless against this novel form of attack.

'Don't we have a bloody air force?' Proud demanded.

'I imagine they have their hands full somewhere else,' Murdoch suggested.

The planes at last withdrew, no doubt to refuel. But now there were more and more men streaming back from in front of them, some even without their rifles. 'There's no hope,' they told the cavalrymen. 'The buggers are everywhere. there's no hope.'

'Here we are and here we stay, lads,' Murdoch said, walking up and down the trenches himself. He wanted them to see him, know he was there, remind them that he was the famous Murdoch Mackinder, who had fought against insuperable odds and won. He had never been so proud of his record, or his heritage. In fact, he had never thought about it in such terms before.

The grey-clad masses arrived in the afternoon, seeping across the meadows in front of them like water. Murdoch had telephoned for artillery support but there was none available, it seemed; several batteries had been overrun. So the brigade engaged with rifles and machine-guns. The Germans flooded right up to the trenches and one or two even got in, but were driven back with bayonets and even fists; the troopers' swords had been left with their horses. Murdoch himself joined the line and emptied his revolver, and at last the enemy faded away as dusk fell.

'All quiet on the western front,' gasped Colonel Cawdray. His steel helmet had a hole in it but miraculously he had not been hit. Some fifty of his men were dead, however, and the other regiments had suffered similar casualties. 'But we beat the buggers,' he said happily.

Murdoch wasn't so confident, remembering the reports of how Gough's advanced positions had been overrun. And sure enough that night a message came through from General Kavanagh to pull out to prepared positions in the rear. Murdoch refused to credit it, after his conversation with the commander-in-chief, and would not allow his men to move until he had spoken with Kavanagh personally. This took some time to arrange, and then the general was not in a good mood.

'Look, Mackinder,' he said, 'you're bloody well all but

123

surrounded. I'm keeping just a lane open for you. Get the hell out of there. Now!'

Murdoch obeyed, sent his men filing back through the darkness. He himself remained with the rearguard until the last trench had been evacuated, then joined the ghostly, silent procession, expecting at any moment to be discovered and subjected to a blaze of fire. It was like 1914 all over again, save that then at least they had turned at bay at Le Cateau. Now the procedure went on for day after day, fighting while it was light, being strafed and murdered from the air while wave after wave of German assault troops crashed against them from in front, and pulling back another few hundred yards at night as the enemy lapped around their flanks, probing, and finding, weaknesses in the ever-changing British position. The only blessing was that the Germans were advancing so fast that they were outrunning their artillery. But still . . .

'How long can this go on?' Colonel Bright groaned as he watched his men trek off into the darkness yet again. 'One morning we're going to find our prepared position is on the beach at Deauville.'

Actually there was intensive behind-the-scene activity going on: Haig's plea to Wilson to have Pétain replaced by 'Foch or some other French general who will fight' had had almost immediate effect, and a very long-ranging effect indeed. On 3 April, when Murdoch and his men had been desperately trying to hold their positions for more than a week, Foch was appointed supreme commander of all the Allied forces, and in fact only two days later the German offensive ground to a halt. By then the Light Brigade was actually dug in in the suburbs of Montdidier, more than forty miles behind the original front line, and were so totally exhausted that Murdoch asked Kavanagh if they could not be taken out of combat for a few days' rest and recuperation; not one of them, himself included, had changed their clothes or even shaved for a fortnight – he could not imagine what the insides of his boots must be like.

The reply was that it was not at that moment possible. The Fifth Army had just about disintegrated, and Gough

124

had been relieved of his command – no doubt, Murdoch thought grimly, that was what Haig had been seeking him for on that second day, to sack him. Now the remnant of his command was being supported by Rawlinson's Fourth Army, hastily being transferred round the rear of the British defences. Once that process was completed, and the additional forces being made ready in England arrived, and the eight American divisions hurriedly being moved up to the line were in position, some relief could be anticipated, but until then there was simply no reserve to utilize. And before that happened, the Germans struck again, this time further to the north, at Plumer's army between the Lys and the Yser. Once again they penetrated deeply, and as they also resumed their advance on the southern front, British morale in general began to show signs of crumpling. It was then that Murdoch received a letter from Haig, addressed to 'All Ranks of the British Forces in France'. Handwritten and mimeographed, it read:

Three weeks ago today the Enemy began his terrific attacks against us in a 50 mile front. His objects are to separate us from the French, to take the channel ports and destroy the British army.

Despite already throwing 106 Divisions into the battle suffering [this word was stroked out] enduring the most reckless sacrifice in human life, he has as yet made little progress towards his goals.

We owe this to the determined fighting and self sacrifice of our troops. Words fail me to express the admiration which I feel for the splendid resistance offered by all ranks of our army under the most trying circumstances.

Many amongst us now are very [word struck out] tired. To those I would say that victory will belong to the side which holds out the longest. The French army is moving rapidly and in great force to our support . . .

There is no other course open to us but to fight it out! Every position must be held to the last man: there must be no retirement. With our backs to the wall, and believing in the justice of our cause each one of you must fight on to the end. The safety from Horror and the Freedom of mankind alike depend upon the conduct of each one of us at this critical moment. But be of good cheer, the British Empire must win in the End. [This last sentence had also been stroked through.]

D. Haig

It was dated Thursday 11 April 1918.

This new attack lasted nine days before it too foundered on the now inspired British defence. General Ludendorff, the German chief-of-staff, then turned east, and launched a savage attack on the still shaken French armies. In a week the Germans were across the Aisne and reaching the Marne, back to where they had been in August 1914. Now it was the turn of the French and the Americans to fight with grim determination. Reinforcements had at last arrived from England, the Fourth and Fifth Armies had been amalgamated – retaining the name Fifth to restore morale to those men beaten in the first German onslaught – and Murdoch was able to lead his battered survivors in search of their horses and a hot bath.

The brigade had suffered severely. Four hundred men, a quarter of their total strength, had been killed or wounded. For those who returned to their cantonments outside Abbeville it was like awakening from a long nightmare. A very long nightmare, for the Germans were still battering away up to the middle of July. But by then it was clear that they had shot their bolt, and when the French and Americans counter-attacked at Noyon and Chateau-Thierry, it was the Germans' turn to have to hold desperately on to the territory they had gained.

On 21 July, feeling fully recuperated, Murdoch was summoned to a senior officers' conference at the head-quarters of General Rawlinson's Fifth Army, where he found himself in the company of the largest assembly of brass he had ever seen. Rawlinson's three corps commanders were present, Lieutenant-General Sir Arthur Currie of the Canadian Corps, Lieutenant-General Sir Richard Butler of the Third British, together with Kavanagh of course, as well as the divisional major-generals and their brigadiers, together with senior officers of both the Royal Air Force – as the Royal Flying Corps had recently been renamed – and the Tank Corps. There was even a clutch of American officers present, headed by a major-general.

'Now gentlemen,' Rawlinson said when everyone was seated, 'it is time to give Jerry a taste of his own medicine. As you probably know, a small counter-attack was launched a fortnight ago, in the direction of the village of Hamel, by the Australians supported by the Fifth Tank Brigade. There was no preliminary bombardment. This operation was a complete success, and it has led Field Marshal Haig to propose to Marshal Foch that we proceed with another counter-attack, on the same lines, but on a much larger scale, with the idea of regaining control of the Amiens–Paris railway, and of course, to drive the enemy back just as far as we can while doing so. Now, as I have intimated, we are going to use the same tactics as at Hamel, on a grand scale, which means we are going to throw at Jerry every man and every machine we possess – with absolutely no advance warning.

'Our dispositions will be as follows. On the left of our position we will have the Third Corps, with the Twelfth, Eighteenth, and Thirty-Eighth Divisions in line, the Forty-Seventh on the extreme left as a flank guard, and the American Thirty-Third Division in reserve; on the right will be the Canadians, with the Second and Third Divisions in line, and the First and Fourth in reserve. To assist in the assault, and I do mean that, gentlemen . . . ' he looked towards Kavanagh and his officers, 'will be the Cavalry Corps, consisting of the First, Second and Third Cavalry Divisions. They will cooperate in the initial breakthrough with our tank forces, the largest tank force ever concentrated on a battlefield to this time: it will consist of the Third, Fourth and Fifth Tank Brigades, and the Tenth Battalion. In general reserve will be the Seventeenth, Thirty-Second and Sixty-Third infantry divisions. And air superiority will be guaranteed, as we have attached to us six corps squadrons of the Royal Air Force, eight scout squadrons, and three bomber squadrons.

'Opposed to us will be the Second and Eighteenth German armies, commanded respectively by General von der Marwitz and General Hutier. General Hutier, I may say, is being given credit in the German press for having

127

invented the tactics used in the recent offensive, the bypassing of strongpoints, leaving them to be mopped by the reserve elements. We will have to see how the general reacts to fighting on the defensive. Individual divisional targets will be assigned later. I just wanted to put you all into the picture. Now, are there any questions?'

'Yes, sir,' answered one of the tank commanders. 'You have said that the cavalry are going to take part in the initial assault, with the tanks. Is that correct?'

'Yes, that is correct.'

'It won't work, sir.'

Rawlinson frowned at him. 'It will work, Colonel Fuller. The tanks will provide cover for the cavalry; the cavalry will mop up when the tanks have broken the enemy line.'

'With respect, sir, the two are not compatible. The cavalry are either going to have to walk their horses the whole way, in which case they might as well be infantrymen, or they are going to be far in advance of anything our men can achieve. While when it comes to fighting, well, sir . . . our tanks will keep out bullets. Horses' flesh will not.'

Rawlinson's frown became imperious, while there was considerable shuffling of feet amongst cavalry officers. 'No flesh will keep out a bullet, Colonel. I am sure every soldier in this army has learned that by now. I am equally sure that the cavalry will give an excellent account of themselves. Now, are there any other questions . . . ?'

'Bloody cheek,' Kavanagh growled as he and his officers assembled outside the conference room. 'Here we are, at last about to be given our chance, and these confounded tank wallahs want us out of it. A service which is hardly a year old.' He looked over the eager faces with which he was surrounded. 'As General Rawlinson said, gentlemen, the cavalry corps will give an excellent account of themselves. Remember that, now.'

It was the most exhilarating news Murdoch had had since Maude had announced his decision to march on Kut-al-Amara. He would dearly have liked to have the regiment under his command, but he had grown to appreciate and have confidence in the Light Brigade, and he had no doubt they would fight with all the verve of the Royal Westerns – he had seen them in action. Yet Colonel Fuller's words hung in his mind. Because they were absolutely true. Of course wars had been fought since time immemorial with horses – and the men who rode them – being cut down by whatever missile weapon happened to be available at the moment. Nothing had changed, save that the missiles available were more deadly nowadays than at any time in history.

And at last a method had been found to save horses from the indiscriminate slaughter to which they had been subjected for so many centuries – by not sending them into battle at all. But to concede that they could be replaced by tanks was to accept the end of the cavalry as he knew it. He was a cavalryman, and the son and grandson and great-grandson of cavalrymen. The concept was impossible. Surely.

He determined to put it out of his mind as he prepared his men at last for battle. And over the following couple of weeks the matter was indeed forgotten, as the whole plan slowly began to change. The more Marshal Foch looked at it, the more he liked its possibilities. The result was that the French Thirty-First Corps was included under Rawlinson's command, and what had begun as a limited operation was to become a massive counter-thrust.

Immediately complications set in. The French had very few tanks, and were not prepared to advance without some preliminary softening of the enemy – so a bombardment, as so often in the past, had to be agreed. This was, however, to be as minimal as possible. What the French did bring with them was more than a thousand aircraft, which, added to the eight hundred odd of the RAF, meant an enormous Allied preponderance in the air.

Complications notwithstanding – and with the plan constantly being changed, so were objectives and require-ments, which meant an inordinate amount of staff work – the preparations went ahead with great verve. The key to the operation, as Rawlinson underlined in his instructions

129

to his commanders, was secrecy. Thus no one below the rank of colonel was to know the objectives or the dates of the offensive until within thirty-six hours of zero hour. It was impossible to conceal the fact that there was going to be an offensive, of course, but the preparations were also carried out with as much concealment as possible: all troop movements had to be made by night, reconnaissance patrols were prohibited in case they alerted the enemy, normal work was carried on during the day, new-laid roads were obscured with sand or straw and all ammunition dumps were camouflaged.

The result of all this was that although the Fifth Australian Division, in complete disregard of orders, at the end of July carried out a raid just north of the Somme, inviting retaliation which duly came in a violent German counter-attack which penetrated eight hundred yards into the British position and all but uncovered the camouflaged material, as well as disrupting the preparations of the Third Corps, by 8 August fourteen infantry divisions, three cavalry divisions, three brigades of tanks and more than two thousand guns had been concentrated just east of Amiens without the enemy, only a few miles away, being the least aware of it.

This was the first opportunity Murdoch had had actually to inspect a tank, and indeed there were five varieties on show, waiting to go into action, while the three main types, the Marks Four, Five and Five Star, were further sub-divided into males and females, although the difference between the two was a matter of armament. These Mark tanks were enormous affairs – the Mark Four measured more than twenty-six feet in length, and the Stars over thirty. All weighed around thirty tons, and were crewed by one officer and seven other ranks. Their armaments consisted mainly of Lewis guns on the smaller versions, and Hotchkiss on the larger, although some had six-pounder cannon. But they were incredibly slow, with a top speed of just over four miles an hour – which ate into their fuel capacity – and an economic speed of not much more than two, and even this gave them a range of only around twenty miles. The idea of their ever replacing horses for screening and scouting had to be a joke.

Slightly more believable as mechanized cavalry were the Medium Mark A tanks, known as Whippets. These were much smaller affairs, only twenty feet long and weighing fouteen tons. They carried one officer and two other ranks, but were yet armed with four Hotchkiss guns, and had twin engines, only forty-five horsepower each – as compared with the hundred-and-fifty horsepower engine of a Mark V Star – but were capable of a top speed in excess of eight miles an hour, and would cruise for forty miles at five an hour. Their main problem, apart from the lightness of their armour, was their limited span, which was only seven feet, as compared with the ten of the Mark IVs and Vs, and the fourteen of the Stars – this meant that the wider trenches were as impassable to them as to wheeled vehicles.

Reservations apart, however, it was, as Rawlinson had promised, the largest armoured force ever to go into action. There were three hundred and twenty-four heavy tanks, and ninety-six Whippets, with forty-two heavies in reserve. In addition the attacking force had available ninety-six supply tanks, and twenty-two gun carriers – huge, even slower monsters. This made up a total of five hundred and eighty machines, to which could be added twelve armoured cars.

The change in the plan meant that the initial assault was to be carried out in the centre, by the Australian and Canadian Corps, with the Third British Corps and the French on either flank to act defensively until the initial breakthrough had been made. The Cavalry Corps was assigned to this assault, in company with the Fifth Tank Brigade, their task being to push through the infantry and secure the Amiens outer defences, and then swing south-east to cut the enemy communications, after which the French would also take up the advance.

'Mark my bloody word,' commented the tank officer beside whose machine Murdoch, mounted on Jupiter, found himself standing. 'You chaps are going to be massacred.'

Murdoch ignored him and looked at his watch. It was three fifty-five ack emma on the morning of 8 August. Zero hour was four twenty, but the movement of the tanks and horses was to begin before that. He drew his revolver and checked that every chamber was loaded, loosened his sword in its scabbard, and felt the adrenaline begin to flow. He looked over his shoulder at Reynolds, but Reynolds was hardly visible. The night, which had begun crisp and clear, had suddenly become shrouded in mist at three o'clock, and the mist had thickened to a dense fog. Which was all to the good. It was the thickness of the fog which had given the German onslaught of 21 March such a send-off.

He listened to growing noise, the roar of a thousand aircraft. He couldn't see the sky, of course, but he knew the planes would be flying low, their purpose at this stage to hide the noise of the tank engines – later, when the sky cleared, they would begin strafing the enemy rear positions.

The tank engines were started, with clouds of exhaust fumes helping to thicken the mist and causing the waiting horses, and there were some fifteen thousand of them, to snort and stamp. Then the machines moved forward, through the gaps left by the enormous mass of infantry in front of them, to whispers of 'Good on you, cobber,' from the Australians.

The horses also rode into the gaps, and out into the morass of abandoned trenches and shell craters that lay beyond. Visibility was still non-existent, and Murdoch, at the head of the Light Brigade, could only just see the tank in front of him. As Colonel Fuller had prophesied, even at a walk it was hard to keep the horses from creeping up on the ponderous machines.

There now came an enormous explosion, quite drowning out the drone of the aircraft, as the Allied artillery opened fire; the time was exactly four twenty ack emma. While the shells wailed overhead, and from in front of them they could hear the enormous crumps as they exploded on the German trenches, tanks and cavalry continued their advance. One or two shots were fired, by nervous German sentries, but they were actually taken completely by

132

surprise. So were the British, at the sudden appearance of the first German trench out of the mist in front of them.

Murdoch caught a glimpse of astonished faces beneath coal-scuttle helmets, of men throwing forward their rifles, and then gasping their horror as the caterpillar treads of the tanks reared above them. The first onslaught was quite sickening. Immediately in front of Murdoch was a machine-gun nest, manned by four men. They had time to loose one burst, the bullets clanging off the steel breastplate of the tank, and then its thirty tons descended on them with a horrifying squelch. The tank never even checked. Its forward tracks had already made contact with the far side of the trench and it rolled on, while Murdoch reined his horse to gaze at what had once been four men, now so crushed into the track-marked mud of the trench wall that only a sleeve here, a helmet there, could be identified. Of the machine-gun there was no sign.

'They're gone, sir,' Reynolds said, riding up beside him. The Germans had abandoned the trench and were fleeing back to the second line, shouting their fear.

Major-General Harrison, commanding the brigade, himself appeared through the murk. 'Now, Mackinder,' he said. 'Now's our chance. Ride through the bastards.'

'The tanks are firing, sir.'

'I've told the buggers to give over and let us have our chance. Fifteen minutes. I've also instructed the creeping barrage to be lifted.'

'Yes, sir,' Murdoch said, and checked his watch, then looked round to find Proud. 'Pass the word to prepare to charge, Major.'

'Yes, sir,' Proud said, and dispatched the three lieutenants who formed his staff left and right to find the regimental colonels.

Murdoch walked his horse forward behind the tanks, which were now assaulting the second line of trenches with equal success. He listened to the guns fall silent, and the tanks too had stopped shooting as the orders reached them on their wireless sets. 'Brigade ready to charge, sir,' Proud reported.

133

'Bugler, sound the advance,' Murdoch commanded, and the notes cut across the morning. A relic, Murdoch thought, of a glorious past, in the midst of a mechanical present.

He touched Jupiter with his spur, and moved forward. It was impossible to raise a gallop, as no one knew when he would come upon a crater or a trench, but the cavalry urged their horses past the tanks and across the open ground beyond, peering into the mist, which was slowly thinning, swords drawn, awaiting at any moment the deadly chatter of a machine-gun. The Germans were still demoralized, however, and perhaps the more so when out of the mist there emerged, not tanks as they had been warned to expect by the men who had fled past them, but sword-wielding horsemen. They were prepared to fight these, but were quickly overwhelmed, although it was often necessary to jump the trenches as they were too steep for the horses to negotiate otherwise.

Inhaling the sweet scent of victory, Murdoch rode on to the next line, which was in and around a shattered village surrounded by his cheering troopers. This too was swept clear of enemy troops, but as the horsemen emerged from amidst the houses the mist suddenly lifted altogether, allowing the morning sun to play on the scene, on a vast mass of cavalry milling about, sabring any Germans who had been left behind . . . and an absolutely magnificent target for the next line of machine-guns.

These opened up immediately. Horses screamed as they were cut to ribbons, men gasped and died. 'Sound recall,' Murdoch shouted. The notes blared across the morning, and he found himself on his feet; Jupiter had dropped like a stone. For a moment he was stunned. Jupiter was the fourth horse shot from under him in his career, and each time it had been almost like being killed himself.

'Here, sir,' Reynolds was alongside him, giving him a hand up into the saddle as the cavalry scampered back to seek what shelter they could find amidst the houses of the village.

'Regroup,' Murdoch bellowed. 'Regroup.' And listened

to the reassuring clanking of the tanks, slowly coming up to take over the advance.

The Battle of Amiens was the beginning of the end for Germany. General Ludendorff was to call 8 August 1918 the Black Day of the German Army. After it the question was not whether or not the Germans would be beaten, but how soon they would admit it.

Yet the battle itself had not been an unqualified success. The Allies achieved their objectives, but little more, all on the first day. By nightfall they had penetrated some ten miles into the German position, but by then they had outrun their reserves of men and had used up all their reserves of tanks, while by then too, as the experience of the morning had proved time and again, it had been realized that the cavalry were only an embarrassment in the forefront of battle, and they were being used to round up the vast numbers of German prisoners left behind in their armies' retreat.

Next day the Germans had consolidated, and there were insufficient tanks to mount another assault; the battle settled down into an old-fashioned slogging match until the necessary repairs could be carried out. But the Germans kept on retiring, back to their newly built Hindenburg Line some distance behind the original front, and the reason was very simply their fear of what the tanks might do next time they were brought into action.

It was more than just the unstoppable juggernaut effect which stayed in Murdoch's mind. That was destructive to morale in a way perhaps nothing in warfare had previously been. But the German High Command was also alarmed by other events on 8 August, such as the feat of the Seventeenth Tank Battalion, Whippets, which had not run out of fuel and had penetrated far behind the enemy lines, catching men at dinner and an entire headquarters staff unprepared, shooting them up, and then returning to their own forces. This was like an old-fashioned cavalry raid indeed, but one carried out by armoured horses accoutred with machine guns. It was like nothing any soldier on either side had ever seen before.

The next three months saw an unceasing advance. While the British regrouped, the Americans launched their first major offensive of the war and pinched out the St Mihiel salient. By the end of September the British were ready to move again, and while the French and the Americans attacked in the Meuse–Argonne area, the British and Belgians, with French support, stormed the Hindenburg Line. Once again this was the task of the infantry and the tanks; the cavalry did the mopping up.

'We'll get our chance, one day, Murdoch,' Kavanagh told him as they sat on their horses and watched the lancers bringing in a steady stream of German soldiers. 'Once we're through the Hindenburg Line, there's open country. No entrenchments, no pillboxes, nothing, all the way back to Berlin. We'll have to cross the Rhine, of course. But we'll swim our horses across that, eh?'

'Yes, sir,' Murdoch agreed, but he knew better. He stroked the neck of Mars, Jupiter's replacement, and thought to himself: You'll never lead a charge, young fellow. So maybe you'll live to a ripe old age.

A month later the Germans asked for an armistice.

PART TWO

THE GENERAL

6
England 1918–23

The world seemed to stand still. The brigade was unsure what to do, caught in the middle of rounding up another batch of surrendered Germans. Were they still to be treated as enemies?

A wireless conversation with divisional headquarters assured Murdoch that they were, but that all German units were supposed to lay down their arms where they were, and await further orders. Obviously there might be one or two who would not do that . . . but those were the responsibility of the line troops.

The brigade returned to its cantonments, and men looked at each other and scratched their heads. Their officers sat down and lit cigarettes and tried to think about what might happen now; more than half of them had joined the army after 1914, would never have dreamed of a military career before then, and did not consider one now. And yet, the thought of returning to university or office, of learning or persuading rather than commanding, of being able to plan what one might be doing in a year's time and knowing that one would be alive to make it happen, of not being constantly afraid, was itself a frightening one.

Murdoch poured John Proud and himself a glass of good armagnac each, and raised his own. 'Peace.'

Proud drank. 'What will you do?'

Murdoch shrugged. 'Same as I'm doing now. Wait for the next one to come along. I've been doing that for nineteen years.'

'Suppose there isn't a next one? Isn't this the war to end all wars?'

'If you'll believe that you'll believe anything. What are

your plans?' He knew Proud was not a regular soldier, but had been a Territorial.

'I have no idea. I was just setting up a little practice as a solicitor in 1914, down in Cornwall. I imagine everyone in Newquay has forgotten my name, by now.'

'Then you'll have to remind them.'

'Yes,' Proud said glumly. He was clearly not looking forward to it, and Murdoch suspected there might be financial problems . . . but he didn't know how to go about offering to help.

They were disturbed by the frantic hooting of a horn.

'Begging your pardon, sir,' Reynolds said. 'It's Mr Caspar.'

'Captain Caspar, you nut,' Harry said, striding into the room with his hand outstretched, and then coming to attention to salute. 'Oops, I almost forgot.'

'Harry!' Murdoch shook hands. Harry wore American army service uniform, and had a revolver slung on his belt – he managed to look like a Wild West gunman. 'Where have you been these last couple of years?'

'Trying to get to you, believe it or not. How I wanted to be with you outside Amiens in August. But . . . duty called. Say, you guys coming out for a drink?' He looked at Proud a trifle uncertainly.

'You haven't met John Proud, my adjutant.'

They shook hands.

'We're gonna celebrate,' Harry announced. 'Weren't you gonna celebrate?'

'Well . . . I suppose we were.'

'So come on. I have some spare cans of gas in the back of that thing.'

Murdoch suddenly realized that he wanted to celebrate, more than ever before in his life. 'You're on. Only, leave that howitzer behind.'

'I'd be improperly dressed. And suppose we met a Jerry?'

'You're in the company of two British officers,' Murdoch said enigmatically.

Harry hesitated, then took off the gun belt and laid it on a chair. 'Just remind me where I left it,' he said.

'Where are we going?' Murdoch asked.

Harry twisted the wheel, and the touring car negotiated both a pothole and stalled lorry. The waiting soldiers cheered the officers. 'A little place called St Omer. It's not far. Maybe a hundred kilometres.'

'St Omer? Murdoch cried.

'Sure, you must know it. Hell, you were stationed just outside it, back in 1915. We used to nip in there for a quick drink. Remember?'

'I remember,' Murdoch said. 'What are we going all the way over there for?'

'What do you think? I'm told it has the best little place in all France. Cleaned up by the British three years ago. You must've heard about it.'

'I've heard about it,' Murdoch said.

'Well, now it caters for officers only. I've been trying to get there for three years. But first, a drink. Say, Johnnie, old fellow, there's some bottles of champagne left in that crate beside you. Break one out.'

Proud obliged, and they drank from the neck. The champagne was warm, but the more bubbly for that. Murdoch's head started to spin, but it was more than the champagne. He was thirty-seven years old, and he was being taken to a brothel for the first time in his life – by his own brother-in-law. The surprising thing was that he wanted to go. It was more than a year's separation from Lee. It was a residue of the simmering emotional upheaval that had been Chand Bibi, and all that she had stood for, deep down in a man's gut.

And he wanted to celebrate. He wanted to let his hair down for almost the first time in his life. As Lee had once told him, he was too much the soldier. But then, his very first colonel had told him that, within a few days of his joining the regiment. He had always been too much the soldier.

Besides, he wanted to see Madame Leboeuf again.

Madame apparently wanted to see him again. She had been engaged in conversation with a major, but she turned away from him immediately the three newcomers entered her crowded salon. 'Monsieur le Colonel!' she cried. 'Oo-la-la,' as she observed the crossed sword and baton. 'Monsieur le général.' She draped her arms around his neck and herself up and down his chest. 'You 'ave been so long, coming to see poor Aimee,' she complained.

Murdoch was astonished as he looked around him, over her head. The dowdy, odorous room had been transformed, with new drapes and cushion covers, new carpets, freshly papered walls, a new chandelier; Madame Leboeuf herself was wearing a splendid gown, slashed in a deep décolletage to expose her small but very attractive breasts, while her auburn hair smelt of expensive perfume; the half dozen young women also in the room were hardly less well dressed; and the place was packed with officers.

'You know the dame!' Harry cried in exasperation.

'We have met, in the line of duty.' Murdoch dutifully kissed Madame, and she reluctantly slid down his chest. 'You have done very well for yourself, Aimee.'

'All because of you, Général. When it became known that I was the only safe house north-west of Paris, why, I had to turn away custom. So, I decided to bar enlisted men, and my business has grown.'

'Poor enlisted men,' Murdoch commented.

'It is all thanks to you. Now for you, it is I, and . . . ' she kissed him again. 'It is on the 'ouse, eh?'

'Oh, I couldn't accept that.'

'On the 'ouse,' she insisted. And lowered her voice. 'I, me, am very expensive, Général. You come with me.' She held his hand.

'Well, I'll be God damned,' Harry remarked.

'The Brigadier has hidden talents,' Proud commented.

'Fifi, Brigitte, look after these gentlemen,' Madame Leboeuf commanded.

'Here, I say, sir,' protested the major on whom she had been lavishing attention when Murdoch and his friends had entered.

'Be patient, Major,' Aimee told him. 'Your turn will come. The Général is my oldest friend.'

142

As old friends go, she was the best. But he found himself thinking of Chand Bibi.

To the family's great disappointment – and his own – Murdoch did not get home for Christmas. The Light Brigade was one of those assigned to overseeing the German surrender, and then to occupying a bridgehead across the Rhine.

'Germany,' Proud remarked, as they walked their horses through the streets of Coblenz. 'To think we have been fighting for four years to get here.'

'We're here,' Murdoch told him. 'That's all that matters.' He wondered how Paul von Reger was feeling now. But more important, he wondered if that other Paul von Reger had survived. He felt that he was entitled to find out, and wrote to Colonel and Frau Paul von Reger, at the address in Prussia he had been given by Margriet. To his surprise, he received a fairly rapid reply – from Margriet:

My dear Murdoch,
What a treat it is to hear from you in these sad times. Not for you. Times have never been sad for you, have they? You are the epitome of British dominance. Here, alas, things are not good any more. Would you believe I have had to queue for bread? I? Things have improved slightly these past couple of weeks, as regards food, but now we are surrounded by red revolutionaries. Only two days ago Paul had to use his revolver and shoot two men who just walked into our house and claimed it was their own, because all property belonged to all men. I was so afraid!

The Paul I refer to is your son. From which you will gather that he is alive and well and restored to his grateful mother. He fought long and well, and wears the Iron Cross. But he was wounded, slightly, at the Battle of Amiens, and sent home to recuperate. He had not yet rejoined his regiment when the Armistice was signed, and I have prevailed upon him to remain here with me, for our mutual protection. I am speaking of the girls and myself, of course. Are you not proud of him?

Of my husband, I have only occasional news. He is in Berlin, I believe, which is not so very far, but has not the time to spare for his family. It is all politics. Who will rule Germany now that the Kaiser has so cravenly fled our country? I wish we were back in South Africa. I wish we had never left.

143

I wish so many things.

But as I am here, and you also are in Germany, Murdoch, I would be so happy to see you. So would young Paul, even if he does not know you are his father. He will, one day, when I can tell him without enraging his legal father. To have you here, for a single night, would make me happy, at least for that night.

Write to me.

Your loving Margriet

Murdoch laid down the letter, and gazed at the wall. She had not changed. He did not suppose she ever would. So beautiful, so proud, so unhappy in her marriage and, he thought, in herself. But he could no longer accept the responsibility of making her happy.

And Paul. A war hero! He had been at Amiens, watching the tanks rolling towards him. Perhaps even watching the cavalry swinging their sabres without knowing that his father was amongst them. Had Paul been one of those who had turned and run? Not Paul Mackinder – even if his name was von Reger.

He wrote back to say that now peace was restored he would certainly visit them when he could – with his wife. And showed Lee the letter when, as he could not go home, she came over to Germany early in the new year. When they had confessed their past experiences on their honeymoon, they had each had only one to confess. And none since? It had never occurred to him to worry about Lee, left alone at Broad Acres so much of the time; he knew she loved him, and that was enough. As she knew of him.

'Oh, Murdoch,' she said. 'I feel so sorry for her. But so proud of young Paul. I really would like to meet him.'

'You shall,' he promised. 'But I think, for everyone's sake, it should be when things really have returned to normal, Reger is back with his family, and some of the bitterness has gone. At least we know he is alive, and not actually starving, and healthy.'

Because millions weren't. There were cases of men and women starving to death in Vienna at the Christmas of 1918, and by then the whole world, it seemed, was in the grip of an outbreak of a new strain of influenza, which killed

144

almost as many people as the war itself had done. Murdoch worried about Lee, and the children, who were all now at school, but her letters were constantly reassuring.

And at last it was time to go home. The Light Brigade was relieved, and sailed for England in the early summer of 1919. It had already been drastically reduced, as conscripts and wartime volunteers had been demobilized as quickly as possible. Each regiment was down to two squadrons of a hundred and fifty men when they left Germany, approximately half the men Murdoch had commanded into the battle of Amiens, and many of these were also due for an early release. John Proud had already left, and Murdoch's adjutant was a captain named Lawrie; he had been a lieutenant when Murdoch had taken command of the brigade, in the Lancers, so at least they knew each other.

There were the usual homecoming parades, the invariable medals. Murdoch's already multi-coloured left breast was enhanced by the even more eye-dazzling colours of the Mons Star, the British Victory Medal, 1914–1918, and the French and Belgian Croix de Guerre – difficult to tell apart.

But going home was the important factor. It was like stepping into a dream world. Given extended leave for the first time since 1913, Murdoch for a few days felt quite disoriented. Even in Germany, with the war over, there had been so much civil strife and so much the atmosphere of a vast military camp, at least in the Rhineland, that it was possible to feel the war had just dwindled, not ended. England had not actually known the war, save for the few zeppelin raids. There had been, and were, privations enough, but few to be encountered down in Somerset. Broad Acres was as he remembered it, peacefully serene, a place of refuge when strong winds flowed across the Somerset moors, a place of sheer joy when the sun shone and the winds were light.

Ian was now ten years old, and Fergus nine. They were attending the prep school Murdoch had been to, which meant they were already boarding, but they were home for the long summer vacation. They wanted to do nothing but play with their lead soldiers, and refight the battles of the war, and they wanted their father to tell them how and why each had been fought. He spent hours lying on his stomach in the playroom, while his mind drifted back to that sand table in Surrey in 1914, and those other lead soldiers. How long ago it seemed. But it was good to know that Swinton had at last received the recognition due to him as the inventor of the tank, and long overdue promotion.

Helen, who was seven, and attending a school in Bath itself, was no less interested in the warlike activities of her brothers, but was seldom allowed to join in. Harry, who was just four, was also permitted only as a spectator.

For Murdoch, to be in the midst of his family was an utter delight. When the weather was fine they played cricket or croquet, and he taught the boys the rudiments of tennis. As he had promised back in 1914, he sold the Rolls and bought a new car, a Daimler drophead. Lee had kept up her driving, and now he took it up as well.

'I'd never thought to see you behind the wheel of a car rather than on a horse,' Philippa remarked.

'Ah, well, according to the powers that be, I may have to find myself behind the wheel of a tank before too much longer,' Murdoch told her.

But no one knew for sure. No one knew anything. The huge army Great Britain had accumulated from all her empire as well as from her own people was being disbanded as quickly as possible, and there were all manner of rumours as to the form the new, post-war army was going to take . . . if any, should the pacifists have their way.

'Same thing's happening in the States,' Harry told him, coming over for a visit. 'Even more so. Seems everyone wants to forget about the war, and about Europe, just as quickly as they can. You know the Republicans are running on a ticket of repudiating the League of Nations?'

'But Wilson will win, surely.'

'Don't quote me, but I wouldn't put money on it, Murdoch. For one thing, he isn't actually campaigning for himself. That might carry some weight, but he can't stand for a third term. And then there's this big feeling that we sorted out your problems for you and now you should be left to get on with it.'

'Sorted out our problems? That's pitching it a bit strong.'

'Sure it is. But to the uninformed masses of Americans – or at least, the trouble is, they *are* informed, by political newspapers – you and the French fought and fought and fought for three years with no result save one hell of a big casualty list. The doughboys arrive, and bingo, the war is won.'

'I suppose there is something in that. It would be rather a catastrophe, though, if you didn't join the League. I mean, it was your idea. Collective security to prevent another war. Collective has to mean everybody. Or at least, everybody who matters.'

'Sure. I agree with you. But most Americans are determined there isn't going to be another war anyway – leastways, not one involving them.' He grinned. 'In another couple of years you wouldn't want us in the League: we won't have an army worth a damn. And when you think that you have to cross the Atlantic to get a decent drink . . . I reckon I'm gonna give up being a foreign correspondent and settle in St Omer and write a novel.'

But whatever the Americans were doing, there would always have to be a British army, that was certain, as long as there was a British empire. The end of the war did not mean any end to the commitments which British soldiers had been undertaking for more than a century. Within the next two years there was confrontation with the resurgent Turkish nationalists across the Bosphorus, and as usual, trouble in the north-west of India, where General Dyer, a fine commander of men, got himself into trouble by opening fire on a Sikh crowd in Amritsar and was cashiered, and even a campaign against the Mahsuds. Murdoch studied the newspapers, and came across the name of Shere Khan often enough. The English treated the 'old devil' with a certain amount of amused respect. But these were newspaper correspondents, who did not know enough about the actual conditions in the valley of the Kurram – or were afraid of reporting them lest they shock even their war-inured readers – and there was no mention of Shere Khan's daughters.

Glad as he was to be home, Murdoch found himself chafing at the relativity light duties of commander of a brigade which was steadily being run down. He was also not terribly amused by the newfangled ideas which were creeping into the army. The one which most affected him, and most annoyed him, was the decision to do away with the rank of brigadier-general. Instead he, and every other brigade commander, became a colonel-commandant. This made a little sense as the brigade idea itself was being phased out in favour of smaller units – mainly for reasons of economy – but the title smacked too much of continental usage.

'I might as well be a bloody German,' he growled to Lee. 'Colonel-Commandant Mackinder, by God! Father must be turning in his grave.'

At least he was still in the army, and prospering as much as anyone. The fall-out amongst his contemporaries and superiors was alarming. Field Marshal Sir John French found himself Lord Lieutenant of Ireland, at a time when the Irish troubles were just raising their head again. Among the casualties claimed by the IRA gunmen was Field Marshal Sir Henry Wilson, who retired as Chief of the Imperial General Staff in 1922, returned to his home in Ireland, and was promptly murdered.

Field Marshal Sir William Robertson became Commander-in-Chief of the British Army of the Rhine, and as such was Murdoch's commanding officer, briefly, in 1919. Field Marshal Sir Edward Allenby, as a result of his triumphs in Palestine and Syria, became a Viscount, Allenby of Megiddo and Felixstowe – but found himself condemned to remaining in the Middle East, as High Commissioner for Egypt.

Sir Henry Rawlinson went to India as Commander-in-Chief. General Sir Horace Smith-Dorien, Murdoch's old commander at the battle of Le Cateau, became Governor of Gibraltar. General Plumer also became a viscount, and was made Governor of Malta. General Byng became Governor-General of Canada. General Gough was retired. General Sir William Marshall, who had succeeded Maude in Mesopotamian command, also found himself in India, commanding the south.

Field Marshal Sir Douglas Haig became Earl Haig, and Commander-in-Chief of the Home Forces in Great Britain. Murdoch wondered what he thought of a situation where all his wartime commanders had been scattered to the corners of the earth.

For Murdoch, the greatest day of 1920 was the return of the Royal Western Dragoon Guards. They had had the thankless task of remaining in Mesopotamia to protect British interests there while the peace was being sorted out.

Murdoch went down to Plymouth to greet them, shook hands with Billy Prendergast, who had after all been confirmed in command. But Billy looked even less confident than when last they had seen each other.

'God,' he said, 'am I glad to be home. We have had one hell of a time.'

Looking over the disembarking men, Murdoch could believe it. They were haggard and worn, and a large number were clearly unwell.

'We had a lot of cholera,' Peter Ramage explained. 'And some fever. It's still about.'

He himself looked as fit as ever. 'Congratulations,' Murdoch said, looking at the crown on his shoulder strap. 'Major Ramage.'

Peter grinned. 'Everything comes to he who waits, they say.'

Murdoch shook hands with Lowndes, looked for Hunter.

'He's buried outside Baghdad,' Ramage told him. 'Cholera.'

The men had lost comrades too. But Yeald was there, saluting as smartly as ever. 'General Mackinder, sir! It's good to be home.'

'It's good to see you, Sergeant-Major.' Yeald was

149

obviously determined to ignore the change of rank; once a general, always a general.

He spotted Destry, and Bryan, but not Collier, who had also died of cholera. And then Ralph Manly-Smith. 'Captain Manly-Smith,' he said. 'Congratulations.'

'I took over Hunter's squadron,' Manly-Smith explained. 'It's good to see you again, sir.' He had never forgotten that his would have been a short war had Murdoch not carried him back from the gas-filled trench.

'What are your plans?' Murdoch asked. He knew Manly-Smith was a product of Sandhurst, like himself, but after six years he might have had enough of the army.

'Oh, I hope to make a career of it, sir. Will I be allowed to do that?'

'I hope so, Ralph,' Murdoch said.

The Westerns returned to their old headquarters outside Bath, marching proudly through the streets of the city behind their colours, which had been kept in storage throughout the war, with the regimental band blaring forth. Sir John French was unable to attend because of ill health, and so Murdoch himself took the salute. He was delighted to have them once again under his wing, for he had been confirmed as Colonel-Commandant of the Light Cavalry, and all four regiments were stationed down in the west country, where they could exercise their peculiar talents on the moors and take part in general manoeuvres on Salisbury Plain with the rest of the army.

When there were general manoeuvres. Anti-militarism and economy were in the air. The Royal Air Force was nearly phased out of existence. In 1922 the Royal Navy accepted terms at the Washington Conference which limited them to thirty-five-thousand-ton battleships and only a specific number of ships as well; the great days when Britain operated the two-power standard, which meant that the Royal Navy was always to be as strong as any other two fleets added together, were gone for ever. For the army there was no new recruitment and precious little new equipment. Even the development of the tank seemed to have been put into a permanent hold position.

'Money, or lack of it,' Sir John said, when Murdoch visited him. The old gentleman was now seventy, and very much the senior soldier in the army. 'And a naive belief that a European war can never happen again. But it will, Murdoch.'

Murdoch grinned. 'Not before I retire as well, Sir John. Last birthday I was forty. I reckon I've seen my career out.'

'Don't believe it,' French said. 'When I was forty the Boer War was still seven years in the future. We hadn't even retaken the Sudan. And if anyone had told me then that twenty-two years later I would command the greatest army Britain has ever put into the field, against the Germans, of all people, I'd have laughed in his face.' He brooded for a few moments. 'Wish I'd made a better job of it.'

'You made as good a job of it as anyone else,' Murdoch insisted. And he meant it. Haig had done nothing French hadn't. If French had been accused of too much caution in 1914 and 1915, Haig could have been accused of far too blatant a waste of life in the following years. He had won because the nation had become geared to total war – which it had not been in 1914 – and because it had been led by a man, Lloyd George, dedicated to total war – which Asquith certainly had not been – and because of the development of things like the tank and the aeroplane . . . things his successor in the next war might well have to do without, if the craze for economy continued.

Winston Churchill, who was now Secretary of State for the Colonies, agreed with him. 'But money has to come first, Murdoch,' he said, when they lunched together at the Cafe Royal. 'Financial stability is the essential for military strength. We have got to get the load of debt we have incurred fighting the war off our backs, get back on the gold standard, let the world see that Britain is again great, again the absolute rock of security she has been for the past hundred and fifty years – then we can start thinking about the next war. Oh, French is quite right. There will be another. I would be a brave man were I to name with whom. It would be Germany, of course, were they ever able to re-

151

arm; they hate our guts for 1914–18. But as they can't re-arm . . . I brood more on Soviet Russia.'

Murdoch frowned. 'Aren't they in the middle of a huge civil war?'

'It's just about over. Again, indecision and lack of funds on our part. We haven't supported the Whites as we should have, and there's no doubt now that Trotsky and Lenin and that whole murderous crew are going to come out on top. Men who can execute their royal family are capable of anything.'

'We executed our king, once,' Murdoch could not help putting in. 'And Cromwell did wonders for the army.'

'Cromwell executed a king,' Churchill corrected him. 'He left the queen and her children alone.'

'Perhaps because he couldn't get hold of them.'

'I hardly believe he would have had them murdered in cold blood. No, no, Murdoch. Watch Russia. You may have to lead your men in a charge across the steppes yet.'

Murdoch did not believe him. If Great Britain was all but bankrupt, the rest of the world, saving only the United States – which was the world's creditor – was in an even worse state. And Russia was in the worst state of all, if only a tenth of the tales coming out of that distraught land were to be believed. There were reports of ten million deaths in the civil war, most of them from starvation, and the concept that the bear could ever threaten the lion again in his lifetime was absurd.

He visited his eldest sister, Rosemary Phillips, when he was in London; they had not seen each other for nine years, since the last pre-war party at Broad Acres.

'It is all a mess, isn't it?' she agreed. 'Geoffrey's getting out.'

'Seriously?' His brother-in-law, several years his elder, had come out of the war a colonel in the Guards.

'Well, what's there to stay in for? He didn't quite make brigadier. No, I think he's right. He's coming out and is going into politics.'

Murdoch grinned. 'As a Tory, I presume.'

'Well, of course. It's time we got rid of these mealy-mouthed Liberals once and for all. You know, it might be an idea for you, Murdoch.'

'Not for me,' he said. 'I'm a soldier. My ambition is to die with my boots on, even in bed.'

He concentrated on training the light cavalry in all the concepts he had built up during twenty-odd years of soldiering, in speed of manoeuvre and use of weapons. He did not know if cavalry would ever be used on a battlefield again, but they would have to be if there were no tanks available.

He also enjoyed becoming the father figure of the young men who followed him, and who clearly worshipped the ground on which he walked. Billy Prendergast retired from the army in 1923. He had found, as Murdoch suspected, the wholesale slaughter of the war, the idea that one wrong decision could cost hundreds, perhaps thousands of lives, too much to bear. He came up to Broad Acres on a Sunday afternoon to say goodbye; one of the great joys of being stationed in the west country as a senior officer was that Murdoch could, for the first time in his life, get home almost every night, and certainly spend every weekend with his family.

'I suppose you feel I'm letting the regiment down,' Billy said. 'But the fact is, I'm thirty-seven, and I doubt I will ever get another promotion, and there's this good job being offered . . .'

'I'm sure you're doing the right thing, Billy,' Murdoch said. 'Promotion has got to be slow in peacetime, with not a lot happening.'

'Of course, if there was a chance of us being sent overseas, India . . .' Prendergast peered at him, seeking any knowledge the Colonel-Commandant might have which had not yet been passed on.

'I'm afraid there isn't, so far as I know,' Murdoch told him. 'Things seem to have settled down over there. The Russians are too caught up in their own problems to be troubling Afghanistan, and this fellow Gandhi seems to be going in for peaceful protests. Even if his followers occasionally get out of hand, there seems to be nothing the police can't handle.' He didn't even know if Shere Khan was alive or dead.

'Yes,' Prendergast brooded, as unsure as ever. 'And Peter will make a good CO.'

'I'm sure he will,' Murdoch agreed. Peter Ramage would have been his choice for colonel of the regiment from the beginning.

'Shame he never married,' Lee observed when Prendergast left.

'Makes a man, does it?'

'Teaches him decision. I mean, surely, getting married at all is a decision.'

'Often taken by the female,' Murdoch pointed out, and ducked the pillow which came his way.

Peter Ramage *was* married, to a dark-haired debutante named Linda whom he had met at a ball in Bath immediately after returning from Mesopotamia. The wedding had been a great affair, and Murdoch had had the pleasure of making the toast to the bride and groom. Linda Ramage was some fifteen years younger than Lee, but the two women got on very well.

Murdoch duly recommended Peter for the necessary promotion, and it was confirmed by the War Office.

'Do you know,' Peter confessed, 'I have waited for this for sixteen years, ever since I came down from Sandhurst. God Almighty, how long ago that seems. Do you remember it, Murdoch?'

'Yes. We were about to leave for Somaliland.'

'With Knox. Poor Knox.' He gave a guilty gulp. Murdoch had killed Tommy Knox himself, to save him from being further tortured by the Somali women. 'And now . . . I feel very humble. And very unsure of myself.'

'You'll grow into it,' Murdoch assured him.

'Do you really think so? When I think of the decisions you have had to make . . .'

He was again thinking of the Knox incident, Murdoch knew; Knox had been Ramage's best friend. 'Making decisions can become a habit,' he said. 'It's one worth

154

cultivating. While you pray they are always the right ones. Incidentally, they aren't always the right ones, Peter.'

He had no doubt that Peter was going to make an excellent colonel. Nor did he have any doubt that the next colonel of the regiment was already to hand. Ralph Manly-Smith was proving a splendid soldier. He had come out of the war with a Military Cross, and tremendous energy and determination.

Energetic men as a rule have an excess of energetic hormones, however, and Murdoch was a little taken aback when Ralph came up to see him one day in his office. 'Permission for a private chat, sir.'

'Of course. Sit down.' Murdoch waited.

Ralph hesitated for some seconds, then he said, 'I would like to get married, sir.'

'Good heavens! Anyone I know?'

'Ah, well . . . I don't think so, sir.' The young man was clearly embarrassed.

Murdoch frowned at him. He had at least a nodding acquaintance with most of the girls who were trotted out for regimental dances. 'Then perhaps you'll tell me her name.'

Ralph licked his lips. 'Her name is . . . Jennifer, sir.'

'Jennifer. That's a nice name. Does she have a surname?'

'Ah . . . Yeald, sir.'

Murdoch stared at him. 'You'd better say that again.'

'She is RSM Yeald's daughter, sir.'

'I thought she might be. Does he know of your desire?'

'Not yet, sir.'

'Have you spoken to Colonel Ramage?'

'Not yet, sir.'

'But you have spoken to Miss Yeald, I take it.'

'Yes, sir.'

'And she, I imagine, is in favour of the idea.'

'Oh, yes, sir.'

'How old are you, Ralph?'

'Twenty-five, sir.'

'Well, then, it's a matter for Colonel Ramage. As you're not yet thirty you cannot get married without his permission.'

'I know that, sir. It's just that I thought, if you were to put in a word . . .'

'Why should I do that, Ralph?'

'Well, sir . . . I love Jennie. I really do. I . . .'

'You are being a God damned young fool,' Murdoch told him in measured tones.

'Sir . . .'

'I know this is the age of democracy. But there is still your career to be considered. You are a highly thought of young officer. I can tell you that you have a brilliant career ahead of you, even in peacetime. Colonel of the regiment, certainly. Very probably field rank afterwards. If nothing untoward occurs. Retirement from field rank can mean a colonial governorship, or even more. But none of those things are likely to happen if you marry the daughter of your own sergeant-major. I'm not being a snob, believe me. I'm presenting the facts of life as they are. You will wind up being retired at thirty-five as a major, with not a lot to look forward to.'

'I accept that, sir.'

'But you're determined to go ahead with it.'

'Yes, sir.'

'She must be a most lovely young woman,' Murdoch remarked, thinking of Yeald's somewhat craggy features. 'How old is she?'

'Eighteen, sir. And she is, a most lovely young woman. But that's not the reason.'

Murdoch frowned at him. 'For God's sake, you're not going to tell me she's pregnant?'

'She is, sir.'

'Holy Jesus Christ! How? I mean,' he added hastily, 'how did you get to know her so well?'

'We met at a non-commissioned officers party, sir. The officers were invited, as usual, and I went along. Well, sir, you always insisted that we shared our men's activities.'

'Yes,' Murdoch said grimly. 'Not their daughters.'

'Well, sir . . . Jennie was there. She really is a most lovely girl, sir. And we got talking, and found that we had quite a lot in common, and . . . well, we sort of agreed to meet again.'

'And you did meet again. A lot in common. What are you, Harrow and Sandhurst?'

'No, sir. Winchester and Sandhurst.'

'And what is she, Bath Grammar?'

'No, sir. Jennie did not attend the grammar school.'

'You are not improving the situation. What does your father do?'

'He is chairman of a company in the city, sir.'

'Does he know any sergeant-majors? Do any of them belong to his club?'

'Well, no, sir.'

'So what is he going to say when he finds out? I don't suppose you've told him yet, either.'

'No, sir, I haven't. He will flip his lid.'

'Quite.'

'But I must do it, sir. I want to do it. And I will do it,' Manly-Smith said. 'Even if I have to quit the army, now.'

'I suppose it's quite a compliment, that he should have come to me before anyone else,' Murdoch said, sitting up in bed with an unread book on his lap.

'Of course,' Lee agreed. 'Everyone who has ever served with you worships the ground you walk on.'

'I hadn't ever expected to play nursemaid to any of them. What the hell am I to do? I mean, how can anyone have been so God damned foolish?'

'I would say he was more unlucky than foolish. Anyway, I seem to remember hearing once about a young lieutenant who fell madly in love with a quite unsuitable young woman. As I recall, he was Wellington and Sandhurst – not quite Winchester, but not far off – and she was from the veldt and . . . did Margriet ever go to school at all?'

He glared at her. 'All right, so you have me across a barrel. I didn't marry her.'

'Wouldn't you have, if they hadn't sent you home pretty damn quick?'

He sighed, and subsided down the bed. 'Of course I would have.'

'Even before you knew she was pregnant.'

157

'Yes. But that doesn't alter the fact that I would have been a God damned fool, and would have ruined my career, to have done so. And I wouldn't have married you.'

'You count that as a good thing?' She smiled.

'I have just been God damned lucky all of my life. Now, how the hell are we going to stop Ralph Manly-Smith from being God damned unlucky?'

Lee closed her own book, and put it on the bedside table. 'Times have changed a little, since 1900.'

He frowned at her. 'You're not suggesting I back him?'

'I'm suggesting we meet Jennie Yeald.'

Ralph Manly-Smith brought Jennifer Yeald to tea at Broad Acres the following Sunday afternoon. He wore mufti, blazer and flannels, and she wore a dress obviously bought for the occasion, in yellow voile with a hemline rather lower than was becoming fashionable; her brown suede shoes were just visible. It was easy to see she had a very good figure. Her hat was a huge straw, which threw one side of her face into shade; this was a pity, because she was also an extremely attractive girl, with somewhat clipped features and very dark brown hair. This, as was the trend, had been cropped and only just covered her ears; it was straight, with a slight wave.

She was very nervous, which was understandable, but not as nervous as Ralph. Murdoch remembered how furious Lee had been at having to be 'vetted' by the colonel's wife when he had proposed marriage, and wondered if this girl was secretly angry underneath. But she was an army daughter, and would understand army ways.

Lee was superb, as ever, dispensed tea and carried the conversation on her own – she had asked Philippa not to appear, because Philippa was a rather awe-inspiring woman. As Murdoch was an awe-inspiring man; Jennifer kept staring at his medal ribbons and obviously relating them to tales told her by her father. Murdoch realized that she probably knew as much about his history as anybody, and had clearly never imagined she would ever sit down to tea with him.

Her accent had a pleasant but unmistakable burr, but she was clearly by no means either simple or totally uneducated; she expressed a desire to see *No, no, Nannette*, which was all the rage in London, stroked the dogs without fear, and admitted that she was fond of riding – astride.

'I think she's absolutely delicious,' Lee said, after they had left.

'So I'm to support the whole thing?'

'Well, the decision must be yours, of course . . .'

His turn to throw a cushion at her.

Colonel Ramage was as taken aback as Murdoch had been when the situation was put to him. So was RSM Yeald. But with the endorsement of the Colonel-Commandant they accepted the idea. The War Office was more querulous, but also accepted Murdoch's recommendation.

More difficult was John Manly-Smith, of Manly-Smith and Partners, who descended on Broad Acres in his Rolls-Royce. 'They tell me you're Ralph's CO,' he announced after the briefest of introductions.

'Not exactly. I'm his CO's CO.'

Manly-Smith glared at him, and Murdoch smiled back. Lee had made him promise to keep his temper.

'Well, you're responsible for what's happening, eh?'

'Now that depends on what you're talking about,' Murdoch said. 'Shall we sit down?'

'I am talking about my son's asinine wish to marry some corporal's daughter.'

Murdoch sat down and crossed his knees. 'Ever read any Kipling?'

'Now, don't give me any nonsense, Brigadier.'

Murdoch decided that, as he was dealing with an habitual bully, he was going to disobey Lee and lose his temper after all. 'I am not a brigadier, Manly-Smith. And as we happen to be in my house, I shall give you any damned nonsense I please. Now, either sit down and discuss this like a gentleman, or get out.'

Manly-Smith's head jerked, and his face flushed. But then perhaps he recalled that this was the man who had led three famous cavalry charges and was one of Britain's best-known soldiers. He sat down.

'George,' Murdoch told Reynolds, who had retired from the army to become his butler-cum-valet. 'Two whiskies. With water, Manly-Smith?'

'Ah, soda.'

'Soda, George.'

George placed a tray with the two glassees, and the soda siphon, between them. Murdoch drank his neat. Usually he took water, but this afternoon he intended to overawe the enemy. 'Have you met Jennifer?' he asked.

'Good Lord, no.'

'And you have no intention of doing so. That would be a mistake. She is an extremely attractive, quiet, well brought up young lady. She is the daughter of the regimental sergeant-major incidentally, not a corporal, and one of the best men it has ever been my privilege to know, much less fight alongside. But even if she were the daughter of a private, she is the woman your son loves, she is to be the mother of his child, your grandchild, Manly-Smith, and I have no doubt at all that she will make him an admirable wife.'

'My son . . .'

'Is one of the privileged few. He is, however, behaving like a gentleman.'

Manly-Smith stared at him. 'Are you trying to insult me, sir?'

'I am trying to bring you down from that impossibly high horse you seem to have mounted.'

They gazed at each other for several seconds, then Manly-Smith lowered his gaze. 'My wife will never accept it,' he muttered. 'She says she will never speak to Ralph again, if he goes through with it.'

'I'm sure she doesn't mean that.'

'You don't know my wife.' He raised his head. 'And what about the boy's career? Won't this kill it?'

'It won't help it, to be sure. But we'll do what we can. I think what you want to remember is that your son is no longer a boy, Mr Manly-Smith. He became a man some

160

time ago. And he is now acting like a man. I suggest, as you're down here, you meet Jennifer, and judge for youself.'

Manly-Smith shook his head. 'No. I couldn't do that. My wife would be furious.'

'Have you ever tried being furious with your wife?' Murdoch asked.

But the Manly-Smiths did not attend the wedding of their only son. It took place in the regimental chapel, and was a small affair. The Yealds and their relatives were there in force, but Ralph Manly-Smith had only one of his lieutenants, Bobby Franklin, as best man, and Lieutenant-Colonel Peter Ramage, Major John Lowndes, and Colonel-Commandant Murdoch Mackinder as guests. Peter and Murdoch were accompanied by their wives.

Once again Murdoch made a speech, toasting the happy couple. Afterwards Yeald took him aside. 'I didn't know what to do, sir,' he said. 'I know it's not right. But in all the circumstances . . .'

'In all the circumstances, it had to happen, Sergeant-Major,' Murdoch told him. 'And who's to say it won't be all right? They very obviously love each other.'

'But his career, sir. Does he still have one?'

'If I have anything to do with it, yes,' Murdoch told him.

Murdoch had anticipated being in official disfavour for some time after his intervention in the Manly-Smith affair, and he was indeed trying to come to terms with being one of the forgotten men of the British army when his forty-third birthday approached and he continued to spend his time training his light cavalrymen. The year 1923 was disturbing, too, as Europe came close to war again, with the French occupation of the Ruhr because Germany had not been fulfilling her reparations payments, and the decision of the German Government to deflate the Deutschmark. They started something they couldn't stop, and soon the most horrendous tales were coming out of that beleaguered land, of how an entire wheelbarrow load of marks wouldn't buy one loaf of bread.

161

With Lee's encouragement Murdoch wrote the Regers to find out how they were faring, and received another adoring letter from Margriet in which she reassured him that they, as landed gentry, were doing all right, although there was a great deal of distress among the middle, or rentier class, whose cash investments had disappeared as if burned. She reiterated her invitation for him, and Lee if need be, to come and stay with them.

The letter arrived just before Christmas, when Murdoch was attempting, like so many people, to reconcile himself to the fact that, Stanley Baldwin's Government having suffered disastrous losses in the General Election just completed, Britain was to be governed by the Labour Party for the first time in its history. As the leader of the Party, and thus the Prime Minister Elect, was Ramsay MacDonald, who had suffered imprisonment during the war for his pacifist views, the outlook for the armed services was distinctly gloomy.

'You'll have to retire after all, and be a country gentleman,' Lee told him.

But on the morning of 1 January 1924, all of that changed. Murdoch found himself a Knight Commander of St Michael and St George.

'I can't imagine why this hasn't happened before,' King George confided after the accolade. 'What on earth have you been doing these last four or five years?'

'Soldiering, sir.'

'But with precious little to show for it, eh? Well, Mackinder, you have something to show for it now.'

There were the usual press cameramen waiting in the palace yard. Murdoch had never felt such a fool in his life, with his white knee breeches and white silk stockings, and his long blue cape with its red lining, and he couldn't help but wonder what the boys, who were now thirteen and fourteen, and both at Wellington College, thought of it all. But the huge heavy collar and seven-pointed star overawed them. Only Helen, an eleven-year-old pigtail-and-braces pupil of Cheltenham Ladies' College, was inclined to giggle.

162

Lee was over the moon. 'I'm a lady,' she said. 'You know, I never expected to be one?'

'That worried me when we got married,' Murdoch confessed, and she bit his ear.

The next morning, after all six of them had been to see Douglas Fairbanks in *Robin Hood*, Murdoch had an appointment with the Earl of Cavan, who had succeeded Sir Henry Wilson as CIGS. He had met Cavan in South Africa, but their paths had taken different directions since then; the Earl had begun the war as commander of the Guards Brigade, and had finished it commanding a British army bolstering the Italians in the valley of the Po.

He was an alert man who wore the moustache still fashionable amongst British officers – a sartorial habit Murdoch had never adopted.

'Sir Murdoch,' he said with a smile. 'Sit down. We should have had this meeting long ago.'

Murdoch waited.

'As of today,' Cavan went on, 'you are gazetted Major-General.'

Murdoch opened his mouth and then closed it again; there was really nothing to say.

'That too should have happened long ago,' Cavan observed. 'But you see, you refused promotion in 1915, to stay with your regiment. I'm not blaming you. I wish more of us had that attachment to our people. But the fact is that once passed over, other fellows got in ahead of you. Still, you remain our most famous fighting soldier, and I'm delighted that you are at last on the ladder of top command.'

'Thank you, sir,' Murdoch murmured.

'It follows, therefore, that you should be where there's fighting to be done. So you're posted to India.'

'India?'

'A famous hunting ground for the Mackinders.'

'Yes, sir,' Murdoch said absently.

'There isn't any actual fighting going on there right this minute, of course, since the Mahsuds have been pacified, but we are hearing disturbing rumours that the Russians, now that they have themselves organized to a certain extent,

163

are again sending missions to Kabul, and that sort of thing. Well, as you know, our historic mission in India has been to keep the Russians out of Afghanistan, and frankly, it can do no harm to let them know that we still intend to carry out that mission. You will be stationed in Peshawar, and you will have approximately a division under your command. Mainly Indian troops, of course, but we thought that you could do with a regiment of British cavalry . . . so the Royal Westerns are also being sent out.'

'Now that is good news,' Murdoch said without thinking.

'You mean the rest isn't?'

'By no means, sir. But if I had any regrets, apart from leaving my family, of course, it would be leaving the Westerns.'

'My dear fellow, this is 1924. We are living in a civilized world. Or we like to pretend that we are. You may take your family with you. Such of them as you wish.'

'India!' Lee shouted. 'Yippee! I've always wanted to go to India. And to be on service with you. Oh, Murdoch, it just gets better and better. I can hardly believe it.'

'Well, it's true,' he told her. He was still trying to get his thoughts straight. Going to India, the North West Frontier, involved so many things.

'And with you a major-general,' she said. 'Oh, it's all too wonderful for words. I'll start packing.'

'Hold on. We don't leave for a couple of months. We have some long leave coming first. To say goodbye to England. Maybe for a few years. What would you most like to do?'

She was suddenly serious. 'Go to Germany.'

'Germany? Whatever for?'

'I'd like to visit the Regers. See Margriet. And see Paul. Both Pauls. Heck, they keep asking us, don't they?'

7

Germany, 1924

Murdoch was amazed. 'Are you serious?' he asked.

'Why not?' Lee demanded. 'You're not still carrying a torch for her, are you?'

'Good Lord, no. But . . .'

'I'd like to meet her. I'd like to meet young Paul. Come to think of it, I'd like to meet old Paul as well.'

'There are several other children, I believe,' Murdoch said. 'Or there were.'

'Well, great, I want to meet them too.'

'I'll write,' he promised.

He found himself looking forward to the visit as well. Equally he was looking forward to seeing some more of Germany than just the Rhineland; as Lee had said, having fought against the Germans for four years it was senseless not to try to understand them.

And presumably Reger would have got over the shock of having lost the war by now.

But Murdoch had a great deal more on his mind than Margriet. He was going to India. He was going to the North West Frontier, specifically. Everything was peaceful up there, and he was not being sent to start a war. Besides, now there was most definitely not a single man in his command who had ever served there. But it had been the comrades of these men, even if unknown to them, who had been murdered by the Pathan women. By Chand Bibi. Would he be able to see her again and not want to throttle her? Or rape her?

Of course, he was hardly likely to encounter her at all. After writing that confession of guilt – and of intent – she would hardly take the risk. He wished he could believe that.

And found himself wondering if he was afraid of her.

Preparations for their departure for India went ahead with preparations for their visit to Germany. Murdoch took the opportunity to take care of Ralph Manly-Smith, by asking for him as his ADC; Lawrie was anxious to get back to regular soldiering. Ralph was delighted, and Jennifer also seemed pleased at the idea of seeing something of the world.

As Lee had never been allowed to accompany Murdoch on an overseas posting before, Broad Acres had been under her care since Florence Mackinder had made the house over to her son, immediately following his marriage, in order to avoid death duties. Florence was now sixty-nine, and although in good health, disinclined to resume the day-to-day running of the establishment. Philippa, however, was more than happy to do so.

She would also look after the children during the school holidays, and see Harry settled at Wellington when the time came, in two years. The boys were taken aback at the prospect of a three- or possibly six-year separation from both of their parents.

'In three years,' Ian said, 'I'll be at Sandhurst.'

'If you pass all your exams,' Lee pointed out. 'And we'll be home in three years, at least on long leave. Now you be sure to write every month . . . all of you,' she said, looking over the other three anxious faces.

'Can't we come out to see you in India?' Helen asked.

'The North West Frontier,' Fergus said. 'That would be wizard.'

Lee looked at Murdoch.

'I'm afraid that won't be practical,' he said. 'Sorry, chaps. You'll just have to do without us for three years. But as your mother says, write regularly. And so will we.'

'I feel such a wretch,' Lee confided as the train took them from London to Harwich, where they would catch the boat for the continent; Margriet had replied in rhapsodies at the idea of their visit, and had expressly added that Count von Reger was looking forward to it, too. 'About leaving them at all. But especially about running off like this, all on our own.'

'I think we're entitled to a little private holiday. We haven't had one since our honeymoon, save for your visit to Germany in 1919 – and I was on duty then.'

'That's why I feel a wretch. I'm so happy. Oh, Murdoch my love . . .' She gazed at his grey Savile Row suit. 'I hardly recognize you in mufti. And India . . . if you knew how excited I am about it . . .'

'You do realize that the North West Frontier can be a dangerous place,' Murdoch pointed out.

'I know. I want to experience a little danger. With you. Because you always win, don't you, Murdoch?'

'Not always,' he said, thinking of Chand Bibi. The concept of Chand Bibi and Lee ever coming face to face was incredible.

'Don't you like your wife to hero-worship you?'

'I love my wife to hero-worship me, my dearest girl. But I have no intention of letting you expose yourself to any danger. The first sign of trouble, and it's you for home.'

'Oh, Murdoch . . .'

'You'll want to see the kids, anyway,' he told her.

They second-honeymooned across the North Sea to the Hook of Holland – the sea was calm although it was February – where they caught the train that would take them to Berlin. Now some of Lee's excitement was beginning to get to Murdoch as well. And some understanding of his achievement. That was taking a long time to sink in. He was a major-general, and a KCMG. Great-grandfather Ian, the hero of the charge against the Baluchis, had wound up as a major-general and a KCMG. So, he had at last equalled the family's most famous member. Only *he* was now the family's most famous member. He was the only one with the VC. It was a thought to make a man light-headed.

And as a major-general, he would have full command of a large body of troops for the first time. He almost hoped the Soviets would encourage the Afghans to start something. But there would be no more leading charges, he thought with a smile; he'd be sitting behind the cavalry giving the command to charge, from safety. Well, perhaps three times in a life were enough – he'd been damned lucky to get away with all of them.

The train took them past the growing port of Rotterdam, and thence across the flat Dutch plain, through a country of canals and windmills and apple-cheeked, smiling people – unaffected by the war. From Rotterdam they swung north through Gouda and then east for Utrecht, north-east for Amersfoort and Apeldoorn, thence Deventer, Almelo and Henglo before reaching the German border at De Poppe.

By now it was late evening, and they had just completed a very good dinner in the dining car; they were glad to get out of their first-class sleeper and stretch their legs on the platform while the various customs officers pored over their passports. They then went to bed, and so slept through the Ruhr – about which Murdoch was rather pleased, as that troubled industrial district was still in a state of some turmoil. He awoke at two in the morning when the express stopped in Hanover, but dozed off again and slept soundly until the steward knocked on the compartment door at five thirty.

'Charlottenberg in half an hour, sir,' he said in perfect English.

Lee was also awake, and they washed and dressed, and raised the blind to watch the suburbs of Berlin rising out of the winter darkness. 'Did you ever really believe you would one day lead your regiment down the Unter den Linden?' she asked.

'Do you know, I think we all did, back in 1914. The illusion didn't last long.'

The train pulled into Charlottenberg Station precisely at six o'clock, and they were on the platform by six fifteen, where a uniformed chauffeur was awaiting them. 'General and Lady Mackinder?' His English was also flawless.

'You must have gotten up at an unearthly hour to meet this train,' Lee remarked.

'It is not so far, milady,' he said, and opened the doors of the huge Mercedes touring car for them.

Rugs were provided for their feet, and they drove over good roads which were clear, although there was snow to either side, and the ponds they passed were covered in thin ice. They travelled south for just on an hour, then turned off to enter a village. Here there was the occasional icy patch on the road itself, and the chauffeur had to drive carefully. But he knew his stuff, and a few minutes later they left the houses behind and were in a driveway leading up to a very solid-looking four-storeyed mansion.

'Oh, my,' Lee said. 'I had expected a Schloss.'

'Count von Reger did own a castle, milady. But it is now in Poland.'

'Oh,' Lee said, and looked at Murdoch.

'Just as well we found out now,' he agreed. 'I think we have to feel our way here.'

'You can say that again,' she said.

The car pulled to a halt before the portico of the house, and was surrounded by barking Alsatian hounds. These were gathered up by the gamekeeper, complete with gaiters and a feathered cap, which pleased Lee. Then they stepped down to face the open doors, and the people who stood there.

There seemed an awful lot of them, and Lee hesitated, until Murdoch came round the car and held her elbow to escort her forward.

'Murdoch! Major-General Mackinder!' Paul von Reger descended the shallow steps to greet them, and apart from the warmth of his address, was also smiling, much to Murdoch's relief. 'And Lady Mackinder! If you knew how long I have awaited this pleasure. May I call you Lee?'

'I'd be hurt if you didn't, Count.'

'And you shall call me Paul,' Reger said. Like Murdoch, he wore civilian clothes. But he had cropped his hair again, and put on some of the weight he had lost in the prison hospital. He looked well, and prosperous – but he was acting. He had to be.

'Margriet,' Reger was saying. 'Our guests.'

Margriet von Reger had waited dutifully until her husband summoned her. Now she too came down the steps.

169

Unlike Lee, who was wearing a mink coat over her travelling suit, Margriet was somewhat simply dressed in a skirt and blouse. She still wore her deep yellow hair long, although it was piled on the back of her head in a chignon. This had the effect of increasing her already considerable height, which was clearly a surprise to Lee – Margriet was very nearly as tall as Murdoch, and in her heels stood a good couple of inches above her husband.

Lee had also not been prepared for her face and figure. The slender girl with whom Murdoch had fallen in love had blossomed into a matron of forty-one, but was still tall and straight, if wide hipped and large breasted. And the face had changed very little. It was still long, and handsome rather than pretty, a trifle solemn in repose but changing when she smiled, as she was doing now. 'Murdoch,' she said, holding his hands and drawing him close for a kiss on each cheek. 'Every time I hear of you, you have become more famous. And Lee.' This time the embrace was slightly longer. 'It is a very great pleasure. Now let us get inside out of this cold.'

Still holding Lee's hand, she led them up the stairs to the porch, where four girls waited. 'Some of my brood,' she explained. 'Anna is eleven. Helga is twelve. Magda is fourteen. And this little rascal is my youngest, Annaliese. She is nine.'

The girls, all brilliantly blonde like their parents, curtseyed and shook hands. Murdoch was astonished to receive a wink from Annaliese.

'Why, isn't that remarkable,' Lee said. 'Ours are just about the same ages.'

'Ah, but I have three more,' Margriet said, escorting them into a huge, armorial hall. 'Ernst is sixteen, and at school. So is Margriet junior. She is eighteen. Klaus is at university. He is twenty.'

'Good heavens,' Lee commented.

'And then there is Paul junior,' Reger said, at her elbow.

'Oh, yes. Paul . . .' Lee looked at Murdoch, flushing as she did so.

'Lee and I have no secrets from each other,' Murdoch lied.

'That is as it should be,' Reger agreed. 'Neither do Margriet and I. So . . . what do you say in English? We can let our hair down. I am sorry Paul is not here to meet you. He is with his regiment, and could not obtain leave for today. But he will be here for the weekend.'

'Oh, great,' Lee said. 'Does he . . .' She bit her lip, and looked at the girls, who were clearly bewildered by the conversation – she had already gathered that their English was not that good.

'No,' Reger said. 'Our secrets we keep at this level.'

'Oh . . . yes,' Lee said.

'Now, I know you will want to make yourselves comfortable,' Margriet said. 'Maria will show you to your rooms.' She nodded in the direction of the waiting housekeeper. 'And breakfast will be served in half an hour.'

'We feel such heels,' Lee confessed. 'Getting you up at this hour.'

'But we always rise early,' Margriet said. 'Even in winter.'

'This place is quite something,' Lee remarked in the privacy of their huge bedroom. 'I thought you said all the Germans were poor.'

'Not all,' Murdoch said. 'In a collapsing economy, land is worth more than gold. Providing you don't have to sell it, except at your price.'

'And a housekeeper. We don't have a housekeeper.'

'You refused to employ one, remember?' Murdoch said. 'Yankee egalitarianism.'

'Mmm,' Lee agreed, obviously considering altering that decision. 'Will we have a housekeeper in India?'

'I should think that will be essential.'

'Can we tell them about going to India?'

'Of course. It's not a secret. All Reger has to do is pick up a *Gazette*.'

'Mmm,' Lee said again. 'Did he really try to kill you at Le Cateau?'

'Well, I led a charge of my dragoons against his uhlans. I suppose we were all trying to kill each other.'

171

'It's difficult to believe. He seems such a nice man.'

'He isn't really.'

'Murdoch! How can you say that! He's our host.'

'And I am sure he is going to be charming. But he has a dark side to his character.'

'Mmm,' she said again. 'Does it bother you that he's father of your son?'

'Yes. But then, I don't know for sure that Paul is my son.'

'I think he is. Murdoch, did you and she, well . . .'

She was thinking of their own lovemaking, he knew. 'We had our moments. But none compared to those I've had since.'

'Do you still find her attractive?'

'Did you come all the way to Germany to be jealous?'

She grinned, and kissed him. 'I think she's very attractive,' she said. 'How old would you say she is?'

'Forty, forty-one. Something like that. I know she was seventeen when I met her, in 1901.'

'Oh, my,' Lee said. 'She's only four years older than me.'

They were overwhelmed with hospitality. Whatever tensions there might still be between Margriet and Reger, none were in evidence for their guests. Or revealed by their children. They seemed to have all the money in the world, judging by the food and wine they served, by Margriet's gowns for dinner, and by her jewellery. Reger had a fine stable – Murdoch remembered that when they had met in Dublin in the spring of 1914 he had ostensibly been buying horses – and the four of them galloped across the open country behind the house, often accompanied by the girls, when they were home from school.

On the Friday night they drove into Berlin to attend a performance of *Tannhäuser* at the Opera House, and Murdoch and Lee were amazed by the splendour of the occasion and the clothes of the people. During the interval Reger took Murdoch up to a mountain of a man, whose face reminded him of a sleepy bear, and who wore the uniform of a Field Marshal of the German army, and had a breast covered with twice as many ribbons as Murdoch himself possessed – although he was wearing none tonight as he was in white tie.

'Field Marshal von Hindenburg,' Reger explained, and spoke to Hindenburg in German.

The great man gazed at Murdoch, looking him up and down. Then he gave a stiff little bow, clicked his heels, made a remark in German, and moved away.

'I have a feeling I have just been snubbed,' Murdoch said, wishing he hadn't held out his hand.

'He lives in the past,' Reger said, with, to Murdoch's surprise, a good deal of contempt. 'He said: "A soldier should be in uniform." '

There were certainly a large number of uniforms on display tonight, for a nation whose army was officially limited to a hundred thousand men by the Treaty of Versailles. Perhaps, Murdoch thought, they are all officers.

'And you don't agree with him? I thought Hindenburg was the most revered man in Germany.'

'He has accomplished some good things. And he may do so again in the future. But Germany will not be rebuilt to its former glory by former men.' Reger smiled. 'Perhaps I should not be saying that to a British soldier.'

'Perhaps you should not,' Murdoch agreed, remembering his last talk with Churchill.

'None the less,' Reger said, 'I am not afraid to tell you that it is the fervent wish of every German to rise above the humiliation of Versailles.'

'As it should be,' Murdoch agreed. 'But you want to take your time.'

'Time. Bah. Time is what you make of it. There is someone I would very much like you to meet.'

Murdoch looked around at the milling crowd. 'Another snub?'

'This man will not snub you. He likes the English. But he is not here tonight. I will take you to see him, next week.'

'I'll look forward to that,' Murdoch said politely. 'I think that's the bell.'

'What did you think of Hindenburg?' Lee asked that night as they went to bed.

173

'Not a lot. But then, he thought even less of me.'

'I wish you had been in uniform. Then they'd have seen all your medals. The Germans don't have a Victoria Cross, do they? Or do they regard the Iron Cross as one?'

'Not exactly. Or there are an awful lot of genuine heroes in Germany. But they do have an equivalent. It's called the Blue Max.'

'What an odd name for a medal.'

'It's a nickname, because the ribbon is blue. The correct name is Pour le Merité.'

'That's an even odder name, for a German medal. How did it come to be called that?'

'Do you know, I have absolutely no idea? I imagine it dates back to when the French were the dominant military power in Europe. But like the Iron Cross, it's not given specifically for heroism, but for military achievement. You could say it's the exact equivalent of your Medal of Honour. I think Britain is the only country in the world which has a medal limited solely to heroism on the battlefield.'

'And you have it.' She hugged him. 'I am so proud of you, Murdoch. I think Hindenburg is a stupid boor. Come to think of it, I always did. Murdoch! Paul is coming home tomorrow. I'm so nervous. Are you?'

'Yes,' Murdoch said.

Paul von Reger junior was as tall and slim as his mother. His blue eyes might also have been inherited from his mother. The real indication that he need not be a Reger lay in his hair, which was dark, in complete contrast to both his parents and his sisters – and, presumably, Murdoch thought, to their three absent siblings.

Twenty-two years old, he looked very smart in his grey uniform with the little Iron Cross dangling at the neck. And even more serious than Murdoch remembered him from their last meeting, in 1914. He clicked his heels and saluted the British general, then bowed over Lee's hand.

'I am so pleased to meet you, Paul,' Lee said.

'It is my pleasure, Lady Mackinder.' His English was

174

perfect. He faced Murdoch. 'And to meet you again, sir. Your career has been a triumph.'

'You say that as though it is over, Paul,' Margriet remonstrated. 'General Mackinder is leaving for India soon, to command the troops there.'

'Well, not all of them,' Murdoch murmured.

'Are you to conquer some more of Asia, sir?' Paul inquired. It was impossible to tell whether he was being naive or sarcastic.

'Our colonial conquering days are over, thank God. No, I'm being sent there to make sure your Bolshevik neighbours don't get any ideas in that direction.'

'Then, sir, I salute you. They are our enemies. The enemies of all mankind.'

Murdoch raised his eyebrows. The young man was peculiarly vehement, his face for a moment almost transfigured.

Paul flushed. 'We in Germany know where our destiny lies. We know it was a foolish mistake to make war upon England and France. Germany's future faces east.'

'Are you sure?' Murdoch asked. 'I was under the impression that your Government and the Soviets were getting on very well.'

'Our Government,' Paul said contemptuously. 'A parcel of Jews and financiers. I tell you, sir, they do not represent the true heart of the Fatherland, the true aspirations of our people.'

'Is that so?' Murdoch asked. 'I had supposed Germany was now a democracy, and that the Government was elected by popular majority.'

Lee squeezed his arm. She didn't want him to quarrel with his son. 'I think we should all go to Russia, some time,' she said. 'And see for ourselves what's happening there.'

'He's terribly intense, isn't he?' she confided to Murdoch in bed.

'Yes. And did you notice how Reger never said a word, just stood there and let the boy do the talking?'

'I thought that was because he had no opinion to offer?'

'Reger has a great many opinions to offer, my dearest. And so does Paul.'

'Oh, my. You mean he's sort of educated Paul himself?'

'Or had someone else do it for him.'

'Oh, Murdoch. Are you terribly disappointed?'

'If I was hoping for anything else I was a fool,' Murdoch said.

'Do you want to leave?'

'Do you?'

'Well . . . not really. I find it all rather exciting here. And Margriet is so sweet.'

'Yes,' Murdoch said. He would never have used the word sweet to describe Margriet Voorlandt. 'Then we'll stay. I am certainly finding it interesting. Besides, Reger has some friend he wants me to meet. That might be interesting too.'

They continued their usual activities during the weekend, in which Paul joined, but there was a tension in the atmosphere which had previously been lacking. Murdoch indeed preferred not to engage the boy in any further discussion – although he would have loved to hear the German point of view on the Battle of Amiens – because Paul was so vehement in every opinion he expressed, Murdoch could never be sure when he was going to explode.

He tackled Margriet instead, as they cantered their horses across the meadows behind the house, letting Paul and his father and Lee gallop ahead. Up to now he had carefully avoided allowing himself to be alone with her. 'Why does Paul wear no insignia on his uniform?' he asked.

'Because he has no insignia,' she replied. 'He is a private.'

'A private?' He was astounded.

She smiled. 'Oh, he was an officer in 1918. A first-lieutenant. At sixteen years old. Is that not an achievement? But when the British and French said that Germany must not have more than a hundred thousand soldiers, Paul, and many thousands of young men like him, had the choice of giving up the army or re-enlisting in the ranks. All the privates in Paul's regiment were once officers.'

'I see,' Murdoch said thoughtfully. 'So, if Germany were ever to be allowed to re-arm, she would have a complete officer corps ready to train her recruits.'

'I do not know about these things,' Margriet said. 'But of course Germany must be allowed to re-arm. The army is the soul of Germany.' She reined her horse, gazed at him with wide eyes. 'Should I have said that?'

He had no choice but to rein also. 'Not to me. I happen to be one of those who believe that German militarism was mainly responsible for the war.'

'And not arrogant British determination to protect her position as the number-one colonial and industrial power in the world, no matter what,' she said, and then leaned across to lay her gloved hand on top of his. 'I do not wish to quarrel with you, Murdoch. I would never wish to do that. But these are my people now. I must share their points of view.'

'Are they your people, Margriet?'

'I could never go back to South Africa, if that is what you mean.'

'No, I did not mean that.'

She gazed at him.

'I can see that you have every material comfort,' he said, wishing that he hadn't asked the question.

'Oh, indeed. Nothing has changed since last we met. There were hard times in 1917 and 1918, but they were temporary.'

'Nothing has changed?' He asked the second leading question before he could stop himself.

Her gaze was steady, but there was a faint glow in her cheeks. 'Nothing. Reger still beats me, if that is what you were thinking about.'

'I find that impossible to believe. Your children . . .'

'Are happily unaware of it. And will remain so. We have a bargain, Reger and I. He gives me everything I wish, in material terms – as you have observed. In return, I give him everything he wishes, in the privacy of our bedroom. He is a sadist. But I think you knew that.'

'And you do nothing about it?'

'It is part of the bargain, that I never complain, and never

177

cry out. He would like me to cry out, of course, because part of the pleasure in inflicting pain is to hear the victim beg for mercy, but we are mutually agreed that it would be bad for the children, so he sublimates by making me move as he beats me.'

'What you are saying is unbelievable. And no one suspects?'

She shrugged. 'I think my personal maids suspect; occasionally he draws blood. And if they suspect, then all the servants do so. But the servants will keep their counsel for fear of losing their jobs. The girls . . . if I ever walk stiffly it is because I have a touch of rheumatism. This is well understood.' She gazed at him. 'You still do not believe me. I have scars. Would you like me to show them to you?'

'No,' he said. 'And Paul does not know either?'

Her face was suddenly bitter. 'Yes. I think Paul knows. I think his father has told him.'

'Good God! And he does nothing about it?'

'I think his father has told him that this is the right way to treat a woman. The Prussian way.'

'And there is nothing you can do about it? Or do you enjoy it?'

'No, Murdoch, I do not enjoy it. The pain does not matter. I do not enjoy the humiliation. But I had to make a choice, long ago, as you well know. Return to my people, and poverty, and eternal disgrace for having borne the child of a British soldier, or marry Reger, and have wealth, and move in high society . . . and be his plaything. That is the lot of a wife. Is not Lee your plaything?'

'I wouldn't suggest that to her, if I were you.'

Margriet shrugged again. 'Because you are an English officer and a gentleman. Perhaps, Murdoch, you are missing something of life. Perhaps you should beat your wife. You might find you enjoyed it.'

'I think we should rejoin the others,' Murdoch said. They were all out of sight.

'Murdoch . . .' She touched him again. 'I apologize. I envy Lee more than any other woman in the world. You ask me why I do not do something about Reger? I would, if I

178

had a man like you to flee to. You are the only man I have ever loved, Murdoch. The only man I will ever love.'

'Now I *know* we have to rejoin the others,' he said, and kicked his horse into a canter.

No one seemed to have found anything remarkable in their stopping for a chat, and Margriet was her usual immaculate, gracious self at dinner.

Now Murdoch did want to leave, but Reger said, 'Tomorrow, as Paul is rejoining his regiment, we will go and visit my friend.'

'You are taking General Mackinder to the Landberg?' Paul asked, suddenly animated.

'Why, yes, Paul.'

'Then you will give the Fuehrer my regards, Father.'

'Of course I will do that, boy. He will be pleased to hear from you.'

'The Fuehrer will tell you of the future of Germany, General,' Paul said, his eyes glowing.

'The Fuehrer?' Murdoch asked. 'Doesn't that mean, the leader?'

'Indeed it does,' Reger agreed.

'What does this gentleman lead?'

Reger gave a shout of laughter. 'Why nothing, at the moment. But he will. You will see, tomorrow. We will be away a couple of days, my dear,' he told Margriet.

'Of course. I will entertain Lee.'

'What did you and Margriet talk about when you dropped back this morning?' Lee asked when they reached their room.

'Paul junior, mainly.'

'And you're not happy about it.'

'Should I be?'

'Is she?'

'I don't think she is. But there's not a lot she can do about it.'

Lee sighed. 'I wish there was something *we* could do about it. I know, Murdoch! We'll invite young Paul to stay

179

with us in England. Heck, we owe them some hospitality, now. And then we can show him how the other half lives. Maybe take away some of that Prussian stiffness.'

'I think that would be a splendid idea, my love,' Murdoch said. 'But . . . we aren't going to be in England again for any length of time for at least three years.'

'Oh, goldarn,' she said. 'There's always something. Well, I'll have a good serious chat with Margriet while you and the Count are away. We'll think of something.'

But not too much, Murdoch hoped.

'I gather it's a long trip, to see your friend,' Murdoch said as he and Reger seated themselves in the back of the Mercedes and the car drove out of the estate.

'We are going down into Bavaria, yes. It is a full day's drive. We shall not arrive at our destination until this evening, and my friend is not available in the evenings, so we shall have to put up at an hotel and see him tomorrow. This does not inconvenience you?'

'I'm looking forward to seeing something of your country.' Even in your company, he thought. It was odd. He knew he should loathe Reger, and whenever he thought of what the man was doing to Margriet, he did loathe him. But then there always came that little niggling doubt as to how much of what Margriet told him was the truth – had ever been the truth. Besides, if she really hated having to live with him, she could undoubtedly secure a very lucrative divorce settlement . . . especially in the new non-aristocratic Germany.

'Good. Tell me, what do you think of young Paul?'

'He is a fine young man,' Murdoch said carefully. 'A very enthusiastic soldier.'

'Oh, indeed. But then, so are you, are you not?'

Murdoch was taken by surprise, both because the observation was so very true, and because it was the first time Reger had ever given the slightest hint that he might accept Murdoch's paternity of his eldest son.

'He is also a very good German,' Reger went on. 'He feels the defeat of his country most severely.'

'As do you, I imagine, Paul,' Murdoch said.

'Well, should I not? You British have never been defeated. I mean, absolutely, your country dismembered and all but destroyed, since 1066. Do you realize that is a unique achievement?'

'Not quite. It goes for Japan and the United States as well.'

'Japan,' Reger said contemptuously. 'They are Asiatics. And the Americans, with respect to your wife, Murdoch, are still in kindergarten as regards world history. Your trouble is, you do not realize how fortunate you have been never to experience such a fate.'

'Maybe not. But I can sympathize with it.' He grinned. 'Anyway, my family are Scottish. Now *we* have been defeated and dismembered, only a couple of hundred years ago. By the English.'

'You think it is all a joke,' Reger said. 'It is not, to us.'

'I do understand that, Paul,' Murdoch said. 'And believe me, it is not really a joke to us, either. I mean, having had to fight you and defeat you. If our terms appear harsh, they are a measure of how much we respected you as fighting men, and how we fear a resurgence of that aggressive spirit.'

'Yes,' Reger said. 'You do well to fear it. Because it is still there. And it seeks revenge.' He pointed out of the window. 'Look at those flowers. It is possible to see the first signs of spring.'

His abrupt change of subject signified a desire to drop politics, for which Murdoch was heartily glad; the idea of talking about Germany's misfortunes over a whole day's drive was daunting. Instead he could now concentrate on the country through which they were passing.

They travelled south at a steady fifty kilometres an hour over amazingly good roads, and as they had left at eight in the morning, were in Leipzig at ten. Murdoch would dearly have liked to stop in the famous old city, which was also the site of one of the most famous conflicts in history, the Battle of the Nations, when Napoleon had suffered a decisive defeat at the hands of the Prussians, Austrians, Swedes and Russians. But they pressed on, and crossed the state border into Bavaria in time to stop for lunch in Kronach.

They resumed their journey at three thirty, and reached Nuremberg just before six. Here Reger had booked them rooms at a very good hotel, in the centre of the town and overlooking the Pegnitz. From the banks of the river, where they strolled before dinner, they could look up at the castle, beneath which the medieval city had grown, and which remained in an excellent state of repair. Reger, when off politics, was a charming companion, a mine of information on the history of his people. But politics was never very far away from his thoughts.

'Once upon a time,' he told Murdoch, 'Nuremberg was the very centre of European trade. People came from all over the continent to show their wares at the Nuremberg fairs, to exchange information, and to purchase goods from faraway lands. But after the discovery of America the centre of gravity shifted from central Europe. It went to London. Is that not so?'

Murdoch sighed. 'I suppose it is.'

'So now, Nuremberg is remembered as the home of Albrecht Dürer, and a residence of Melanchthon. And for much activity during the great witchcraft trials. Still, I suppose it is good to be remembered for something.'

They left Nuremberg at nine the following morning, passed through Donauworth at eleven, and then took to country roads. Murdoch had had the impression, from their route, that they were making for Munich and the Bavarian Alps, but he realized he was wrong as they came in sight of the River Lech, which rose in the high land to the south and divided Augsburg before joining the Donau as a tributary a few kilometres east of Donauworth. The road turned along the bank of the river and they found themselves looking at a fortress perched high above them.

'Our destination,' Reger explained. 'The Landberg.'

'Your friend owns that imposing pile?'

'Ah, no.' Reger smiled. 'The Landberg is owned by the Bavarian Government. It is a prison.'

Murdoch turned his head in surprise. 'Your friend works in a prison?'

'As a matter of fact, he does. But not in the way you mean.'

Murdoch was content to wait; Reger was obviously enjoying his little secret. They drove up to the castle, and Reger spoke to the uniformed men on the gate. There was no objection to their entry, apparently, as a few minutes later they were in the centre courtyard, looking up at the high walls which surrounded them, before being taken inside, up several flights of stairs and along a corridor which had small barred windows let into the various doors they passed, to be sure, but bore very little other resemblance to a prison.

When they finally stopped before one of the doors, the gaoler knocked before turning the key.

'Your friend is in prison?' Murdoch could restrain his curiosity no longer.

'Indeed. He is in this cell.'

Standing in the doorway was a young man with dark hair and a craggily handsome face. His eyes were earnest and his whole manner tense, but he was rather incongruously dressed in alpine clothes, with braces and bare knees. The prison was heated, but even so Murdoch suspected he couldn't be all that warm.

'Herr Hess,' Reger said, and spoke rapidly in German; Murdoch heard his name being mentioned. When Reger was finished, the man named Hess clicked his heels and offered his hand. 'He speaks no English. Neither does the Fuehrer. But he is glad to make your acquaintance.'

Murdoch shook hands, at the same time realizing that they were here to meet this mysterious Fuehrer. In a prison?

He was escorted inside and found himself gazing at another man, who stood by the window. Also dark, and wearing his hair brushed half across his forehead, this man had a little black moustache – he made Murdoch think of his favourite film star, Charlie Chaplin. He also wore alpine clothes, and he and the other man had apparently been working on some kind of manuscript, because the table by the window, which had a most pleasant view out over the river and the surrounding countryside, was littered with papers.

'Adolf,' Reger said, and spoke in German. The man advanced into the centre of the room, politely. 'Adolf Hitler,' Reger said. 'My friend. Major-General Sir Murdoch Mackinder.'

Murdoch shook hands, while his brain stirred. 'I have heard that name before.'

'Of course. Last year.'

Murdoch snapped his fingers. 'The Munich putsch. This man attempted to overthrow the Bavarian Government.'

'Exactly.'

Hitler had been waiting patiently, but he had recognized the words Munich and putsch, and now he frowned at Reger, who hastily interpreted. Hitler replied. 'Adolf says he is sorry to appear before you in the guise of a gaolbird,' Reger said.

'He doesn't look the least like a gaolbird to me,' Murdoch said. 'But . . . he is your leader? The leader of what?'

'Of a political party which will one day rule Germany. The National Socialist Workers Party.'

Murdoch was astounded once again. 'You, Paul, supporting a leftist group?'

Reger smiled. 'It is the National that counts, in our estimation. Come, sit down.' He spoke to Hitler, and they all seated themselves.

Murdoch studied the imprisoned politician. Hitler was several years younger than himself, he estimated. He was well groomed and had regular if undistinguished features. And knobbly knees. Anyone less like a Bismarck or a Hindenburg, or indeed, a Paul von Reger, could not possibly be imagined.

Now he was holding out his hand again. 'I have been telling Adolf that you wear the Victoria Cross, and he wishes to congratulate you. He himself has twice been awarded the Iron Cross.'

'Has he?' Murdoch shook hands with more warmth.

184

'Unlike you, he finished the war in hospital. He was badly gassed.'

'Was he now. Tell him my regiment was one of the first to suffer a gas attack, back in 1915.'

Reger translated and then turned back to Murdoch. 'He observes that you survived. I told him you always do.'

'How long will he be in prison?'

'Another year, perhaps. He was sentenced to five, but it will be reduced for good behaviour. And when he comes out, then you will see a startling change overtake Germany.'

'And then he'll wind up in prison again.'

'Not this time. No more putsches. It will all be legal from here on. We shall win by the votes of the people.'

'And you will support them. With money?'

'And time.' But Reger could see that Murdoch was neither impressed with Hitler nor able to understand why a Prussian Junker should wish to support such an irrelevant and unsuccessful political movement. He spoke to Hitler again. For a moment Hitler demurred, but Reger pressed his point. Hitler gazed at Murdoch, then he began to speak. He spoke quietly at first, but gradually his voice gained both power and passion. Then he was on his feet, arms outflung and then folded, fists clenched and then unclenched, as his voice flowed across the room, sometimes high-pitched and angry, immediately afterwards dropping to a caress. Murdoch glanced at Hess and Reger, both quite lost in the magic of their leader's voice, and no doubt at his words as well. Murdoch could not understand what he was saying, but he certainly understood that he was listening to a charismatic speaker.

Hitler paused, looked at Murdoch, and sat down. He made a remark to Reger. 'The Fuehrer wishes to know if you understood anything of what he said.'

'I caught a few words, like "Juden", several times, and "England", I think.'

'He was telling you of our plans. He was saying how everyone knows that the German army was not truly defeated in the last war, but was betrayed by the treachery of the Jews and politicians at home. He was saying that he

185

has no quarrel with England. The Germans and the English share a common racial heritage; they are both of Aryan stock. He was saying that England should be the friend of Germany, as she always has been historically, and not attempt to trample her out of existence. He was saying that England needs Germany far more than she needs France, because only a strong Germany can hold back the Russian hordes. He was saying that when Germany is strong again, she will turn against the Bolsheviks and wipe them out of existence. He was saying that in the great plains of the Ukraine and Byelorussia is where the true future of Germany lies. He was saying that when Germany stretches from the Rhine to the Don, then will the peace of Europe be assured for all time.'

'Quite a programme. When is all this supposed to happen?'

Reger smiled. 'In the course of time. But not too much time.'

They shook hands with the Fuehrer again, and returned to Donauworth for lunch. 'That was a most interesting meeting, Paul,' Murdoch said.

'But you think nothing will come of it. I mean of our hopes for the future?'

'I don't know enough about your party, or your organization and your strength. I am bound to say, however, that Great Britain and France would never stand by and watch such a programme being carried out.'

'Not even if it means the destruction of Bolshevism? Of Lenin and all his crew? I think they will.'

'I cannot see them doing so. I also must tell you, Paul, that as a serving British officer I feel it my duty to repeat this conversation to my superiors when I return to London.'

'Even if you do not believe it will ever happen?'

'I feel they should know that there is a current of such thought flowing through Germany, even if on a very small scale.'

'A very small scale,' Reger said thoughtfully. 'Well, you are welcome to put the Fuehrer's thoughts before your

186

leaders. He intends to do it himself. You saw the papers in his cell. He is writing a book, with the aid of Rudolf Hess. Rudolf is his secretary.'

Murdoch had assumed they had both been prisoners. 'You mean he's allowed a secretary, in prison?' he asked in amazement.

'But of course. In that prison. And for that man. It was a political offence, against a socialist government. We do not care for socialist governments, in Germany.'

Murdoch scratched his head as he tried to envisage such a situation in England.

'The book will be published, and if you like, I will send you a copy. But I am sure it will be translated into English.'

'And he intends to say in it what you have just told me?'

'Amongst other things, yes. He will outline our entire programme, and invite your people to join us.'

Murdoch scratched his head some more. It was not until the next day, when they were nearly back at the house, that he remembered he had a question to ask. 'Paul has met this man, Hitler, hasn't he?'

'Oh, indeed,' Reger said with a smile. 'Paul is one of his most fervent admirers. He will be one of the new elite, when Germany rises again.'

8

India, 1924

'So what did you and Margriet talk about?' Murdoch asked as the train sped them westward across Germany.

'Everything you can imagine. You know what? I think she's still carrying a torch for you.'

'Um,' he agreed.

'She didn't make advances, did she?'

'She always makes advances.'

It was Lee's turn to say, 'Um. I'm glad you decided to cut the visit short. I guess it was a stupid idea in the first place. I so wanted to see young Paul . . . but he's not your son any more, is he?'

'No,' Murdoch said.

'Was that man Hitler really frightening?'

'Good Lord, no. He's just a propped-up demagogue. No, it's Reger and people like him, Hindenburg as well, who are frightening. I really thought, when we arrived, the way Reger greeted us, that things had changed. That the Germans, or at least the German militarists, like Reger, had said to themselves, we fought and lost. That really was the war to end all wars, simply because the world, Europe anyway, cannot afford another war like that. So let's make the best of it. Instead, you have Hindenburg apparently living in the past, and Reger ready to jettison that past in favour of the future, willing to support anyone who might be able to sway a mob to get at that future, and openly planning the wars he is going to fight to re-establish Germany's greatness. That is frightening.'

She squeezed his hand. 'Can they ever do it, Murdoch?'

'Well, of course they can't. They're limited by treaty to nothing more than a token military establishment. All they're going to get is a smart slap across the knuckles.'

But he wasn't as sure as he had pretended to her. 'Can they ever do it?' he asked Churchill, when they lunched together.

'Well, of course they can. If we let them.'

'But we won't.'

'Now that is an imponderable, right this minute, Murdoch. What this Socialist Government is going to do next is anyone's bet. They're even recognizing the Bolsheviks. However . . .' He grinned. 'The best bet anyone has is that they're not going to remain in power a full term. Tell me, you parted from Reger on good terms?'

'Oh, indeed.'

'Well, if this friend of his does get his book published, and he sends you a copy, I'd like to read it.'

'It'll be in German.'

'I can have it translated. I've heard of the fellow, Hitler, of course. Read about him when the putsch failed. He had Ludendorff on his side, you know, so he can't be quite such a put-up job. Of course, Ludendorff disowned him when the whole thing collapsed. One would hardly expect anything else of that gentleman. But I'd like to have chapter and verse, as it were.'

'You shall,' Murdoch promised.

'When do you leave for India?'

'Next month.'

'I envy you.'

'Do you?'

'Aren't you looking forward to it?'

'Well, yes, I am. But for purely selfish reasons. I'm looking forward to retreading the steps of Father, and Grandfather. And Great-Grandfather for that matter. And I'm looking forward to being my own boss, to all intents and purposes. But I do gather it's rather a beastly assignment when there's trouble.'

'Most trouble is, beastly. But you never want to forget, Murdoch, that India is the jewel in our crown. Defend it with your life, if you have to. But defend it. Should Great Britain lose India, ever, on that same day will she lose the appellation "great".'

Churchill was a man of unusual vehemence, in certain directions. But it was a thought to carry with him, Murdoch supposed.

'Well, Ralph,' he asked Manly-Smith. 'Ready to head east again?'

'Gosh, sir.' Manly-Smith looked distinctly embarrassed. 'I never did thank you properly.'

'For what?'

'Well, for making me your ADC. For giving me a chance.'

'One should never waste talent, Ralph. Now, is Jennifer looking forward to it?'

'She's wildly excited, sir.'

'And little Albert?' The baby had been named after Jennifer's father.

'I think he'd be excited too, if he understood what was happening.'

'I think we're all excited,' Murdoch agreed.

Because they would be travelling with the regiment. And for the first time, ever, with their wives. At least, the officers would. The age of true democracy had not yet arrived.

As it was peacetime, it was no longer possible to requisition an entire luxury liner, and so they could not all sail together in one ship. Murdoch and Lee, with Murdoch's staff and Reynolds, were accompanied by A Squadron, Captain Bryan. Colonel Ramage, with Major Lowndes and B Squadron, Captain Destry, were on a separate ship, and C Squadron, Captain Rostron, on a third. RSM Yeald sailed with Colonel Ramage, which was a relief to both him and Manly-Smith, and his daughter.

Captain Bryan was not married, so Lee and Jennifer were the only two officers' wives on the first ship. Already good friends, they became almost intimates as the voyage progressed, despite the considerable disparity in their ages – Lee was just old enough to be the girl's mother. The four of them, indeed, made up a very happy party, sometimes joined by Bryan, as they explored Gibraltar, and then Malta

– where there was time for a picnic excursion to the marvellously clear waters of Camino – before reaching Port Said and beginning their journey down the canal.

This was of course familiar territory to Murdoch and Manly-Smith, but not to the ladies, who were fascinated by everything they saw. Lee's only disappointment was that they did not have time to go up to Cairo and look at the pyramids. 'When we're returning on long leave,' Murdoch promised her.

From Aden it was very nearly two thousand miles almost due east across the Arabian Sea to Bombay. 'Almost like crossing the Atlantic,' Lee said as they steamed for four days without sighting land. 'Except for the weather.'

As it yet wanted a month or so to the start of the monsoon season the sea was unfailingly smooth and the sun unfailingly hot. Lee and Jennifer and some of the other ladies retired to the boat deck in bathing costumes and began turning brown.

'You want to watch that,' Murdoch said, 'or you'll be mistaken for Indians when we land.'

He had never felt so relaxed. The somewhat traumatic visit to Germany seemed very far away, and the possibly traumatic situation he might have to face in Peshawar equally far in the future. This was really the first genuine holiday he and Lee had ever shared, and it was sheer bliss. Especially in the company of two such delightful people. Ralph Manly-Smith was proving an ideal ADC, always ready with information or maps as required. While Jennifer was a revelation, good-humoured, surprisingly well-read, and, more obviously, steeped in the history of the regiment. Her baby was also a jolly little fellow, who was no more than fretful even when he came down with a bad case of prickly heat.

Even their first glimpse of India was like a holiday. They steamed round Colaba Point and into Bombay Harbour and disembarked to cheering crowds who had apparently been advised of their imminent arrival. The crowds were composed mainly of English and Anglo-Indians to be sure, but there were quite a few dark skins amongst them.

191

The other two ships had not yet arrived, nor had the regimental band, but A squadron made a proud show as it marched in column of twos to its cantonment. Murdoch and Lee were immediately besieged with invitations, but they could accept very few of them, as, while Bryan and his men would await the arrival of their comrades before travelling north, Murdoch was under orders to report to Delhi as rapidly as possible. After only two days in Bombay, therefore, which allowed them just time to pay a visit to the Bhendy Bazaar and get a taste of the atmosphere of true India, they found themselves again in a train, and embarked on a much longer journey than across Germany.

They boarded at Central Station at eight in the morning and were shown to their first-class sleeper, which adjoined that shared by the Manly-Smiths. Reynolds and Sergeant Denning, in charge of communications, shared a third. The train skirted the racetrack and began a long haul up the eastern shore of the Gulf of Khambhat. Progress was slow, mainly because it stopped with monotonous regularity, and the countryside was flat and uninteresting, and terribly poor.

It was three that afternoon when they pulled into Surat, where there was a lengthy stop, and then they chugged on again. Darkness fell as they reached Baroda, and they retired to bed soon after dinner, exhausted as much by the boredom as the heat. Unfortunately the train continued until eleven, when it stopped for the night in Ahmedabad. The clanking and banging and the noise of the disembarking passengers woke everyone, and then the hot stillness of the night, which was accentuated by the barking of dogs and the many odours which drifted through the city, made sleeping very difficult. For the first time Baby Albert would not stop crying, and when they met for breakfast the following morning, served as the train finally pulled out, having been joined by it seemed thousands of passengers garbed in every manner of clothing from business suits with rolled umbrellas to saris and even dhotis, the four of them looked as if they had been on a binge.

'Is the whole journey going to be like this?' Lee asked.

'I certainly hope not,' Murdoch said.

In fact at ten o'clock, when they reached Siddapur, they could see higher land to the east, and an hour later, at Palanpur, the line definitely began to climb. Instantly it became cooler, and they lunched looking up, to the west, at the Guru Sikhar, a mountain which rose some five thousand feet.

'Now this is splendid,' Lee declared.

They reached Beawar at seven and Ajmer a couple of hours later. The Anivalli mountain range had been on their right all afternoon, and in Ajmer they were some two thousand feet above sea level. The train stopped here for the night, but there was no difficulty in sleeping; in fact they used blankets for the first time.

Next morning the journey resumed at seven, as usual, and after a long but interesting day, climbing up and then down, winding round hills and often seeing mountains in the distance, they chugged through the suburbs of Delhi at six o'clock, as the sun was setting in a blaze of light to the west.

They had apparently been expected earlier, because at their hotel there was an invitation to dinner that very evening. As it was from the Viceroy, Rufus Isaacs, Viscount Reading, it could hardly be refused, so it was necessary to have a quick bath and unpack somewhat crushed mess jackets and even more crushed evening gowns. Jennifer was overawed at being so quickly introduced into the highest society in India. Lee was unamused by the whole thing, until she discovered that Reading had been a special envoy of the British Government to the United States at the end of the war. Then they had a great deal to talk about.

Also present was General Sir William Birdwood, who had just taken over as Commander-in-Chief, India. He was one of the few senior serving officers whom Murdoch had not actually met, for although he had been in South Africa at the end of the Boer War, as Kitchener's military secretary, he had arrived after Murdoch had already been sent home in disgrace. During the World War he had been commander of the Australian forces, first of all at Gallipoli and then on the western front, but there again they had not come into contact.

Murdoch knew, however, that he came of an Anglo-Indian family, whose father had been a judge famous for his independence of thought. Birdwood himself was a tall, spare man who yet had a twinkle in his eye.

'I'll expect you in my office tomorrow morning, General Mackinder,' he said as the party broke up. 'To put you in the picture.'

'Good morning, gentlemen,' Birdwood said, when Murdoch and Manly-Smith arrived at his office. 'I hope you slept well?'

'Like tops, sir,' Manly-Smith said enthusiastically.

'Splendid. And what are the ladies doing today?'

'Exploring, as they don't know how much time we have here.' Murdoch said. 'They've gone with a guide to somewhere called the Jami Masjid.'

The hotel had provided an ayah for Albert.

'Ah, the Jami Masjid. Yes, it's a splendid edifice. Fairly recent, of course, built by the Muslim emperors, the Mughals. But then, this is Mughal country. Actually, you're welcome to spend a week or two here. It might pay to get acclimatized. I would take a run down into the valley, if I were you. Go to Agra and show your wives the Taj Mahal; it's only a hundred and twenty-odd miles by rail. To come to India and not visit the Taj Mahal would be like going to England and never visiting the Tower.'

'Then we might just do that. I had got the impression that there was a certain amount of urgency for me to get up to the Frontier.'

'Things are very quiet there, right now,' Birdwood said. 'And we would naturally like them to stay that way for as long as possible. As to whether they will, no man can say, since the Viceroy was advised to release Mr Gandhi from prison last January. He may preach non-violence, but a good many of his followers don't believe in it. There have been some quite nasty incidents, such as shooting up of police stations, and the murder of their inmates, in the past

194

few years. The trouble is, you see, that the Hindus and the Muslims hate each other more than they hate us. Gandhi keeps trying to unite them in antagonism to the British, but he hasn't been very successful, and every time a Muslim murders a Hindu, or vice versa, there is a fresh outbreak of violence. However, this is really outside your terms of reference. Now, here is the area of your command.' He got up, and they walked with him to a huge wall map which had just been unrolled by one of his secretaries. 'North-west India. Here's Delhi down in the right-hand corner. You'll see that we're never very far away from you; it's only five hundred and fifty miles from here to the Khyber Pass, as the crow flies.

'North-west of us from here to the Afghan border is mainly inhabited by Muslims, with the very big exception of the Punjab, of course, which is the home of the Sikhs. The Sikh enclave, as you know, has played a very big part in the military history of India. In the old days they were a hostile and very efficient enemy. After we conquered them, in one of the hardest wars ever fought out here, they became our firm friends, and of course they supported us entirely during the mutiny. It is a thousand pities there was that trouble in Amritsar in 1919. I'm not blaming Dyer. I would probably have done the same thing in his shoes. But it still is a pity. However, things have quietened down there now. It is north of the Punjab, Waziristan and Kashmir, where the border abuts that of Afghanistan, that you have to concern yourself with.

'All the tribes up there, the Mohmands and the Afridi, the Wazirs and the Mahsuds, are independent-minded, and have lived since time began by robbery and violence. They know no other way of life. Ever since we defeated the Sikhs and came into contact with the hill tribes we have been forced to engage in punitive expeditions against them whenever they have come down to pillage peaceful people who were supposed to be under our protection. This is what the North West Frontier has always been about, and when it was a matter of sending a regiment after a single recalcitrant khan, levying and collecting a fine or burning

195

his village, it was not very serious. Occasionally, however, several of the tribes have buried their differences and got together, and then a major campaign has been necessary to restore order. You will know about those, Murdoch; your father and grandfather both fought in such campaigns. I may say that it was the opinion of most military men that although the fighting was always dirty, if you take my meaning . . .'

'Yes,' Murdoch said.

'It was also of great value in training troops. And of course, Waziristan provided a natural buffer between anything that might be happening in Afghanistan, or beyond, and British India.

'However, two years ago, after the Amritsar massacre, and more trouble up there, the Government came to the conclusion that the time-honoured system was uneconomic, bad for British prestige, and somehow, one gets the impression, untidy. They decided to annex Waziristan.'

'Ah,' Murdoch said, beginning to understand why he was sitting there.

'The annexation was undertaken, I may say, over the advice of the Chief Commissioner for the province, Sir John Maffey, but he was presented with a fait accompli. Now, it is early days yet, and no one knows for sure what the reaction of the tribesmen is going to be. I mean, we didn't, we couldn't, take over the entire province. A proclamation was made, and garrisons installed at certain key points. This was the lynchpin of the Government's plan, that permanent garrisons would restrain the habitual lawlessness of the tribes. Maffey was of the opinion that permanent garrisons provide a permanent irritation, and a permanent target for the tribes to attack, should they get in the mood. Well, in a sense he has been proved right; last year there was a serious uprising of the Mahsuds. On the other hand, the Government can also claim a point – apart from the Mahsud insurgence, which was speedily dealt with, the area has been quiet for the past year. But, and this is an important point, it is extremely doubtful that all the tribes are yet aware that they belong to Great Britain. In any event, having heard Maffey's point of view and digested the facts of the Mahsud rising, the Government decided that it might pay to strengthen their hands up there, as it were.'

'So they chose me. And the Royal Westerns,' Murdoch observed.

'Quite. Britain's most famous fighting soldier, who also has a name well known and feared in Waziristan, and one of Britain's most famous regiments, which is also remembered and respected in the area. It is assumed that your presence, and that of the Westerns, will make the Pathans pause to think before starting anything.'

'Or act like a red rag to a bull.'

'There is that possibility. There is no suggestion, of course, that you attempt to police such a huge area with six hundred men. You have more than a full division up there. They are mainly Indian troops, and they are scattered about in garrisons, but they are a sizeable force, and can be concentrated in time of trouble.'

'Hm,' Murdoch said. 'Where are these garrisons?'

The secretary handed Birdwood a wand, with which he pointed at the map. 'There is a strong one here, at Razmak. That is in the very heart of the Mahsud country. The Mahsuds, who are themselves an enclave surrounded by Wazirs, have always been the most warlike of the hill people. Presumably they have had to be, to survive. So Razmak is garrisoned by a brigade of six battalions, including one British, and also has a mountain artillery battery. To the north, along the River Tochi, is another brigade, of seven battalions, and there is yet another brigade concentrated around Wana, in the south. You will of course have another brigade in garrison at Peshawar as a general reserve, and it is anticipated that you will make there your headquarters, as it has good rail and radio links with us here.'

'And these are all seasoned troops?' Murdoch asked.

'Ah. No, I'm afraid I cannot say that they are. And there is another factor of which you must be made aware. It is the Government's policy, wherever possible, to recruit on the ground, as it were.' He paused, gazing at Murdoch.

197

'You can't be serious.'

'There can be no doubt that the tribesmen are natural soldiers.'

'So are the Irish. What you are saying is the equivalent of the British garrison in Ulster being forced to recruit only from members of the IRA.'

'Well, it worked very well with both the Sikhs and the Nepalese. The Sikhs and the Gurkhas are the best soldiers in the Indian army.'

'With respect, sir,' Murdoch said. 'They became so after their armies had been utterly defeated by the British. We have never actually smashed the Wazirs or the Mahsuds, have we? We've won some punitive actions, nothing more.'

'That's a good point. Believe me, I don't disagree with you, Murdoch. But we are here to implement Government policy, and must do what we can. However, you will be aware that the loyalty of certain troops has not yet been proved. You will also have gathered that your main problem is lack of cavalry. This it is hoped the Westerns will remedy. But obviously we have always suffered from lack of mobility where the Pathans are concerned. Oh, by the way, you also have at your disposal a brigade of armoured cars. But these are stationed in Peshwar. They aren't really of too much use in the mountains.'

'No, sir,' Murdoch agreed grimly.

'However, what you do have, and is of inestimable value in the mountains, is a squadron of De Havilland Nine As . . . they call them Ninaks. They are bombers which can winkle out any enemy lashkars, even in places inaccessible to troops. They are, of course, only to be used offensively in cases of open warfare.'

'Yes,' Murdoch said.

'So there you have it. You'll want to see the situation for yourself, and make your own dispositions, of course. However, if there is anything else I can tell you, please ask.'

'There is one thing more, sir,' Murdoch said. 'Is Shere Khan still alive?'

'Shere Khan? Oh, you mean that old Mahsud reprobate. Oh, indeed he is, so far as I know. He's fairly ancient now, of course, and I believe he leaves the day-to-day running of tribal matters to his son, Abdul.'

'He also had some daughters, I believe,' Murdoch said.

'I'm sure he did. Most of these fellows have more children than they can count. I would leave him well alone, if I were you, as long as he leaves you alone. He wasn't involved in last year's business, which was a relief to us all. As you probably know, he isn't a real Mahsud at all, nor are his people. They're kindred, and it suits us to give them that name, but Shere Khan's people live away from the main body of the tribe, in the valley of the Kurram, which is really Turi country. It is also of course right up against Afghanistan, and in the old days Shere Khan would whip across the border when the pressure got too heavy.'

'Yes,' Murdoch said. 'What is the situation in Afghanistan now? I was told in London that there was some Russian penetration.'

'There is always Russian penetration into Afghanistan. What we don't know, nowadays, is whether it is imperialistic, as in the days of the Tsars, or whether they are merely trying to convert the Afghans to communism. The fact is, Amanullah, the amir, signed a treaty of friendship with Soviet Russia three years ago. Now, in 1919, after that little war we had with him, he signed a treaty of friendship with us as well, and in fact we then recognized the complete independence of Afghanistan, for the first time, I may add. Reports from our agents indicate that he does seem to have rather a large number of Russian advisers in residence, but, as he is an independent monarch, we have no say in that. Afghanistan I would also leave well alone, Murdoch, unless they start something. And even if they do, remember that it would be a matter for the Government to decide what action should be taken. There is a difference between tribal warfare and international warfare.'

'And if I find it necessary to undertake a punitive expedition against a Pathan tribe, and they flee across the border?'

'I would consider very carefully before pursuing. Certainly I think you ought to be in touch with GHQ before acting on your own. But hopefully, Murdoch, you won't have to undertake any punitive expeditions. You are here to overawe, sufficiently to prevent any trouble. If you manage to get through your tour of duty and return home without having fired a single shot in anger, you will be a very popular man.'

'I'll bear that in mind,' Murdoch agreed.

'What do you think?' Ralph asked as they sipped whisky and soda and waited for Lee and Jennifer to return to the hotel.

'I think we're on a hiding to nothing,' Murdoch said. 'I've been given military command of an occupied country which doesn't yet know it's been occupied. I've been given a large number of troops, of which many are unreliable. And I've virtually been forbidden to take any preventive action, or even to shoot unless the other fellow shoots first and I've ascertained that he was actually shooting to kill.'

'Hm,' Ralph said. 'What are you going to do?'

'The job, of course,' Murdoch answered. 'That was what I was sent here to do. But I intend to use my judgement, not theirs. Here are the girls.'

Lee and Jennifer were exhausted, but excited and delighted with the sights and sounds of Delhi. So much so that Murdoch decided to take advantage of Birdwood's offer, and they all went down to Agra, taking the ayah and the baby. He wanted time to assimilate everything he had been told, in any event, and he also wanted time to find out what had happened to the regiment; he had telegraphed Bombay and learned that C Squadron had still not arrived.

However, thoughts of the job in hand were driven from his mind as he and Lee stood inside the red standstone walls and gazed at the red and white marble of the Taj Mahal. Lee consulted her book.

'This says it took twenty thousand workmen eleven years to build the mausoleum, and another ten years to finish the whole place. At a cost of forty million rupees.'

'And the rupee was worth somewhat more then than it is now,' Murdoch pointed out, gazing at the four gleaming minarets which rose one from each corner of the grave, and at the marble screen which guarded the entrance, studded with precious stones.

'When I die, do you suppose you could build something like this over me?' Lee asked.

'I'm sure George and I can manage something. Let's see . . . Taj means tall hat, doesn't it? So this is literally the tall hat of Mahal. I suppose, the crown of the Begum Mumtaz Mahal is what old Shah Jehan had in mind. We could erect your riding hat on a whip stuck in the ground on the croquet lawn, and surround it with bits of broken glass, tastefully arranged, of course.'

'You brute. But really, can you imagine the power that man had, to spend all of that time and money on a grave for his wife?'

'And it was only four hundred years ago,' Murdoch said thoughtfully. 'He used to rule these people we're going to live with. I'll bet they still remember that kind of power.'

'Which we can't match. Not even the British empire.'

'No,' Murdoch agreed. 'Because the true ruler of the British empire is the Chancellor of the Exchequer.'

To his great relief, on his return to Delhi Sergeant Denning was able to tell him that Colonel Ramage had reported the entire regiment now assembled; they would travel north by special train. Murdoch sent off a message immediately instructing them to proceed direct to Peshawar by the quickest possible route, and then put an end to the holiday and took himself and Manly-Smith, and their wives, north.

From the capital it was a fourteen-hour train journey to Lahore; they left at dawn and arrived at nine that night. The route was through high land most of the way, and was intensely interesting, however slow, for it took them by way of Panipat, where the Mughal Conqueror Babur had decisively defeated the Hindu kings of Delhi, and founded the empire which was to last, officially, for more than three hundred years, and then, as they swung west, just on dusk, Amritsar itself. But they caught only a glimpse of the Golden Temple and the Pool of Immortality. 'We'll come back to it when we've settled in,' Murdoch promised.

From Lahore it was a nineteen-hour run to Peshawar, and as this was the end of the line the run was done in one, with the usual stops at various wayside stations and some fairly large towns, including Rawalpindi. The country undulated, and they descended to the bridge over the huge Chenab, one of the tributaries of the Indus, before climbing again to the high plateau, and as the day went on they could make out the peaks of the Hindu Kush away to the north.

'Pathan country,' Murdoch said.

'How close are we to where your ancestor made the charge?' Lee wanted to know.

'Oh, a long way. That was in Baluchistan, south-west from here. We might have a look at it when we've time.'

'There's so much exploring to be done,' she agreed. But now she was more interested in Peshawar, and the bunga-low which was to be her home for the next few years.

As they arrived in the middle of the night they could do little until morning, and in fact Murdoch elected to sleep on the train rather than move themselves at that hour. The next day they found themselves in a sizeable city set in the middle of an intensely irrigated plain, the water coming from the Kabul River to the east and the Khyber River to the west; the rivers reminded Murdoch that Kabul itself, the capital of Afghanistan, was only two hundred miles away – two thirds less distance than Delhi – and that the Khyber Pass, through which the rivers flowed, was under forty. Indeed the name Peshawar means, simply, frontier town.

The plain, although some six hundred feet above sea level, lay in a depression between two much higher areas, and was warm enough to support crops of sugar cane as well as wheat and maize – there were cane mills outside the city. The city itself contained many splendid buildings, domin-ated by the pure white Mahabat Khan Mosque, one of the treasures of Muslim architecture, built in 1630, and, on a more prosaic level, Government House, built by the British quite recently. There were also, naturally, a vast number of shanty areas, but the streets were wide and the air clean.

Lee was fascinated, and by the inhabitants, who were mainly Pathan – tall, fair-skinned people. She was less pleased when they were taken outside the city itself to the huge, forbidding fortress of Bala Hissar. This had been built by the Emperor Babur in 1526, and rebuilt by the Sikhs in 1830 when they had attempted to hold this country. Now it was very much a British cantonment, with the Union Jack floating lazily above the white walls and the garrison encamped in and around it.

'We're not going to live in a fort?' she demanded.

Actually the officers' residential area was extremely pleasant, and Lee's humour was quite restored when she saw the commanding general's 'bungalow'. Murdoch had always understood a bungalow to mean a single-storey dwelling, but this had two storeys, the living area on the ground floor, which was surrounded by wide, shady verandahs, and the bedrooms on an upper floor which rose out of the centre of the building and overlooked the verandah roofs. The windows also overlooked an extensive garden, dominated by multi-coloured hibiscus hedges.

'Now this is rather nice,' she remarked.

Ralph and Jennifer had a smaller bungalow close at hand, and the other officers were all virtually within shouting distance.

A perfect retinue of servants lined up on the first morning for Lee's inspection. 'What on earth am I to do with all these people?' she asked Murdoch.

'I'd let them get on with whatever they were doing before you came,' he suggested. 'The British taxpayer is footing the bill.'

Fortunately the butler, whose name was Kohar, spoke good English, and if Lee was rather taken aback to discover that it was he, and not the housekeeper, with whom she would be dealing, on all subjects, the pair of them and George Reynolds soon became the best of friends. Lee went trotting off to the bazaar most mornings in search of Indian delicacies such as saffron, and learned how to concoct vast, mouth-burning curries, but also some of the exquisitely flavoured Kashmiri dishes like murg massalam, or baked spice chicken, in which the various curry flavours were very lightly used, the bird being marinated in honey, almonds and raisins before being baked in the oven, or Raan, the magnificent spiced leg of lamb. Every evening she and Jennifer compared notes to see who had learned more during the preceeding twenty-four hours. As there were quite a few other officers' wives in the cantonment, there was a lot to be learned.

Murdoch was delighted to see her so happy. It removed one possible burden from his mind. There were enough others. If Maffey was pleased to have such a distinguished soldier as his general officer commanding, Murdoch's immediate subordinates were not quite so enthusiastic. It was easy to see that they wanted nothing more than a continuance of their pleasant garrison life, with its cocktail parties and bridge parties, and polo matches and cricket on Sunday afternoons, and were unsure how the arrival of a famous fighting man was going to affect their lives.

'Relax, gentlemen,' Murdoch told them at his first staff meeting. 'I'm here to enforce peace, not wage war. But we'll have peace more easily if we tighten things up a bit.'

Because it was, still, a frontier, and a certain amount of laxness had spread through the garrison. This consisted of two battalions of Indian infantry, one of British – the Northamptonshires – and a battery of artillery. All were under the command of Colonel West, who was, in fact, what would once have been called a brigadier. He was a capable officer, with Great War experience, but Murdoch soon realized he did not have the greatest confidence in his sepoys. He telegraphed Birdwood and requested that one of the Indian battalions be replaced by a battalion of Gurkhas.

'Things will improve when the Westerns get here,' he promised the Colonel. 'But if you don't mind, I will keep Colonel Ramage and his men as an independent entity, I will need them to show the flag.'

He then persuaded Squadron-Leader Eccles to take him for a flight in one of the Ninaks. This was a relatively large aeroplane with an enormous wingspan. Murdoch was carefully strapped into his cockpit and given a flying helmet and goggles, and held his breath as the aircraft raced along the grass runway and then soared into the sky. Lee was green with envy as neither of them had ever flown before.

As instructed, Eccles flew north to the Khyber Pass itself, low enough so that Murdoch could look up at the mountains to either side, and then banked off to the west. It was utterly exhilarating, to be several hundred feet above the ground, watching the country unfolding beneath him, the rushing rivers, the valleys and sudden peaks, the little villages, the pasturage covered in sheep and goats . . . and the herdsmen looking up at the plane. Murdoch had his binoculars with him, and he could see that every man had his rifle slung on his back – and these were modern rifles, not the old long-barrelled jezails which his father had fought against.

After an hour Eccles pointed down at the river flowing beneath them, and Murdoch realized it was the Kurram, which came down through the Peiwar Kotal Pass eventually to join the Tochi River before they both flowed into the mighty Indus. There was little difference in the country, the size or architecture of the villages, or the composition of the herds down there, but Murdoch felt his pulse quicken – somewhere below him was the land of Shere Khan's Mahsuds.

He passed his notebook forward with the query, and Eccles nodded and turned his machine. They flew close to the mountain wall which marked the border, then banked again, and the Squadron Leader pointed to a sizeable town, guarded by a fort perched on a hill to the north. Murdoch saw a mosque, and several goodsized buildings clustered in the centre of the other, smaller houses. 'Mahrain', Eccles wrote, and passed the notebook back.

Shere Khan's capital, Murdoch thought, and wondered if Chand Bibi was down there, looking up at him. If she was alive, and in India, she would know who the new general officer commanding in the province was. He wondered what she would think about that.

He had been more or less warned not to go near her. But he was his own boss up here.

They flew on for another hour, and swooped low over the camp at Razmak. This *was* a camp, with neat rows of white tents stretching for almost a mile, although Murdoch could also make out the foundations for the permanent buildings which would, hopefully soon, be completed. The soldiers mustered to wave at the plane, a lone emblem of Britain's might, and then they returned to Peshawar for lunch.

'It certainly gives you a different concept of time and space,' Murdoch confessed as he stepped down and patted his wind-numbed cheeks. 'How far did we travel?'

'Three hundred miles,' Eccles said. 'It's about a hundred and fifty down to Razmak, as the crow flies. Or an areoplane. That's actually about the safe limit for this one. We're just about out of fuel.'

'I'm glad you didn't mention that earlier,' Murdoch said. 'One hundred and fifty miles, in two hours. How long do you think it would take this command to march that, Eccles?'

The Squadron Leader shrugged. 'As you saw, there are virtually no roads, once you get any distance away from Peshawar. I don't think you could allow more than three miles a day for a foot force.'

'One month, to reach Razmak?'

The airman grinned. 'That, sir, is if you weren't opposed.'

At the end of the week the regiment arrived. Murdoch took the salute, and it seemed the entire city turned out to admire the dragoons and listen to the march from *Aîda* played by the regimental band. Several prominent Indian citizens told Murdoch at the reception after the parade how they remembered the Westerns here in 1906, and how respected they were. Murdoch thought it a shame that Billy hadn't stayed with them for such a relative homecoming.

But they weren't there for show; as far as he was concerned they were a major component of the only reliable troops he had – and their commanding officer was the only true confidant he had, as well, apart from Manly-Smith.

206

'The first thing we have to do,' he told Peter Ramage, 'is get your fellows absolutely fighting fit. Then we are going to take a tour of the whole province. If we are here to overawe, then we are damned well going to overawe. It's certainly our best chance of keeping the peace.'

'Give me a fortnight,' Peter asked. The combination of the long sea voyage and the train ride up from the coast had left the men, and the horses, soft and lazy, but he set to work with a will, and Murdoch greatly enjoyed watching them riding, and shooting, themselves into top form – he noted that they were also watched by both the rest of the garrison and large numbers of civilians.

Their presence introduced an immediate complication, as Lee decided to throw a large garden party to introduce herself, Jennifer Manly-Smith, Linda Ramage and Coralie Rostron to the locals. 'Do I invite Mr Yeald?' she asked.

'Good Lord, no,' Murdoch said.

'Won't he be insulted?'

'He'll be relieved. I don't think the fact that he is Jennifer's father should be publicized.'

'Isn't that rather hypocritical? It's sure to become known.'

'Of course. But we will by then have established a pattern. There is nothing hypocritical about it. Jennifer has married above herself, and has to live the part. Yeald knows this, and accepts it.'

Lee accepted his decision, although she was clearly unhappy about it. But Jennifer fitted well into the social whirl of the cantonment.

A further complication arose when Murdoch announced he was taking the regiment on a grand parade through the entire province. This didn't actually happen until October, because the rains set in soon after the regiment arrived and the locals told him the hill country would be quite impassable until they stopped. But when they did, Lee was immediately interested.

'I am coming with you, I hope,' she said.

He considered. He hadn't really thought of it, and his initial reaction was rejection. But then he changed his

207

mind. He had to display to the Pathans at once the panoply of a famous warrior and the confidence of a man who had never been defeated; that was his sole reason for being in India. Besides, he had every intention of calling in on Shere Khan; it might be very necessary to have Lee along if Chand Bibi was still there. Chand Bibi, he reckoned, would be in her thirties now – but he didn't suppose she would be any the less compelling a woman. As for safety, he was travelling not as a lieutenant command-ing a patrol, but as a general accompanied by six hundred of the best fighting men in the world. As Chand Bibi would know. He did not consider safety came into it. On the other hand, he was deceiving Lee as to the real purpose of the parade.

'If you would really like to, I should love to have you along,' he agreed. 'It'll mean living rough. And maybe, seeing rough,' he added, having been reading various reports.

'I've been looking forward to that for years,' she said.

'There is also a fair chance that by the time we get back it'll be pretty chilly, according to the experts,'

'I'll have you to snuggle up to,' she reminded him.

Jennifer of course could not leave the baby for what might be a two-month jaunt, and Linda Ramage was not keen on the idea, so in fact Lee was the only woman to ride out of the cantonment with the regiment. In her khaki breeches and jacket and brown boots and with her khaki topee strapped beneath her chin, she looked very nearly as military as the troopers. She rode a mare named Calliope, while Murdoch was on his new horse, Brutus, who had replaced the ageing Mars.

There actually was a fairly good road south from Peshawar through the Kohat Pass to Kohat, and then south-west to the Bannu Pass and on to Tochi. The cavalry made a steady ten miles a day, and reached Tochi in a fortnight.

It was a fascinating journey. They rode north-west to begin with, up the Bazar Valley to inspect Jamrud Fort, only a few miles from Peshawar, and the real defence of the Khyber Pass, and then on to the pass itself.

'Can't we go through it?' Lee asked, gazing at the huge, overhanging cliffs above them.

'I'm afraid not,' Murdoch said. 'Just a few yards over there is Afghanistan.'

Lee had been reading her history. 'Well, what about Jellalabad? Isn't that where the sole survivor of the massacre rode into, in 1842? Let's go look at that.'

'Jellalabad is north of the pass,' Ramage told her. 'To go there really would be an invasion of Afghanistan.'

As it was they were attracting a great deal of attention from watchers posted in the hills above them, and Murdoch could make out the flashes of heliograph signals being dispatched north. He was quite happy about that; he wanted to let the Afghans know he was there as well.

But his purpose lay in Waziristan, and he turned the column south-west. Even after they left the vicinity of the famous pass, the land was never less that six hundred feet above sea level, and so the nights were cool enough for blankets, especially under canvas. The scenery was wild in the extreme, and always they were conscious of the looming mountains to either side; Murdoch, indeed, treated it as a reconnaissance in hostile territory and had a squadron out as advance guard, another as rearguard, and flankers. This thrilled Lee, who could imagine she was actually taking part in one of the campaigns she had only ever read about in books or the newspapers.

She was equally thrilled by the relics of British rule, various hill fortresses, either abandoned and crumbling into dust, or garrisoned by a dozen sepoys and a havildar or sergeant, just keeping an eye on the tribes. Murdoch rapidly concluded that these men were useless, as being assimilated into the society they were supposed to watch.

The Pathans themselves also turned out en masse to watch the famous regiment ride by, and the first time they camped by a village invitations were sent to Murdoch and Ramage, Lowndes and Rostron, Destry, Manly-Smith and Bryan to dine with the local khan. Murdoch caused a considerable sensation by informing the khan, on the first of these occasions, that he would be attended by his begum. Of course Lee was accepted, watched by whispering, veiled ladies from the back of the room in which they ate. Murdoch had explained that not all the food might be to her taste but that it all had to be eaten, and she coped splendidly with sheep's eyes and goats' testicles, although afterwards she confessed that she had nearly been sick on more than one occasion.

What was more important to Murdoch, at the next village, and all of them from there on, the invitations included the general's lady. Obviously the various Pathan tribes were in closer communication than an ordinary day's ride for his cavalry.

Lee found other reasons for nearly being sick. Whenever they camped near any Pathan village, they had to accept the risk of pilferage; this was carried out by naked young men, whose bodies were greased to enable them to slide silently through the night in their search for, preferably, rifles and cartridge belts. When shot at, and occasionally hit, they made distressing sights. Even more distressing, however, were the women the regiment occasionally came across. Like their men, the Pathan women were fair-skinned and handsome, but no women can be handsome with her nose cut off.

'They have been unfaithful to their husbands, memsahib,' Manilal, their head guide, explained. 'It is the recognized punishment for infidelity.'

'Gee,' Lee whispered to Murdoch. 'Remind me to think twice before jumping into bed with anyone but you, lover.'

Tochi was a large town, to reach which they had to ford the Kurram itself, along which one of the brigades of troops were encamped. Murdoch cast a long look up the hill country to the north, but there was no one who truly understood his interest there.

In Tochi they were welcomed and invited to make use of apartments in the town itself, but Murdoch preferred to camp with the garrison by the river, although he and his officers and the colonel in command, Gwyn Evan-Jones, and of course Lee, accepted the invitation of the khan to dine and to attend an entertainment. Lee squeezed Murdoch's hand as the bare-breasted nautch girls postured in front of them, and as she took in the richness of the drapes and carpets, and conversed with the khan, who spoke excellent English.

'I had no idea soldiering could be so much fun,' she whispered to Murdoch.

Murdoch managed to have a few words with the khan himself. 'You have Mahsuds to the south of you,' he remarked.

'That is so, General,' the khan agreed.

'How are your relations with them?'

'Excellent, General. We are all good friends up here.'

'I'm glad to hear it. But you have also Mahsuds to the north.'

'Ah. Terrible people. Their khan is a bandit. But this is well known.'

'Do you have much trouble with them?'

'No no. Shere Khan is an old man now. He has a white beard. All he wishes is to live in peace.'

From Tochi it was necessary to climb some four thousand feet, or five thousand above sea level, to reach Razmak. Now for the first time the going grew really rough, and the nights truly cold. Although the distance was only about twenty-five miles, it took them a week, most of the time on foot leading their horses.

'Gee, I'd hate to have to do this and fight as well,' Lee remarked, panting at Murdoch's side.

'You are echoing the thought of every man in the regiment,' Murdoch assured her.

But at Razmak they were made welcome, with a roaring fire to keep out the chill, and a magnificent lamb korma to warm their stomachs.

'It has all really gone off rather well,' Colonel Cormack told Murdoch. 'There was that spot of bother eighteen months ago, but really the Mahsuds seem to have learned their lesson.'

211

'Including Shere Khan's bunch,' Murdoch remarked.

'Even them. In fact, they have been the quietest of the lot, recently.'

'Don't tell me. Shere Khan is now an old man with a white beard.'

'Well, yes, sir, that is a fairly accurate description. I have no doubt the old adrenaline still flows from time to time, and will be doing so now, when he hears the Royal Westerns are in the area, but that son of his, Abdul, is a sensible fellow and has no wish to take on machine-guns and bombing aircraft. I think we have these people sorted out.'

Murdoch felt he was being unduly sanguine, especially after inspecting the garrison. The British battalion, the Cheshires, was everything he could have wanted, and there was also a battalion of the famous Guides, the regiment raised by Lawrence in the previous century, sepoys who had time and again proved their worth in battle. The other four battalions were Pathans. They looked the born soldiers they were, in their smart turbans and puttees . . . but they were the brothers and sons and cousins of the people they were meant to overawe.

Murdoch would have left Lee in Razmak while he made the last part of the journey south, but she wanted to come along, and so they proceeded to the fortress at Wana. This was a further thirty miles, and was a fairly easy journey there, as it was downhill, but it would involve the climb back up.

All was well with the Wana garrison, and the return journey was commenced. They regained Razmak a week later in a blizzard, as icy winds swept down from the mountains of Afghanistan.

'Good idea to remain here over Christmas, sir,' Cormack suggested. 'It's going to be a bitter journey back.'

'It's a journey I may have to make, some time, Colonel, in these very conditions,' Murdoch told him. 'So I'd better get used to it.'

The weather improved after a couple of days and they set off again, descending to Tochi. 'I think,' Murdoch told Ramage, 'that instead of heading straight back to Kohat, we'll follow the border round a bit.'

'You want to take a look at the other Mahsuds,' Ramage said.

'Why, yes, so I do. They're old enemies of the Westerns.'

'You don't think we might stir things up?'

'I don't see why we should. They're supposed to be the most peaceful of the hill tribes, at this moment. But if our presence is going to stir things up, then the sooner we find out about it the better, as we're going to be here for some time.' But he didn't intend to take any risks. He got Sergeant Denning to raise Peshawar on the radio, and tell Squadron Leader Eccles that six of his bombers were to make a run over the Kurram Valley one week hence at fifteen minutes past noon. But what he had seen had changed his mind about taking Lee into the lair of Chand Bibi.

'We're going to take a swing through some very rough country,' he told Lee, 'and the weather isn't getting any better. I propose to detach a troop to return direct to Peshawar and would be very happy if you'd accompany them.'

'Why are you detaching a troop?' she asked.

'Well . . . I . . .'

'To escort me. For heaven's sake, Murdoch. I'm not afraid of a little cold. I used to go skiing in Vermont every winter as a girl.' She peered at him. 'Or do you think there's going to be trouble?'

'Well, since you ask, I'm intending to pay a visit on Shere Khan. He's supposed to be old and peaceful, nowadays, but less than twenty years ago he was a bitter enemy of the Westerns.'

'This I have got to see,' she told him. 'Forget about the troop going back to Peshawar. If they do, they can go without me.'

Once again he accepted her decision, actually with some relief. It was a march of about thirty miles to the Mahsud town, but it was fairly easy country compared with what they had just left. Their only problem lay in fording the Kurram, which had swollen with the snow of the previous week; they all got thoroughly wet.

213

By now their progress was being overseen by watchers in the hills, as they could tell easily enough by the heliograph signals being exchanged. On the fifth day the advance guard of Lieutenant Winton sent back word that Mahrain was in sight. Murdoch himself rode forward to inspect the area, and chose to camp on a wide pasture about half a mile to the east of the walls. The regiment came up, and the usual precautions were taken; a perimeter was set up and guarded by the Lewis guns, the horses were tethered in long, straight lines, the tents were pitched and sentries posted.

All of this was watched by an interested crowd of men and boys. It was now fairly late in the afternoon, and the mountains were lost behind the sweeping clouds. 'Do you think we'll have an invite, here?' Lee asked.

'I'm damn sure we will,' Murdoch said.

They had just sat down to supper when the messengers arrived, bowing low when Murdoch and Lee left the command tent to meet them.

'Great General,' their leader said. 'My master, the mighty Shere Khan, sends to inquire the purpose of this invasion of his lands.'

'As your master well knows,' Murdoch told him, 'I am the new commander-in-chief of the British army in the North West Frontier Province. I am thus engaged in inspecting the country which is my responsibility.'

The man bowed again. Clearly he had known what the answer was going to be. 'Then my master, the mighty Shere Khan, invites the great English general, and his officers . . .' his gaze flickered over Lee, 'and his lady, to eat with him tomorrow, at the hour of noon.'

'Tell your master we shall be pleased to do so,' Murdoch said.

'I'm quite nervous,' Lee confessed. 'Is he really as formidable as people say?'

'I have no idea,' Murdoch said. 'I have never met him.'

'But the regiment fought against him, in the old days.'

'Yes,' Murdoch said. 'And gave him a damned good thrashing. Let's hope he, and his family, remember that.'

There were eight of them in the party that rode up the shallow hill to the town the following morning, accompanied by Sergeant Matheson and twelve troopers. Lee had wondered if she should wear the one dress she had brought with her, but Murdoch preferred her to remain in khaki. They were welcomed at the gate by the same man who had delivered the invitation, and inside the wall, where there was a large crowd gathered, there was also a guard of honour of some hundred men, very smart in short red jackets and white turbans and breeches, and armed with Lee-Enfield rifles, waiting to be inspected. There had been similar guards of honour in several other places where they had stopped, and of course in the British cantonments, but these were about the smartest of the lot.

'My army,' said their commander, and saluted Murdoch with his sword. 'You will see, General Mackinder, that it is but a fraction the size of yours. I am Abdul Hussein ibn Shere ibn Ali ibn Muhammad. I am the son of the khan.'

He was about forty years old, tall and strongly built, like his sister, and handsome too, beneath the full beard.

'I have heard much about you,' Murdoch said, 'and am pleased to make your acquaintance.' He shook hands, introduced Lee and his officers.

'You travel in much state,' Abdul Hussein observed, gazing at Lee.

'I am ruler of North West India,' Murdoch reminded him.

They left their horses with the troopers and walked up a narrow, winding street of steps to reach the palace, which was situated in the central square Murdoch had observed from the air, opposite the mosque. The town was less impressive from the ground, the houses being old and in many cases dilapidated, and the streets dirty. People gathered to either side to stare at the white officers and, even more, at the white woman. 'I would say you are the first they have ever seen,' Murdoch remarked.

'That is so, General Mackinder,' Abdul Hussein agreed. 'The very first. But perhaps, as your influence spreads, Lady Mackinder will not be the last.'

215

However decrepit the town as a whole, the palace remained a place of splendour. They entered through a white marble portico, surrounded by bowing servants and nautch girls, walked by a large pool of translucent water, and mounted a flight of broad steps. At the top a curtain was held for them by two guards in red tunics and they found themselves in a splendid reception chamber where the marble floors, now black, were covered with priceless rugs. Here there were gathered several Mahsud chieftains, who bowed to the British party. At the far end of the hall there was another short flight of steps, and at the top sat Shere Khan. He rose as Murdoch approached, still tall and well built, richly dressed, but with the lower part of his face and neck concealed by a full white beard.

He held out both his hands. 'General Mackinder,' he said. 'Many years ago, thirty years ago, I fought against your father.'

'I know,' Murdoch said.

'He died in these hills, of fever.'

'Yes,' Murdoch said.

'And you have come to take his place. You, an even greater warrior than your father. I have heard much about you, General Mackinder.'

'Indeed, your excellency? From what source?'

Shere Khan smiled. 'I have many sources, General. And this is your charming wife?' He bowed over Lee's hand. 'You are blessed with great good fortune, General. As am I, that you have come to visit me, in peace. With so many men.'

'My escort,' Murdoch told him.

'The Royal Western Dragoon Guards. Yes, I remember them well. My people think of them as their enemies, but I have reassured them that you have come in peace. Otherwise my warriors would have entered the town, and caused a disturbance.'

Lee caught her breath, although Shere Khan continued to smile.

But Murdoch also continued to smile. The time was twelve fourteen. 'That would have been unwise, your

216

excellency,' he said. 'Who knows, it might have caused the destruction of your city.'

Shere Khan's nostrils flared. 'You are so bold, with six hundred men, General?'

'My strength is limitless,' Murdoch told him, and listened to the drone of the aeroplane engines.

Several of the Mahsuds ran outside into the courtyard to stare at the six bombers, flying low over the town, waggling their wings at the British camp before swinging away to the south and east.

'Those too, are part of my escort,' Murdoch told Shere Khan.

'You sure scored off him,' Lee confessed when they regained the camp. 'I didn't know you'd arranged for the planes.'

'It pays to surprise.'

'Even me? I really had the willies there for a moment. That man was threatening you.'

'Yes. He's not quite as benevolent as he appears. Still, now we know where we stand.' Except that he didn't, personally. No women had appeared at the meal, save for the serving girls. But next morning, as the dragoons were breaking camp and preparing to resume their march, the major-domo again appeared.

'My master bids you farewell, Great General,' he said, 'and utters a prayer to Allah that the British and the Mahsuds may always remain in peace.'

'Tell your master that I reciprocate his desire,' Murdoch said.

'I am also asked to give you this, Great General.'

It was a single sheet of folded paper. Murdoch felt his pulse quicken as he took it; almost, he thought, he could smell her perfume.

'Thank you,' he said, and opened it.

Chand Bibi had written:

You come in glory, Murdoch Mackinder. As I always knew you would. And you are accompanied by your lovely wife. You have

217

men, and machine-guns, and bombing planes. We have nothing but our wits and our courage. But you are in our country now, my Murdoch. And you are my enemy, and the enemy of my people, now and for all eternity. I will yet see you again. On my terms.

9

The North West Frontier, 1925–29

Murdoch showed Ramage the note; Peter did not know what had actually happened in the tent between Murdoch and Chand Bibi in 1916, but he knew the crimes of which she had been accused by Morton.

'God damn,' the colonel said. 'So we know she's there. What are you going to do about it?'

'There is damn all I can do about it,' Murdoch said. 'Even if I arrested her, there is no one left able to give evidence against her. And she is no more guilty than any member of her tribe. But at least we know where we stand. We know that Shere Khan hates us as much as he ever did. We know that his people would love to go to war against us. So we are just going to wait and see, Peter. Every day we are here is going to make them just a little more edgy. And the moment they step out of line . . .'

'You are going to wipe them off the face of the earth. You'd really like a war to begin up here,' Peter said.

'Wouldn't you? If Johnnie Morton was right about what those savages did to our people?'

'If he was right,' Ramage pointed out.

'We know it happened, Peter. Bodies were found. Too horribly cut up for anything but immediate burial.'

'I know that, Murdoch. And I would like to take it out of those blighters, and their beastly women, as much as anyone. But for God's sake . . . let them make the first move.'

'I shall,' Murdoch promised. 'Believe me.'

He was confident that Shere Khan's Mahsuds would make the first move, eventually, out of sheer frustration. Especially after he replied to Chand Bibi's letter, giving his note to one of the Mahsud shepherds they encountered as they rode out of the valley of the Kurram. He wrote: 'As you say, Chand Bibi, I have come to you, and you know my purpose. It is to destroy you, and all those people who are guilty of the murder of my soldiers. It is but a matter of waiting, until the time is ripe.'

He did not sign his letter either, but she would know who it was from.

'There is something going on,' Lee remarked as they walked their horses through the valley towards the Kohat Pass. 'Between you and that Shere Khan character.'

'We hate each other's guts, if that's what you mean.' Murdoch said.

'But he can't do anything about it. And you . . . you're trying to make him do something about it, aren't you, Murdoch?'

'Let's say I'm trying to anticipate the future,' Murdoch told her. 'That is a good soldiering principle. It's nothing for you to worry your head about.'

But he was disappointed. He kept the garrison at Peshawar virtually under arms well into 1925, as well as those at Razmak and Tochi and Wana, and had his aircraft make regular patrols over Waziristan, but, perhaps because of this, the North West Frontier remained quieter than anyone could remember. Later that year General Birdwood left, and was replaced by Bill Ironside. Ironside was only a year older than Murdoch; they had been at Sandhurst together. Now he came up to Peshawar to inspect the troops and greet his old friend; they had not seen each other for some years, but Murdoch knew Ironside had had both a busy and successful war, in which he had commanded troops in the Middle East and on the western front, as well as in northern Russia following the collapse of the tsarist government.

'Murdoch!' The two men clasped hands at the railway station. 'I can't tell you how pleased everyone is with the situation here. Whitehall is wondering why the War Office didn't send you out in 1919.'

Murdoch grinned. 'It's not for want of trying.'

'Oh, we hear all about it. Riding with the Westerns the length and breadth of the country. Having your bombers make fly-pasts over likely trouble spots. It's not everybody's cup of tea, of course. You're probably lucky the Socialists only stayed in power a year, or they'd have had you back out of here. But right now you're Stanley Baldwin's blue-eyed boy. I think you always were Churchill's.'

Churchill was now Chancellor of the Exchequer in the recently elected Conservative Government.

'We happen to see eye to eye on most things, that's all,' Murdoch confessed. 'You remember Lee?'

They had met, briefly, before the war. Lee was all smiles. She was enjoying life in Peshawar more than she ever had before. When she had first married Murdoch she had, as an American, found both the structure of army society, and the structure of Edwardian imperialistic society, a little hard to take. Reserve had changed to admiration during the Great War, and here in India, especially with Murdoch in a position of such authority, she had discovered the true pleasures of imperialism. And of conservatism. As wife of the general officer commanding, she was able to set fashion, and she had no intention of being caught up in the bobbed hair and short skirts which were becoming prevalent in both England and America. She had always worn her hair short when very long hair had been in fashion. Now, perversely, she had grown it in her early forties, although she wore it up except when in bed. Just as she kept her hems well below the knee, and by example encouraged her officers' wives to do the same.

But they were a happy community. The initial stiffness had passed off very rapidly, and however much Lee enjoyed her retinue of servants, and the deference paid her by all and sundry, even by Lieutenant-General Ironside – he might be Murdoch's superior but he had not been knighted – she could yet let her hair down, and by her own happiness inspire it in those around her.

She was also finding in India an inexhaustible treasure house of things to do and places to visit. Once the winter

221

was over she persuaded Murdoch to take time off occasionally. They went back to Amritsar properly to explore the Sikh holy city, and then she talked him into a long trip down to Quetta in Northern Baluchistan.

Quetta was actually only two hundred miles further south-west than Wana but it was an impossible journey to make on foot or by horse, as the way was barred by the mountains of Zhob. However, Murdoch himself was keen to visit an area so rich in British military history, and having ascertained that the garrison in Quetta had laid down an airstrip, he used one of the Ninaks, with Lee and himself crushed into the rear cockpit.

It was a tremendous flight, with mountains higher than ten thousand feet rising to either side, and Quetta itself was all they had hoped. Lying where it was, between the Bolan and Khojak passes, Quetta had always been of supreme military importance. What interested Murdoch was that just north of it, in Afghanistan beyond the Khojak Pass, were both Maiwand and Kandahar. Maiwand was where in July 1880 a British army in the field had been virtually annihilated, and Kandahar was where Field Marshal Lord Roberts had marched his army of ten thousand men, over three hundred miles from Kabul, across the mountains, in twenty-two days, to avenge that defeat. It had been 'Bobs's' greatest military feat, and had culminated in the crushing victory of Kandahar which ended the Second Afghan War. Murdoch's father, as a subaltern, had been on that march.

'We simply have to get into Afghanistan, one day,' Lee said. 'I know, let's invade.'

Ironside was impressed with what he saw of Murdoch's control of the North West Frontier Province, and so was his successor when he too was removed for other duties after a year. Ironside was clearly one of the men of the future, in the eyes of the War Office. Sir Charles Harington, who replaced him, was a man of the past. His principal claim to fame was of having averted war between Great Britain and the resurgent Turkey in 1921, by his firmness at Constantinople when in command of a handful of troops. He was far senior to either Ironside or Murdoch, and was aware that this would be his last important military posting before the pre-retirement round of colonial governorships began.

Like his predecessor he toured the North West Province, by air, and seemed pleased with what he found. Murdoch had by now become thoroughly familiar with all the aspects of his command, and had commenced implementing the various ideas which had come to him during *his* tour of inspection: he had had airstrips laid out at Tochi, Razmak and Wana, and fuel dumps installed, to give his air force vastly increased mobility, and he had also made the camps, wherever possible, into permanent fortifications.

'You certainly seem to have these fellows licked into shape, Mackinder,' Harington said. 'I'd like you to take another tour of duty, if you will.'

It had never occurred to Murdoch not to take another, but he was somewhat surprised to discover that he was at the end of his first three-year tour of duty. If he felt reasonably satisfied at what he had achieved, it would be intensely galling to leave and immediately have the rising he felt was simmering under the surface explode the moment his train pulled out of the station. Besides, he was enjoying the life, the independence, the totality of command. He had now had two of the native Indian regiments replaced with Gurkha battalions, and felt he had a really powerful little army under his orders . . . and one which was devoted to him as well.

As for the Mahsuds, it seemed obvious that they were not going to try conclusions after all. No doubt the days of death and glory on the frontier were gone, for ever. Equally, no doubt, he had demonstrated that too conclusively on his visit to them back in 1924. Shere Khan had understood that his tribesmen could not take on bombers, at least where they could not find shelter across the border in Afghanistan. No doubt even Chand Bibi had had to understand that. He had not heard from her for well over two years. He did not expect ever to hear from her again.

And he had not seen her for ten years. He wondered if she was still as beautiful.

But it had to be a joint decision. 'Harington has invited me to take another tour of duty,' he told Lee after the Commander-in-Chief had left. 'Think you can stand another three years up here?'

'Well, I wasn't planning to move, in a hurry,' she said. 'I've only just got the garden licked into shape. And there's a whole lot more of India I want to see. Anyway, Ian is coming out to join the regiment here, isn't he?'

'Yes,' Murdoch said.

'You're not bothered about that, are you?'

'No, I'm not. Peter Ramage knows the score. Ian will be treated as any other subaltern, no better and no worse. But I'd like you to remember that as well.'

She blew him a kiss. 'Surely I can have him to tea, now and then.'

There was also Manly-Smith to consider. 'I imagine you're ready to return to active duty,' Murdoch said, having told him his plans.

'With the regiment? Are they being moved?'

'I don't think so. Starting this year one squadron is going to be returned to England each year for a year, for training and replacements, before coming back out here. So we'll be down slightly on our establishments. But I think they are due to remain here for another tour, as well. They're doing too good a job.'

'Then I'll be with them if I remain with you.'

'That's true. You'd probably get promotion quicker if you were with them, though.'

'I'm happy the way things are,' Ralph said.

He was indeed. Despite his reassuring words to Lee, Murdoch had been a little worried as to the relationship between Ralph and his father-in-law, but Ralph and the sergeant-major had struck up a perfect friendship, which never transcended the difference in their stations and yet permitted Bert Yeald to visit his daughter once a week, have a cup of tea, and play with the grandchildren. Ralph had in fact taken to life on the frontier as if he had been born to it, and his unceasing energy had led him into some remarkable hobbies. The most surprising, and the most dangerous, in Murdoch's eyes, was jumping from one of the Ninaks by parachute. The airmen had of course been trained to it, but why anyone should want to do it for pleasure defeated Murdoch. He was, however, delighted to find his ADC such a continuing source of interest and support.

So was Jennifer, who had again become a mother. But Murdoch was determined to do something about Ralph, and had him promoted major while the Mackinders were home on long leave; Ralph remained in Peshawar to handle the day-to-day business of the command – he and Jennifer and the children would take their long leave after Murdoch and Lee returned.

It was a magnificent trip. They took their time, as it was their time, and did all the things they hadn't been able to do on the voyage out. At Port Said they left the ship to spend a week in Cairo, and Lee had her long-awaited look at the pyramids. Then from Alexandria they took a ship to Piraeus, and spent a week in Athens so that she could look at the Acropolis.

Then they voyaged to Naples, and inspected the ruins of Pompeii before going up to Venice, where they joined the Orient Express for the trip to Paris and then Folkestone.

It had all been timed to get them to Sandhurst in time for Ian's passing out parade.

'I'm so proud,' Lee said. 'I can just imagine you standing there . . . how long ago was it?'

'Twenty-eight years, by God,' Murdoch said.

'I bet you were just as handsome, too.'

Fergus had a year to go. 'But I'm coming out to India too,' he announced.

'I'm not sure India will be able to stand it,' Murdoch said.

Ian was more serious. 'You've no objections, I hope, Dad,' he said when they had a chance to be alone.

'I'm delighted. So, I can tell you, is Peter Ramage.'

'Is there any chance of action?'

'None whatsoever. The natives are strictly non-revolting.'

'Oh. Still . . .' He brightened. 'I suppose if there's no chance of action on the North West Frontier, then there's no chance of action anywhere in the world, what with all these pacts outlawing war . . .'

'And let's hope they make them all stick,' Murdoch said. 'You don't want to get that nice new uniform all messed up.'

They gazed at each other, and grinned. They understood one another perfectly. Murdoch could remember how when he had been a boy his sole dream had been to serve in the regiment under his father. It had never happened. Father had died while he was still at Wellington. But it would happen to his sons. All three of them.

They all went down to Broad Acres together, picking up Helen and Harry as well. Helen was fifteen, and a proper beauty. Harry was twelve, and had just completed his first term at Wellington. 'I hate it,' he confided.

'Well, we all hate our first years,' Murdoch told him.

But he felt Harry was actually rather unhappy.

'I don't blame him,' Lee said. 'I'd hate to be shut up most of the year with several hundred other boys. I don't suppose you'd consider . . .' she pinched her lip.

'He'll grow out of it,' Murdoch promised her. 'Mustn't baby the baby.'

'I hope you're right,' she said.

Broad Acres was exactly as they remembered it. As Murdoch had always remembered it, in fact. Nothing would ever change Broad Acres. But nothing could stop people changing, and animals. 'Had to put Buccaneer down,' Philippa confessed. 'The poor chap could hardly stand.'

He was buried in the field behind the house, and she had erected a monument. Murdoch stood there for some time. Perhaps because he was now serving in India he could remember so vividly the year in Somaliland, the cavalry charge which had really made his reputation. Buccaneer had carried him on that charge.

There were other looming changes as well. Mother was now seventy-two, and more frail than she should have been.

'It's good to have you back, Murdoch,' she said. 'When are you coming home for good?'

'Three years,' he said.

'That long?'

He discussed the matter with Rosemary, at her London flat; Geoffrey Phillips had left the army with the rank of colonel, and had done as he had always intended and entered politics as a Conservative MP. Rosemary had always been much more sensible than Philippa.

'Of course mother hates to think of you being away for all those years,' she said. 'But she should be used to it. And you have your life to live, your way to make, Murdoch. Anyway, she's a lot tougher than she looks. She'll be here when you get back.'

While in London he lunched with Churchill, as was now becoming quite a habit. His friend seemed to have achieved the pinnacle of his career in being Chancellor of the Exchequer, as he recognized. 'They'll never have me leader of the Party,' he said. 'I'm too radical, too outspoken for them. Maybe I'm too imperialistic for this mundane age. Still, I've got us back on the Gold Standard. I'll rest on that. Now tell me about India.'

'It's all very quiet out there. You must have had more excitement here last year in the General Strike.'

'You think so? What about this damn fool commission?'

The commission had been set up by Parliament the previous year to inquire into every aspect of Indian political life.

'They don't seem to be accomplishing much,' Murdoch said. 'Mainly because the Indian leaders won't talk to them.'

'I think it's the thin edge of the wedge,' Churchill growled. 'I voted against it, but was overruled. India needs to be governed, by us. Start giving them self-government and God knows what will happen. Have you met Wood?'

Edward Wood, Lord Irwin, had replaced Reading as Viceroy.

'Why, yes,' Murdoch said. 'I had lunch with him in

227

Delhi on my way to Bombay. Seems a very decent sort of chap.'

'He is. And very good at his job, too. He'll make a top-class viceroy, if the politicians let him. But they probably won't. So he's wasting his time. So are you, Murdoch. You should come home. Then we could see about making you CIGS. That would cause a stir. All the world would assume we were about to go to war. That mightn't be a bad thing.'

Murdoch raised his eyebrows. 'Problems?'

'The usual rubbish. We're all friends with the Germans now, you know. They even belong to the League of Nations.'

'Surely that's a good thing. It has to be better to talk than shoot. And haven't they signed the Locarno Treaty guaranteeing perpetual friendship with France?'

'Oh, certainly. All these pacts are very fine, as long as they are adhered to and not made a wordy cover for something else. Did you ever read *Mein Kampf*?'

'I've never even heard of it.'

'It's that book your German friend Hitler was writing when you visited him in prison.'

'Good Lord! You mean he got it published?'

'Oh, indeed.'

'And is it as rabid as it seemed it might be?'

'I would say it is the most rabid thing I have ever read. Were he the leader of a sovereign country one would have to think about it very seriously. I'm not sure he shouldn't be locked up, anyway. For all our sakes. But they don't do that sort of thing in Germany, nowadays.'

'So what is he doing now, if he isn't locked up?'

'What he said he was going to do. Running a political party, which is preaching hate and damnation. He even has a few seats in the Reichstag.'

'Good heavens,' Murdoch commented. 'And no one is doing anything about it?'

'Well, how can they? His people have been legally elected. As I say, only a few. But it is significant that the book has been quite a success. So there must be a lot of Germans who enjoy reading it. Also, there can be no doubt that the Germans, and I'm talking about the army rather than the Nazis, are doing a good deal of secret re-arming. There is evidence of it everywhere. Gliding clubs to train pilots, regiments in which every private is an officer, that sort of thing.'

'I saw something of it when I was there. Why don't we put a stop to it?'

'Put a stop to it? My dear fellow, there are too many people in this country saying: "Poor Germans, why *shouldn't* they have an army?" Too many people in the Government, too. Do you know we're pulling out our occupation forces in a couple of years?'

'We were supposed to stay twenty, weren't we?'

'At least. But now everyone thinks it's unfair on the Germans. I don't agree with the decision, and I've said so. Another reason for not being entirely popular with my Cabinet colleagues. Then there's trouble brewing in the Far East as well. The Japanese are getting increasingly aggressive towards China. Oh, there are a good many reasons why we could use a real fighting man as CIGS. And if there's nothing happening in India, well, why stay there?'

'I like it there,' Murdoch said. 'I'll come home when my second tour is up in 1930. You can make me CIGS then.' He grinned. 'If anything crops up before then, you can always send for me.'

Reger, he thought, must be having the time of his life. And young Paul?

'Holy Smoke!' Lee commented, opening her mail just the day before they were due to depart again. 'It's from Harry.'

'Brother, or son?'

'One day, when he takes up writing letters, it could be from son,' Lee said sadly. 'He's gone and got married.'

'Brother, or son?'

'Oh, you . . . would you believe it? How old is he, for God's sake? Heck, I'm forty-one . . . he has to be in his mid-fifties.'

'How come we didn't hear about this before?'

'Because he's eloped! With another man's wife, would

229

you believe it? Ye gods and little fishes. If Ma and Pa were alive they'd be turning in their graves.'

'If they were alive they'd almost certainly be doing something else,' Murdoch pointed out. 'What you mean is, they *are* turning in their graves. But let me get this straight: your brother has eloped with a married woman? Then how can he have married her?'

'Oh, she's divorced now. They went down to Reno. I wondered why we hadn't heard from him for a while. He's been carrying on with this . . . this . . .'

'Scarlet woman,' Murdoch suggested.

'Scarlet woman. Then her husband found out, and all hell let loose. So now he's married her.' Her cheeks were pink with indignation.

'Now let's be reasonable about this,' Murdoch said. 'How old is this woman?'

'Ah . . .' Lee re-read the letter. 'Thirty-two.'

'And Harry is fifty. It's just possible the boot is on the other foot, and this dirty old man of a brother of yours has invaded the marital nest and seduced an innocent matron.'

She raised her head to gaze at him with her mouth open.

He grinned at her. 'And good luck to him. But I do think we should withhold judgement until we meet the girl.'

'You may do that sooner than you think. He says he wants to bring Veronica . . .'

'Is that her name? Veronica?'

'Yes. Bit of a mouthful, isn't it? And she . . .' she handed Murdoch a snapshot.

'She's a bit of an armful too,' he agreed, gazing at a decidedly statuesque blonde young woman, who was at least six inches taller than Harry, standing beside her.

'Her hair is dyed, I'm sure,' Lee remarked bitchily.

Murdoch didn't think that would have mattered, to Harry. Not unless her bust was padded as well.

'Murdoch, he wants to bring her to visit. So he wants to know whether we are going to be here for the foreseeable future or in India.'

'Tell him India.'

'Do we really want Veronica dropping in on Peshawar?'

'Peshawar isn't a place you can "drop in" on.'

'That's what's worrying me. She could be there for months.'

'Think of all the things you'll be able to show her,' Murdoch pointed out. 'In the meantime, do cable Harry congratulations on becoming a husband.'

The trip back out to Bombay, however familiar it was now becoming, was rendered the more enjoyable because of the presence of Ian. He was naturally excited to be tracing the steps taken so often by his father and grandfather, just as he was in a perpetual heaven at the thought of joining the regiment and wearing that famous uniform – even if it was only khaki on service nowadays. Murdoch indeed had difficulty in persuading him not to wear uniform on board ship. 'It's a matter of convenience,' he explained. 'Once you put that on, you have to start calling me "sir" and all sorts of things like that. In mufti, we're father and son. Remember that.'

The journey north from Bombay was made twice as long as usual, and twice as uncomfortable, by a strike of railway workers. It took them nearly two weeks to reach Delhi, and while Lee enjoyed herself thoroughly, exploring each of the towns at which they were forced to wait for a train, both her menfolk chafed at the delays when they wanted to be on station.

'The whole bloody country seems to be on strike,' Harington said when they finally made the capital. 'It's all an offshoot of that damned stupid commission. The textile workers are out, as you saw one can never tell when the railway is going to be working or not . . . the people have been properly stirred up.'

'Are you expecting trouble?'

'No, I'm not, to be frank. Nothing the police can't handle. At least down here.'

'But on the frontier?'

'I'm damn glad you're back, Murdoch. Oh, this commission thing has had little effect up there. I don't think the Pathans want to be governed by Indians any more than they

231

enjoy being governed by us. But there are some disquieting reports coming out of Peshawar.'

Murdoch frowned. 'What kind of rumours?'

'That there are mullahs trying to stir up the tribes. I suppose we have to accept that this thing happens every few years. And it's a compliment to you that the agitators waited until you were out of the way.'

'What tribes, sir?'

'The Mahsuds. They were the ones who caused the trouble in twenty-three, you remember. However, nothing actually seems to have happened as yet. And then there is this talk of trouble in Afghanistan.'

'Afghanistan?'

'Yes. The rumour there is that all is not well with Amanullah's government. Seems there could be financial problems. As well as communist agitation. It may all be a storm in a teacup, but I'll be damned glad to have you back up there, and to let any hotheads across the border know that you're back.'

'So Shere Khan, or Chand Bibi, is making a move at last,' Murdoch commented to Peter Ramage when he regained Peshawar. 'I assume I am correct in supposing it is those Mahsuds that have been preaching jihad?'

'Absolutely correct. But they haven't had any joy, so far. No one seems to want to budge.'

'They have more sense. I must say, though, this rather blows a hole in my estimation that it is me they're after. Waiting until I've left, I mean.'

'Ah, but they knew you were coming back.'

'Eh?'

'Well, everyone in the province knew that. You know how impossible it is to keep a secret in this place. But in fact the Mahsud mullahs have been using this as a prong, telling the other tribes that you have been sent here to cause their destruction, and that you will be coming back, and that this time you will act against them, if they do not act first.'

'I see,' Murdoch said thoughtfully.

'As I say, they haven't had any joy,' Peter went on. 'And

232

West has kept the garrison, all the garrisons, in a state of readiness. But really, it seems to me that Shere Khan has shown his hand, Murdoch. Why don't we move in there and arrest him and his whole family? We may not be able to hang them, but we could certainly lock them up.'

'On what charge?'

'Well, incitement . . .'

'There isn't a khan in Northern India would accept responsibility for what his mullahs say or do. And there isn't a court would attempt to force him to. As you say, he's showing his hand, but he's going to have to show it much more clearly than this before we can move against him. He will. Or she will. And on the first attack on a police or military post, we move.'

'I am looking forward to that,' Peter said. 'So are the men. They thought they were coming here to fight. And all they've done is parade up and down the country.'

'So keep your fingers crossed. Now what's all this about Afghanistan? It does occur to me that Shere Khan may be hoping for some support from there, or may even be in touch with the dissidents in Kabul.'

'There are rumours of meetings and underground societies being broken up by police. But the Afghans coming through the Khyber seem happy enough. And what's happening up there doesn't seem to be having any effect on the province. Even cattle raiding has died down these past couple of months.'

'Which could mean something, or it could not. Well, I suppose we'll just have to wait and watch, just as long as too many Afghans don't come through the pass at the same time. What do you think of Ian?'

Ramage grinned. 'Chip off the old block.'

'I'm not sure you mean that as a compliment. You know there's another one coming out next year, if there's a vacancy.'

'Oh, there'll be a vacancy. Roberts has had enough. He'll stay until the first squadron goes home. But he won't be coming back.'

'Had enough?'

Ramage grinned. 'The old story, Murdoch. Got involved with a bint and fell in love with her. I had to play the old Dutch uncle, and he saw my point of view, but he's not happy any more and I would say he's right to quit. How was England?'

'Fine up to June, then it started to rain. It could have been the monsoon. When are you due for leave?'

'Well, we all are, right now. But I'm letting Destry and B Squadron have first crack. As I said, Roberts – he commands B Troop – is an urgent case.'

'Linda happy with that?'

'Linda's happy,' Ramage said.

She certainly appeared to be, was even prettier than when she had been a girl, and as vivacious as ever. Yet Murdoch wondered why she and Peter had never had children, and if their domestic life was as blissful as it appeared. It was odd how, although he and Ramage had now been close friends for more than twenty years, they had never been intimates. The reason, he was sure, was that Ramage and Tommy Knox, the two subalterns who had accompanied him to Somaliland, *had* been close friends – and Ramage had had to watch while Murdoch had killed Knox, to save him from further torture at the hands of the Somali women. That deed had haunted him throughout his life. It had clearly haunted Ramage too. Neither of them doubted it had had to be done. But Murdoch had been the man to do it, and Peter had been left always unsure when that streak of ruthless determination which lurked in Murdoch's character was going to surface again.

But Murdoch genuinely liked the man, and worried for him. 'How do you think Linda and Peter are doing?' he asked Lee, who saw a lot more of Linda than he did.

'Funny you should ask,' Lee said. 'There are, well . . . one or two problems, maybe. I didn't expect you to notice.'

'I have noticed she's never had a child. Don't they ever have sex together?'

'Of course they do. But . . . I guess Linda isn't very keen on, well . . . you know what I mean.'

'Do I? All my women have been very keen. On everything.'

234

'So you're just lucky, Murdoch.'

'Anyway, surely you don't have to have "everything" to conceive.'

'Of course you don't. But I'm sure it helps if you really are enjoying what you're doing. And you have to enjoy it enough to do it regularly. It's a shame about Linda. She's such a lovely girl. And Peter is such a nice chap.'

'Why don't you talk to her?' He grinned. 'Why don't you lend her your copy of the Kamasutra?'

He had given it to her as a joke, when they left England – the book was banned there. But Lee, with her seriously excited interest in any new experience or sight, had read it from cover to cover – and then wanted to put its precepts into practice, even if Murdoch had been growing a little old and stiff for some of the recommended positions. But he was actually more serious now himself than he pretended; as he had recognized in France back in 1914, and in fact long before then, a man had to have sex – and he hated the thought of Peter Ramage becoming 'involved with a bint'.

Now she made a thoughtful moue. 'I might just do that. Let me think about it.'

Ralph Manly-Smith was another officer reluctant to take his leave. Not, in his case, because of any sexual problems – he and Jennifer were obviously as happy in bed as Lee and Murdoch. But he was aware of what was going on.

'I would shoot myself if I was in England and something started up here on the frontier.'

'It's extremely unlikely that anything is going to devolve for a while, Ralph,' Murdoch said. 'And you have to have leave. Listen. I'll promise not to go to war with anyone until you get back. How about that?'

Ralph grinned. 'I'll hold you to that, sir.'

He and Jennifer and the children accompanied B Squadron when it left at the end of the year. They would arrive in England in midwinter. But as they had six months' leave, they would enjoy a good part of the summer as well before having to return. They would also attend Fergus's passing out parade as representatives of his parents, and then return to India with him.

Murdoch felt quite confident of being able to keep his word about fighting a war, for the agitation of the Mahsuds appeared to dwindle with his return, and rumours of possible trouble in Afghanistan died right away over the turn of the year, so much so that in January 1928 the Amir Amanullah and his queen left Afghanistan for an extended visit to Europe. The British agents reported that the trip was undoubtedly intended to seek financial support for the costly reforms the Amir was inaugurating – he was attempting to counter the spreading communist influence in his country by improving the lot of everyone, introducing socialism from the top, as it were – but the mere fact that he could afford to leave the country for any length of time had to be reassuring.

Equally significantly, the Amir chose to leave Afghanistan by way of India. Murdoch was apprised of his intention well in advance, and he took the two remaining squadrons of the Westerns up to the Khyber Pass to escort the royal procession. They had not of course taken their full-dress uniforms with them to India, but they were very smartly turned out, and the band was there to play music which had been chosen hopefully to please the Afghan ear.

To Murdoch's surprise, the Amir turned out to be a very Western-looking gentleman, clad in a brilliant uniform, wearing not a beard but a little toothbrush moustache which reminded Murdoch of Hitler's – or Charlie Chaplin's – and travelling in a procession of very expensive motor cars which bumped and rattled over the uneven road.

He greeted Murdoch warmly. 'General Mackinder,' he said. 'This is a great pleasure. Yours is a famous name on the frontier.'

'You are very kind, your excellency,' Murdoch acknowledged.

'Having you in command down here has been a great relief to me,' the Amir continued. Murdoch wasn't sure in what sense he meant, but presumably it had kept his own turbulent people under control. 'I would like you to meet my wife.'

Murdoch saluted and then bowed over the offered hand. The Begum Suriya was a handsome woman with a somewhat pronounced chin, who was dressed in the height of fashion, revealing an amazing amount of calf, for a queen. When the introductions were over and the cavalcade was moving off, escorted by the dragoons, Murdoch hastily placed himself alongside Peter. 'You have a radio back there?' he muttered.

'Of course. Why?'

'I'd like to send an urgent message to Lee. And to Linda for that matter. Tell them to prepare for Garbo out of Banky.'

Peter looked puzzled for a moment, then grinned. 'You're on.'

Lee had laid on an enormous party which overflowed into the empty garden of the Manly-Smiths. She had received the message and was dressed for the occasion in a short frock and a huge picture hat. Linda Ramage matched her. The Amir and his wife were suitably impressed, especially with Lee and Linda, regardless of what they were wearing. Their visit was a great success, if a little exhausting, for the Begum spoke almost no English and had to be accompanied by an interpreter all the time. But finally they were seen off on the train to Delhi, by another guard of honour.

Lee did her curtseying and Murdoch his saluting for the last time, and she fanned herself vigorously as the train pulled out of the station. 'Life gets more and more interesting. What's next on the agenda?'

'Well . . . supposing they actually get to Delhi and don't wind up back here in a couple of days' – the strikes were getting worse – 'it should be the arrival of B Squadron, with replacements.'

'And Fergus. Oh, I'm so excited about that.'

So was Murdoch. It would be very nearly unique to have two brothers serving in the same regiment – under the overall command of their father. He had, of course, worried from time to time about Ian, about his relations with his brother officers, who would be well aware that most Sunday

237

afternoons he took tea with the Major-General, and more, about his relations with Indian women. This was a problem with any young officer, of course; Lieutenant Roberts' predicament had merely highlighted the situation. Murdoch could well remember when he had first joined the regiment, in 1899, how his fellows had tried to get him down to the local brothel just as soon as possible. And that had been in Bath, Somerset, England.

He had refused to go, and had earned the reputation of not being a 'sport'. He had found it hard going, but the almost immediate onset of the war in South Africa had changed all of that, and the combination of his Victoria Cross and his affair with Margriet Voorlandt had made him about the most popular officer in the regiment. Ian was, as Ramage had spotted, a chip off the old block, a professional soldier from his toes to his forehead, and the odds were that he would, that he had already, refused to accompany his fellow subalterns into the bazaars of Peshawar – it was not something Murdoch would ever ask him, or Ramage, or even Lowndes, who as adjutant would know most of what was going on. That would make the boy's way harder, but would also make him the stronger.

Fergus was a different character. He had less sense of duty and more of Lee's bubbling enthusiasm to learn and to know, to accept every new experience. And perhaps, God forbid – much as Murdoch liked his brother-in-law – he had something of his uncle's sensuality. He wondered if he should discuss it with Lee, but as she seemed blissfully happy at the prospect of having at least half her family with her again he decided against it. He reminded himself that his sons were both men, now, and would have to take life as it came, as he had always done.

Fergus Mackinder and B Squadron – together with the Manly-Smiths – arrived just in time to greet the returning Amanullah, another splendid occasion. The Amir and his wife conducted themselves like old friends now, and their journey had obviously been a great success.

'And everything is quiet on the frontier, eh, General Mackinder?' Amanullah said. 'Just as it should be?'

238

'Just as it should be, your excellency,' Murdoch agreed.

'Remember,' the Amir said. 'We are friends, you and I, Afghanistan and Great Britain. I have been to London. I have seen the greatness that is Britain. I know the value of your friendship, and I deplore the stupidity of my ancestors, who fought against you for so long. I shall never go to war with Great Britain, General. Rather must we always vow to help one another.'

He peered at Murdoch as he spoke.

'I am sure my Government would heartily reciprocate such feelings, your excellency.'

'So, if I ever should need the assistance of you and your fine soldiers, I will send for you, eh? And you will ride to Kabul, as did your famous ancestors.'

Murdoch frowned. 'Providing you have made a prior arrangement with my Government, your excellency.'

'That I will do.'

Murdoch escorted him back to the Khyber Pass, thinking very deeply. Was that a straw in the wind, or did the Amir really feel he might need the assistance of British troops at some time in the future? He made a full report of his conversation to Delhi, and six weeks later, presumerably after Delhi had had a chance to be in touch with Whitehall, received a directive, 'that under no circumstances whatsoever will His Majesty's Forces, or any part of them, become involved in Afghan affairs, or cross the Afghan border, no matter what the appeal or the provocation'. The letter was signed by Lord Irwin himself. So, he thought, Amanullah, old chap, you will have to sink or swim on your own.

That autumn, immediately after the monsoon ended, a letter arrived from Harry Caspar to say that he and his bride would be arriving at the end of October.

'But it's the end of October now,' Lee complained.

'The letter must have been delayed. Everything else is delayed nowadays. Relax. Harry and Veronica will almost certainly be delayed as well.'

Lee decided not to chance that, and there was a great

239

turning out of the spare room. In fact, Harry didn't appear until the end of November. Lee and Murdoch had no idea exactly when they would be arriving, so Lee sent Palraj, the chauffeur, down to the station with the general's official Bentley to meet every train. Palraj was a new addition to the staff, a big, handsome, genial Pathan who actually was a very good driver. The original driver had been a small Indian from the south, who had made Lee very nervous. He was on her conscience because she had shouted at him on occasion, and when they had returned from long leave he was simply not there any more.

'He just left, one day, memsahib,' Kohar explained. 'Said he was going home to his people. But this new man, Palraj, he is a very good driver.'

Murdoch had not been very pleased to have his servants changed, and selected, in his absence, but Lee had reminded him that the whole staff had been selected before they had ever arrived, and it had worked very well. Besides, she had liked Palraj from the start; he was so genial and helpful, and, she felt, trustworthy.

'I don't know what the woman looks like,' she told him. 'Except that she's yellow-haired, and fairly tall, judging by her photograph. But the man looks like me.'

'I will bring them, memsahib,' Palraj promised.

And he did. Although, Murdoch realized when he came home from the headquarters office at almost the same time the guests were being delivered at the front door of the bungalow, there was no way he could not have done so. Women like Veronica Caspar did not disembark at Peshawar station every day of the week. Or every week of the year. Or, come to think of it, every year of the century. Her photograph had hardly done her justice. She was not conventionally pretty, or even handsome, really; her face was too long and her mouth too tight. But her figure might have been carved by some Grecian sculptor who believed in size, as well as perfection, and she wore her silky yellow hair long on her shoulders. She was indeed at least twice the size of Harry, and Murdoch's first reaction was to wonder how they might get on with the Kamasutra, and survive.

240

Harry was like a cat with two tails. 'Murdoch,' he cried, shaking hands vigorously. 'Brother, am I glad to see you. What a journey. What a journey. Say, are you guys governing this country or letting it go to pot? I thought the old New Haven-New York line was bad, but this has got to be the pits. Meet my wife.'

'Oh, General,' Veronica said. 'Harry has told me so much about you. And you are just like he said.'

'I am, am I?' Murdoch asked, and kissed the presented cheek, while looking past her at Lee. While his mind was roaming over Greek allegories he found himself thinking of Medusa.

'And I just adore your place here,' Veronica continued. Her voice was rather high, and was the least attractive thing about her. Superficially. 'And Lady . . .' she released Murdoch to throw an arm round Lee's shoulders. 'Harry won't tell me if I should call you Lady Lee. I think that sounds kinda nice, don't you?'

'I don't,' Lee said grimly.

'I think she'll settle for just Lee,' Murdoch suggested.

'Aw! Now that's a real shame. I've never been related to a real-life lord and lady before.'

'I'm not a Lord,' Murdoch pointed out.

'You're a sir. Next best thing. And Lee sure is a lady. Right?'

'Right,' Murdoch agreed, beginning to feel a little tired. 'Perhaps you should show Veronica to her room, Lee.'

He felt very nearly turned to stone by her glance. 'I'll do that,' she agreed. 'Come along, Veronica. Kohar, you'll see to the bags.'

'Right away, memsahib.'

'Memsahib!' Veronica cried. 'Oh, I love it. I just love it.'

Murdoch poured himself a whisky, and as an after-thought poured one for Harry as well. 'Welcome. It's been a long time.'

'Too long. Here's how. Murdoch, what do you think of her? Ain't she fantastic?'

'Ah . . . yes,' Murdoch said, giving a considered

241

opinion. 'Where did you pick . . . I mean, how on earth did you and she get together?'

'These things happen.'

'She's about half your age, isn't she?'

'A bit more than that. What the hell has age to do with it? I'm not past it, if that's what you mean.'

'I didn't suppose for a minute you were past it, old boy. Well, how long are you staying?'

'A while. There's so much I want to see, and do. The North West Frontier. Heck, I've been reading about that since I was a kid. Murdoch, I want to see everything.'

'You going to write about it?'

'Well, I think I might. I thought of a book.'

'What about the paper?'

'Oh, I've quit the paper. I'm freelancing now. And it's time I wrote a book. All the other top-notch war correspondents have written books. I should've done one on the Great War, back in 1919. Now it's too late; everyone else has done it already. What I want is a good war. And you know something, there isn't a damned one in sight.'

'Well, don't look at me,' Murdoch said. 'My brief is to prevent war, not start one.'

But next day he discovered he might have been wrong.

He had left Lee and her houseguests at breakfast – 'Tiffin,' Veronica cried. 'Oh, I love it. I just love it' – at which they had been joined, by special request from Lee, by Fergus – Ian was on duty at Jamrud Fort – 'And this is your son?' Veronica had cried. 'Oh, he's just lovely. You mean you have another one just like this?' – and settled himself at his desk to read the various reports when Sergeant Denning hurried in.

'Radio message from Lieutenant Mackinder, sir.'

Murdoch raised his head.

'Lieutenant Ian Mackinder, sir, with B Troop, B Squadron, on duty at Jamrud.'

Murdoch frowned. 'Yes?'

'Message reads: "Refugees coming through the pass claiming considerable civil disturbance in Kabul and surrounding areas. Please advise." '

'Tell him to hold them until further notice.' Murdoch pulled a pad of paper towards him and wrote rapidly. 'Then get that off to Delhi. And ask Colonel Ramage and Brigadier West to see me here, right away.' This year the much disliked title 'colonel-commandant' had finally been abandoned, and 'brigadier' restored . . . albeit without the 'general' attached.

'Yes, sir.' Denning hurried from the office.

Ramage and West were with him in ten minutes.

'I want you to take all your men out to Jamrud right away, Peter,' Murdoch said. 'Put another troop into the fort, and then send a squadron up the pass itself, and close it. We can't let a whole lot of Afghans into the province without Delhi's say so, and there may be trouble when they're stopped. But . . . no bloodshed unless it becomes absolutely necessary.'

'Yes, sir.' Ramage saluted and hurried for the door.

'You'll place the garrison on alert, Jimmy,' Murdoch said to West. 'Cancel all leave. And be prepared to move to the dragoons' support should it become necessary.'

'Yes, sir.'

'Send messages to Tochi and Razmak and Wana to do the same. And alert Eccles to have his planes standing by. A few low passes mightn't harm, either.'

'Will do.' West also hurried from the room.

Delhi was on the air in fifteen minutes. Murdoch spoke himself, to a first secretary. 'The Viceroy is unavailable right this minute, General.'

'Well, get hold of him and put him in the picture. I am acting on the assumption that he wants these people checked and sent back, and I want him to know that this may involve force. If he has any alternative instructions, I wish to have them as soon as possible. Understood?'

'I will do the best I can, General.'

Murdoch handed the set back to Denning. 'I'm going up to Jamrud. If anything comes through, I want to know about it, immediately. Oh, and have someone go up to the bungalow and tell Lady Mackinder I won't be in for lunch.'

He rode out with the regiment, and they reached Jamrud

before noon. Here things were better than Murdoch had expected, with the Afghans squatting on the pasture outside the fort in apparent equanimity, and Ian and his eighty-odd men in complete control of the situation. Murdoch interviewed the best-dressed of the Afghans to find out what had happened.

'Much trouble in Kabul, sahib,' they told him. 'Much shooting, many dead.'

'What is the cause of the trouble?'

'It is the mullahs, sahib. They are saying the Amir is wrong to be changing the way of our people. They are saying they do not want to be like the West. We are the East.'

'But the Amir has the army,' Murdoch said, hopefully.

'Many soldiers in the army believe that the mullahs are right, sahib.'

Murdoch followed Ramage up to the pass, where Destry's squadron was being dug in and machine-guns mounted. Already they were confronting nearly a hundred refugees who were trying to continue down the road.

'We could have a serious situation on our hands,' Murdoch said. 'But keep the pass closed, no matter what.'

Ramage nodded, and Murdoch returned to Peshawar.

'A real-life revolution, right on our doorstep,' Veronica said. 'I love it. I just love it.'

'Any chance of seeing some of the action?' Harry wanted to know.

'No chance at all,' Murdoch told him. 'There is no one going or coming through the Khyber Pass as long as I can help it.'

'Of all the cock-ups,' Lee complained when she could get him alone. 'The only hope I have of staying sane is to keep that dame on the move.'

'Well, do that,' Murdoch told her. 'There is no trouble in the province, and I intend to keep it that way. Just continue as normal.'

'But you won't be able to come along.'

'I'm afraid not,' Murdoch said. 'Call on Jennie and Linda. I'll take care of Harry.'

244

'You reckon I want to be alone with her? Maybe she'll just love it, she really will. But I won't.'

'You'll have Jennie and Linda,' he told her.

'It's going to be a great Christmas,' she grumbled.

In fact, it was. The trouble in Afghanistan grew worse, but none of it spilled over into Waziristan. Murdoch made several flights up to Wana, Tochi and Razmak – and buzzed the Mahsuds en route – just in case anyone was feeling agitated, but the province remained peaceful.

The Viceroy himself came up to see what was going on, concurred with the blocking of the pass, but decreed that a limited number of refugees could be allowed in. However, he recognized that this was a civil rather than a military matter, and a special commissioner, Mr Humphrey, arrived to set up a camp and vet the various applicants for asylum. Murdoch rather felt it was on a cash or usefulness basis, but it was not his responsibility any more. He had to supply guards for the camp, and he had to keep a much stronger force than usual at the pass and in Jamrud, while he also had to keep his various garrisons on the alert, but his mini-crisis was good for the men, and as December drew to a close the position seemed to have become stabilized.

He wondered if he was disappointed. He had no real desire to invade Afghanistan to assist Amanullah. Too many British armies had come a cropper in those mountains, even if he did not doubt he could emulate his boyhood hero, Bobs. But with authority in decline across the border he had suspected the Mahsuds might have been able to encourage other dissidents to chance their arm. They hadn't, and now the chance seemed gone, as reports of fighting in Kabul died down. Yet Chand Bibi and her father and indeed all her people remained nagging at him like a sore tooth. It was unreasonable, he knew. All the Pathans fought in the same way; they expected no mercy and they gave none. There was not a tribe in the province which had not at some time in the past mutilated British soldiers, and he had no great hatred for any of them. But he did for the Mahsuds. And for Chand Bibi.

245

Or did he just want to see her again?

In January news arrived that Amanullah had abdicated, in favour of his brother Inayatullah. This was a surprise development, as he had seemed to be getting on top of the situation. Murdoch expected to see his friend and the Begum appear at the Khyber Pass, seeking asylum, but they did not – he had apparently fled to the south-west of the country, around Kandahar – and three days later there was a sensational development: Inayatullah was also deposed and power seized by a bandit chieftain named Bacha-i-Saquao, who had himself proclaimed Amir as Habibullah Ghazi. Amanullah immediately broadcast from Kandahar that he withdrew his abdication and would be leading an army against the usurper.

'It's just absolute nineteenth-century chaos up there.' Humphrey complained.

'The difference is that even thirty years ago we would have marched in and sorted them out,' Murdoch reminded him. 'Now we just sit and watch.'

But he intended to watch very carefully.

'Now this is really something,' Harry Caspar said. 'I sure would like to get into that country, Murdoch. You gonna let me go up the pass?'

'I can't stop you going anywhere you want to, Harry,' Murdoch told him. 'You're an American citizen. I must warn you, though, that there is no way I can come to your rescue . . . and those fellows have a nasty habit of doing things to their prisoners which would leave Veronica a very frustrated young woman.'

'You serious? In 1929?'

'I am very serious indeed.'

'Heck! I reckon I'd better have a chat with the girl first. Where are they today?'

'Looking at some tomb,' Murdoch told him.

'This is the tomb of the Ghazi Anatollah.' Lee read from her guidebook as the Bentley bumped to a halt beside a stand of trees through which the mausoleum could just be glimpsed.

246

She had actually been here before – they were only a few miles along the valley south of Peshawar – but she didn't want to get any of her facts wrong; Veronica had a habit of repeating everything that was told her to Murdoch and Harry. 'Born 1782, died 1872. Preached war against the British the whole time. Britain didn't own up here then, of course.'

'Let's take a look at it,' Veronica decided.

Palraj immediately got out and hurried round to open the door for her. George Reynolds was already opening the other door; it was Murdoch's instruction that George accompanied Lee whenever she went exploring on her own – and that he was armed.

'Come along, Linda,' Lee said.

Jennifer had not accompanied them today. Linda lit a cigarette. 'I'll stay with the car, if you don't mind, Lee,' she said. 'Ancient tombs give me the creeps.'

Lee hesitated, then shrugged, and followed Veronica, already striding out towards the weathered marble. Giving Linda the Kamasutra to read had not been one of Murdoch's better ideas. She had returned the book within a week. 'I'm afraid yonis and lingams aren't really my style,' she had said. And yet, it had had an effect on her. Not sexually, Lee felt; Peter Ramage, for all his good humour and relaxed personality, was, she was sure, a pretty desperate man. But Linda had got the message that her friends were trying to tell her something, and had decided to modernize herself. She had shortened her skirts until they were just below the knee, and had taken up smoking cigarettes, neither of which habits Lee approved, especially in India, where she considered it was essential that white women set an example. But she had done nothing about it. To have openly criticized the girl would have caused a quarrel, and that would in turn have caused a rift between Murdoch and Peter. Lee was determined not to do that.

But she thought she might just start leaving Linda behind on future excursions. Jennifer, always cheerful, always willing to please, and always most respectably dressed, was a far better companion. Anyway, Harry and

Veronica would be leaving in another week, and life could get back to normal.

'I sure would like something like this over me,' Veronica remarked, poking at the tomb with her stick. 'I love it. I really do.' She sighed. 'But Harry believes in this crematorium thing.'

'So let him,' Lee said. 'He's certain to die before you. Then you can cremate him and do what you like. Just make sure your third husband is an undertaker.'

Veronica gave her a suspicious glance. She had slowly been coming to realize that her leg was being pulled a lot of the time, but she was never quite sure when, or how much. Then she looked past Lee. 'Oh, my,' she said. 'What tough-looking guys.'

Lee turned to look back at the car, and saw Linda getting out in some haste, to stand beside George; Palraj was behind them. The two of them were gazing at some twenty men, on foot, who had suddenly appeared from beyond the road. They were armed, and they were clearly Pathans.

Her heart gave a peculiar lurch, even as she reminded herself that she was Lady Mackinder, wife of the general officer commanding, and that no one, but no one, would dare lay a finger on her. She stepped towards them, to ask in her most imperious voice what they wanted, and had her arm gripped by Veronica.

She turned back, irritated at the check, and saw that there were another twenty Pathans behind them, also armed. In front of the men stood a veiled woman.

'Lady Mackinder,' the woman said in perfect English. 'I have long wanted to meet you. I am an old friend of your husband's. My name is Chand Bibi ibn Shere ibn Ali ibn Muhammad.'

10

The North West Frontier, 1929

'The memsahibs not back yet, Kohar?' Murdoch asked as he and Harry entered the bungalow.

'Not yet, General sahib.' The butler bowed.

Murdoch looked at his watch; it was just past five. 'Did Lady Mackinder say she was going out for the day?'

'No, General sahib. It is very strange. The Major's memsahib has been here also, inquiring about the memsahib; she said they were to play the cards together this afternoon.'

'Hm,' Murdoch commented.

'You mean they didn't come in for lunch?' Harry demanded.

'Not at all, sahib,' Kohar said, adding, unnecessarily, 'Neither did the car come back.'

'They were going to the tomb of that holy man,' Harry said. 'Is it far?'

'Not more than a dozen miles. But it is off the main road a way. They must have had a breakdown. Kohar, get me another car. And ask Major Manly-Smith to join me here, with you.'

'Right away, General sahib.' The butler hurried from the house.

'Gee, Veronica will be upset,' Harry muttered, pouring himself a scotch. 'She hates things to go wrong. And missing lunch . . .'

'Yes,' Murdoch said absently. He could not see Lee sitting passively in a car waiting for someone to come looking for her. Not for several hours. She'd have started to walk back . . . twelve miles, in the midday sun?

Ralph hurried in. 'Thank God you're back, sir. Jennie's worried stiff. Seems they had a bridge date this afternoon, and Lady Mackinder never turned up.'

'So Kohar was telling me. Well, let's go find them. Was Linda with them?'

'Yes, sir.'

'Well we won't worry Colonel Ramage at this stage.' Peter was out at Jamrud. 'Is the car here?'

'Yes, sir. I'll just tell Jennie, if I may.'

'Do that,' Murdoch agreed, and drummed his fingers on the car bonnet until he returned. Then Ralph sat in the front beside the sepoy driver, Murdoch and Harry in the back.

'Say,' Harry remarked as they were about to leave. 'You guys don't reckon we should be armed? I mean, heck, they could've been held up or something.'

He seemed to think he was still in the States, didn't understand that being 'held up' would have a far more different, and ghastly, connotation on the frontier than merely losing one's handbag. But he had a point.

'Yes,' Murdoch decided.

'I'll get them,' Ralph volunteered, and returned a moment later with three revolvers.

They drove out of town, took the road south. On the uneven surface it was impossible to do more than twenty miles an hour, and it was nearly six, and getting dark, when they reached the track down to the tomb. On the journey, once they left the suburbs of Peshawar behind, they had encountered but a single bullock cart and team; they had stopped to ask the driver if he had seen any memsahibs on the road, but he had not.

'Veronica is going to be hopping mad,' Harry moaned.

The tomb was about two miles off the main road, and they bumped their way even more slowly.

'There's the Bentley,' Ralph said as the car loomed out of the dusk.

'What's that?' Harry snapped, his voice high, as there was a whirring sound and a dark shadow rose above them.

'A vulture,' Murdoch replied, *his* voice harsh, as he opened his door and stepped out, revolver in one hand, torch in the other. He played the beam over the Bentley, but it was undamaged. Nostrils dilating, he went towards it, shone the torch into the open windows. The car was empty, and the interior was unmarked.

'Sir!' Ralph's voice was urgent. And strange. 'Oh, my God, sir!'

Murdoch went to his side, about twenty feet from the car, and looked down at Reynolds. Ralph's torch beam was playing on the naked body. Murdoch looked at the tortured, twisted features; the severed genitals had been stuffed into the mouth. He felt quite cold. He and George had been friends, intimates, for thirty years.

'Holy Jesus Christ!' Harry stood beside him. 'Is that . . . oh, God!' he fell to his knees and vomited.

There was a piece of paper pinned to the dead man's chest. Murdoch bent and pulled it free, shone the light on it.

Chand Bibi had written:

Not one, not two, but three! Am I not the most fortunate woman on earth, my Mackinder? Or is it that you are the most foolish man on earth, so to allow your women to wander? Did you know that I have kept you under surveillance for more than a year? Did you not realize that Palraj is a member of my own personal guard, that we have waited patiently for the right moment? Yes, you are a fool, my Mackinder, because you are too confident, too arrogant. It is foolish to be arrogant.

The cold was being replaced by heat.

Now I am embarrassed for pleasure. I can hardly make up my mind what to do first, to whom. Would you like a nose to help you make up *your* mind what to do? But I think the body of your man will act as a spur.

His fingers were beginning to curl into fists, carrying the paper with them; he had to straighten them with an effort.

What will you do, my Mackinder? Will you mount at the head of your dragoons and come galloping into our country, guns blazing? I hope you will do that, my Mackinder. For two years I have tried to rouse my people and their allies to make war upon you, upon the British. But their warriors are grown old, and afraid. Mackinder

251

does not trouble us, they say. Why should we trouble Mackinder?
But you are going to have to trouble them now, are you not, my
Mackinder? To what avail? But I will make a bargain with you.
When you commence to war upon us, I will send you the skins of
your women, that you may have them stuffed and remember what
you are fighting for.

Now the heat was beginning to fade into cold again, leaving
him clammy with sweat.

Or will you come by yourself, the great hero, and offer yourself in
exchange for your wife? I should like that best of all, my
Mackinder. So I will be generous. Come by yourself, and I will let
the women go. I will not even make them suffer, more than a little,
for a week, to see if you come. But I do not think even you have the
courage for that, my Mackinder, much as I dream that you might.
So, you will plunge the frontier into war, and we will all be happy.
Except your masters, my Mackinder. They will repudiate you.
And your wife, who will die screaming your name. But I will send
you her skin.

Murdoch stared into the darkness. She was right, of
course. He had been a fool. An arrogant fool, supposing he
held all the trumps. Whereas he held none at all. Save the
ultimate trump, that of vengeance. But it would be a bitter
vengeance, and it would accomplish her purpose just the
same.

'Sir?' Ralph stood at his elbow. Murdoch gave him the
letter.

'What is it?' Harry wanted to know. 'Some kind of
ransom demand?'

'Yes,' Murdoch said. 'You could say that.'

'Oh, God,' Ralph muttered. 'Oh, God.' His voice was
trembling.

'What the hell is in that thing?' Harry demanded.

Murdoch gave it to him in turn, then walked to the
waiting cars and found a blanket in the boot of the Bentley.
He and the sepoy driver wrapped George's body in it, and
laid it on the back seat. By then Harry had read the note and
was just about in tears.

'They can't be far,' he said. 'Let's turn out the cavalry and go get them, Murdoch. Let's tear this country apart.'

'Presuming they were taken almost the moment they arrived here,' Murdoch told him, 'and that was nine hours ago, they could be thirty miles away by now. And we don't know in what direction they've gone.'

'Thirty miles? Veronica can't walk thirty miles.'

'We would need the entire army to cover the ground,' Murdoch went on, 'and we do know that Chand Bibi is quite capable of killing her prisoners if cornered. Losing our heads is not going to solve anything. Let's get back to Peshawar,' he said, and sat behind the wheel of the Bentley.

He called Ramage back from Jamrud, and summoned him and West and Humphrey, as well as Squadron-Leader Eccles, to the bungalow where Ralph and Harry and himself waited, showed them George's body, gave them the letter to read, watched their horrified expressions.

'Christ,' Peter said. 'Linda, in the hands of that devil.'

'We are going to get her back,' Murdoch said. 'We are going to get all of them back.'

'I want to ride in there and shoot the whole God damn lot,' Harry growled.

'I think we would all like to do that, but not until the women are safe. And we have to act quickly.'

'The only way we can regain the women, according to this letter, is for you to surrender yourself,' West said. 'You would be committing suicide, sir. In a most unpleasant way. And we do not have any guarantee that Chand Bibi will keep her word.'

'Agreed. But we must believe that, or we must believe that our wives are already dead. And I refuse to believe that.'

'But you cannot surrender yourself, sir,' West repeated.

'It is the only way, Brigadier. But I don't intend to commit suicide if it's possible to avoid it; and if I do, I want to be avenged, and immediately. So we will lay a few plans, here and now.'

253

'If you are contemplating offensive action, General,' Mr Humphrey said, 'then the matter should be referred to Delhi. The lady is quite right about the possibility of your action being repudiated by HM Government.'

'The matter isn't being referred anywhere, Humphrey, until it is done. They can cashier me afterwards, but I happen to be in command here at this moment, and I want that clearly understood. I also want it clearly understood that no one outside this room must know the contents of that letter, or what we are going to do. We cannot unfortunately keep secret the fact that the three women have been taken, or that Reynolds has been murdered. Our driver knows what happened. But the official line must be that they have been kidnapped by bandits – not by Mahsuds – and that we have already received a ransom note, and that the ransom is being paid.' He looked at Peter. 'This is especially important as regards my sons.'

Peter nodded. 'What are you going to do?'

'At dawn tomorrow morning we bury Reynolds. We don't want a crowd, but I do want full military honours.'

'Leave that with me,' West said.

'Thank you. Now, Peter, how soon can you make Tochi Camp, by forced marching.'

'Six days.'

'Good. You will set off tomorrow, immediately after the funeral. Brigadier, you will have to replace the regiment at the pass.'

'Will do. I'd like some of my men involved in your campaign.'

Murdoch shook his head. 'If this business does stir up all the tribes, you will need a full garrison here. We will also need you as a general reserve, depending on how things go. And incidentally, Jimmy, should things *not* go well, command of the province devolves on you as the senior brigadier until you hear from Delhi. Understood?'

'Understood,' West said grimly.

'Tomorrow morning, Squadron Leader, I would like your people airborne at dawn.'

'They will be, sir.'

254

'Good man. I shall be accompanying you. We will search the country between here and Tochi as thoroughly as we can. I do not think we are going to find anything; Chand Bibi will have allowed for the use of planes. But we may be lucky and we must try.'

'Yes, sir. But even if we do spot them . . .'

'Oh, quite. There's not much we can do about it, from the air. We can't bomb or strafe them. And the cavalry will be far behind. Still, I want it done.'

'Of course, sir.'

'Once we have completed our search, you will land me at Tochi airstrip. From there, after I have briefed and instructed Brigadier Evan-Jones, I will proceed to the Mahsuds.'

'You can't, sir,' Ralph muttered. 'It . . . it's unthinkable.' He was thinking of Reynolds' body.

'He's right, Murdoch,' Peter said. 'We can't let you.' He was remembering Tommy Knox.

'It is a calculated risk,' Murdoch told them. 'And I am the only one who can take it. Chand Bibi has a woman's weakness for talking, or writing, too much, and we have a few cards up our sleeve. She would like to lay hands on me, I agree. Thus I think she may well not harm the women for six days. Before then, I will ride into the Mahsud camp.'

'I'll come with you,' Ralph said.

'You'll do no such thing. I will ride in alone. Study the letter, gentlemen. Firstly, Chand Bibi does not believe I will do that. Her plans are based on an assault by me at the head of my troops. Secondly, you will observe that she has been trying to raise the tribes for two years, without success. It is she who has been sending out the mullahs. But again, no one wants to listen. I do not believe even her own brother has wanted to listen. He struck me as being a very sensible man. I think she may have acted on her own initiative here, taken a gambler's chance on at last achieving her objective. Thirdly, while I know how fast the Pathans can move about their mountains, she cannot regain Mahrain for at least six days. Therefore, by using the aircraft, I will be there before her, and I think I have a very good chance, if I ride into the Mahsud village and demand to be taken before Abdul Hussein ibn Shere, of having him return both myself and the women, unharmed, when he is told exactly what the consequences of our deaths will involve. Because fourthly, unless I achieve my objectives, I do intend to use force. I will inform Brigadier Evan-Jones in Tochi of my decision, and he will mobilize his troops. On the sixth day the Westerns will arrive. The punitive expedition will move out on the eighth day, that is Wednesday of next week. That will give your men twenty-four hours to rest up at the end of their march, Peter. Brigadier Evan-Jones will be in command of the operation, and I will not pre-empt his tactical dispositions. But I would expect the relief force to be across the Kurram and assaulting the Mahsud positions by dawn on Friday. Before then, on the Thursday morning, Squadron Leader, you will make a series of low passes over the town, and on the Thursday afternoon you will return, only this time you will carry out a bombing raid and lay Mahrain flat.'

'With you and the ladies in it, sir?'

'If you have to bomb, Eccles, then the ladies and I will probably be already dead. Because I intend to inform Abdul Hussein of the exact sequence of events I have ordered. Thus, unless he has already freed us, he will learn that the troops have moved out of Tochi Camp at dawn on Wednesday morning, as I will have told him they will. Then, if he has still not released us, he will see the planes make their low passes over Mahrain on Thursday morning, and he will know that the punitive column is virtually on his doorstep. As I say, if he has not released us by then, it will mean that I am wrong and he means to fight. In which case the four of us will be dead anyway. But I do not think he will fight.'

'If he does release you, say on Thursday morning, how will we know in time to call off the bombing raid?' Eccles asked.

'Good thinking. I will take a Verey pistol and a box of flares with me. The flares, if I am released and safe, will be fired in a pattern of three, two, three, two. Anything else will mean I am dead and the Mahsuds are using the pistol. Understood?'

'Three, two, three, two,' Eccles repeated. 'Understood.'

'God, the way you can just sit there and weigh chances,' Harry moaned. 'You're talking about my wife . . .'

'And mine,' Murdoch reminded him. 'And Peter's.'

'The General is also talking about his own life, Mr Caspar,' Ralph pointed out quietly.

'And if the bombing raid is carried out, and we undertake an assault on Mahrain on Friday morning?' Peter asked.

'You will also act on the assumption that I am dead. Brigadier Evan-Jones will understand this. In which case, your orders will be to raze that town to the ground. And if you manage to get hold of Chand Bibi, to hang her from the highest tree you can find. I wouldn't like her to be brought to trial and sentenced to ten years in gaol.'

'No chance of that,' Peter promised. 'I rather think I'll hand her over to the dragoons for an hour first, though.'

'I cannot believe that I am sitting here and listening to British officers, senior British officers, discussing murder, mayhem and rape in such cold-blooded terms,' Mr Humphrey protested.

'Perhaps you would be able to appreciate it if your wife was involved,' Jimmy West suggested.

'I am not married, Brigadier,' Humphrey said coldly. 'You also seem oblivious to the fact that you are likely to set the entire frontier ablaze, which is exactly what this woman wants. The other tribes, peaceful though they may be, are hardly likely to sit by and watch British troops destroy a tribal society. For heaven's sake, it is only six years since we were last at war with the Mahsuds. I must warn you again, gentlemen, that you are taking your careers in your hands. I must also tell you that I refuse to adhere to any of the decisions taken here today. In fact, I entirely dissociate myself from them, and I intend to put that in writing to the Viceroy.'

'You are welcome to do that, Mr Humphrey,' Murdoch said. 'But if you don't mind I would prefer it not done until after the expedition has carried out its purpose.'

'I'm afraid, sir, I cannot agree to that.'

'Very well. Then you leave me no option. Brigadier West, will you place Mr Humphrey under house arrest until further notice.'

'With pleasure,' West said.

'You can't arrest me,' Humphrey declared, his voice shrill. 'I am responsible only to the Viceroy.'

'Then you may include a protest at my action in your letter to him,' Murdoch said. 'I will give you written instructions, Jimmy, so that there can be no doubt where the order came from. Thank you, gentlemen. I suggest we all have an early night. Peter, do you think you could spare both Lieutenants Mackinder to have dinner with me?'

'Good lord!' Ian said. 'Mom, kidnapped? It doesn't sound credible.'

Fergus said nothing, just scratched his head.

'I agree, it's a colossal piece of check,' Murdoch said. 'And believe me, it is not going to go unpunished. However, I'm sure you agree that the first thing to be done is to get your mother, and Mrs Ramage and your Aunt Veronica, back, as rapidly as possible. This is what we are setting out to do. The regiment is moving down to Tochi just to overawe the populace, as it were, until Lee is returned. Then we are going to seek and destroy in a big way. Understood?'

'Yes, sir,' Ian said. 'Do you think . . . she's in any danger?'

'No, I don't,' Murdoch lied. 'These rascals just saw an opportunity and took it. They know that if they actually killed a white woman, much less the wife of the GOC of the province, there would be hell to pay.'

'But they killed George,' Fergus put in, his voice resonant with misery. George had been around ever since any of them could remember.

'They're saying he was, well, mutilated,' Ian put in.

Once again Murdoch had to lie. 'George attempted to defend your mother, and was cut down. His body is a mess, yes. It was a brave but perhaps unwise act, as there must

258

have been quite a few of the bandits. He will be buried with full military honours at dawn tomorrow. And then he will be avenged. I give you my word on that. Now return to your quarters and get some sleep. And don't worry, everything is going to be all right. That's an order.'

Words. How easy to use. He had been using words, giving orders, occupying his brain, since six o'clock. He had not allowed himself time to feel. To be afraid. Of so many things. To be horrified.

To think of George. But to think of George was to go mad. Because he could suffer the same fate? Of course he could. He was taking the biggest chance of his life. So would he scream and gasp and beg as he was shown the knife? And make Chand Bibi laugh, deep in her throat? But when a man was about to die, it didn't really matter what he did.

Then, to think of Lee, in the hands of that she-devil. To think of them all. He did not know them well enough. He did not even know Lee well enough. Would she scream and beg, as *she* was shown the knife? They would not be shown the knife for six days. He had to believe that. But Chand Bibi had said she would make them 'suffer a little'. That too was an impossible thought.

He would only stay sane by thinking positively. By believing that his estimation of the situation was right, and that Abdul Hussein was far more sensible than his bloodthirsty sister. Or by envisaging the destruction of the Mahsuds should he be wrong.

And his career? There would undoubtedly be the most frightful repercussions. But there again, only positive thinking was possible. If he was right, and returned with Lee and the others, unharmed, then they could cashier him and he wouldn't care. If he was wrong, well, they couldn't cashier a dead man, either.

And what of the third possibility, that kept nagging at his brain all the time? That he might very well be right in the calculations, and Abdul Hussein be aghast at what had happened – but that by the time Chand Bibi regained

Mahrain the women might already have been mutilated, or at least raped?

But that too was an unthinkable thought.

Towards dawn he fell into an uneasy sleep, and awoke at first light; there was no Reynolds waiting with a cup of coffee. But before he had finished dressing, Kohar came up to tell him that Mrs Manly-Smith was downstairs. Murdoch knotted his tie and went down to her. She was fully dressed, her expression a mask of anxiety and fear.

'Oh, Sir Murdoch . . . I don't know what to say.'

She looked on the verge of tears. He took her in his arms and held her close.

'I should have been with her,' she sobbed. 'With Lee. I only stayed because Bert had a colic. I should've been there.'

'To have been taken too?' Murdoch asked.

She threw her head back. 'What will they do to them, Sir Murdoch? Ralph won't tell me.'

'Hopefully they'll do nothing to them, Jennie. If we can act in time.'

'But if . . .'

'If, they'll be avenged.'

'My God! Lee . . .'

He kissed her forehead. 'Thanks for coming over. I know Lee will appreciate it.'

'If there is anything I can do . . . anything . . .' She gazed at him, eyes enormous.

Almost she seemed to be offering him physical comfort. But he knew that she was utterly distraught. 'I'll come running,' he promised. 'If there is anything. But Jennie . . . it is going to be all right.'

She might have been his daughter. But she and Lee had been such close friends. What was he thinking? She and Lee *were* such close friends.

Reynolds was buried at half past six, and at seven o'clock Murdoch was strapped into the cockpit of Eccles' Ninak. A place was found for Harry in another machine, and the squadron was airborne five minutes later. They flew, low and widespread over the scene of the kidnapping and then

to the west and north. They swooped in and out of valleys
and over hills, frightened herds of sheep and goats, had the
shepherds shaking their fists at them. They saw various
bullock carts on the tracks, some of them accompanied by
several men and some women . . . but none of the women
looked under restraint.

They searched to the limit of their fuel, and then
returned to Peshawar for a hasty lunch. Ralph and West
were there to greet them; they had passed the regiment on
the road beneath them, already several miles away.

'No luck,' Murdoch said. 'So as soon as Eccles is
refuelled, I'll be down to Tochi Camp.'

'Can I at least come down there with you, sir?' Ralph
asked.

Murdoch nodded. 'All right. We're taking the entire
squadron down anyway, so it'll be right on hand. You're in
command, Jimmy, until further notice. How is Humphrey,
by the way?'

'Swearing he will have every one of us cashiered.'

'You keep that letter of instruction handy. All right, you
chaps, let's go.'

'And about time,' growled Harry, who had been jumping
around like a cat on hot bricks all day.

Jennie, somewhat more in control of herself, stood with an
almost equally upset Coralie Rostron to wave them off, and
they landed at Tochi in the middle of the afternoon.

Brigadier Evan-Jones listened to what Murdoch had to
say with consternation. 'The woman must be mad,' he said.
'She must know she is going to bring down the wrath of God
on her head.'

'I think she wants to do that. But we must hope her
brother has more sense. You are quite happy with my
instructions?'

'I'm happy with them, General Mackinder. I'm not
happy with you wandering off by yourself into those hills.'

'I'll take an escort up to the Kurram; it can act as your
advance guard. My appearance in Mahrain will have shock
value.'

'I still would prefer you here, sir, commanding operations.'

'I know this is where I should be,' Murdoch said. 'But that wouldn't save the lives of the ladies, would it? Operations are your responsibility, Brigadier. I have every confidence in you. You'll have the finest cavalry regiment in the world under your command next Tuesday. Use them well.'

He slept better that night, now that he was about to go into action, as it were, and set off at dawn next morning, with an escort of a company of mounted infantry, Gurkhas, delighted if confused at being ordered to undertake a march to no fixed destination – under the personal command of GOC. They forded the Tochi River and made their way over the undulating but steadily rising ground towards the Kurram. The herdsmen they passed gazed at them incuriously, but Murdoch had no doubt that their presence was being reported deep into the mountains which rose in front of them.

That night they camped on high ground, and were swept by an icy wind, but the next day, Saturday, they descended to the valley of the Kurram. Now the mountains loomed so high above them they seemed almost ready to topple over, and they were looking at Afghanistan. They camped for the night on the banks of the river, and next morning Murdoch took Lieutenant Chambers aside. 'Here is where you stay until further orders. Be sure you fortify your position.'

'Yes, sir.' The Lieutenant was totally bewildered, but he was not going to argue with a Major-General . . . until he realized Murdoch wasn't staying with them. 'You can't go into Mahsud territory without an escort, sir,' he protested.

'They're expecting me,' Murdoch told him, not sure whether or not he was lying, on this occasion.

'Yes, but I mean, sir, these Mahsuds . . .'

'I know which Mahsuds these are, Lieutenant. Now be a good chap and do as I wish. Your business is to hold this ford, either until I return, or until brigade arrives to take over from you. Understood?'

'Yes, sir,' Chambers said unhappily.

Murdoch checked his saddlebags, mounted. The company was drawn up in parade-ground order to salute him, and he saluted them in turn. Then he splashed across the shallow ford and walked his horse up the other side. At the top he looked back. The Gurkhas were already at work, digging in and emplacing their machine-gun. But they were still watching him. He raised his hand, and then turned his borrowed horse – Brutus was coming down with the regiment – and walked it down the next slope, out of sight of the river.

He was, he knew, within twenty miles of Mahrain, and was thus very much inside the territory ruled by Shere Khan. Soon he passed a herd of goats, and the herdsmen gazed at the tall, mounted figure, the khaki uniform, the Sam Browne belts and highly polished brown boots, the topee and the red tabs on Murdoch's lapels, the rows of ribbons on his breast, the sword and revolver, in total amazement, then peered behind him to discover the whereabouts of the army this imposing figure must be leading.

Murdoch continued on his way, aware of a very odd feeling as he turned his back; the Mahsud carried a rifle slung across his shoulder. But he was in that type of situation from here on. And as the sun rose higher he became aware of flashes of light passing from hilltop to hilltop; Shere Khan's sentries were signalling news of his arrival.

He rode through the shallow pass which took him back down to the bend of the river, and looked at Mahrain, its white houses rising out of the opposite bank, beneath the fort. There were banners flying from the fort, and men on the battlements, pointing at him. Closer at hand there were women down at the water, washing, beating the wet garments with rhythmic thwacks of their heavy sticks; the sound echoed up the valley like gunfire. Around them small children, naked save for a brief skirt or jacket, played games. The women stood up to watch him ride down to the ford and splash across.

He rode the slope towards the white walls. Now there were men gathered outside the gate, every one armed, staring at him. He could not tell whether they were expecting him or not.

He walked his horse up to them, reins lying in his left hand, right arm straight at his side, resisting all temptation to unfasten the flap of his holster. 'I come to see Abdul Hussein ibn Shere ibn Ali ibn Muhammad,' he said.

The man peered at him, and he wondered if none of them spoke English. But at least one understood what he had said. He spoke in Mahsud, but took Murdoch's bridle, and led the horse towards the gate. The other men followed.

The gate was open, and the man led the horse up the suddenly crowded street. People pressed close to peer at the English general, and there was a hubbub of conversation. Murdoch was led up to the palace and through the inner gate. Here there were no crowds, but a dozen red-jacketed guardsmen, who stood to attention and presented arms, for all the world like their English counterparts.

Murdoch dismounted, looked towards the palace porch, and the man who stood there. His face was unfamiliar, and he was not an Indian. Murdoch's heart gave a little leap as he saw the boots, the green breeches and jacket, the little fur cap. The man was clean shaven, and had heavy and rather coarse features. But he was looking pleasant enough at the moment, or at least, pleased to see Murdoch.

'General Mackinder,' he said. He did not offer his hand. 'I did not believe you would come. You are as brave a man as they say.'

Murdoch gazed at him. 'Who are you?' he asked. He knew it was essential to maintain his facade of arrogant confidence, project a total certainty that no one would dare harm him.

The man gave a slight bow. 'I am Sergei Wittvinov.'

'Ah,' Murdoch said. 'And what are you doing in British territory? Communist agents are not welcome here.'

'British territory?' Wittvinov asked. 'I think you will find the Mahsuds do not agree with the estimation, General. And I am not a Communist. I fought for the tsar, and will do so again, God willing. As to what I am doing here, this is my home. I live with my wife.'

'Your wife?' Murdoch knew the answer before he finished asking the question . . . and in that instant knew the answer to a great many other things, as well.

'My wife is the Princess Chand Bibi.'

Murdoch nodded. 'Yes. Well, I have come to see Abdul Hussein ibn Shere. Will you inform him of my presence, please.'

'Alas, General, I cannot do that. It is possible, however, that you may be able to see Abdul in the near future. He is in hell. He died four months ago.'

Murdoch felt as if he had been kicked in the stomach. He had indeed committed suicide. But he kept his face rigid with an effort. 'Allow me to offer you my condolences, Mr Wittvinov. In that case, I must speak with Shere Khan himself.'

Wittvinov shook his head. 'Shere Khan is in his dotage. He no longer rules the Mahsuds. They obey the commands of his eldest daughter and heiress, Chand Bibi.'

Bluff, bluff and again bluff, Murdoch told himself. 'Then you had better let me see the princess. It is a most urgent matter.'

'I am sure it is, General. But my wife is not here at this time. As I think you know. She did leave instructions, however, that were you to pay us a visit before her return, you were to be entertained.'

'I am too busy a man, Mr Wittvinov,' Murdoch told him. 'As your wife is not here, I will leave, and return on a more suitable occasion. When do you expect her back?'

'Not for a few days yet. But I cannot let you leave, General Mackinder. Chand Bibi would be very angry were I to do that.'

Murdoch felt rather than heard movement, and realized that two of the guards stood on either side of him.

'I think you should know,' he said evenly, 'that you are committing an act of war.'

'But that is my intention,' Wittvinov said.

Murdoch stared at him. 'An act of war which I anticipated, Mr Wittvinov. There is a brigade of British and
Indian soldiers leaving Tochi Camp next Wednesday
morning to march on Mahrain. If I do not return to meet
them, they are going to raze this town to the earth.'

'With you in it, General? Not to mention your wife,
perhaps? Come now, I am not such a fool as to believe that.'
His voice suddenly hardened, and he spoke in Mahsud.
Before Murdoch could react his arms were seized, and
another of the men was unbuckling his Sam Browne belts to
remove the revolver holster, cartridge case and sword. He
made no effort to resist them. At forty-eight he remained as
tough and as fit as at any time in his life, and he had little
doubt that he could, probably, take on these four. But there
were another dozen standing behind him who would
certainly be able to overpower him, and he wanted neither
to risk his dignity nor any injury; he was going to need all
his strength during the next few days.

Still holding his arms, the guards marched him into the
palace itself, and through the outer court. Here they were
surrounded by whispering, giggling women, and some
children. Murdoch made himself ignore them, but he could
not help but turn his head when one of the children, a
startlingly lovely girl of perhaps eight or nine, ran forward
to hold Wittvinov's hand. She looked like her mother, he
thought.

He was taken through a corridor to one side of the throne
room, down several flights of steps, until he realized he was
in the very heart of the hillside on which Mahrain stood.
Here there were guttering torches set in the walls, and the
walls themselves damp and cold. There were several cells
on this level; he did not know if any were occupied, for
there was no sound apart from the scuffling of their own feet
and their breathing. At least one of the doors was opened
and he was thrust inside.

'Your quarters, until my wife returns,' Wittvinov said.

Murdoch's arms had been released, and he looked at the
wooden cot against the wall; the mattress was wooden too,
and there were no covers. There was nothing else in the

room at all, and there was no window – a shaft let into the wall reached up to a faint light, a long way away. He turned to face his captor; the little girl had come down with her father, and still held his hand.

'You have just signed your death warrant,' Murdoch said. 'And that of all your people. Including your daughter.'

'The death warrant has your name on it, Mackinder. No one else's,' Wittvinov said. 'Strip.'

Murdoch frowned at him.

'Undress,' Wittvinov commanded. 'Or would you rather my men did it for you?'

Murdoch gazed at him, then took off his tunic and pulled his tie loose.

'You may think my objective is to humiliate you,' Wittvinov said. 'Well, of course it is. But it has a practical purpose. I cannot risk you despairing and strangling yourself with one of your garments before my wife returns. She would never forgive me. You will be uncomfortable, of course, and a little chilly. But you will not freeze. Everything, Mackinder.'

Murdoch gazed at the little girl as he removed the last of his clothing. One of the guards gathered up the garments, almost reverently. Another took the boots.

Wittvinov smiled. 'She will see more of you than this, in the course of time, General. Now we will leave you, to anticipate the coming of Chand Bibi.' He drew the girl out of the room, and the guards slammed the door.

The cell was almost dark; the faint light just enabled him to see. But there was nothing to see. He discovered another shaft in the floor at the far corner, which, from the stench, he gathered was his lavatory.

He sat on the bed, and tried not to shiver; already the chill was striking at him; if Chand Bibi did not return for another two days he would be a shuddering wreck. But no doubt that was intended.

He tried to think, but he could only feel; his brain was overwhelmed by the knowledge that he had not allowed for the one, or perhaps two, eventualities which would leave him helpless. The death of Abdul Hussein, and the possibility that Chand Bibi was obtaining outside help. Outside help; if Wittvinov was that girl's father, then Chand Bibi must have married him by 1920, almost immediately after returning to *her* father.

Therefore, with her brother dead and Shere Khan a nonentity, there was no check at all on Chand Bibi's ambitions. He had not a weapon left to play with, save vengeance – and Chand Bibi was looking forward to that vengeance. And the frontier would explode into flames. And Lee . . . my God, Lee! Would they die together? Or would Chand Bibi make Lee watch her husband being torn apart, before executing her in turn?

It was incredible, that a week ago they had been playing bridge with Linda and Peter Ramage, while Harry mixed martinis and Veronica prattled aimlessly in the background, in the total security of the Bala Hissar. It was even more incredible that there were earnest politicians sipping their beers in the House of Commons Bar, clad in sober suits and clean underwear, discussing India as if it was an abstract mathematical problem, to which there had to be a solution simply because every problem had to have a solution, who had no idea of the realities of life on the frontier, of the depths of hatred and anger . . . on both sides, now. He did not doubt that the Westerns would destroy this place, if they knew that their beloved erstwhile Colonel, and his no less admired lady, had been murdered in it.

And what would the newspapers say? They would not wish to disturb their readers. 'Shocking crime in the North West Frontier Province. News has been received that Major General Sir Murdoch Mackinder, known as Britain's finest leader of light horse, and Lady Mackinder, have both been murdered by revolting Pathan tribesmen. (No details, of course: perhaps an 'in horrifying circumstances'.) A reprisal raid has since been carried out, and a Pathan village burned to the ground. Major-General Mackinder will be remembered, etc, etc, etc.'

He could recall reading similar reports himself, before

the war; and they had made very little impression on him. He had not been there.

The door opened, and he was fed; the gaoler was guarded by four armed men. Even naked, he was still the famous Murdoch Mackinder. The curry was quite palatable, and there was a jug of cool mountain water to drink. The meal warmed him up, somewhat, then the door was shut and he was again left to his thoughts. But now he had to concentrate entirely on vengeance, on imagining himself at the head of the dragoons as they stormed those white-washed walls. There was no other way he was going to survive the next few days.

Keeping track of time was difficult. He had left Tochi Camp on Thursday morning, and he had entered Mahrain on Saturday morning. He wondered how fast Chand Bibi was travelling. On foot he did not see how she could make more than ten miles a day. That would mean ten days from Peshawar. But she had spoken of a week, therefore she must have had horses, or at least mules. So perhaps six days. The kidnapping had taken place on Tuesday morning, therefore she could be back on Monday. Until then life had no meaning; his entire being was concentrated on trying to keep warm. He made himself walk up and down his cell until he was exhausted – this had the advantage of making him sleep. But he awoke shivering, teeth chattering, and soon began to sneeze and his nose to run.

Cold and mental state apart, he was not ill treated. He was fed twice a day, always curry, and he was visited once a day, by Wittvinov, although to his relief on these visits the Russian was not accompanied by his daughter. The visits enabled him to keep track of the days.

And as he had calculated, when the door opened on the Monday afternoon, he gazed at Chand Bibi.

She must have arrived some time before, for she did not look in the least travel weary. She had clearly just bathed, and she wore a green and gold sari. He had not seen her for thirteen years, and thus she had to be very nearly forty years

269

of age, but she looked magnificent, bathed in the light of the lanterns held by two of the guards behind her.

He forced himself to his feet, tried to keep from shivering. 'You made good time,' he said, and sneezed. 'You must have had horses.'

She looked him up and down. 'Always debonair, my Murdoch. Oh, indeed, we made good time, despite having to take shelter when your planes were overhead. But they made so much noise we could hear them coming long before they could see us. I'm afraid the ladies did not enjoy their journey. I tied them to their horses, on their bellies across the bare backs. It was great sport. But I have never heard so many complaints. The large blonde lady was the worst. I finally had to have her beaten.'

Murdoch swallowed. But imagining Veronica Caspar being beaten did not help him at all. He dared not imagine Lee being tied on her belly across a horse's back. 'Where are they?' he asked.

Chand Bibi smiled. 'They are being given hot baths. Is that not kind of me? They are being bathed by men. Is that not even kinder of me?'

Murdoch refused to be drawn. Lee was alive, and that was what mattered. What happened to her, in the way of insults or humiliation, was irrelevant. They were down to fundamentals, and only the ones who survived would have any right to smile.

'But you,' Chand Bibi said. 'You also need a hot bath. I'm afraid my dear Sergei has been cruel to you. He is really afraid of you, I think.'

'You mean you did not command my imprisonment?'

'I did not expect you to come, my Murdoch. I really did not. Your courage amazes me. Come.'

She stepped outside and waited for him. The corridor was full of guards, but it would not have mattered. He could do nothing until he could reach Lee.

They escorted him up the various uneven stairs, led by Chand Bibi, and he thought he was going to be taken out into the courtyard, naked and shivering, but she turned aside, through a curtained doorway, and he found himself in a world of women.

270

This was an Indian, not a Turkish harem, and this was a world of fighting men and women as well – there was no room for eunuchs. Although he was now clearly in the private apartments of Chand Bibi herself, the guards entered with him, and marched him to a great enamel tub set in the centre of the floor. This was filled with steaming water, and in this he was made to sit. It was clearly a tub used on occasion for more sinister purposes, for there were stout steel rings set into the sides, and to these his wrists were secured, leaving him quite helpless. Then the guards bowed and withdrew.

'You will forgive my caution, my Murdoch,' Chand Bibi said. 'But you are a famous warrior, are you not?' She studied him. 'It is remarkable, the effect heat has on a man. I suppose it makes the heart pound, and this affects the penis. Is your heart pounding, my Murdoch?'

'Yes,' he said. However she might enjoy watching him, he was enjoying the magnificent sensation of warmth spreading through his limbs.

'I will have you bathed again, immediately before your execution.'

'Chand Bibi,' he said, 'you are destroying your people.' Looking at her, at her face, at once so intelligent and so calm and so beautiful, it was impossible to believe that she could not listen to reason, that she really lived only to destroy.

'Have you met my daughter?' Chand Bibi brought the child forward to stand by the side of the tub with the other women. 'Her name is Yasmin, and she is nine years old. Do you not think she looks like me?'

'Yes,' he said. 'Do you wish me to see her lying dead?'

'She will not lie dead,' Chand Bibi said.

'There is a brigade leaving Tochi Camp on Wednesday morning to march on Mahrain,' Murdoch said. 'Unless I and all three of the ladies are released unharmed and meet them on the way, they are going to burn your town to the ground, and kill anyone they find in their way. Can you understand that? They will be here on Friday, and the assault will be launched immediately. But before that, on

271

Thursday morning, my aeroplanes will fly over your heads. That will be your very last chance. If I do not signal them with the Verey pistol which was in my pack, a signal known only to me and their commander, they will return that afternoon and they will bomb your village flat.'

'With you and your wife in it?'

'They are under orders that if I have not signalled them by noon on Thursday, they must assume I am dead.'

'Ah,' she said. 'I was going to execute you on Friday, when your soldiers came in sight. Now I will bring forward, as you say, to Thursday. Of course, I could torture you into telling me the agreed signal. Could I not?'

'Do you think I would tell you?'

She gazed at him for several seconds, then said, 'Probably not. So let me see, I must work things out. Leave us,' she commanded.

The ladies bowed and left the room, taking the little girl with them. Then Chand Bibi took off her sari. Her body was as splendid as he had always known it would be, firm-muscled from the life she lived as a hill woman, and yet voluptuously overflowing with sexuality.

'I will bathe you myself, my Murdoch,' she said, and knelt beside the tub. 'I would prefer much more, but I know you would wish to strangle me.'

'I am trying to save your life,' he said. 'All of your lives.'

She gave one of her low, throaty laughs as her fingers guided the soap over his chest and round his back, her thick black hair flopping against his face. 'You are trying to save your own life, you mean, and the life of your wife.'

'You promised that, if I surrendered.'

She turned her attention to his stomach and thighs. 'What is a promise, to an infidel? No, no, I will execute her, just after you, I think. I will execute them all together. Until Thursday, they can be used to entertain Sergei. He is an insatiable satyr. He makes me quite tired.'

'Are you really so evil, Chand Bibi?'

'I am not evil, my Murdoch. It is you who are evil, with your dreams of conquest. I tried to explain this to you once. I hate. That is my reason for being. I hate you and all you

272

stand for. And yet, I could love you. Do you know, when I cut away your manhood I will weep.' She soaped his feet.

'And then die? Will it be worth it?'

She gave another laugh. 'I shall not die, my Murdoch. Some of my people, perhaps. But it is what they dream of, to die in battle against the British. But I, and Sergei, and Yasmin, and my guards, will simply flee before your soldiers, across the border. We have no battle honours to wave and forbid us to run away. Let your people burn my town. They have done so before. I will rebuild it. And from the safety of Afghanistan we will raid as often as we wish, and cause havoc from one end of the province to the other. But the havoc will already have commenced, when word is spread how the Mahsuds have executed the British general officer commanding when his troops moved against them. I will have your castrated body photographed, and prints circulated throughout the frontier. The khans will not be able to restrain their people after such a triumph.'

'Afghanistan,' Murdoch muttered.

'You thought the border was closed to us, did you not, my Murdoch? For a while it was. A long while. But all things change. It is only necessary for one to be patient. So, have I answered all of your questions? I know, you see, that your men are under strict instructions not to cross the border. *You* might disobey those instructions, my Murdoch, because you are that kind of man. But with you dead, your people will not. Am I not right?'

He stared at her, because he could think of no reply. She knew too much.

She laughed, and clapped her hands. He was to be spared no humiliation. The women returned, and with them was Lee. Like him, she was naked, and her hands were bound behind her back. She did not look ill-treated in any way, although there were bruises on her thighs and stomach, no doubt caused by the horse's back, and her face was drawn with tension and exhaustion. And now with horror, as she saw him as helpless as herself.

'Oh, Murdoch,' she said. 'Oh, Murdoch.'

Chand Bibi laughed, and turned her attention to his genitals.

All she did was hate, she claimed. Well, then, he must cultivate hate himself. He would need it. Hating, he might even die well.

He had never hated before. He had been angry. He had killed in anger; Mulein. When he had killed male enemies, be they Boers or Somalis or Germans or Turks, it had been a dispassionate act of war. But now it was necessary to hate, and hate, and hate again.

Futilely. There was nothing he could do. And there was nothing Chand Bibi spared him, as on Tuesday and Wednesday she made him watch the three women being raped by her guards, one after the other. Veronica was on Tuesday morning, screaming and moaning. Linda was on Tuesday afternoon, silent and almost somnambulistic, her lips moving as she begged some disinterested deity for mercy. Lee was Wednesday afternoon, having been forced, like him, to watch the others. She kept her eyes on his face, throughout, and never uttered a word of protest.

'And tomorrow,' Chand Bibi said, smiling at them. 'Tomorrow is the great day. Oh, by the way, my watchers tell me that your army is encamped on the banks of the Kurram. They have made good time. My people are looking forward to the fly-past of your planes tomorrow morning. As soon as they have left again, we shall begin our evacuation. I will leave just enough men to tease your people into continuing their advance. Tell me if I have forgotten anything, my Murdoch. You are a professional, and I am only an amateur.'

'I am sure you have thought of everything, Chand Bibi,' he said. He seemed to have known her all of his life.

That night he was not returned to his cell. Instead he was tied to one of the beds in the harem, and Chand Bibi spent most of the night with him. 'I wish you to die at least sated, my Murdoch,' she said, lying on his stomach and kissing his face. 'Oh, what beautiful lovers we could have made. And who knows, with you as my consort, I could perhaps have re-created the Mughal empire, here in the mountains.'

He strained at his bonds. To get one arm loose would be to strangle her, and at least avenge Lee. But he could not get free, and she gave her throaty laugh as she satisfied herself.

She left him just after midnight, exhausted. He was hardly less so, as he remembered the scent of her perfume, the feel of her body on his, of her fingers. The last night of my life, he thought. The last night of all of their lives. What a waste. What criminal negligence.

He knew he would not sleep, and yet did doze, to awake to a droning sound. His head jerked as he identified it. Planes, flying low over Mahrain. In the middle of Wednesday night? He had ordered no such demonstration. He listened, to shouts from above him. But no explosions. What on earth was Eccles playing at, he wondered?

The noise grew louder and louder, until the aircraft were clearly immediately over the palace, then it started to fade again. But now there were other sounds. The shouts became screams, someone was blowing a bugle, and the night was punctuated with the reports of rifles.

Once again Murdoch strained at his bonds, heart pounding, not daring to hope, not understanding what could possibly be happening. But the noise was growing all the time, and suddenly it was in the corridor outside his room. He watched the door collapse, kicked in by booted feet, gazed at one of Chand Bibi's women, her face a mixture of terror and pain, because someone was holding her arm twisted behind her back . . . someone? RSM Yeald. And by his side, Ralph Manly-Smith. And behind Manly-Smith, three other men, but not dragoons. Two were Gurkhas and one was a British private of the Cheshires.

'Murdoch!' Ralph gasped. It was the first time he had ever used his Christian name. 'Thank God!'

Murdoch couldn't speak for a moment.

'Come on, sir, let's get you up?' Yeald said, cutting the ropes holding him to the bed.

'The women . . .' Murdoch felt he had to be dreaming.

'We have them safe,' Ralph said. 'You stay here, bint.'

He thrust the girl into the room, removing her sari as he did so, and handed it to his general. 'You'll feel happier in this, sir.'

Murdoch wrapped it round his waist. 'I'd feel happier with a weapon.'

A revolver was pressed into his hand, the door was shut on the unfortunate girl, and they ran outside. 'That was a remarkable march,' Murdoch gasped. 'Two days, from Tochi? And yesterday afternoon Chand Bibi said the brigade was on the other side of the Kurram.'

'I think they still are, sir,' Ralph said. 'The brigade.'

'But . . .'

There was a burst of firing from outside, and they ran into the main room of the harem. Here Murdoch found another eight men. There were two dragoons, two more Gurkhas, two sepoys from the Guides, another English infantryman, and Harry Caspar – armed to the teeth: he had two revolvers as well as his rifle. They were divided into two groups, one at the doorway facing the corridor to the throne room, and the other at the doorway opening into the courtyard, and had apparently just driven off a counter-attack by the Mahsuds; several bodies were heaped in the arched doorway leading to the courtyard, and the scented atmosphere was heavy with cordite.

'Where is your main force?' Murdoch snapped.

'This is it, sir,' Ralph said. 'Do you wish to see the women?'

Explanations would have to wait. Murdoch was already running across the floor, bursting open the door to the inner apartments and finding Lee, crouching on the floor beside the bed as she had been told to do by Manly-Smith, but scrambling to her feet at the sight of him.

'Murdoch!' she screamed. 'Oh, Murdoch.'

He held her close, looked past her at Veronica and Linda. Veronica had already been reunited with her husband, but tears continued to roll down her face and every so often she sobbed.

Linda stared at Murdoch, then at Ralph Manly-Smith. 'Is Peter here?' she asked, her voice a quiet murmur of despair.

'He wanted to come, but there wasn't room, and he has to command the regiment. He'll be here this afternoon.' Ralph looked at Murdoch. 'They're forced marching, all night. All we have to do is hold until then.'

A renewed flurry of shots came from the other side of the apartment, and they made the women lie down again, while they hastened to the scene of action. There were Mahsud riflemen in the throne room, firing along the corridors, but doing little damage.

'Chand Bibi,' Murdoch said.

'She must have got out when we broke in,' Ralph told him. 'It was a marvellous bit of work by Eccles. We actually landed in the courtyard.'

'He put a plane down in the courtyard?'

'Oh, no, sir. We parachuted.'

Murdoch was speechless.

'All volunteers, of course,' Ralph told him. 'In fact, I had enough volunteers to fill a hundred planes. Brigadier Evan-Jones suggested I split the company up as much as possible. Do you know, sir, I was the only one ever to have done it before?'

'You mean you parachuted into an enemy fortress? And Evan-Jones gave you the go-ahead? Good God!'

'Well, sir, we felt that things might go wrong. But we couldn't come any earlier, because we have to hold until the brigade gets here.'

'Things went wrong, all right,' Murdoch said. 'I owe you my life, Ralph. And so do the girls. But . . . parachuting into an enemy position . . .'

'It was a piece of cake, sir,' Ralph told him. 'The real work will start when they get their courage back. If only we'd got Chand Bibi.'

'Yes,' Murdoch agreed. 'But we will.'

Ralph was right about the real work. With the coming of daylight the Mahsuds guards made a concerted effort to rush the harem. But they were driven back from both doors by the accurate fire of the defenders. Each man of the volunteers was carrying two hundred cartridges, and they made every one tell. The once-elegant apartments were torn and riddled by bullets, and the women had to remain crouched by the floor, but Lee refused to stay hidden, and crawled about to pass water to the defenders, searching out what food there was to be had – there was no lack of water because of the pool, but the only food was sweetmeats and biscuits. They did, however, find Murdoch's uniform, laid out on a bed in a spare room. When he was dressed he felt a much happier man.

'Now we're commanded by a general,' Lee said, and looked into Murdoch's eyes.

He squeezed her hand. 'Nothing matters, save you and me.'

'And winning,' she said fiercely. 'Oh, I want to win now, Murdoch. I want to win, at your side. I have never wanted anything so badly in my life before.'

'You are going to win,' he promised her. 'At my side.' And at the side of men he had trained and who would follow him anywhere. As they had.

Veronica and Linda did not ride their hellish experience so easily. Veronica kept saying, 'I want to go home,' over and over again. She was at least speaking. Linda never said a word after asking about Peter.

The sniping continued for some hours, until the middle of the morning. Then there was a rush at the courtyard door. Murdoch left three men to hold the inner door, and the remaining ten of them manned the barricades and sent volley after volley into their assailants. By now several of the defenders had been hit, but none seriously. Lee tore drapes of splendid silk and brocade into strips to make bandages. And while the battle was at its height, the drone of the planes was heard again, followed soon after by the crump of bombs. Eccles' men were flying low over the town, and dropping their deadly cargoes with total precision, carefully avoiding the palace, but utterly demolishing the fort.

The bombing was too much for the Mahsuds, and the firing died down and then ceased altogether. One of the Gurkhas crawled outside, and reported that the enemy had withdrawn. But Murdoch, taking no chances, used the opportunity to strengthen their defences, gather up discarded rifles and bandoliers from the dead men scattered about the courtyard, and bring in some food. He had to assume Chand Bibi would send her people back to the assault the moment the planes were gone, because unless she could murder him and prove her leadership to the khans, her hopes of a general rising were finished. He did not in any event know how much longer they could hold out, as the sun rose and the flies came to attack the corpses; the stench inside the harem would soon become unbearable.

But the attack was not resumed, and soon they knew why, as they heard the drums and fifes of the brigade approaching, and before them, the jingle of harness as the dragoons rode up the slope. At last the defenders could leave their shot-scored harem and go out to meet Evan-Jones, and Peter, and the other battalion commanders.

'That was a brilliant operation, Gwyn.' Murdoch shook hands.

'Thanks to Ralph Manly-Smith.'

'I haven't forgotten that,' Murdoch said.

'And nobody else is gonna, either,' Harry Caspar promised.

Ian and Fergus were embracing their mother. 'Are you all right, Mom? Are you all right?'

'I'm fine,' Lee said; she was wearing a sari and actually looked as if she had just stepped out of her own bedroom in the Bala Hissar.

'You mean they didn't harm you.'

'No,' she said. And looked at Murdoch. 'They didn't harm me.'

'Linda?' Peter Ramage held her in his arms. 'Linda?'

She wouldn't look at him, buried her face in his tunic and wept.

There was so much to be said, and understood. But now was not the time.

'The Mahsuds have regrouped across the border, sir,' RSM Yeald reported. He had ridden out to scout on his own.

279

'Well, that's that,' Evan-Jones said despondently. 'We'll have to wait for a change of government in Kabul.'

'Which may never happen,' Murdoch said. 'I intend to get Chand Bibi, now.'

'Delhi won't like it, sir.'

'Delhi can do what it damn well likes,' Murdoch told him. 'Very well, gentlemen, we'll have to snare her. If the whole brigade crosses she'll just keep on withdrawing. It has to be a force small enough so that she'll reckon she can beat it. I'll take the two squadrons of dragoons, and two squadrons of Guide cavalry, as we have to travel fast. I'll also take one field battery. You'll clean this place up, bury the dead, and hold it until we return, with the main body. Then we'll burn it.'

'Yes, sir,' Evan-Jones said doubtfully. 'Do you really reckon four hundred men will be sufficient? My reports indicate she may have as many as two thousand fighting men.'

Murdoch grinned at him. 'Four hundred was all my ancestor had in Baluchistan. It's going to be enough for me to sort out that bitch. Will you fall the men in, Colonel Ramage?'

'Yes, sir. Are you coming yourself?

'Yes. Do you mind?'

'I'd be delighted.' He looked at his wife.

'The ladies will remain with brigade,' Murdoch said.

'I hope you're not figuring on leaving me behind,' Harry said.

'No. I want you, Harry. We're going to need all the good press coverage we can get.'

'He'll be killed,' Veronica wailed.

'I've never been killed yet,' Harry reminded her.

'I wish I could come with you,' Lee said.

'I'm afraid that's not possible, my dearest girl.'

'I know,' she said. 'But . . . you will get that woman, Murdoch. Promise me.'

'We will get her,' he promised.

The regiment had brought Brutus along with their

remounts, and Murdoch could settle into his saddle again. Peter fell the men in, the two squadrons in column. The Guides followed and the artillery brought up the rear. Cheered by the rest of the brigade, the small force walked their horses down to the river and forded it, then made their way into the pass. They were in Afghanistan.

An advance guard of Guides was sent up, and flankers thrown out to either side as they proceeded through a succession of ravines, watching the hilltops to either side. The Mahsuds were up there, and as soon as they saw the British emerging from the pass they opened a desultory fire at long range. But one or two men were hit, and Murdoch called a halt and unlimbered his artillery. Half a dozen shells bursting on the hills drove the tribesmen to take shelter, and the small force proceeded, until they debouched on to a level plateau about four miles inside the border. Here they were met by enemy artillery fire.

Murdoch commanded his men to dismount and seek shelter, while he, Peter and Colonel Briggs of the Guides surveyed the Mahsud position through their glasses.

'They're well dug in.' Peter observed. 'How many guns, would you say, sir?'

'They had three,' Murdoch said. 'And they're old pieces. But they want to stand and fight, which is what we hoped Chand Bibi would do, now I've been identified as leading the brigade myself. Very good, gentlemen, we are going to winkle them out.' He looked at the sun. It was about to disappear behind the western hills. 'Colonel Briggs, feed your men now, and then dismount them, and climb that hill to the left. Can you do that in the dark?'

Briggs grinned. 'My Guides can go anywhere in the dark, Sir Murdoch.'

'That's what I thought. Proceed quietly until you are flanking the enemy position, then hold until dawn. Commence firing at eight ack emma, and commence your advance. We will carry out a frontal assault at that time. Understood?'

'Yes, sir.' Briggs hurried off to assemble his officers.

'While we wait,' Peter said.

'Have some sleep. I'm sure we all need it.'

'Suppose she pulls out in the night?' Ralph asked pessimistically.

'She's not going to do that. She has staked her reputation as a woman who can lead men on this coup. Right now she's lost all along the line. But she can still re-establish her position if she can claim that she has defeated us, and that she has killed me.'

'You mean you're going to charge with us?' Peter asked.

'Any objections?' Murdoch grinned. 'It could be for the last time.'

But, like Ralph, he was haunted by the fear that Chand Bibi would after all run away. She had certainly lost her nerve when thirteen desperate men had dropped out of the sky into her midst, had fled from the harem when, had she immediately rallied her men, Ralph and his daring party must have been overwhelmed. He hardly slept, was up well before dawn, surveying the far side of the plateau, and breathed a sigh of relief when he saw the flags still flying over the Mahsud army.

Chand Bibi had confidence in her position, and in having established that he had crossed the border with only half his force. No doubt, as Evan-Jones had estimated, there were probably two thousand warriors opposed to his four hundred odd.

But he reckoned those odds were about right.

'It'll be hot work,' he reminded his officers as they mounted. 'And you're staying here, Harry. You can have an overall view of the battle and write us up after.'

Harry didn't object. He knew he lacked the experience for what was about to happen. The Mahsuds had seen the British preparations, and again opened fire, but the range was very long. The two squadrons lined up, and Murdoch walked his horse out in front, Ralph at his side, to where Colonel Ramage sat at the head of his men.

'It's your show, Peter,' he said.

'No, sir,' Peter replied. 'The Royal Western Dragoon

282

Guards would take it as an honour and a privilege if you would lead them.'

Murdoch looked over the ranks, at so many familiar faces, at RSM Yeald, waiting immediately behind his colonel, then Harry Lowndes; at Captain Destry sitting his horse in front of B Squadron, and Lieutenant Ian Mackinder, immediately behind him. Further back, behind Captain Rostron and in front of C Squadron, Lieutenant Fergus Mackinder also waited, gazing at his face. He had never imagined that he would one day lead his sons into battle. And they were avenging the wrong done their mother. He could ask for nothing more.

Then the entire regiment realized he was going to lead the charge in person, and gave a cheer. He wheeled Brutus and faced the Mahsuds, looked at his watch. It was five to eight, and he looked up at the hill on the left, saw the flash of the heliograph catching the rays of the rising sun.

He drew his sword and raised it. 'May the great God of battle,' he shouted, 'who has guided the fate of this famous regiment on many a hard-fought field, and never failed to lead it to distinction, grant that on this day, faced as we are with a host of enemies of our King and our Country, every man will do his duty, so that should we fail in our ordained task, it will yet be said of us, they were the Royal Western Dragoon Guards, who fought and died according to the ancient valour of their regiment and their blood.' He pointed his sword. 'Gentlemen, there is your enemy.'

He walked his horse forward, and listened to the so familiar jingling of harnesses behind him. Immediately the Mahsud artillery opened fire, and shells burst overhead. The shooting was for the moment wild. They would gain in accuracy long before the dragoons could reach their position, but they were not going to be allowed to do that. For the time was eight o'clock, and suddenly the hill to the left exploded in flame.

A great hubbub arose from the enemy lines, as fire was returned against this unexpected attack. It was incredible that Chand Bibi had not allowed for the possibility, but as

283

she had said so contemptuously, she was an amateur at war; he was a professional.

In any event, the gunners were distracted as Briggs' men poured bullets into the Mahsud battery.

'Bugler, sound the charge,' Murdoch commanded.

The hooves drummed as the call rang through the morning and the horses moved to the trot, then the canter. Now they could see the faces of the men in front of them, some firing at them, some at the Guides, who were advancing down the hill, returning fire as they did so – but more were moving to the rear, many throwing away their weapons.

Murdoch gazed straight ahead as he galloped at the line. Because now he could see a group of horsemen behind the position, shouting orders and gesticulating, and at least one of them was a woman.

A man appeared in front of him, levelling a rifle. Brutus brushed him aside and trampled him down as he screamed. Another man swung at Murdoch with the butt of his weapon and was thrust down. A third threw himself to the ground to attempt the old Pathan trick of hamstringing the horse with a cut from his sword as it passed. Murdoch swerved to the left and left the man lying there, to be trampled by the horses behind, then he was through and riding at the Mahsud horsemen. They scattered as he approached. Chand Bibi and her daughter rode for the rear, but Wittvinov held his ground and levelled his revolver. Murdoch ducked low over his horse's mane, and drove on behind his levelled sword. The point took Wittvinov in the chest and hurled him from the saddle, dead before he hit the ground.

Carried on by the impetus of his charge, Murdoch was up to the woman and the girl before they could gather speed. Brutus bumped into Yasmin's horse and she tumbled from the saddle with a wail. Chand Bibi drew rein to look down at her daughter, then up at Murdoch, her beautiful face a mask of rage and despair. Before she could make up her mind what to do she was surrounded by dragoons, and her arms pinioned.

'What shall we do with this fellow, sir?' RSM Yeald asked.

Murdoch gazed at Palraj, held by two of his troopers. The erstwhile chauffeur was trembling with fright.

'Hang him,' Murdoch said.

'And the woman, sir? The men would like to have her, for fifteen minutes. Just for what she did to Lady Mackinder, sir.' Yeald didn't know what had been done to Lee . . . but he could guess.

'You cannot permit that,' Chand Bibi said in a low voice.

'Are you begging me?' Murdoch asked.

Chand Bibi licked her lips. 'Imprison me. I have lost. But do not . . .' she licked her lips again. After all, she was just a frightened woman.

Murdoch hesitated. He had come here to destroy a monster. Now he could only look at a lovely woman who hardly more than twelve hours ago had lain naked on his chest. He turned his head left and right, looked at Ramage and Ian and Fergus and Lowndes and felt his heart give a little skip.

'Where is Ralph Manly-Smith?' he asked, his voice harsh.

'He's dead,' Ian said. 'He was right behind you when that fellow shot at you. The bullet hit him in the head.'

Now Murdoch's heart was constricting, as he looked at Harry, who had joined them when the charge was over. Harry's face was set and hard. So were the faces of all the men around him, including his sons.

He looked back at Chand Bibi, who read her fate in his eyes. 'You are a devil,' she said in a low voice. 'A devil!' Then her shoulders sagged. 'I would beg you to spare my child.'

Murdoch looked at the girl, who had been picked from the ground by one of the dragoons, and now twisted in his arms. 'Let the girl go,' he said. He pointed at Chand Bibi. 'Hang that woman.'

PART THREE

THE VETERAN

11
England, 1929–33

'Your action was high-handed.' Lord Irwin was obviously choosing his words with great care. 'It was also ill-timed, General Mackinder. Here we are, trying to get Gandhi and his people to agree to a conference on the future of India, a future in which Indians will govern their country according to the precepts of English law as laid down by us over the past century – and one of our generals starts shooting up the frontier . . .'

'Was I supposed to allow my wife to be tortured to death?' Murdoch asked quietly.

'Without reference to this office,' Irwin finished.

'There wasn't time.'

'And then, this invasion of Afghanistan, in direct contravention of orders . . . there could be the most serious international repercussions. And there was no necessity for it; you had already rescued your wife and the other ladies. And a drumhead court-martial, of a woman . . .'

'Who had murdered my men, and who was dedicated to stirring up the frontier against us,' Murdoch pointed out.

'It was still a drumhead execution. And then, placing my representative under arrest . . .'

'I had no choice, sir. Mr Humphrey was attempting to interfere with a military operation.'

'An unauthorized military operation,' the Viceroy reminded him. 'The furore . . . and with a general election pending at home. Add to that these articles your brother-in-law is writing in America . . . you may be the last of the old-fashioned heroes who "made Britain great" to him and his readers, but American governmental opinion is as shocked as ourselves by your behaviour. And of course there is the ethical question of giving detailed information

289

of an irregular campaign to a newspaper reporter at all, much less an American one. Really, Sir Murdoch, I don't know what to say.'

'I did not give any information to anyone, Lord Irwin,' Murdoch said. 'Mr Caspar happened to be there.'

'I'm not sure allowing him to accompany you wasn't actually worse.'

'He was there because his wife was also in the hands of the Mahsuds. However, in view of the, as you say, furore this thing seems to have caused, you will have my resignation this afternoon.'

'My dear fellow, I can't accept your resignation. And I think it would be most unwise for you to become a private citizen at this moment. No, no. You are being recalled for consultation with the War Office. A new GOC of the North West Frontier will be installed to act in your absence, and will be confirmed in the post in due course, when you have, ah, been assigned to other duties.'

'And my recommendations?'

'Well, they have been forwarded, of course. I don't know that the circumstances will permit Major Manly-Smith to be considered for a VC, however . . .'

'He gave his life in action against an enemy, sir,' Murdoch pointed out, 'having risked it to save his commanding officer as well as three civilians. The action in which he was killed was a regular one. Five of my men were killed, and fourteen wounded.'

'Which is another point,' Irwin commented. 'The fact is that Mr Manly-Smith's action in, ah, parachuting into the Mahsud town was certainly irregular. It is not covered in any military manual I have ever heard of. As for Military Medals for all the men of his party . . .'

'They all took the same risks.'

'Yes,' Irwin said again. 'Well, I can only repeat that your recommendations have been forwarded. We will have to wait and see.'

'I intend to make sure that the bravery of those men, and particularly Manly-Smith, is recognized, Lord Irwin,' Murdoch said.

'Well, I will wish you the best of luck in your future career, General,' the Viceroy remarked.

The regiment paraded as a guard of honour to say goodbye to Murdoch and Lee. Harry and Veronica had already left, but they were being accompanied by Jennifer Manly-Smith and the two children, bewildered little souls who did not yet understand that they were fatherless.

Also accompanying them was Linda Ramage.

'I'm really quite worried about her,' Peter confessed to Murdoch and Lee. 'She, well . . . she won't speak, and she hardly eats. When you think how Jennie is bearing up . . .'

'It was a quite horrible ordeal,' Lee told him. 'Especially for someone . . . well, as sensitive as Linda. I guess Jennie is just a shade tougher. And besides . . .' she bit her lip. Murdoch knew she had nearly said, 'Jennie wasn't raped.' Was that worse than losing a husband? It was something he had to find out, urgently. 'We'll look after her, Peter,' Lee said. 'Until you come home.'

'Which won't be very long,' Murdoch reminded him. 'The pundits seem to feel that like me, you and your men are too dangerous to be left loose on the frontier.'

'I can't say I'll be sorry to go,' Peter said.

'I can't say I'm sorry to be leaving, either,' Murdoch agreed.

Ian and Fergus came up for dinner on their last night. Like everyone else, except those actually involved, the two young men had no idea what had really happened in Mahrain before it had been razed. But they had gathered that Chand Bibi had been a dangerous enemy of the British Raj, responsible for kidnapping their mother. They accepted that their father had done what had needed to be done – even if they had been taken aback by the grim figure he had displayed in the Afghanistan mountains.

'They can't possibly sack you for quashing a rising that rapidly and that successfully,' Ian argued.

'Governments can do anything they like,' Murdoch reminded him. 'They believe in expediency.'

'If they sack you, we're coming out as well,' Fergus declared.

'Don't be a chump,' Murdoch told him. 'The army, and the country, needs men like you.' He grinned at them. 'I can't tell you how thrilled I was to be riding into battle with you.'

'Or how scared I was,' Lee said. 'All three of you in action at the same time.'

They had not spoken about the things that really mattered, yet. There had hardly been time, with Murdoch having to go down to Delhi and with the preparations for their departure. Besides, they had not wanted to talk about it, while still surrounded by the sights and sounds and smells associated with the frontier, and all it stood for. Then it was a matter of looking after Jennie and Linda on the train journey down to the coast – they didn't want to talk about it either. Jennie was by no means as strong as she pretended. In fact she had been suffering from shock since she had been told of her husband's death after he had so magnificently rescued her dearest friends. The presence of her father had helped her to appear to ride the blow, but now the shock was wearing off, and she was facing the fact that at twenty-five she was a widow with two small children and only an army pension. Murdoch had every intention of helping her, but he hadn't yet worked out how.

Linda was the more serious problem. For a woman with her psychological repugnance for the more earthy side of human relationships, to have been stretched naked on the floor before a crowd of laughing men and women and forced to submit to several of them had driven her close to madness. Or perhaps over the edge. She gave no visible signs of it, replied when spoken to, even smiled from time to time, and then withdrew again into the hidden cellars of her mind. She never picked up a book or a newspaper, never even looked out of the window on the train journey, just stared in front of her. Remembering, Murdoch wondered? Or trying to forget?

He knew Lee was having the same nightmares. She had reacted so bravely, with such determination not to be beaten, but she was a woman just like the others, and she had been as humiliated as they, just as like them she had had to watch Reynolds murdered. And unlike them, she had had to suppose that she would also have to watch her husband mutilated while still living.

That he, they, had triumphed at the end was perhaps only just sinking in. He knew it was, for both of them, a matter of timing . . . but he had the experience of having survived captivity and the threat of torture and even near death before: she had not. They had not touched each other, sexually, since their return from Mahrain, and he understood that she was at least partly afraid to be alone with him. He counted that mood as affected by India as well. But at last they stood together at the rail to watch Bombay drop astern. Jennifer was feeding the children, and Linda had retired to her cabin immediately. There were people around them, but it was the first time since Chand Bibi's death that they were actually alone with each other, mentally; even in their bedroom at Bala Hissar they had always been surrounded by the sounds and smell of India.

'I thought the frontier was going to be a huge adventure,' Lee said, looking down at the wake. 'I guess, when one dreams of adventure, one never understands that it needn't all be fun.'

'No,' he agreed.

She glanced at him, then looked back at the sea. And gave a little shiver. 'I keep thinking of that woman . . . so much beauty, so much hate.'

'Yes,' he said.

'What did you think of, when you hanged her?' She gave him another glance.

'I'm not sure I thought of anything.'

'But . . . you had known her a long time. And . . .' she flushed and bit her lip and he knew she was remembering Chand Bibi masturbating him.

'I never slept with her, willingly, if that's what you mean. I won't pretend she wasn't a fascinating creature.'

'And yet you hanged her.'

'Some snakes are fascinating creatures,' he pointed out.

293

'To look at. But you still have to blow their heads off if they get too close.'

'Um.' She hugged herself and looked at the sea. 'There are so many parts of your life I know nothing about.'

'Not any more,' he said.

Another glance. 'Tell me, about her,' she said.

'What about her?'

'Well . . .' she licked her lips in a quick, nervous gesture. 'How did she die? Did it take a long time?' She was working towards some private watershed, he knew. And he wanted her to get there.

'No,' he said. 'We didn't strangle her, you know. We tied her wrists and put a noose round her neck and then placed her horse beneath a tree and drove it away. She died instantly of a broken neck.'

'And while all this was going on, she didn't say anything?'

'No, she didn't. She just stared at me.' His turn to give a little shiver. 'It's a good thing I don't believe in ghosts. And then, when she saw Yeald about to hit the horse with the whip, she looked at her daughter.'

'Oh, my God!' Lee gasped. 'The girl was there?'

'Yes, she was.'

She was silent for a few moments. Then she asked, 'What happened afterwards?'

'We took her down and buried her. Hanging is a ghastly death to watch. All death is pretty ghastly, but hanging is the worst. There may be no blood, but everything else in the body is liable to let go.'

'Ugh! Do you know, Murdoch, until poor George . . . I had never seen a human being die? And then that fight outside the harem . . . I suppose it's all commonplace to you.'

'No,' he said. 'Death is never commonplace.'

She gazed at him. 'You have lived, so much, seen so much. Murdoch, when those men were . . . lying on me, what did you think?'

'I thought that I hated them, and I hated Chand Bibi. And that I loved you.'

'Oh, Murdoch.' There were tears in her eyes. 'Can you ever want to make love to me again?'

'I want to make love to you, right now, my dearest.'

'Right now,' she said.

He held her hand and they went to the cabin.

'So there it is,' Churchill said, lighting a cigar. 'We have another Socialist Government, and one with a proper majority, too. It may be more difficult to get rid of than the last one. And we have our best soldier in disgrace. It's a rum world.'

'I don't know I'm in disgrace, yet,' Murdoch told him. 'I've only just completed a very long leave. Eight months. Maybe I've been retired and don't know it yet. But I still get my salary.' He grinned. 'Under instructions not to give any interviews to the press.'

'Rather like shutting the stable door after the horse has run off,' Churchill grunted. 'I've read your brother-in-law's articles. Next thing they'll be wanting to make a film of your exploits. You really are a little old to be leading cavalry charges, you know, Murdoch.'

'Old? I'm only just forty-nine. And I'm as fit as a fiddle.'

'I must say, you look fit. It's a damned shame.'

'What is?'

'That all this has happened. Oh, not only your adventure in Afghanistan, but this Labour victory at the polls. You should be our next CIGS. But I don't see it happening, now.'

'I didn't see it happening at all. As you once said, they don't really want a fighting soldier as the boss. It might alarm too many people.'

'I'm not sure that would be a bad thing. Your friend Hitler is still breathing hell and damnation, you know.'

'Is he? And is he getting anywhere?'

'No. Not at the minute. But politics is a funny business. Were anything to happen to tilt the applecart, a political crisis which brought another humiliation on Germany, or another financial crisis, who can say? You know we're in the process of evacuating the Rhineland. And there can be no doubt that the German military men are starting to sound aggressive again. Bruening won't have anything to do with them, but if someone equally aggressive were to become chancellor, a fighting CIGS might be a very useful asset.'

'By then they'll probably have sent me off as governor of some colony.'

Churchill smiled. 'As long as it isn't somewhere you can cause trouble. How is Lady Mackinder?'

'She's fine.'

'Must have been quite an ordeal.'

He was probing. Although the events at Mahrain were now nearly a year in the past, and Harry had developed his articles into a book, the central figure of which had been Murdoch, he had not described what had actually happened to the women, merely related to how they had been in the hands of the Mahsuds for a week, allowed his readers to envisage, according to their knowledge and imaginations, just what that might entail. Churchill had served in India, and had more knowledge and imagination than the average man.

But Murdoch was not going to be drawn, even by him. 'Yes,' he agreed. 'It was, quite an ordeal. But Lee can take it.'

It was quite an ordeal, every time he drove through the gates at Broad Acres and looked out at the meadow and up at the house. India, Mahrain, Chand Bibi, even Peshawar and the Bala Hissar, seemed so very far away, a long nightmare which had now ended.

Because it had, at last, ended. He parked the car, ran up the steps. He had been more tired than he had admitted to Churchill, but it was a mental tiredness, born of frustration and the fear that he would never be employed again. But that had been swept away, the following day, when he had gone to the War Office. That was only yesterday – it seemed like a hundred years ago. But a hundred happy years.

'Lee!' he shouted. 'Lee! Philippa! Where is everyone?'

They came in from the garden. 'What's happened?'

He took Lee in his arms and kissed her, then did the same to his sister. 'Everything. Everything good.'

'You mean you haven't been sacked?' Philippa asked. They had regarded his summons to London with some apprehension.

Murdoch felt in his pocket and produced the new badge, the crossed swords and baton now surmounted by a crown.

'Oh, Murdoch!' they screamed together. 'A lieutenant-general?' They hugged and kissed him again.

'I've even been given another medal.'

'Let's see.'

'Oh, it's simply the General Service Medal. Everyone who has served out there gets one.' He showed them the ribbon, dark blue edged with green.

'The colours clash,' Philippa complained.

'You won't even notice it, amongst all the others,' Lee told her.

'But best of all,' Murdoch said, 'Ralph is to get his posthumous VC, and the others their Military Medals.'

'Oh, Murdoch,' Lee said. 'I am so glad. I'll go down to the village right after lunch and tell Jennie.'

Jennifer had been living with her mother since her return.

'But how on earth did it happen?' she wanted to know.

'Well . . . what was principally upsetting the powers that be was the reaction of the Afghans to my "invasion" of their territory. The last thing the Government wants is another full-scale war on the frontier. So . . . Habibullah Ghazi has been overthrown and executed.'

'Oh, good heavens. You mean Amanullah is back in charge? How splendid.'

'No, he's not. I'm afraid Amanullah is a refugee. The new amir is the man who got rid of Habibullah, a general named Muhammad Nadir Khan. He now calls himself Muhammad Nadir Shah. And he is so delighted that I chased the Mahsuds and walloped them he wants to give me a medal himself; they were allies of Habibullah, you see. On top of all that, there's been serious trouble in the province, riots in Peshawar, armoured cars on the streets, you name it.'

'Oh, good heavens!' Lee exclaimed, trying to envisage it.

'Thus there are people saying, "This would never have happened had Mackinder still been in command." So I'm a blue-eyed boy again.'

'And CIGS?' Philippa asked.

'Ah, no. One can't have everything, I suppose. I think they feel that to put me in charge of the army would be to show their approval of my "reckless behaviour". No.' He pulled his nose. 'I've been put in charge of converting the cavalry from horses to tanks.'

'From what?' Lee was aghast.

Murdoch grinned. 'I'm not sure I wouldn't rather be fighting the Mahsuds again, to be sure.'

He had not yet taken up his new duties when the collapse of the American Stock Exchange began to spread across the Atlantic. It happened in fact only a couple of weeks after his promotion. The resulting chaos naturally affected the army: mechanization was put on ice. It affected everyone. Murdoch's own investments, created by his father and grandfather, were mainly in government stock, and as he did not have to sell and continued to receive his dividends, he was not affected by their fall in value – even if his salary, and that of everyone else, was soon cut in the interests of the national economy. Harry was in deeper financial trouble, and Murdoch offered to lend him money, but his brother-in-law reckoned he could manage, although, having written his book, he had to go back to work for his paper. The book, however, was quite successful. He did not inform either Lee or Murdoch of his relationship with Veronica since her catastrophic Indian adventure, but early the following year they were divorced.

'Second casualty,' Lee remarked. 'I reckon there are going to be more.'

'Jennie?' He was concerned. 'I thought she was settling down quite well.' He knew she had got herself a job, allowed herself to sink back down the social scale to being a sergeant-major's daughter instead of an officer's wife.

'Oh, she is. I was thinking of Linda Ramage.'

Murdoch hadn't seen Linda since their return – she had

gone back to her parents as well – but he knew Lee had kept corresponding with her.

'I think she wants a divorce too,' Lee said.

'Does Peter know?'

'I don't think so. She's waiting until the regiment gets home this year. But I don't think she'll ever be able to bring herself to sleep with a man again.'

'Um.' He squeezed her hand. 'I'm so glad you're you.'

'I'll second that motion. What a foul world it is.'

'It's only foul if you let it get on top of you. You've never done that.'

But Linda Ramage had. The night before the regiment landed at Plymouth, she died from an overdose of sleeping pills.

'If only she'd waited,' Peter said. 'I'm sure we could have worked something out.'

'I think she died in Mahrain,' Murdoch said. 'She was only going through the motions of breathing and moving. I wish there was more we could have done. I am so terribly sorry, Peter.'

Peter sighed. 'And here I am, a brigadier.' He had handed over command of the regiment to Colonel Lowndes. 'I was so proud of that, so wanted to make her proud of it, too. What the hell am I going to do, now?'

'You're going to give me a hand, turning our dragoons and hussars and lancers into mechanics.'

With the fall of the Government in 1931, as the depression became worldwide, and the formation of a National Party which was swept to power on a wave of optimism, the mechanization of the cavalry at last got under way.

Murdoch had used his time over the previous two years, when he had been without a command, to study the whole question of mechanization, and had found his research utterly fascinating. If his every instinct was against the phasing out of horse cavalry, his experience told him it was inevitable, and his concern was to make the British cavalry again the best in the world – he was appalled at the amount that needed to be done.

The main issue between the various tank experts, in various armies, was whether the tank of the future should be a heavily armoured slow-moving gun platform, like the Stars of the Great War, or more lightly armoured but capable of considerably more speed and manoeuvrability, like the Whippets. The British had developed the idea of the tank, but they had largely been overtaken by the French even during the Great War; at the end of 1918 the French army had actually had about half as many tanks again as the British – close to four thousand. No other country had any sizeable tank force at all.

The main French tank was built by Renault, and to Murdoch's mind combined the worst features of either alternative. Although about the lightest in existence, weighing only six tons as against the Whippet's fourteen, it was also very slow. But then, the entire French concept of war was different to that of the British. The French army was dominated by the infantry, and tanks were intended only for close support of the foot soldier, not for combat on their own. Pursuing this theme, the French had also been building, during the twenties, huge sixty-eight-ton monsters, armed with a turret-mounted seventy-five milli-metre cannon, truly moving fortresses. By the early thirties they had ten of these, far heavier and more heavily armed than anything dreamed of by the British.

The British concept was truly of mechanized cavalry. Even before the end of the war they had developed the Medium D which could travel at twenty miles per hour – for brief periods. Built by Vickers, some hundred and sixty of them went into service by 1928. But they were lightly armoured, and lightly armed, with not more than half the firepower of the giants, and by the time Murdoch became involved the British too were making slow, heavy tanks for infantry support.

Murdoch was naturally not involved in the infantry's plans, but he was concerned at the proliferation of ideas about medium and light tanks. The Vickers were officially described as medium, but now along came absurdly little things, called 'tankettes' which carried two men and were armed only with light machine-guns. They were faster than anything else, and were undoubtedly useful for reconnaissance, but were really of little use in battle.

His dream was of a corps of medium tanks, sufficiently well armed and armoured not only to devastate enemy positions, but to engage and defeat enemy tanks. He sought to re-create the cavalry battle of the past, only with vehicles instead of horses. And with the development of a Vickers-Armstong six-tonner, armed with a thirty-seven millimetre gun, he began to realize his ambition. These vehicles remained lightly armoured, and could not stand up to enemy artillery, but their speed and striking power made them a potentially brilliant weapon in the hands of an aggressive commander.

Far more difficult than choosing the tanks with which to replace the horses was finding the men to man them. For the most part the cavalry was scandalized at the idea. And at the training involved. Training a cavalry trooper was basically a business of drilling him and teaching him how to ride, and in the case of the dragoons, how to shoot as well. Once he had mastered those fairly straightforward arts he could be as thick as a brick, for from then on his every action was governed by the commands of his officers.

Training men to operate in tanks was a different matter. They had to be mechanically minded as well as tough minded, for the inside of a tank was no place for psychological hang-ups which might not be noticeable galloping along in the fresh air on the back of a horse. The psychological factor was indeed of prime importance, because the operative word was 'in' a tank. It was quite possible for a cavalry trooper to be at odds, however temporarily, with the men to either side of him; it was not possible for seven men to spend hours at a time cooped up in a tiny, odiferous, noisy and highly dangerous compartment unless they all got on extremely well.

'I have to thank God I'm retiring, Sir Murdoch,' Yeald said. 'I could never adapt myself to riding in one of those things.'

Ironically, they sat on their horses to watch the tank

crews manoeuvring their vehicles beneath them; Murdoch could legitimately spend more time with the Westerns than any other regiment, for they had done him the great honour of choosing him as their new colonel-in-chief.

'I'm not sure I could either,' Murdoch agreed. 'It's a young man's game.' He was delighted that both Ian and Fergus had accepted the necessity of change, albeit reluctantly, and were proving adept tank commanders. So were Colonel Lowndes and Major Destry. 'But the regiment still won't be the same without you, Sergeant-Major.'

'Thirty-three years, sir, man and boy.'

'I'm only six months your junior, in length of service. There were some good times.'

'And some pretty sticky ones, sir. But I enjoyed them all, with you riding in front.'

'What are you going to do?'

'Buy a newsagent's shop in the village, sir. Jennie's keen. She'll help me run it. And the kids'll soon be old enough to make the deliveries.'

'She should get married again,' Murdoch said. 'She is such a lovely girl.'

'She won't ever marry again, Sir Murdoch. Not after Mr Manly-Smith. Do you know she keeps that Victoria Cross on her bedside table, and she says her prayers to it every night.'

The depression gripped ever more relentlessly and coldly during 1931 and 1932 – to Lee's disappointment she had been unable to throw a really big party for Fergus's twenty-first birthday in 1931, while Ian's had been celebrated in India, just before the regiment's return – but by the end of 1932 there were signs that the worst might be over. Of principal importance seemed the election of Franklin Roosevelt to the presidency of the United States in November 1932. Lee, whose family had always voted Democrat, was tremendously excited, and Murdoch also felt that the promotion of this strong, clear-minded, and above all optimistic man was going to provide America with the leadership she had seemed to lack during the previous four years.

302

There were, of course, less happy appurtenances of the financial gloom. Japan undertook open aggression in Manchuria, desperately seeking outlets for her manufactured goods which were now being closed in the West as tariff walls went up. The West, politicians and newspapers, screamed their indignation, a commission was set up which condemned the Japanese for aggression – and the Japanese responded by leaving the League of Nations and in effect thumbing their noses at the rest of the world . . . who did nothing about it.

Then in India the disturbances grew as a conference called in London, and attended by Ghandi, ended in disagreement. Churchill had not been offered a ministerial post in the Coalition Government, partly because he was anathema to the Socialists who formed part of it – MacDonald was still Prime Minister – but equally because of his outspoken views on India, which he had outlined to Murdoch back in 1924 and which he never changed.

But the most startling event occurred at the end of January 1933, when Adolf Hitler was appointed as Chancellor of Germany.

Hitler's position had dramatically improved as the world, and most of all Germany, had again been plunged into financial chaos. Too many people remembered 1923, only six years before the American stock market crash, and were not prepared to put up with another slow haul back to prosperity, with the possibility of another crash a few years further on. Hitler promised an end to all that. As to exactly how he was going to do it, he remained vague – on the hustings. And while a great many people had read *Mein Kampf*, which had become a bestseller, few seemed to take his vision of the Nazi – as his party was now called – world, in which Germany would initially finance itself by expropriating Jewish property, and then seek its future in the east, at all seriously.

The twelve seats he had held in the Reichstag in 1928 – these did not include himself as he was still an Austrian citizen – had grown to a hundred and seven in 1930. Two years later he secured more than eleven million votes when contesting the presidency against Hindenburg. Thus he had clearly become a politician to be taken seriously, but with Hindenburg in power for another seven years, and his known dislike for the 'Austrian corporal', his sudden surrender to Hitler's demands for the chancellorship took everyone by surprise.

Equally surprising was an invitation which came the following week for Murdoch to visit Germany. It was signed by Reger, but was actually from the new Chancellor, who looked forward to renewing their acquaintance, in these 'changed circumstances'.

'He's being backed by the army, of course,' Churchill said. 'They see in him their best hope of making Germany again a world power. Well, they are probably right, if we are stupid enough to sit back and let them. They also suppose that he will be nothing more than a puppet in their hands. Would you agree with that estimation?'

Murdoch considered. 'Reger certainly thinks he can be used, I would say. The point is, should I go?'

'I think you should, if the War Office will give you permission. It's always worthwhile listening to the other chap's point of view.'

The War Office thought it might be a good idea for Murdoch to visit Germany, especially after, at the end of February, a fire which was said to have been set by the Communists burned down the Reichstag. There seemed some possibility of civil war between the Nazis and their rivals, and the Government was interested in a first-hand appraisal of the situation. He was, however, required to travel strictly as a private individual, but to his delight they agreed that he might take an ADC, and that the ADC could be one of his sons. He took Ian, recently promoted to first-lieutenant. Lee went as well, of course, looking forward to renewing her acquaintanceship with the Regers after nearly ten years.

'Do we tell Ian that Paul is his half-brother?' she asked Murdoch.

'No. Because we don't know that he is,' he insisted.

'Oh, you are a wretched man,' she grumbled.

They went immediately after Easter, because they wanted to be back for Harry's final speech day, which would be in June; he was due at Sandhurst in September. They also had to make the necessary arrangements for Helen's twenty-first birthday, which would be in the summer, and for which Lee was planning a huge ball to make up for what she felt she had missed with Ian and Fergus – Helen was currently at Girton.

The three of them repeated the same route as Murdoch and Lee had taken in 1924, from the Hook of Holland to Berlin. But they had barely crossed the border when they became aware of considerable differences between now and then. They were surrounded by evidence of the bite of the depression, but they were also aware of a kind of throb, echoing through the nation. It was evident in the crisp salute and the heel-clicks of the border guards; everyone seemed to have suddenly quickened their pace.

'Do I get to meet Mr Hitler on this trip?' Lee asked. 'I should like to.'

'Then you shall. Why, do you count him a good thing?'

'He certainly seems to be doing wonders for Germany.'

'Yes,' Murdoch said thoughtfully.

They were met in Berlin by Paul junior as well as his father. Paul was now wearing the uniform of a captain, and was graver and more intense than ever. Reger was also in uniform, that of a general.

'You see,' he said with a smile. 'I have caught you up, Murdoch.'

'Congratulations,' Murdoch said, deciding not to ask him what he was general of: the German army was still officially limited to a hundred thousand men.

Margriet hardly seemed to have changed, was as boldly beautiful as ever. Perhaps her eyes were more watchful, her manner more thoughtful, but she was as gracious a hostess as in 1924.

The change lay in her family. Three of the girls were now married. One of her sons, Klaus, was a storm trooper, as

305

Reger told them proudly, one of the brown-shirted supporters of the Fuehrer, as Hitler was now widely called. The other, Ernst, was a member of the Fuehrer's own personal bodyguard, the Schutzstaffel, and wore a black shirt.

'You see,' Reger smiled. 'It is all happening, as I told you it would.'

'And is it all going to continue to happen, as the Fuehrer said it would?' Murdoch asked.

'Of course.' Reger continued to smile.

The only child remaining at home was Annaliese. At seventeen she was startlingly lovely, for while she had her mother's pale complexion and flowing hair, her face was rounder and her features not quite as regular – thus she avoided the solemnity of expression which had always marked Margriet. Her character was also as ebullient as he remembered from that wink nine years before.

'I think Ian is quite smitten,' Lee remarked that night.

'Well, he'd better not be,' Murdoch said. 'I don't think it would be a good idea for any British officer, much less a son of mine, to get entangled with a German.'

'You almost sound as if you think we are going to have another war with them.'

'We can hardly have that, as they have nothing to fight with. But I do think we are bound to have a confrontation with them in the not too distant future, put up our hand and say, you've gone just about far enough.'

'What would happen then?'

'I would say, as he has risen to power by telling the people how great he is going to make them, that that would be the end of Mr Hitler. And his supporters. Which wouldn't make Reger very happy.'

'Um,' she said. 'What a shame. I think Annaliese is an absolute charmer.'

'Anyway,' Murdoch said. 'It would be virtually incest.'

'Oh, come now. They're not related at all.'

'You know what I mean,' Murdoch said.

They're were the ususal gallops across the country, and

dinner parties, and a visit to the opera. On all these occasions Annaliese was included, to round up the numbers. At the opera Murdoch was presented to Hitler, and Lee was also introduced. The Fuehrer had changed somewhat from 1924. He had put on weight, gained in confidence, looked like a gentleman in his white tie, and smiled a good deal more easily.

'He would like a private conversation with you,' Reger interpreted. 'I will arrange it, if you do not mind.'

'I was under the impression that is actually what I'm here for,' Murdoch agreed.

'General Goering would also like to see you.'

'Goering?' Murdoch raised his eyebrows. He knew that Hermann Goering was virtually Hitler's right-hand man in the Government, and that he was chief minister of Prussia, but he also knew that he was an airman. Indeed, he was a very famous airman, a holder of the Pour le Merité medal for his exploits in the Great War; he had succeeded Manfred von Richtofen as commander of the famous 'circus'. 'What can he want with an army man?'

'I am sure he will tell you, Murdoch,' Reger said.

Murdoch felt the growing influence of the Nazis more in Berlin than anywhere he had yet been. And he could not help but feel, too, that it was a malign influence. Following the destruction of the Reichstag building and the consequent threat of a communist coup, or so it was claimed by the Government, Hitler had pushed through the reassembled parliament – which now met in the opera house – a series of laws giving him and his party virtually dictatorial powers until the emergency ended. This was itself sinister as, being open ended, it left the decision as to when the emergency was at an end with Hitler himself.

More disturbing, however, was the use being made of the laws by the Nazi rank and file, and it was no unusual thing to see gangs of youths wearing military-style kepis and armbands with the swastika insignia engaged in beating up those suspected of being Jews or Communists, or even ransacking houses belonging to their opponents.

307

'I'm amazed those people put up with it,' Murdoch told Reger.

'A lot of them do not. The Jews are emigrating in droves.' He grinned. 'Fortunately, as Germany is a bankrupt nation and forced to apply severe exchange-control restrictions, they have to leave most of their worldly possessions behind.'

'And?'

'Oh, they are confiscated for the good of the state.'

'Good God! Anyway, what I meant was, why don't they go to the police?'

'Because it would do them no good. The police are all Nazis.'

Murdoch stared at him. 'What you are really saying is that the rule of law has completely broken down in Germany.'

'Quite the contrary, my dear fellow. The law is more strictly enforced in Germany than anywhere else in the world.'

'But it is Nazi law, and it is only enforced for the good of the Nazis. And you approve of this?'

'Yes, Murdoch, I do. It is a necessary transitional stage in our crawl back to greatness. No nation ever became great under democracy and total equality. Britain rose under an oligarchy of rich country gentlemen, who knew what needed to be done, and did it, regardless of the squeals from a few minorities who felt they were being trampled on. Almost everyone agrees that Britain is in decline. Why is that? It is because you now have full democracy, that is why. Here in Germany we tried full democracy, for a dozen years. And the results were disastrous. Now we must use the stick. In a classroom of unruly boys it is the only way to restore discipline, and purpose – and there must be no restrictions on the use of corporal punishment by the master. But for those who behave, and contribute to the common good, why, no rewards will be too high. You wait and see, Murdoch. In a few years, when we have got rid of or disciplined all our malcontents, Germany will be the happiest, most prosperous nation on earth.'

'Presuming your party retains power at the next election.' Murdoch suggested.

Reger smiled. 'Oh indeed. Whenever the next election may be.'

'It really is quite terrifying,' Murdoch confided to Lee. 'It is like a town being taken over by a totally corrupt council. Only this isn't a town; it's a nation of sixty-odd million people.'

'So what are we going to do about it? It seems to be the government they want.'

'I doubt that. As for what we are going to do, we are going to watch and listen for a few more days, then we are going to go home and report.'

'I have read Mr Caspar's book,' Goering said. 'It is fascinating. One longed to have been with you in those mountains, Sir Murdoch, fighting against those savages for the honour of your women.'

There wasn't much of a reply to be made to that, and in any event Murdoch was still taking in the baroque splendour with which he was surrounded. They had all been invited down to the castle Goering had appropriated as his own. The building alone was awe-inspiring, the interior more so, for the German police chief had furnished it with apparently everything he fancied from amongst the paintings and other works of art confiscated from emigrating Jews. A good deal of the work was of a distinctly erotic nature, but Goering was not embarrassed as he escorted Lee and Margriet and Annaliese through the various galleries.

'I am a widower,' he chuckled. 'I am not a fortunate man like your husband and General von Reger, Lady Mackinder. I must live on my memories.'

From the number of attractive young women who seemed to have jobs in the castle, Murdoch decided that Goering's memories did not play as large a part in life as he claimed. But he was here for a more important purpose than to look at nudes, and now he and Reger were closeted in Goering's private study.

309

'What I find most interesting,' Goering went on, 'is the way you were rescued, by the gallant Manly-Smith. Mr Caspar merely states that Manly-Smith and his little band were dropped from aeroplanes. Did these planes land, or were parachutes used?'

'Oh, they used parachutes. There was no place for the planes to land.'

'But how many men could each plane carry?'

'Only two, apart from the pilot. That was why the force was so small.'

'Ah. As an airman, you will understand, Sir Murdoch, I am interested in these things. I have used a parachute myself, of course, and what I find difficult to understand is how this intrepid band were all dropped within a relatively small area. Normally, when one leaps from an aircraft, one has very little idea of where one is going to come down. It is a matter of the winds.'

'There was almost no wind that night,' Murdoch said.

'But still, from several thousand feet . . .'

'The planes flew at no more than a thousand feet.'

'Good heavens. Is that possible? Were none of your men dashed to pieces on the earth? The free fall before the parachute opened would have been very nearly a thousand feet, surely.'

'Not more than six or seven hundred,' Murdoch told him.

'But then . . . three hundred feet? Was there time?'

'Apparently. Once the parachute opened and checked their descent, it didn't seem to matter all that much how close to the ground they were. Oh, they suffered various bumps and bruises, but they all survived.' He smiled. 'It's not something I would have cared to do myself, but I'm damn glad those men were prepared to.'

'Oh, indeed. I find the whole episode incredible,' Goering remarked. 'But also, incredibly interesting. Shall we join the ladies?'

'What do you think of the progress we are making?' Reger asked, acting as Hitler's interpreter.

310

'I think you are doing remarkable things, your excellency,' Murdoch said. 'I am sure the world is looking forward to seeing the new Germany play an important part on the international stage.'

Hitler looked pleased. 'Indeed we shall. It is our intention. It is also our birthright. But more important, it is our responsibility, to ourselves and to Europe. You will not deny, General Mackinder, that the greatest threat to peace at this time is Stalin's Russia.'

'I would have thought Stalin had too many internal problems to be capable of foreign adventures, your excellency.'

'He is capable of anything,' Hitler said. 'The Russians are Mongols. It is only six hundred years since Genghis Khan watered his horses in the Danube. This is not so long.'

Murdoch decided against attempting to correct the Fuehrer's somewhat muddled history.

'Thus it is the business of Germany to be strong,' Hitler went on. 'So that the next Mongol invasion may be met and thrown back. Or better yet, prevented from ever developing. I have said this for ten years. I have said this to you.'

'I remember, your excellency.'

'But we are prevented from being strong, by that millstone which has been hung around our neck, the Versailles Treaty. We cannot permit this to continue.'

His voice was growing more strident, and Reger's translation was matching it.

'Presumably,' Murdoch suggested, 'the time will come when certain aspects of the treaty can be renegotiated.'

'Time? I have no time, General. You must tell your Government this. The world has no time. The time must be now.'

'Now would be rather a bad time,' Murdoch said.

Hitler frowned at him, and Reger began to look worried. But Murdoch had something on his mind, and he was determined to say it. 'You are getting rather a bad press at the moment, you see,' he explained. 'This harrassing of the Jews, which almost amounts to a persecution, is upsetting a good many people. If you wish a sympathetic hearing from the French and British governments, you would be making a very good move by restraining your storm troopers, by giving back the Jews their time-honoured place in German society.'

Hitler stared at him, and Murdoch became aware of throbbing veins in the usually calm face. Then the Fuehrer suddenly exploded, screaming at the top of his voice. 'The Jews! Do not mention the Jews to me. They are the scum of the earth, pests, rodents. I do not deal with the Jews, I crush them under my heel as I walk by.'

He paused for breath while Reger translated.

Murdoch gazed at Hitler, uncertain whether the display of anger had been genuine or calculated. 'Then, your excellency, I am afraid public opinion in Great Britain and France may make it very difficult, if not impossible, for our governments to undertake any re-negotiation of the Versailles agreements.'

'Public opinion,' Hitler sneered. 'What do I care for public opinion? What does Germany care for public opinion? There is only one opinion which matters in Germany. Listen to it, General Mackinder.'

He flung out his hand to point at the window, and as if a switch had been turned Murdoch heard the tramp of marching feet, the roar of a thousand voices singing the Horst Wessel song.

'You tell your Government,' Hitler said, speaking now in a low and calm voice, 'that it is my most earnest wish to be Britain's friend. More, I would be her closest ally. I would sign, tomorrow, a treaty of perpetual friendship and mutual support with Britain. All I would ask is the return of our colonies. But I have a duty to my people. They have called me from obscurity to lead them to greatness. I shall not fail them, no matter what it may entail. You tell your Government that, General Mackinder.'

'I imagine you'll be glad to get home,' Murdoch remarked as he and Ian finished the packing.

'Well, of course,' Ian agreed. 'But I have enjoyed

312

myself.' He had not been present at any of Murdoch's private conversations with the Nazi leaders.

'With the fair Annaliese,' Murdoch agreed.'Where did you go last night?'

The young couple had been out on their own on several occasions, and the previous night had been their farewell engagement.

'Well . . .' Ian looked somewhat embarrassed. 'We went to this night club. Apparently it's all the rage in Berlin at the moment.'

'Any good?'

'Damned embarrassing, as a matter of fact. They had a floor show, half a dozen quite beautiful girls. Then they stripped.'

'To a mixed audience?' Murdoch was shocked.

'Oh, well, the Germans don't look at these things the way we do. I mean, they take off their clothes the moment the weather warms up. The thing was, these girls took theirs off, and then at the end, they turned out to be boys. Well, men.'

Murdoch gazed at his son. 'You took Annaliese von Reger to an obscene show?'

'Steady on, Dad. She took me. She's been there before.'

'A seventeen-year-old girl?'

'As I said, that's the way it is, in Germany.'

'And you approve.'

'Well . . . I don't disapprove. She's a most lovely girl.'

'I suppose *she* has stripped for you, like her compatriots.'

'I only wish she had.' Ian grinned. 'I guess it's still a shade cold. But she and her parents have always gone naked at their summer cottage in Bavaria, in the summer. Didn't you know?' he asked innocently.

'I've never been here in the summer,' Murdoch growled.

'Everyone does it,' Ian continued. 'Last summer Anna went to camp with her friends. Boys and girls. And took everything off to swim. That's why they're all so healthy-looking.'

'Tall, tanned, terrific, and taken,' Murdoch suggested.

'Maybe she is. But does that matter?'

He was right, of course. Lee had not been a virgin on their wedding night, and it had not mattered to him. In fact Lee's girlhood experiences had no doubt helped to create the strength that had enabled her to withstand the worst Chand Bibi could have done to her. While poor Linda Ramage had undoubtedly been a virgin on *her* wedding night.

But he wasn't going to approve. He didn't want to approve of anything in this new, Nazi-controlled Germany.

'It had been so wonderful having you to stay,' Margriet told him. 'I only wish there had not been so much business. We have had no time to talk. But I also hope it won't be another nine years before you visit Germany.'

'Well . . .' Murdoch temporized. 'You should try visiting us, in England.'

'I would love to do that, Murdoch. But Reger would never come now, when there is so much happening here. And he would not let me go alone.' She smiled. 'He is positive I am just awaiting the opportunity to jump into bed with you.'

'Wherever could he have got that idea?'

'Don't you even like me a little?'

'You are a most beautiful woman, Margriet. But our time was more than thirty years ago. We were children.'

'Children.' She sighed, and looked across the hall to where Ian and Annaliese were saying goodbye to each other. 'How I wish we were children again.'

'It might be quite fun,' Murdoch said, without thinking. And found himself imagining Annaliese naked. He felt quite ashamed of himself.

'I reported all my conversations to both the War Office and the Foreign Office, of course,' Murdoch said.

'And what was their reaction?' Churchill asked.

'They varied between two extremes. One was of the opinion that the Germans have every right to re-arm. The other seemed to feel that Hitler is going to be a passing phenomenon. In the middle there was total indifference about what is happening in Germany.'

314

'Yes. When you think that the Oxford Union recently voted, almost unanimously, that they would never be prepared to fight for King and Country, it really makes you wonder what we are coming to.'

'I'll tell you something, Winston. I wish to God you had a ministry. Preferably the War Office.'

Churchill grinned. 'I can make a damned nuisance of myself, even from a back bench. Why don't you give me some facts and figures, and I'll ask a question or two. What are your plans now?'

'Back to the grind. And I mean that literally; the grind of tanks. But first . . .' his turn to smile. 'I have a fun family summer coming up.'

The ancient rafters of Broad Acres rang to the roar of the singing voices, 'Never been twenty-one before, now you've got the key of the door.' Helen Mackinder beamed at her brothers and parents, her aunts and uncle and cousins, and Lee's eyes were unashamedly moist.

Murdoch saw Harry step outside on to the porch, and quietly followed him. He had been aware, since his return from Germany, that his youngest son had something on his mind. It was difficult to determine what it could be. Harry had had a far more brilliant scholastic career at Wellington than either of his brothers, and had done well at sports, too. He was tall and strong and as fit as any young man of seventeen and a half should be. But he was not the confiding kind.

Murdoch found him leaning against one of the uprights, looking out over the meadow, and the graves of Buccaneer and Mars; Brutus was still at stud.

'Bit noisy in there,' he commented.

'Bit,' Harry agreed.

'Still, one of the pleasures of growing old is having several children and celebrating their various events,' Murdoch said. 'Your mother and I are inclinded to anticipate them, one after the other. I suppose there is always the chance that Helen will suddenly produce a fiancé, but barring that, I would estimate the next event of importance will be your

315

passing out parade from Sandhurst.' He paused, but as Harry made no comment, he continued, 'I imagine you'll just make that before they pass me out of the army, for good.'

'I don't think I will,' Harry said.

Murdoch frowned at him.

Harry continued to look at the graves of the horses. 'Dad, I don't want to go to Sandhurst.'

Murdoch was too surprised to speak.

'I mean,' Harry said, 'don't you think two Mackinders in the army at one time, I mean as junior officers, is enough?'

'I hadn't thought about it,' Murdoch confessed. 'Every male Mackinder has always gone to Sandhurst, since it was founded. But I suppose Colonel Lowndes would feel a little overloaded with the brood. You could try the Guards. Your uncle-in-law did well at that.'

'Dad, I don't want to go to Sandhurst,' Harry repeated.

'Well . . . is it the navy? Or the air force. I'd have no objection, you know.'

'I don't want to go into the forces at all,' Harry said. 'I don't want to have to fight anyone. I don't want to see people killed and be torn apart myself, Dad.'

Murdoch could only stare at him. 'But . . .' He meant to say, 'What *do* you want to do?' but instead it came out as, 'Why on earth not?' Again, he meant, what is your objection to battle and warfare, but it didn't sound like that.

Harry's face twisted. 'Just let's say I'm too God damned scared, Dad. Because that's the truth.'

316

12
England 1933–38

Murdoch was again quite struck dumb.

'So there it is, Dad,' Harry said. He gave a little shrug, then went back inside to where his sister was being kissed by everyone in the room.

Murdoch followed more slowly. That a Mackinder would not want to join the army, eventually, he supposed was inevitable. That a Mackinder would ever make a confession of cowardice was unthinkable. It was in any event absurd. How could a boy like Harry have any idea of the many facets which went to make up courage – or cowardice? He knew them all himself. He could remember the rolling gut and the dry throat of his first South African patrol, when he had been only a year older than Harry was now. His principal fear had been of proving a coward, when the shooting started. His CO, dear old Tom Holt, had reassured him that when the first shot was fired at him he would think of nothing else but killing the man who had fired it. Holt had been absolutely right.

That determination to beat the other fellow to the exclusion of all else had carried him upwards throughout his career. He had known no fear when standing over Colonel Edmonds' wounded body with bullets flying around him – only anger. That had earned him the VC. Again he had not been afraid when captured by the Boers. He had not immediately known that his old friend Reger was fighting with them, but his emotions had again been anger, that he had been careless. Apprehension, as to what they might do to him, had followed later. But the fear had never outgrown the anger – or the determination to escape, by any means to come to hand. And the means had been there . . . an eighteen-year-old-girl named Margriet

317

Voorlandt. How that act of courage had come back time and again to haunt his conscience.

After that he had recognized and anticipated the pattern, knowing that all doubts, all apprehensions, would vanish the moment he saw his enemy in front of him. He had not even known actual fear when riding into Mahrain, alone, to face Chand Bibi. Again, he had been angry, and aware that a job had to be done. It was that anger, and grief over Manly-Smith's death, that had led him to execute her without trial. He did not regret what he had done; he had meant to do it ever since she had written him that first letter, confirming Johnnie Morton's accusation. But all that was experience. It was not something of which you could convince a seventeen-year-old boy.

'I guess maybe it's a throwback to my side of the family,' Lee suggested, as they lay awake next morning. 'We've been peaceful people for generations.'

'Oh, yes? I seem to have spent half of my life trying to keep your brother from getting his head shot off. And how about you, in Mahrain, rushing around like an aggressive houri?'

'Well . . . I was angry, I guess.'

'That's what it's all about.'

She rose on her elbow to look at him. 'Murdoch! You're not going to take it out on him?'

'Of course I'm not. I'm going to pretend to be as proud as hell of him, proud as hell to have an academic in the family. Which university has he chosen, Oxford, or Cambridge?'

Lee lay down again, stared at the ceiling. 'He doesn't want to go to either Oxford or Cambridge.'

'So maybe he is more American than British. That's okay by me, too. I've always had a high regard for Harvard.'

'Not Harvard.'

Murdoch turned his head. 'Then what does he want to do?'

'He wants to write.'

Murdoch sat up. 'Write? Write what?'

'Well, novels, I guess.'

318

'How the hell can you write novels at seventeen? For God's sake, what is he going to write about? Schooldays at Wellington?'

'He must have something he wants to write about. We haven't discussed that.'

'Well, he has to learn how to write, hasn't he? So he must go to university somewhere.'

'That's the whole point. Harry claims no really worthwhile novelist ever went to university. He says the whole point about being a novelist is having a totally individual point of view. He says it is hopeless trying to belong to a clique or a school or a body or a faculty, because then you're just reproducing the views of that body or whatever.'

'Where'd he get all of these theories?'

'I have no idea. But he must have been thinking pretty deeply about it. He wants to leave school, and get out into the world, and travel, cut all ties with home, and learn about life.'

'Because to be a writer means he can't belong to a family either, is that it? Especially one with as pronounced views as his.'

'He didn't say that. But it could very well be true.'

'And how does he propose to live, while he's on this worldwide grand tour?'

'He said he'd earn a living. But . . . I promised him an allowance.'

Murdoch looked over his shoulder at her.

'Well,' she said. 'We can't let him starve. It won't be much of an allowance. He won't be able to afford any luxuries. I always want him to remember that home is best. But it'll keep the wolf from the door.'

'And you approve of the whole idea?'

'No,' she said. 'No, I hate it. I hate the very thought of it.' She sat up too and put her arm round his shoulders. 'But he is a human being, Murdoch. He has a right to live his own life the way he wants to. I'm counting on the fact that he's also a product of you and me. He'll come round, given time.'

★

319

Ian and Fergus were more amused than annoyed by their little brother's odd fancy. Helen was more annoyed. 'Oh, really, Harry,' she protested, 'you are utterly absurd. What will my friends say?'

'Well,' Harry replied. 'Maybe you'll find out who *are* your friends.'

He left that autumn, on a ship for America. He had letters to his Uncle Harry, and Lee felt fairly sure he would be well looked after. In fact, she wrote and asked her brother to do that. Harry Caspar had not married again, following the disaster of his first attempt. Now in his early sixties, and with the stock market gradually recovering and business in general improving, he was back to writing, a novel this time; he would be, Lee felt, the perfect foster parent for her errant child.

Murdoch had to hope she was right in her estimation of Harry's character. In any event, by the end of the year he was more concerned with watching events in Germany, and with continuing his training of the mechanized cavalry. Because he had the oddest feeling that they were going to be used, before too much longer. International tension seemed to be increasing every day, and if the British Parliament and newspapers seemed to be doing their best to ignore continental problems, he did not feel those problems were going to go away.

They arose in the main from the successive acts of the new German Government. Harry Mackinder had barely left Southampton when Germany withdrew from the League of Nations and from the Disarmament Conference which had been sitting now for some years without reaching any positive decisions.

The following year came the sensational news of the elimination, by Hitler and his black-shirted Schutzstaffel, of a large part of the brown-shirted storm troopers, the street fighters who had first carried the Nazis to power. If world opinion was shocked by the idea of the German Chancellor decreeing the murder of his principal associates, the German people apparently were not, and when Hindenburg died that August, they almost unanimously

320

elected Hitler President in the General's place. Murdoch wondered how the Regers had fared in the Night of the Long Knives, as he remembered that one of their sons had been in the SS and the other in the storm troops. But no word came out of Germany to him, personally.

That Christmas tensions shifted in another direction, as Italian and Ethiopian troops clashed at the wells of Ualual, on the borders of Italian Somaliland. This was well remembered territory to Murdoch, and to retired RSM Yeald, with whom Murdoch often had a glass of beer in the village pub, and like the old war horses they were, they reminisced about their campaign against the Mad Mullah thirty years before.

'Those were the days, General,' Yeald said sadly. 'When cavalry were cavalry.'

'And when we were young men,' Murdoch reminded him.

'That, too, sir.'

'I wasn't even married,' Murdoch said thoughtfully. 'But you were, Sergeant-Major.'

'Oh, indeed, sir. That girl of mine was just a year old when we sailed.' He peered into his beer. 'It's a rum world.'

For the Yealds more than anyone else, Murdoch supposed. He made a point of driving into the village every day to buy a newspaper from Jennie, who grew prettier every day, it seemed. Until the morning when the paper was sold him by young Bert, eleven years old.

'Mum's gone off,' he said. 'She's joined up.'

Murdoch was astounded, but a few days later Jennie herself came up to Broad Acres to call. 'I've joined the army,' she said defiantly. 'Well, everyone thinks there's going to be a war, and there was this advertisement for volunteers for the new women's army, and . . . ' She looked from Lee to Murdoch, and flushed. 'I wanted to do my bit. I'm to train to be a driver. Who knows, Sir Murdoch, one day I may be your driver.'

'I'd like that,' Murdoch said.

Jennie's flush deepened. 'I'd like that too, Sir Murdoch,' she said.

'That girl,' Lee observed after Jennie had left, 'just worships the ground you walk on.'

'And it should be the other way around,' Murdoch said. 'She's Ralph's wife.'

'I prefer it the way it is,' Lee said.

The clash at Ualual remained a subject of discussion and negotiation about rights and wrongs and indemnities for most of the year, while in Germany the Saar, under the government of the League since 1921, voted by an overwhelming majority to be reunited with the Fatherland. No sooner had that been done than Hitler denounced the disarmament clauses in the Versailles Treaty, and announced his intention to re-arm Germany just as quickly as he could.

This again shocked the world, and there were vigorous protests by France, Britain, and Italy . . . but only protests, and while accusations were still flying back and forth, Hitler concluded a naval agreement with Britain, by which he promised not to build a fleet in excess of thirty-five per cent of the strength of the Royal Navy. While the English newspapers were carrying headlines about Herr Hitler's earnest desire to remain friends with Britain – as shown by this treaty – and French newspapers were carrying headlines about British betrayal of the alliance – by signing the treaty at all – Murdoch was in London, and lunching with Churchill.

Churchill had remained out of power, both because of his refusal to accept any idea of dominion status for India – in which direction Murdoch felt he was rather trying to do a Canute – and because of the repeated prodding questions he asked in the House of Commons regarding Hitler and German re-armament, which he knew, from various information gathered from friends, including Murdoch, had been proceeding even before Hitler denounced the Versailles clauses. Today he was absolutely furious.

'I cannot believe how eminent politicians, clever men, can so delude themselves. Do you know, I had a chat with Chamberlain the other day' – Neville Chamberlain was

Chancellor of the Exchequer – 'and he was positively preening himself. All Hitler is suffering from is a bad press, he told me. Of course he wants to be strong vis-à-vis the rest of Europe, and especially Russia, he said. I entirely agree with him on that. But he has no intention of ever taking us on. Or he wouldn't have signed this agreement. With the German navy no more than thirty-five per cent of the British, we have absolutely nothing to fear from him. Can you believe it?'

'But doesn't he have a point?' Murdoch asked.

'The point, my dear Murdoch, is this: has Germany a navy at all at this moment?'

'Well, no. A few river launches.'

'Quite. Therefore Hitler is starting from scratch. Now, how long do you think it will take him to build a fleet thirty-five per cent our strength? We have eighteen battleships; that means he can build six. We have ten aircraft carriers; that means he can build three. We have fifteen heavy cruisers; that means he can build five. We have sixty light cruisers; that means he can build twenty. We have two hundred destroyers; that means he can build seventy. We have seventy submarines; that means he can build twenty-five. Now that is quite a programme.'

'Yes, it is,' Murdoch agreed. 'It's going to take him several years to complete.'

'Exactly.'

'So?'

Churchill showed signs of erupting. 'Murdoch, don't you realize that what we have really done is tell a chap, who is certainly a potential enemy, but who at this moment has no fleet at all, that for the next six or seven years he can build ships just as fast as he can get them on and off the slips?'

'Ah,' Murdoch said. 'Good God! No, I hadn't realized that.'

'And who can tell what the situation is going to be in seven years? It is the most absurd, and dangerous, thing any government could possibly have done. And when I tell them that, they look at me as if I was mad. As I said, it drives me to despair. What is even more soul-destroying is

323

that we could put an end to Hitler's schemes, and possibly him too, right this minute, just by sending you with an army corps, including your armoured brigade, to France and having it take up a position on the Rhine. The French would welcome it. Indeed, they'd put one of their armies alongside ours.'

'It won't happen,' Murdoch said.

'I know. Blithering idiots.'

'I mean, it won't happen, because I was informed yesterday that I no longer am responsible for armoured troops.'

'Don't tell me they're retiring you?'

'No. I'm only fifty-four, dammit. I'm coming up to Aldershot for a spell at the Staff College.'

'Now that may be a good thing. You could still be the next CIGS.'

'I'd like to think that, but I know it won't happen. Not with my reputation and after that Afghan business. Still . . . it'll give Lee a chance to get to know London; as we'll be so close we're going to buy a flat – I'll spend my weekends in town. And . . . ' he grinned. 'There will still be Mackinders with the armoured brigade. Ian has just been gazetted captain.'

But he was deeply sorry to have turned his back on the regiment, and its new colonel, Colin Destry, who had fought with him right through the war and had been at his back when he had charged the Mahsuds. And this, he knew, had to be for the last time. He was now merely filling in time until his retirement; a couple of years at the Staff College, and then a colonial governorship, and then . . . old age. The future was brought home to him forcibly that Christmas, when his mother died. Florence Mackinder had been weakening gradually over the years, although her general health had remained remarkably good. Now, at the age of eighty, she just stopped breathing on Boxing Day.

Cables were sent to America, but Harry had left his uncle's to go south into Mexico, and no one knew where he was. Murdoch knew Lee worried about it, but as an army wife, not knowing the whereabouts of her menfolk was not an unusual experience for her, and she was more concerned with their imminent move to London.

By that Christmas, Italy and Abyssinia were at war, with Italy being denounced by the League, and threatened with sanctions. It sounded very like a possible European war, as Mussolini defied the League, but it all fizzled through the inability of the British and French to agree on imposing oil sanctions, which would either have forced Mussolini to pull his men out of Africa, as they could not be supplied with that essential ingredient of modern warfare – or try to shoot his way through the Royal Navy. The only real result of the fiasco was to turn Mussolini from an ally of the British and French against German resurgence into a potential friend of Hitler – a friendship which grew steadily over the next year, and culminated in a treaty which Mussolini grandly described as forming the axis of Europe.

During this critical period, British minds were distracted by the death of King George. Murdoch, like a great many officers in all the armed forces, felt it as an almost personal blow, and was honoured to be one of those required to stand guard at the catafalque in full-dress uniform and black armband. Then during the following year there was the Abdication Crisis. Murdoch had only met King Edward a few times, and had not been taken by his personality. Again, however, like most serving officers, he was concerned by the possibility of having to renounce his oath to serve King and country. He was heartily relieved when in December the King decided to abdicate and leave the throne to his brother.

By this time Hitler had reoccupied the Rhineland, again in total defiance of the Versailles Treaty, and a brutal civil war had broken out in Spain, between the Nationalist forces of General Franco, who were avowedly fascist and received support from Germany and Italy, and the left-wing government, which was very close to being communist, and received support from Soviet Russia. The British Government determined to keep its distance from all of these sinister developments, but by now it was pretty obvious to any thinking man who was not a blind optimist that all of

325

Europe was on a collision course with itself, a course from which Britain could hardly step aside.

The trouble was, from the point of view of the army, that they suddenly found themselves third in line for funds and therefore equipment. Obviously the navy had to be kept up to scratch in view of the fact that Germany was now building monster battleships and that Italy, a probable ally of Hitler if it came to bullets, possessed a powerful battle fleet. Equally obviously, the Royal Air Force had to be expanded just as rapidly as possible, as horrendous reports arrived from Spain of the damage done by German bombers over defenceless cities. The army was told to do its best with what it had.

Thus the discussions at the Staff College became concerned with the here and now. Down to only a few years previously all the British armed forces had been ordered to budget, and plan, on the assumption that Great Britain would not become involved in a general conflict with any other sizeable power for a period of ten years. This period had been extended year by year. But now at last it was scrapped in favour of preparing for an imminent confrontation with Germany.

After such a lengthy period of 'peacetime manoeuvres' it was rather like starting from scratch. Murdoch was delighted again to be working with men like Bill Ironside, and the new Chief of the Imperial General Staff, Lord Gort, even if it was a little disturbing to know that Gort was five years younger than him – he also held the Victoria Cross. What was more disturbing were certain assumptions drawn by the British Staff, the most important being that the French army was the finest in the world, and the second being that a war with Germany, if it came, was being envisaged as an essentially defensive operation.

The basis for this was again the French principle. Every leading soldier in the French Army had had personal experience of the bloodbath on the western front in the Great War, and was determined that it should never happen again. Equally were they haunted by the rapid German mobilization and invasion of their country in 1870. Ever since then they had been building forts where the two countries abutted, and indeed these powerful fortifications had been chiefly responsible for the German decision that any future invasion of France had to take place through Belgium – the decision that had precipitated the World War. Following their narrow victory in that conflict, the French had again turned their minds to limiting German options. To this end their erstwhile minister of war, General Maginot, had begun the construction of a vast system of fortifications, which bore his name, in effect linking the existing forts with miles of concrete and steel, and which now stretched from the Swiss border to the forest of the Ardennes. In this continuous fortress it was proposed that the French would maintain themselves while the German forces pounded themselves to pieces against iron and steel and lead; it would be Verdun all over again, only on a greatly increased scale. The theory was that after a very brief period of this the Germans would collapse as in 1918.

When Murdoch questioned the validity of maintaining an army, any army, much less that supposed to be the finest in the world, in a strictly defensive posture, with its inevitable effect on morale and loss of initiative, he was told he did not understand French élan. When he pointed to the historical record that troops which stood on the defensive had not usually been victorious, he was told to study Waterloo.

'When we will no doubt play the part of the Prussians,' he commented, 'and come up on the flank to save the day. But the Prussians arrived attacking.'

That remark did not increase his popularity, but the British Staff were having thoughts about what happened where the Maginot Line ended. The Forest of the Ardennes was regarded as being impassable to large bodies of troops. It had proved difficult in the Great War, and the French, who still dreamed of Napoleonic victories, reminded everyone how the Duke of Brunswick's army had become bogged down in the forest back in 1792. When Murdoch reminded them of the catastrophe of Sedan in 1870, he was reminded in turn that the Prussians had then come upon the

French from the east and south, that is, after crossing the border in open country – this was now obviously impossible, because of the Maginot Line.

What then of Belgium? Belgium was neutral, and both Germany and France, and Britain, had again reiterated that neutrality after the Great War. But the Germans had violated Belgian neutrality in 1914, and Murdoch, from what he had seen in Berlin, had no doubt that Hitler was a far more pragmatic politician than Bethman-Hollweg; if the Maginot Line could only be turned by a wheeling movement through Belgium, then there would be a wheeling movement through Belgium.

In this respect he was at last entirely at one with his colleagues, and strenuous efforts were made to induce Belgium at least to enter into secret military discussions as to what would be done should another war with Germany break out. But the Belgians refused to contemplate such a possibility affecting them; they had another solemn treaty to rely upon. The British Staff therefore went ahead with their own contingency plans based on the assumption that, if Hitler did invade Belgium, the Belgians would again call for help, as in 1914. Careful calculations were made as to the possible rate of German advance, having regard to the powerful Belgian fortifications which had held up the Germans in 1914, and it was determined that, using Sedan and the 'impassible' Ardennes as a hinge, as the Germans crossed the Belgian border in the north-east, the British, with French support, would cross the border in the south-west, and advance as far as the River Dyle, where they would stem the German onslaught.

This nearly drove Murdoch to despair. 'They are advancing to defend,' he grumbled to Churchill. 'It will be Mons all over again. But then we knew we were both outnumbered and facing high-quality troops. Now we are supposed to be part of the finest army in the world, and the strongest numerically, and we are still doing nothing more than looking for positions to be held. Why in the name of God have we created what is really one of the best armoured divisions anyone has, if we are going to keep it in reserve?'

'Maybe the Germans will also have a defensive mentality,' Churchill commented. 'And will just sit and glower at us.'

'Do you really believe that, Winston?'

'Of course I don't. I believe Germany is governed by a bunch of gangsters, who, if they gamble, or are forced to gamble, will gamble everything. If even half of the rumours one hears about what is going on in that country are true, they are the biggest thugs on the face of the earth. The tragedy is that it could so easily have been prevented. Ah, well, we will just have to put our faith in the French.'

However much he feared Germany's growing military strength, Murdoch had always taken the rumours of summary executions, concentration camps, torture and mistreatment of the inmates, which were carried by escaping Jews, with a large pinch of salt. He recognized that people like Reger, if Margriet was to be believed, had a good deal of the sadist in them, and being imprisoned is never a very pleasant experience – as he knew, personally. But imprisonment and mistreatment of minorities or political opponents by a civilized European state in the twentieth century seemed absurd.

He was now to discover differently. Early in 1937 Helen had become engaged to a naval officer, Lieutenant Commander Stephen Cross. The wedding was to take place at St James's, Piccadilly, and the reception would follow at the Café Royal. It was to be a splendid occasion, in which many old friends from the regiment, as well of course as the bride's two brothers, came up from the west – and to the delight of everyone but more especially Lee, young Harry arrived, from Paris, where he was living and working on his first novel. He looked fit and well, and much more sure of himself than four years earlier.

Murdoch was very tempted to tackle him on the subject of changing his mind about the army, confident that he would have grown out of his boyhood – he had, apparently, had some fairly grim experiences in his wanderings – but Lee asked him not to.

Steve Cross had his stag party in a Soho nightclub, and it was a riotous affair which went on until well into the morning. By midnight, however, Murdoch had had as much wine, dirty stories and nearly nude waitresses as he could stomach for one night, and went outside to find a taxi. There wasn't one in the neighbourhood, so he turned up Greek Street for Oxford Street, where he was sure he would find one on the prowl. He had walked about fifty yards away from the restaurant when he became aware that someone was following him.

He slowed slightly, while considering the matter without looking round. He was not apprehensive; he remained perfectly fit and he had his rolled umbrella as a weapon. On the other had, he had had a lot to drink, and there was a dark alley in front of him. So if there was to be a confrontation with a footpad, it was best done now, while there was still a street light handy. He therefore slowed some more, took a deep breath, and turned.

And found himself looking at a woman. A young woman, he estimated, from a hasty glance at her ankles; the rest of her was concealed beneath a bulky cloth coat, but the general impression was rather one of run-down gentility.

It was Soho. Murdoch smiled at her. 'You're wasting your time, my dear. I really am not in the mood.'

'I would like to speak to you, please, Sir Murdoch,' the woman said, in a distinctly foreign accent.

He frowned at her, trying to place her, because she was certainly familiar, even in the gloom, as she came closer. She again said, 'Please!' And gave a little tremble which without warning developed into a kind of paroxysm. He caught her as she fell, and realized she was Annaliese von Reger.

Her eyes had shut as she fainted, now they opened again, for a moment stark with terror.

'Annaliese?' he asked, unable to believe his eyes.

'Please,' she said again.

Holding her in his arms, Murdoch could feel her body trembling, but he could feel more than that – even through

330

the coat her ribs could be counted, and her arms were pencil thin. 'When did you last eat?' he asked.

'I . . . I had something this morning.'

'I meant a square meal?'

'I . . . don't know, Sir Murdoch.'

Murdoch did some hasty calculations. It was past midnight, and the pubs were closed. Several restaurants were still open, but he didn't fancy taking Annaliese into one; he was a fairly well-known figure, and there could easily be a newspaper reporter around. Nor did he fancy taking her back to the stag party; she'd be terrified out of her wits at being surrounded by drunken soldiers and sailors. He put his arm round her waist, hurried her along the alleyway and into Oxford Street, and to his great relief was able to hail a taxi immediately. He gave the address of his London flat, and placed Annaliese on the back seat beside him.

She huddled against him, whimpering, while the taxi driver tactfully kept his glass screen closed. 'How long have you been in London?' Murdoch asked.

'Four days.'

'Four days? Where have you been staying?'

She pulled away from him but remained hunched, elbows on knees. 'I have managed. Where are you taking me?'

'To my home. It's not far.'

'I cannot go to your home. I cannot . . . ' fear was rising in her voice again.

'Nobody is going to harm you, Anna. Least of all me,' Murdoch promised her. 'But you need a square meal and a warm bed, in my estimation. And safety.'

She made no reply, just stared out of the window as they swung into Mayfair. He didn't press her. There was time enough for that.

The taxi stopped and Murdoch paid him. The doorman peered at him. 'Good night, Sir Murdoch,' he ventured.

'Good night, Burton. Is Lady Mackinder in yet?'

Helen's hen party was also taking place tonight.

'No, sir,' Burton said, regarding Annaliese with an

expression which suggested that that was a very fortunate thing.

'Ah,' Murdoch said. 'Thank you, Burton.' He half carried Annaliese towards the lift.

'That man,' she whispered as the door closed on them. 'He will report my presence to the police. You will be arrested.'

'That'll be the day,' Murdoch said.

'It does not matter if you are a general . . . ' she shuddered.

'It does here. As a matter of fact, it matters if you're a private. The police can't arrest anyone for taking a young lady to his flat . . . as long as she doesn't shout for help.'

She looked up at him, then down again, and the lift was stopping. He found his latch key and let her in.

'Not quite as sumptuous as your mother's house, I'm afraid, but it does for us. Now . . . ' He guided her into the lounge and sat her on the sofa as close to the central heating radiator as he could. 'Bacon and eggs?'

'Bacon and eggs?'

'Why not? I'm going to have some. Just sit there. First, some medicine.' He went to the bar, poured two goblets of brandy, gave her one. 'It's very good to see you,' he said, and sipped.

She sipped also, staring at him, and he went into the kitchen. It took him fifteen minutes to prepare a meal. As he carried the tray into the dining room he looked through the arch at the sofa, and saw that she had drunk the brandy and was fast asleep, the goblet drooping from her fingers.

He removed it, stood looking down at her. She had unfastened her coat, and her dress was crushed and soiled. Her stockings where laddered, her shoes scuffed. She smelt of sweat and fear, and misery. He knew what needed to be done with her and debated whether he should do it, then breathed a sigh of relief when he heard a key in the latch.

'Hello,' Lee said. 'You were early.'

'Perhaps fortunately,' he said.

She came into the lounge, looked down at the sleeping girl. 'Your Christmas present? She looks a little tatty.'

'Don't you remember her?'

Lee frowned. 'Good Lord! Annaliese von Reger. Where on earth did you pick her up?'

Murdoch told her.

'But what is she doing here?'

'That she hasn't told me yet. She's terrified, she's hungry, she's exhausted, she's cold, and she's filthy.'

'Yes,' Lee agreed. 'And you wish to keep her here rather than send her to a hospital or a police station.'

'I would like to do that, yes,' he agreed. 'At least until we find out what she's running away from. If you have no objection.'

'Good lord, no. I'm as curious as you are. Right. First thing, a hot bath.'

'I thought of that, but . . . '

'The idea of undressing a nubile young woman didn't excite you.'

'It excited me very much. Which is why I was hesitating.'

She stuck out her tongue at him. 'Well, then, tonight is your lucky night. I bet she looks like her mom did, forty years ago.' She blew him a kiss. 'Who knows, maybe it'll turn out to be my lucky night as well. I'll run the bath. Is that breakfast I smell?'

'It's untouched.'

'It won't be for long. I'm starving.' She hurried into the bathroom, turned on taps. Murdoch remained looking down at Annaliese. She really was a most beautiful girl, even more so than when last he had seen her. The suggestion of emaciation had removed some of the fullness from her cheeks, and the slight down-turn of her lips gave her expression a seriousness it had previously lacked.

'Okay, lover, bring the victim in,' Lee said. She had also undressed, wore a dressing gown with the sleeves rolled up. Between them they removed Annaliese's clothing, Lee wrinkled her nose as she dropped each garment on the floor. 'I don't think she's changed any of these for at least a week. Where's her suitcase?'

'She didn't have one.'

She raised her head to look at him. 'Curiouser and curiouser. Holy cow!'

She had noticed something, and now she half rolled the girl on to her side, to show him the weals on her buttocks.

'Great God in the morning. The bastard!' Murdoch said.

'What bastard?'

'Her father. Has to be her father.'

'Her *father*?'

'He beats Margriet. I never told you that, but she told me.'

'I can't believe that. Can you put her in the bath?'

Murdoch took off his dinner jacket, rolled up his sleeves, picked up the naked girl and carefully lowered her into the hot water.

Annaliese awoke with a start and screamed.

'Just relax,' Lee told her. 'We're old enough to be your parents. And we're your friends.'

Annaliese stared at her, and then at Murdoch, who was holding her head and shoulders to prevent her slipping beneath the water.

'Think you can soap yourself?' Lee asked.

Annaliese's head moved up and down, slowly.

'Well do it. Nice and slow. And soak. Let some of that warmth get to your bones. Oh, and wash your hair as well; there's shampoo in that bottle. We're going to leave the door open, just in case you fall asleep again. When you've had a good bath, put on that dressing gown and join us. We'll be eating.'

She went outside, and Murdoch followed her. He opened his mouth, but she shook her head. They ate in silence, and Lee was making another breakfast just as Annaliese appeared, a glow of soap and shampoo.

'Sit down here,' Lee told her. 'And chew each mouthful forty-two times.' She poured coffee, and sat beside her. Murdoch sat opposite.

Annaliese took a mouthful, and Murdoch could almost feel his own saliva burning his mouth as he watched her expression. 'You must think I am terrible, coming here like this,' she said.

334

'Eat first, talk after,' Lee commanded. 'And you didn't come here. You were brought.'

Annaliese gave Murdoch a shy glance, and ate some more. 'I had to come,' she said. 'I had to get away . . . ' she shuddered.

'From your father?' Lee asked. 'You mean you've run away from home?'

Annaliese gave a little sob, and drank some coffee. 'From home, yes. From Germany. It is so terrible.'

'Tell us,' Murdoch said.

She sighed. 'It all seemed so splendid, when Herr Hitler took power. Father was suddenly a very important man, with a position on the General Staff, and a confidant of the Fuehrer. All of us were important. We were invited to all the official functions . . . '

'I remember, when we were there,' Lee said.

'And then . . . Klaus was murdered.' Annaliese's shoulders hunched.

'Klaus? Your eldest brother? I mean, after Paul.'

'Yes,' Annaliese said. 'He was in the Sturmabteilung. The storm troopers. He was with Herr Roehm at the spa on the night they were all shot. Ernst was one of those who killed him.' Her voice contained a sob.

'Ernst?' Lee asked.

'Her other brother,' Murdoch said. 'He was in the SS, wasn't he, Anna?'

Her head flopped up and down.

'Let me get this straight. The SS were the guys who executed the SA, right?'

'Yes,' Murdoch said.

'So Ernst . . . ' she gazed at Murdoch with her mouth open.

'Father went to Hitler to protest about Klaus's murder,' Annaliese said. 'He came back . . . oh, Sir Murdoch, it was terrible. He looked . . . broken. We were all broken. Except for Paul and Ernst. They said Klaus had been a criminal and deserved to die. Mama wept and wept and wept. But then Father changed. He became more of a Nazi than ever. He said Paul and Ernst were right, and Klaus *had* been a

335

criminal. He insisted we start going to receptions again. He made me accept dates with Nazi officers.' Another sigh. Her plate was empty.

'You'd better go to bed.' Lee said. 'We'll talk some more in the morning.'

'I must tell you,' Annaliese said. 'I must. There was a party. A great ball. Then we went to a nightclub . . .' she glanced at Murdoch. 'One of those places where men pretend to be women.'

'Good heavens!' Lee commented. 'Do they?'

'They're called transvestites,' Murdoch told her.

Lee looked as if she wanted to know more, but she didn't want to interrupt Annaliese, who was now talking as if under hypnotism, her voice a flat monotone, her eyes half shut.

'We stayed there until dawn, then . . . we were all drunk, I suppose . . . we went to a camp.'

'A camp?' Lee asked.

'A prison.'

'A concentration camp,' Murdoch explained.

'Yes.' Annaliese shivered. 'It was just light, and the inmates were being lined up for roll call. They were women. They wore pyjamas. Striped pyjamas. Oh, Sir Murdoch, it was terrible.'

'What had they done?' Lee asked.

'They were Jewesses, and the wives of opponents of the government.'

'And they had been locked up for that?'

'Yes. And they were made to stand there . . . it was cold. They stood there for more than half an hour. I wanted to leave and go home, but the others made me stay. They said we would see something very amusing. Oh, Sir Murdoch . . .'

'Go on,' Murdoch said. 'You have to say it.'

Lee stared at them both.

Annaliese sighed. 'One of the women fell down. She was not old, I don't think. I don't think she was much older than me. But she fell down because of the cold. So the guards held her wrists and dragged her out of the line. They took away her pyjamas . . .'

'My God!' Lee commented.

'She was blue, and she was screaming, and they they began to beat her. They tied her wrists to a stake in the ground, and they flogged her, with whips.'

'You can't be serious,' Lee protested. 'Not even . . . ' she bit her lip. Murdoch knew she had almost said, 'Not even Chand Bibi had done that.'

'They beat her,' Annaliese said. 'They beat her and beat her and beat her. There was blood running down her legs. When she fainted they poured cold water on her face and beat her again. I could not stand it. I was sick.'

'I should think so,' Lee said. 'Those men must have been savages.'

'They were women, Lady Mackinder.'

Once again Lee stared at Murdoch with her mouth open.

'I went home,' Annaliese said. 'I burst in on Papa and Mamma and I told them what I had seen. I told Papa he had to see Herr Hitler and have such things stopped.'

'Good for you,' Lee said.

'Then he beat me.'

'What?' Lee screamed.

'You have undressed me. You have seen the marks.'

'Your own father did that to you?'

'He tied my wrists to the bed, just like the woman in the camp. Then he flogged me with his riding crop.'

'Oh, my God! But your mother . . . '

'She tried to stop him, and he hit her. She fell down. She begged him to stop, but she could not get up. Then . . . ' her shoulders slumped.

'Then he beat your mother as well.' Murdoch said quietly. 'In front of you.'

Lee was speechless.

'Yes.' Annaliese raised her head. 'How did you know?'

'He's been beating her for years. But they always managed to keep it a secret.'

'But . . . he didn't say anything, while doing this?' Lee asked.

'He kept saying that whatever the Fuehrer did was right. That it was necessary for Germany to be strong, and for those who did not wish a strong Germany to be punished. He was raving like a madman. Then he let me go. I went to my room and I wept. But Paul was home. I went to Paul's room and I told him what had happened.'

'Paul,' Lee said. 'Yes. He was the one to tell.'

'He told me Papa was right to beat me,' Annaliese said. 'And Mamma.'

'He said *what*?'

'That is what he said, Lady Mackinder. My brother. I loved him.'

'So you ran away,' Murdoch said.

'Yes, Sir Murdoch. I could not stay there any longer.'

'How did you run away?' Lee asked.

'I left that night. I could not take much. Just a small case, with some clothes.'

'Where is it now?'

'It was stolen.'

'You poor kid. You have had a time. But you had money.'

'A little,' Annaliese said.

'Enough to get you here, anyway.'

Annaliese looked at Murdoch. There were pink spots in her cheeks.

'You mean there wasn't?' Lee pressed.

'She got here,' Murdoch said. 'That's what matters. Now you have to go to bed, Anna. Sleep is the most important thing in the world for you right now. And remember, you're with friends.'

'You won't send me back?' Annaliese begged. 'If I go back Papa will send me to a camp. He threatened to do so. I will be flogged like that woman. Please don't send me back, Sir Murdoch.'

'No one is sending you anywhere, Anna,' he promised.

Lee tucked her up in the spare room, came back and poured herself some more coffee. 'Three thirty. Jesus, the mother of the bride is going to look like a wet dishcloth. Murdoch, what are we going to do?'

'I'm brooding on it. She's over twenty-one.'

338

'So she can do what she likes.'

'Here. Not apparently in Germany.'

'Oh, I know we can't send her back. But . . . shouldn't we let Margriet and Paul know where she is?'

'That's what I'm brooding on. If what she said was true . . .'

'I can't believe it,' Lee declared. 'Any of it. I just can't.'

'Well, I'm afraid I do believe it.'

'You mean Margriet did tell you about Reger's treatment of her?'

'Yes. Yes, she did.'

'And showed you her scars, I guess.' Lee squeezed his hand. 'I apologize. That was a shitty thing to say. And that girl certainly has scars. So I guess Paul did come over the heavy father. But that story about the camp, in front of visitors . . . that has to be imagination.'

'I wonder,' Murdoch said.

'I mean, she's lying about so much else,' Lee pointed out. 'She has only a little money, but she manages to walk or whatever right across Germany, and Holland, and get to England . . . how the hell did she get in and out of two countries with no passport and no money? There has to be more to it than meets the eye.'

'I wonder,' Murdoch said again.

Lee frowned at him. 'I hope you're not meaning what I think you're meaning. That little girl?'

'She's not a little girl, my darling. She's twenty-two years old, she's been brought up in a society whose moral values aren't quite the same as ours, and she's been terrified out of her wits.'

'You are telling me she has prostituted herself across half Europe?'

'I don't know. And I don't intend to ask her. But I would certainly say the only way she got a ship's captain to smuggle her into this country was by offering to share his bunk for the voyage.'

'Jesus Christ! I don't think I could do that.'

'Here's hoping you never have to. But I reckon anyone can do anything if it's a case of survival.'

339

'Um.' She was again thinking of the events at Mahrain, he knew. 'So what are we going to do about her?'

'I'd like to help her.'

'How?'

'Well, when she wakes up, I'll have her write down everything she's just told us. If it's still as horrendous, I'm going to see the Home Secretary and ask that she be granted political asylum. Meanwhile, I'd like her to go down to Broad Acres to recuperate. Philippa can look after her. Give her something to do.'

'You mean we take on another daughter.'

'Hopefully not. When she gets back her health and her nerves, and is accepted into this country, well, hopefully she'll be able to stand on her own two feet.'

'Hopefully,' Lee said. 'And what about the Regers?'

'We'll get her accepted here first, then we'll write and tell them where she is. If she's already been granted asylum, they won't be able to pull any strings to get her back out.'

'All very devious. Did I ever tell you that marrying you was the most exciting thing in my life? And it doesn't seem to change.'

'Even if there are some experiences you could've done without.'

'No,' she said seriously. 'Now we've survived them all, I wouldn't change a thing.' She gazed at him. 'Does that make me a fallen woman?'

He grinned. 'Like Annaliese? It makes you a very brave woman, my dearest girl.'

'Like Annaliese,' she commented. 'Don't you think we should get to bed? You have a bride to deliver in ten hours' time.'

Obtaining political asylum for Annaliese von Reger was not a difficult task, once her statement, which differed in no way from what she had told Murdoch and Lee, was read. Lee took her down to Broad Acres and installed her there, telling her to stay as long as she wished. Philippa was delighted. So were Fergus and Ian, when they discovered there was a lovely young woman in residence at the family

340

home. Lee was less happy about that, but reassured herself with the thought that neither of them could marry without their commanding officer's permission until they were thirty, which was not for another couple of years – and she intended, if necessary, to have a word with Colonel Destry.

Murdoch duly wrote to Margriet to inform her where her daughter was – but he never received a reply. In his letter he asked her to confirm or deny that what Annaliese had told them was the truth, but as she did not reply, he showed Churchill a copy of the statement.

'They are absolute Huns,' Churchill said. 'How on earth Chamberlain believes he can deal with them is a mystery to me.'

For on the retirement of Stanley Baldwin, Neville Chamberlain had become Prime Minister, and had immediately left no doubt that he regarded the peace of Europe as his principal objective, which was admirable, and that he believed that he and Hitler could sit down and discuss their differences and come to a lasting settlement, which was debatable.

'I think he should see this,' Churchill decided.

He made an appointment, and the Prime Minister met both Churchill and Murdoch in his office at the Commons. Murdoch had of course met Chamberlain before, at various official functions, but they had never been more than acquaintances. The Prime Minister was most courteous, however, and read Annaliese's deposition with grave attention.

'I agree,' he said when he had finished. 'The Nazi Party is behaving in a most barbaric way towards its dissidents. However, that is an internal matter. No doubt, hopefully soon, the German people will have the good sense to replace Mr Hitler, and his cohorts, with someone more civilized. But I have no responsibility for Germany. What I do have is responsibility for this country and empire, and the people who live in it. And in this regard, keeping the peace in Europe, so that not one drop of British blood has again to be shed to enforce that peace, has to be our principal, our only

341

objective. And that objective can only be reached by attaining an agreement with Herr Hitler.'

'And do you really believe that a man so sunk in moral turpitude as Hitler will honour any agreement, Neville?' Churchill demanded.

'I believe he will. He needs peace as much as we do. And let's face it: some of his demands are entirely reasonable. We would be quite upset if several million Englishmen had been forced to live, say in France, and were being deprived of their civil rights by the French Government.'

'And you don't reckon all of this hoo-ha about the Anschluss and the Sudeten Germans is just a screen to get his hands on the Czech armaments works?'

'No, I do not. I thank you, gentlemen, for bringing this document to my attention, and I shall remember it, but I repeat, it is not my intention to interfere in internal German affairs . . .'

'The man is blind,' Churchill growled over lunch.

'It might work,' Murdoch said. 'Surely Hitler knows he can't take on England and France together?'

'I think Mr Hitler doubts whether either England or France, under present management, is in a fit state to go to war with anybody,' Churchill said.

In the event, he was proved right. The British and the French made warlike noises, but at the end they acquiesced in the German occupation of both Austria and the Sudetenland. For all that, 1938 was a time of open preparation for war, with gas masks being issued and reservists told to stand by. Murdoch had some hopes of being given command of the Expeditionary Force, if it was necessary to send one to France. He was certainly the senior active general, and he had a battle record second to none. He had also been intimately involved with the formation of the armoured division, which he was sure was going to play a vital role in the coming conflict – because he had no doubt there was going to be a conflict now. Of course he was fifty-seven, but he still felt he could give points in fitness to most officers in the army.

On the other hand, next year he would be fifty-eight, and sixty was looming. He felt almost disappointed when in November Chamberlain arrived back from the final Munich meeting to announce that he had secured 'peace in our time'.

He happened to be alone at the London flat at the time, Lee having gone off to stay with Helen down in Portsmouth; she was expecting her first child.

He telephoned Lee there. 'Looks as though my dream of commanding a British army in battle has gone for good,' he said.

'You poor darling,' Lee sympathized. 'But don't you really feel you have fought enough battles for one lifetime?'

'Have a drink,' he suggested. 'Because I'm going to have several.'

She was right, of course, he thought as he poured himself a scotch and water; he had given his new man, Bartlett, the night off, and the other servants had left some time ago. He had fought enough battles. And of course to want to lead a British army into battle was cruelly selfish, when he thought of the casualties which would be involved; if Chamberlain had secured peace for the foreseeable future he would deserve all the praise going.

But the thought of having such a command . . . that had to be the dream of every soldier.

He finished his drink, poured himself another, and decided to go to bed, pleasantly tight. He went into the bedroom, took off his jacket and tie, and heard the doorbell ring.

He went into the lounge and thence the lobby, unlocked the door, blinked at the young woman standing there. She was not very distinct, because the hall light was not very bright, and his immediate reaction was, oh, no, not another Reger daughter fleeing the Nazis.

'General Sir Murdoch Mackinder?' she asked. She certainly had a foreign accent.

'Yes,' he said.

'May I speak with you, please? It is very important.'

He hesitated, then held the door wide, and she stepped

343

inside. Now he could see her more clearly, he realized that she was certainly not a Reger – she was far too dark. On the other hand, there was something familiar about her, and she was a remarkably beautiful girl – because he did not think she was much over eighteen.

She wore a trench coat and a beret, and carried a handbag, in both hands. He closed the door, and she smiled at him. 'You do not remember me, General Mackinder.'

'I'm afraid not,' he said.

'Well, I was only a child when last we met.'

He stared at her, and knew who she was. Who she had to be. And who she resembled. He stepped back, and her smile became cold.

'Ah,' she said. 'Now you remember.' Her hand came out of the bag, holding a small automatic pistol. In the same movement she levelled it and squeezed the trigger.

13

Holland 1939–40

With the instincts born of a lifetime under fire Murdoch
was moving the moment he saw the gun, both to the left and
forward. Even so he was all but knocked over by the impact
of the bullet. But he still reached Yasmin in the one long
bound, sweeping sideways with his right hand. He struck
her on the shoulder with such force that she was hurled
against the wall and dropped the gun, shouting something,
either in Russian or Mahsud, as she did so.

He found himself on his knees, reaching for her again, as
she tried to regain her weapon. They closed and rolled
across the floor, the front of the trench coat now stained
with blood. His blood! Her fingers reached the pistol, and
he rose to his knees and swung his left fist with all of his
fading strength. It hit her on the jaw and she struck the floor
in a crumpled heap.

Murdoch picked up the pistol and put it in his pocket. He
pulled off his shirt and held it against the wound in his side,
but the pain was now intense and he knew he did not have
very much consciousness left.

He rolled the girl on her back, unbuckled her belt and
dragged it from the trench coat, pulled her wrists behind
her and used the belt to secure them. Then he did the same
to her ankles with his own belt.

She was stirring by now, moaning with pain from the
blow on her jaw, eyes opening and then flopping shut again.

Murdoch held her ankles and dragged her across the
floor. Her skirt rode up and she woke up some more.

'Bastard!' she said in English. And then smiled. When
she smiled, she looked more like Chand Bibi than ever.
'You are bleeding to death.'

'You could be right,' Murdoch agreed. He got her to the

345

dining table, left her there while he took the cord from one of the drapes. Then he propped her against a table leg, and passed the cord round her throat.

She stopped smiling; her eyes were wide with horror. 'Do you mean to strangle me as you did my mother?'

'That's up to you.' Murdoch secured the cord to the table leg sufficiently tightly so that if she wanted to roll about and try to free her wrists she would indeed strangle herself. 'But if you just sit there like a good little girl you should be all right when the police come.' He grinned at her. 'On the other hand, if I happen to die before they get here, they will most certainly hang you. Just like your mother.'

She hissed at him, again in a language he didn't understand. He sat in the armchair by the telephone. The room was going round and round. He picked up the phone.

'Nine, nine, nine,' he said to the operator. 'There has been an attempted murder at this address.' Then he fainted.

'Murdoch,' Lee said. 'Oh, Murdoch!'

Murdoch gazed at her, and slowly the black spots cleared from his eyes. He realized he was in hospital, swathed in bandages round his chest.

'You promised you weren't going to get wounded again,' Lee reminded him.

He licked his lips; his throat was parched. She held a glass of water for him to drink.

'This one took me rather by surprise,' he confessed.

She kissed him. 'It's this habit you have of picking up strange young women. But why would she want to kill you?'

'Because she's Chand Bibi's daughter.'

'That nine-year-old kid?'

'Nine-year-old kids grow up. Where is she now?'

'In prison, I suppose. Oh, Murdoch, she all but got you. Two broken ribs, several pints of blood lost . . . they weren't at all sure you were going to pull through.'

'Well, I did.'

'I hope they hang her,' Lee said fiercely. 'Be sure you tell

346

the policeman that. By the way, you're a grandfather. His name is Murdoch.'

The policeman turned out to be a Scotland Yard inspector named Bloomfield, who looked unhappy. 'If you feel strong enough to make a statement, Sir Murdoch . . .'

'Yes,' Murdoch said, and did so.

Bloomfield studied what he had written. 'You'll understand that the young lady's statement doesn't tally.'

'Oh, yes? What did she say?'

'That you invited her to your apartment, and there tried to rape her. That she happened to have that pistol in her handbag and managed to get it out, and shot you in self-defence. Whereupon you beat her up, tied her up, and called the police with the story that she had tried to murder you.'

'How very interesting,' Murdoch agreed. 'Do young ladies in this country normally carry loaded automatic pistols in their handbags?'

'Of course not, sir. Mind you, she isn't English.'

'I have just told you that,' Murdoch pointed out. 'What passport is she using?'

'Oh, Russian. She's travelling under a student visa.'

'Do the Soviets give their students a lot of visas to visit England?'

'Well, sir, they don't. Not on their own, certainly. It seems when her application came through the Home Office felt it might be a breakthrough. It's important that we are friendly with the Russians, right now.'

'Oh, quite,' Murdoch agreed. He knew that the whole British defence plan was based on the assumption Hitler would at least have to watch his eastern border.

'The point is, sir, can you positively prove that the young lady is the daughter of this . . . ' he glanced at the statement, 'Chand Bibi. That would mean she was an Indian, wouldn't it?'

'Half Pathan. And half Russian. Virtually the same racial background on both sides. No, Inspector, I don't think I can prove the young lady is Chand Bibi's daughter. What name is she travelling under?'

'Ah . . . the inspector opened his notebook. 'Yasmin Bogoljubova. The first name fits, of course.'

'But not the second. Her real name is Wittvinov. I suppose, correctly, Wittvinova. So tell me, am I to be charged with rape?'

'Oh, good Lord, no, sir. I mean . . . well, you hadn't well, if you know what I mean . . . '

'Oh, quite. You mean you had me examined while I was unconscious and discovered I hadn't ejaculated recently. So the charge will be attempted rape.'

'I do not propose to charge you with anything, Sir Murdoch. You? I'd lose my job. However, having consulted the Director of Public Prosecutions, I must tell you that it is our considered opinion that it would be best if the case did not come to court. Defence counsel could make a meal out of the facts. I mean, the girl's clothes were disarranged . . . '

'But also, I think, covered in blood,' Murdoch pointed out. 'Does that mean I went on trying to rape her after being shot?'

'Well, no, sir. There obviously was a struggle while you were tying her up. The point is that there would be quite a hoo-ha, which would involve a very senior and well-known British officer, might cause trouble with the Russians . . . we have a watertight charge against her, that of carrying a weapon without a licence. The Home Office feels the best thing would be just to deport her.'

'So she can have another crack at me when she feels like it.'

'Good Lord, sir, she'll never have that. We'll make sure she'll never be re-admitted to this country.'

'How very reassuring,' Murdoch said. 'Remind me to give up travelling.'

'I'm very glad you see it our way, Sir Murdoch,' Bloomfield said, rising. 'We'll do our best to keep the facts out of the newspapers, of course. Oh . . . we will have to submit a full report of the incident, with your and her statements, of course, to the War Office.'

★

The War Office made no comment, at the moment, but Bloomfield was not entirely successful with the newspapers, whose comments ranged from the sedate *'MYSTERIOUS SHOOTING AT FLAT OF WAR HERO'* in *The Times* to *'WAR HERO CAUGHT WITH HIS PANTS DOWN BY GUN-WIELDING FEMALE'* in the *News of the World*.

Lee was furious. 'Of all the cheek. They're virtually calling you a liar.'

'They're trying to sell newspapers,' Murdoch pointed out.

'And when you think they've just sent her back to Russia,' Lee said. 'She should have been horsewhipped at the least.'

Harry Caspar wrote, 'Shame you didn't wring her neck.'

Helen was annoyed, Harry didn't comment from his Paris hideaway, Fergus was amused, Ian naturally more serious. 'She would hardly have been working on her own,' he pointed out. 'She was probably sent by the Russians.'

'Why should the Russians want to bump off a has-been soldier?' Murdoch asked.

'Probably some sinister red plot. Or she could be in the pay of the Nazis?' He looked across the bed at Annaliese; Murdoch was recuperating at Broad Acres, and Annaliese had virtually appointed herself as his nurse. He suspected she was going to be something of a problem, because although he was sure she had recovered from her traumatic experience, she showed no sign of attempting to resume her life, seemed perfectly happy being general dogsbody at Broad Acres. And patently worshipped him.

'Ian could be right, Uncle Murdoch,' she said.

'In that case, they're scraping the bottom of the barrel,' Murdoch told them.

He was in a hurry to get well, because Europe was getting more and more tense. It was March of 1939 before he was sufficiently recovered to return to work, and in that very month Hitler swallowed the rest of Czechoslovakia, in complete defiance of what had been agreed at Munich. By then even Neville Chamberlain recognized that he had been hoodwinked by a man to whom treaties meant nothing, and now he issued unconditional guarantees of support to both Poland and Romania, the countries which most seemed to be threatened by German ambitions. Britain prepared for war.

'Glad to have you back, Murdoch.' Ironside shook hands.

'Glad to be back, Bill. And congratulations.' Ironside had just been appointed CIGS. 'Whatever is Gort doing?'

'Ah . . . he's to command the BEF, if and when it has to go to France. As most of us agree, it's a when rather than an if, and the when could be at any moment, it's a matter of getting everything together.'

Murdoch gazed at him. 'Gort is getting the BEF?'

'Well . . . ' Ironside looked embarrassed. 'There is a precedent, of course. Sir John French was CIGS up to 1914, and was then given the Expeditionary Force.'

'Yes,' Murdoch said, and sighed. 'Well, I'm quite willing to serve under Gort.'

Ironside played with the pen in front of him.

'You mean I've been sidestepped, totally.'

'For God's sake, Murdoch, you are fifty-eight years old.'

'I beg your pardon. I won't be fifty-eight for another two months. And how old are you?'

'Fifty-nine.'

'So?'

Ironside sighed in turn. 'I'm CIGS. All right, maybe it should have been you. But you weren't around, were you? And frankly, that business with the Russian girl . . . well, some eyebrows were raised.'

'Indeed? She was Chand Bibi's daughter, out to avenge her ma.'

'Oh, quite. But suppose we had set out to prove that? Then the whole business of your summary execution of her "ma" would have come up. We could hardly have you as CIGS after that.'

'So give me a field command.'

'It is simply not on, at your age, Murdoch. You know the rules. Forty is the usual top line for combat in subordinate positions.'

'So what command am I to have? Chelsea Hospital?'

'We have a very important posting in mind for you, Murdoch. And I'd be deeply grateful if you'd accept it. We'd like you to head a military mission to Holland.'

'Holland?'

'We're trying to get all our potential allies to realize the seriousness of the situation. There's even a military mission going to Russia.' He grinned. 'I hope you'll agree that in all the circumstances we could hardly send you there.'

'Holland is a neutral. Was a neutral last time. And will certainly be a neutral this time.'

'If left to themselves, maybe. But we have it much in mind that the original Schlieffen Plan for the defeat of France in 1914 was to wheel through both Holland and Belgium. This was watered down to a wheel through Belgium alone, but there can be no doubt that the German General Staff are in possession of Schlieffen's plans, and that if they do decide to invade France they may very well come through both the Low Countries.'

'Damn difficult, with all those canals and polders.'

'Nevertheless, it could happen. The Dutch happen to feel, like you, that it'd be too difficult to try. We believe Hitler will try anything and everything, when he decides to move. We want you to convince the Dutch of this. You speak Dutch, don't you?'

'Good Lord, no. I had a few words of Afrikaans once, but I've forgotten them.'

'Well . . . most of them speak English. Will you take the assignment, Murdoch?'

Murdoch considered. But it seemed evident that he was not going to be offered anything better. 'Oh, very well.'

'That's splendid. You have a staff, of course. Any choice as ADC? One of your lads?

'Ah, no. If there's a war they'll want to be on the shooting side of it. Find me some young fellow who won't mind serving with a has-been.'

'You can never be a has-been, Murdoch. There isn't an officer in this army wouldn't jump at the chance of serving with you. Oh, and you can take Lee, of course.'

'She'll be tickled pink,' Murdoch growled.

Lee was, tickled pink. 'Holland,' she said. 'I've always wanted to live in Holland. How long will we be there?'

'God knows. Until something happens, I suppose.'

'Murdoch, you're all grouchy.'

'It is a hundred years since anyone fired a shot in anger against Holland,' Murdoch pointed out.

'Well, thank God for that. The place is growing on me every minute. I'll be able to see Harry whenever I like. We both will.'

'It's over two hundred miles from The Hague to Paris, my love.'

'A comfortable drive,' Lee said.

Annaliese was less happy than Murdoch. 'You are going away,' she sobbed. 'Cannot I come with you?'

'I'm afraid not. It would complicate your becoming a British citizen.' Her papers still had not come through. 'But I'll be only just across the North Sea,' Murdoch told her. 'We'll be home almost every weekend.'

'It is so close to Germany,' she said.

'And that's another reason why you're staying here.' He gave her a hug. He really did look on her as his daughter, now. 'Keeping the home fire burning.'

A week before they were due to depart, Lieutenant Paul Standing, Royal Western Dragoon Guards, arrived. Murdoch had met him two years previously, when as the junior subaltern the young man had uttered the regimental prayer at the annual dinner. Murdoch had seen him several times since when visiting the Bath depot in his capacity as Colonel-in-Chief. 'Are you sure you want to do this?' he asked.

'Oh, yes, sir,' Standing said. 'The other fellows are green with envy.'

'What, at you going to Holland? It's the third most neutral country in Europe.'

'Ah, sir, but with you, there's sure to be action.'

Murdoch scratched his head; it was the first time he had ever been embarrassed by his reputation.

Next morning who should appear but Jennifer Manly-Smith, looking very smart in her khaki uniform, with its khaki stockings and heavy brown shoes, and her khaki forage cap perched on the side of her head. She was driving a staff car, saluted as she was ushered into Murdoch's presence. 'Private Manly-Smith reporting for duty, sir.'

Murdoch gazed at her in amazement. Jennie was thirty-four now, and the pretty girl had grown into a most attractive woman, her dark hair gathered in a snood on her neck. 'For duty? With me?'

'I'm your driver, sir.'

'Well, I'll be damned.'

'I volunteered, sir,' Jennie said, continuing to stare straight ahead of her. 'I am a very good driver, sir.'

'I'm sure you are,' Murdoch said, and shouted, 'Lee, look who's here.'

Lee was delighted. 'Now I know we are going to have a good time,' she said.

Murdoch still felt disgruntled at having been shunted aside when he had no doubt at all he was as physically fit and mentally alert as any of the young major-generals – Alexander, Montgomery, Auchinleck – who were getting commands in the fighting forces. He was even more disgruntled by events that summer. It was the beginning of July when they finally got to Holland, to be received with grave but sceptical protocol, and they hadn't been there a month when news arrived of the Soviet-German pact. Everyone knew this meant war . . . between Germany and Poland, and therefore between Britain and France and Germany. But the Dutch, charming hosts as they were, remained totally confident that they would be able to sit on the sidelines, as they had in 1914. In fact Murdoch, as soon as he got down to staff discussions, realized that his hosts were not going to be of very great use even if they did have to fight. The Dutch army mustered only eleven divisions, some two hundred and seventy thousand men, possessed no armour, and only one hundred and twenty-six planes. They had a useful navy of over seventy ships, but a large percentage of these were in the East Indies.

Lee, however, was very content. They were given a pleasant flat in The Hague, overlooking the sea, and as they were right next door to the fishing port of Scheveningen, there was every prospect of being able to do some boating before the winter closed it; she had sailed a good deal in her youth, but Murdoch never had, so she was looking forward to being on the teaching end of experience, as it were, just for a change.

She was also very happy to have Jennie back with her on a whole-time basis. They immediately reverted to Christian names, and went everywhere together. Nor could this raise a single eyebrow, as it was Jennie's duty to drive the English General, or his wife, wherever they wanted to go. As Murdoch was taking his assignment seriously, however useless he felt it to be, it was Jennie whom Lee took with her when she wanted to explore, and Holland of course was as much a treasure trove of new sights and sounds and smells as India; together the two women drove up to Amsterdam, boated on the Zuider Zee, visited the old seaport of Hoorn, and then went on into Zeeland, to such delightful spots as Sneek. While Murdoch remained in the office he had been given, studying documents and making appointments to see people who always listened to him politely and then dismissed his apprehensions or ideas as impractical.

He had been given a staff of nine, including Jennie and Standing, and also including another ATS girl, Sergeant Withie, a plump blonde who rather obviously rapidly became very friendly with every other man on the station. The Dutch assignment was clearly the perfect receptacle for people who weren't very keen on ever having to fight a war. Murdoch did not feel this applied to Standing, but certainly to everyone else; he found his office as depressingly pacifist as the various officials he fruitlessly lobbied.

Lee also had Jennie drive her down for a weekend in Paris, to see Harry.

'Tell him it's time to give up this writing business and join up,' Murdoch suggested.

'He is just not going to be a soldier, Murdoch,' Lee said severely. 'You have to get that through your head.'

But on 3 September the holiday came to an end; following the German invasion of Poland two days earlier, Britain declared war.

'I am totally wasting my time here,' Murdoch said on the phone to Ironside. 'I'd be better off filling sandbags at home.'

'You stay where you are,' Ironside told him. 'Until we see how this thing develops.'

Murdoch sighed and hung up, and went off with Lee to attend a reception at the home of the Spanish ambassador.

When they got back to the flat, the telephone was ringing. 'Murdoch!' Philippa shouted down the line. 'Murdoch, is that you?'

'Yes, it's me,' he said. 'There's no need to shout.'

'Murdoch, the most terrible thing has happened.'

'What? Has there been a raid?'

'No, there hasn't been a raid,' she snapped. 'Annaliese has been arrested.'

'What did you say?'

'A dirty great policeman arrived with a warrant. She's an enemy alien. Murdoch, the poor girl was distraught. *I* am distraught. How can she be an enemy alien? For God's sake, she came here to get away from the enemy.'

'Red tape,' Murdoch said. 'I'll sort it out.'

As Lee had a hair appointment and didn't really want to get involved with Annaliese's problems – she regarded the girl entirely as Murdoch's protégée, especially since the manner in which she had escaped from Germany had sunk in – he gave himself a three-day pass and took the ferry across to Harwich the next day, where he found Ian waiting for him.

'I think it's just lousy,' Ian said.

'Why aren't you in France?' Murdoch asked.

'We aren't ready yet. I don't think we're going to get across until next month. So I gave myself some leave.' He had recently been promoted major and was now adjutant of the regiment; Fergus was a captain.

'Snap,' Murdoch said. 'Where is she now?'

'In a detention centre in Taunton.'

They drove down to London, first. The signs of war were already spreading across England; barrage balloons dotted the sky, and although there was as yet no petrol rationing, the garages were reluctant to give any car more than a few gallons.

In London, Murdoch went to the Home Secretary. 'Of course, Sir Murdoch,' Sir John Anderson said. 'These are sad times. But the girl *is* an enemy alien. I mean to say, her father is a well-known Nazi, one of Hitler's most prominent supporters, and a general in the German army.'

'She fled her father, because she could no longer stomach his views,' Murdoch pointed out.

'Oh, quite, and all this will be taken into consideration. I am setting up special tribunals to deal with every enemy alien in the country. They will investigate the alien's background, record in this country, family connections, and so on. Fraulein von Reger will receive a sympathetic hearing, I do promise you, and it may well be that she will be released unconditionally.'

'Have you any idea how many enemy aliens there are?' Murdoch asked.

'As a matter of fact, I do: there are more than fifty thousand in the London area alone.'

'And something like ten times that in the country as a whole. To process them all could take months.'

'Yes, I'm afraid it is an enormous task.'

'And for all that time this innocent girl is going to be locked up.'

'She will be in a detention camp, Sir Murdoch.'

'I'm not sure that won't be worse,' Murdoch growled, remembering the detention camps in South Africa.

'I'm sorry, but there is nothing else I can do. You may know, and I may believe you, that Fraulein von Reger is innocent of any desire to harm this country. But I am afraid we also know that a large number of the German aliens in Britain are pro-Nazi, and even that some of them were sent here with the specific purpose of sabotaging our war effort in every way. They have to be found.'

356

'And as they are found they are going to be locked up with Annaliese. Don't you realize, Sir John, that if any of those people are Nazis, or Nazi agents, they will know all about Annaliese's defection? They will give her a very hard time. They might even murder her.'

'This country is at war, Sir Murdoch. You, as probably our most famous living soldier, must understand the implication of that. We are fighting for our very existence against a hideous tyranny. The comfort of one individual, even the life of one individual, cannot be more important than the life of the nation. However, I do assure you that Fraulein von Reger is receiving every protection we can afford.'

Hitherto Ian had taken no part in the conversation. Now he said quietly, 'Would it make a difference if Miss von Reger was a British citizen?'

'Well, of course it would, Major Mackinder.' Anderson said, somewhat wearily. 'But she has not yet obtained her naturalization papers. I may say that the delay has been just because of her Nazi connections.'

'She hasn't had a Nazi connection in two years,' Murdoch snorted.

'Would it make her papers easier to obtain if she were my wife?' Ian asked.

Murdoch started to turn his head, then checked himself.

'Your wife?' Anderson asked.

'We are engaged to be married, yes.'

'I have no record of it.'

'We are engaged,' Ian said. 'It only happened a few days ago, and with one thing and another, I have not even bought a ring. We had intended to get married next spring, but in the circumstances, we will get married immediately. Now, Sir John, are you going to refuse to grant British citizenship to the wife of a serving officer in HM forces?'

'Well . . .' Anderson stroked his chin. 'Of course not.'

'Then, sir, will you release my fiancée into my custody? I give you my word that we will be married within the week.'

Anderson looked at Murdoch.

'He has my blessing,' Murdoch said.

357

'Just when did you actually become engaged?' Murdoch asked as they drove down to Taunton.

'Ah . . . half an hour ago.'

'That's what I thought. Therefore Anna doesn't actually know about it yet.'

'Well, no. She knows I'm very fond of her.'

'And is she very fond of you?'

'Well . . . I think she is.'

Ian was driving, so Murdoch could study the road. And a few other things. 'Has she told you why she left Germany?'

'Yes. And I have to say that if I ever get Reger in the sights of a gun she is going to be an orphan.'

'Quite. Did she also tell you how she got to this country?'

'Not in detail.'

'She travelled from just south of Berlin, across Germany, across Holland, and then by sea to Harwich, and then from Harwich down to London, and existed in London for several days while trying to find out where I was. In fact, she only found me by the merest accident; she was standing on the corner of Greek Street, saw me going into that nightclub for Steve's stag party, and waited for me to come back out.'

'Some determination. She is a most incredibly tough girl.'

'Yes,' Murdoch agreed. 'She made the journey, which took her several weeks, without any money.'

'That must have been tricky. How did she eat?'

'Ian,' Murdoch said, 'she earned her keep as she went along.'

The car slowed as Ian turned his head.

'I think she did a very brave thing,' Murdoch said. 'It's not something everyone would have done, however. And much as I love her, and I do love her, Ian, that experience must mean that she has a few mental scars locked away. Coming across them might prove traumatic for both of you.'

The car gathered speed again. 'Are you advising me not to marry her because she's been to bed with a few other men?'

'I am not advising you,' Murdoch said. 'You are old enough to make your own decisions. I am putting you in possession of all the facts. There is also the fact of your career.'

'Billy Rostron isn't going to object.' Rostron was the new colonel, Destry having been promoted to brigadier. 'He's met Anna, and likes her. So does Coralie. As regards the future, this war can't last very long. Then we'll all be friends again, just as you and the Regers became friends again after 1918. Any more objections?'

Yes, Murdoch thought. The biggest objection of all: if Annaliese loved any Mackinder, it was himself. But he didn't dare say it. 'No.'

'Then I am going to marry her.'

'To get her out of a detention camp, or because you love her, warts and all?'

'Because I love her, warts and all. I think I fell in love with her when we were there in 1933. I have thought of her ever since. I love her, Dad.'

'Then you have my blessing,' Murdoch said. 'And I'll tackle your mother.'

'You have got to be joking,' Lee said. 'My son, marry that tart?'

'Our son,' Murdoch reminded her. 'Is going to marry the girl with whom he is in love.'

'A German?'

'So what's wrong with being a German?'

'Only that they're trying to kill us.'

'Anna isn't trying to kill us, Lee. And if you'd just simmer down you'd see that they really are a perfect match. Heck, when we were in Germany you were in favour of it.'

'And you weren't. It's a crazy old world, isn't it?' She smiled. 'Okay, so I was being heavy. I'd better nip across to Bath and have a chat with them both.'

Murdoch went across too, for the wedding, which took place a week later. In all the circumstances it was a small affair, but Annaliese looked radiant.

359

'Oh, Uncle Murdoch,' she said, 'this is the happiest moment of my life. Actually to belong to you . . . I mean, your family.' She flushed as she gazed at him.

He held her close, kissed her on each cheek. 'He loves you very much,' he said. 'And he's half my age. Don't be a chump and spoil it all.'

Yet he felt somehow guilty as he watched them set off for their brief honeymoon. Suddenly it seemed that all the fame of which he had been so proud, the glamour which had surrounded his youthful exploits, and which had made people either love him or hate him, was coming home to roost.

He took the opportunity to visit the Admiralty, where Churchill had been reinstated almost the day war broke out.

The First Lord was not in a good mood. 'I knew we were unprepared, but this situation is ridiculous,' he growled. 'Everyone is in a complete twitter. Here we have one of our submarines torpedoing another . . . do you know, there were only two survivors from *Oxley*?'

'I didn't know anything about it,' Murdoch said. 'It wasn't in the papers.'

'Well, it's not the sort of thing you put in the papers, is it? And then the German U-boats are having a great time with our shipping, knocking it off all over the place. We'll get it right, but it'll take time. And we don't know how much time we have. And then, these farcical raids over Germany, dropping leaflets. Are we fighting the Hun, or supplying him with toilet paper? As for that French 'offensive' in the Saar, it's a joke. They seem to have met no opposition, so they are withdrawing again. My God, the French army should have smashed their way right into the Ruhr, and dug in there, while Hitler's people were all in Poland. Without the Ruhr he'd have been in trouble from the start.' He sighed. 'All of these are mistakes which are going to cost us dearly. How are things in Holland?'

'Quiet,' Murdoch said. 'I have never felt more like a square peg.'

Things remained quiet in the west as the winter dragged on.

360

Philippa wrote to complain that the standard rate of income tax had gone up from five shillings and sixpence to seven and six. By the first week in October the British Expeditionary Force of one hundred and sixty-one thousand men, together with twenty-four thousand vehicles and tanks, had safely been transported to France and was moving up towards the Belgian border. By then Poland had finally been crushed out of existence and everyone was expecting a German assault in the west, but it didn't happen. Things were so quiet it was almost uncanny, as Murdoch discovered when Jennie drove him down to see how the lads were getting on.

'Familiar territory to you, I suppose, sir,' Colonel Rostron observed.

'I seemed to recognize one or two villages,' Murdoch agreed. 'But the scenery is different.' He looked out of the window of Rostron's farmhouse – where was Madame Bosnet? he wondered – at rows and rows of medium tanks instead of rows and rows of horses.

'Yes,' Rostron agreed. 'I tell you what, Sir Murdoch, war has become a damned sight more noisy since the last time.'

Murdoch lunched with Fergus and Ian, and managed to have a word in private with his eldest son. 'How are things going?'

'Couldn't be better.'

'Honestly?'

'Honestly, Dad. We only had a week together, of course. I wish it could've been more. But I have never been so happy. Or let's say, I will never be so happy as when I get home again.'

Maybe I was imagining things, Murdoch thought thankfully, and went on down to Paris to see Harry.

Who was packing up.

'Well, thank God for that,' Murdoch said. 'I'm afraid, having rejected Sandhurst, you'll have to start at the bottom. But in view of your name I have no doubt at all you'll be commissioned in six months.'

'Dad,' Harry said, 'I'm not going to England.'

'Not going . . . then where the devil are you going?'

361

'I'm going back to the States.'

'The States? Now?'

'Yes. My novel is going to be published over there, and the agent says it'll be good for my career to be on the spot.'

'Harry,' Murdoch said, as patiently as he could. 'There happens to be a war on. Hadn't you realized that?'

'Of course I had, Dad. That's another reason I'm getting out. I don't want any part of it.'

Murdoch stared at him. 'Your brothers, your brother-in-law, our country is part of it.'

'I respect that, Dad. But I think you are wrong.'

'You think we are wrong to oppose Nazi Germany? You've heard what Anna had to say.'

'I heard. Anna is a somewhat hysterical young woman, in my opinion. But even if everything she said was true, I do not see how we are going to make matters better by killing people. Or by being killed ourselves.'

'I cannot believe it.' Murdoch said. 'I do not believe it.'

'I'm sorry, Dad.' Harry attempted a smile. 'Call me a coward, if you like.'

'Yes,' Murdoch said, finally losing his temper. 'If you won't fight for your King and Country, there is nothing else I can call you.'

Harry's face stiffened. 'Well, then, that's that. If you don't mind, I have another dinner engagement.'

'But I suppose you want me to pay your passage across the Atlantic.'

'That won't be necessary,' Harry said. 'Mother has already done so.'

'Mother? Lee knows about this?'

'Mom approves,' Harry said. 'She thinks fighting a war is crazy, too.'

'What are you doing tonight, Jennie?' Murdoch asked as he got into the back seat of the command car.

'I'm for an early night, sir,' she said. 'It's a long drive back tomorrow.'

'Bugger that,' he said. 'Come with me to a show. You've no objection to nudity, I hope?'

'Well . . . I suppose not, sir.'

'Right. Do you have a dress?'

'Well . . . no, sir.'

'That shouldn't be a problem.' They were driving down the Champs Elysées. 'Those shops are still open. Pull in.'

She obeyed, got out to open his door, frowning at him. 'Are you all right, sir?' She hadn't previously inquired into his meeting with his son.

'Probably not,' he said. 'I have never been so God damned angry in my life. But I also happen to feel like taking a pretty woman out to dinner. Any objections, Private?'

Jennie hesitated. Then she said, 'No, sir.'

He took her into a dress shop and bought her a white georgette evening gown with wine-coloured lace trimmings and velvet sash. 'Oh, Sir Murdoch,' she said. 'I have never owned anything so lovely in my life.'

'Handbag and shoes,' he said. 'Now there's just time to have your hair done. There's a salon at the hotel. We'll eat at the show.'

'Sir Murdoch,' she said, 'are you sure . . . well, that Lee would approve?'

'Lee,' he said savagely, 'approves of everything. She has told me so. And Jennie, once you take off that uniform, you can start calling me Murdoch.'

He had a bath, shaved, and dressed; he was staying in uniform. Then he went down to the hotel bar and had a stiff scotch. He did not recall ever having been so disturbed in his life, so questioning of all the values he had ever held and maintained. Life had always been a simple matter, for Murdoch Mackinder, holder of a famous name. One did one's duty, without looking to right or left, without accepting the possibility of death, sure that if one did die, one's reputation would remain, like the scent of a woman's perfume, to remind others that one had passed that way.

He had always accepted nothing less from anyone else, certainly all the members of his own family. Now he felt he had been stabbed in the back. Not least by Lee herself. He loved her. He had never loved anyone else, since Margriet. And he did not doubt that she loved him. But she had a

363

different sense of values. He had known that when they married, but had felt that her values had merged with his during the war. Now he thought that perhaps they never had.

He gazed at the door, and Jennie Manly-Smith standing there. 'You look quite gorgeous,' he said.

'Thank you, Sir Murdoch.'

He held up his finger, and she smiled. And flushed. 'I have never called you Murdoch before.'

'Well, enjoy yourself for tonight.'

He bought her a drink, and then they took a taxi to the Moulin Rouge. He asked her about her boys, during dinner.

'Bert is in the army,' she said. 'With the Dragoons, remember?'

'Of course. You must be very proud of him.'

'Just so long as he doesn't get his head shot off. Joe is only fifteen, of course, but he hopes to follow Bert.' She smiled through her champagne. 'We're going to have a tradition like yours, Murdoch.'

'Something to be proud of. Jennie . . . don't have any more.'

She gazed at him. 'I'm not likely to do that, Murdoch. I'm a widow.'

'I meant, there'll always be one rotten apple, if you go on long enough.'

'Oh,' she said, the penny suddenly sinking in.

'Show's starting,' he said.

They spent three hours watching the bare-breasted young women, laughing at the comics, who were mainly visual as the management were well aware that at least half of their audience were English soldiers, and drinking champagne. There were three empty bottles on the table by the time they filed out to find their cab.

The hotel was blacked out, of course, and the bar was closed. 'Oh, great,' he said.

'I don't really feel like anything else, to drink,' Jennie said.

The hesitation had been only a split second, but it had

been enough to have them gazing at each other, as they stepped into the lift and the doors closed.

Jennie licked her lips. 'I . . . when I was a little girl, I used to go up to Bath and watch the regiment drilling, or going over the jumps. I . . . ' another quick lick of the lips. 'You were always there. You rode better than anyone else, and you looked better. I suppose you were better.'

Murdoch took her into his arms and kissed her on the mouth.

'Are you going to tell Lee?' she asked.

She lay against him, a brief white wisp of a woman. Her breasts were small, her hips were slender, her legs perhaps a trifle thin. But her passion was beautiful.

The odd thing was, he realized, that she could have been anyone. Anyone in the sense that there were others, such as Annaliese or her mother, who would willingly have been here in Jennie's place; and worse, anyone in the sense that had she not been here he would tonight have picked up a whore on the Champs Elysées. He had been in that kind of mood.

'I think I have loved you, Murdoch, since I was six years old,' she said.

He kissed her forehead, where it rested on his shoulder.

'But I think I have loved Lee as well,' she said. 'I always envied her. Mrs Mackinder, Lady Mackinder . . . '

'Do you envy her still?'

She smiled; her breath tickled the hairs on his chest. 'More than ever. She has you every night.' She was silent for a few moments, then she asked again, 'Are you going to tell her?'

'No. She wouldn't want that.'

Another silence. Then she asked, 'Are you going to have me transferred?'

'Not unless you wish it.'

She raised her head, then rolled on to his stomach, enclosed him in those thin, strong legs. 'I would hate it.'

They gazed at each other, and he kissed her again. 'Then you'll have to stay.'

365

'Did you see Harry?' Lee asked.

'Yes,' Murdoch said.

'So, I guess you're mad at me.'

'Yes,' he said. 'I was very mad at you.'

She sighed. 'I guess I'm a bit of a coward too, Murdoch.'

'You are one of the bravest women I have ever met.'

'But I'm still a woman. That means I'm a coward, where my children are concerned. I want at least one of them to survive this war, Murdoch.'

'And Harry is your choice.'

'No,' she said. 'They would all be my choice. Harry is the only one I can really hope for.' She undressed and lay down, watched him pick up his book. 'I guess you're sated,' she remarked.

He looked at her. 'Does that make you mad at me?'

She gave a twisted smile. 'Nope. Never mad at you, Murdoch Mackinder. I guess I had it coming.' She kissed him on the forehead, and picked up her own book.

She knew what had happened, but had no idea it was Jennie, he was sure. And the honourable thing to have done would have been to send the girl away. But that would be to indicate her guilt; Lee was too smart not to be able to add two and two. Yet keeping her here seemed to enhance the cheat, especially as he knew he was going to cheat again, if Lee went away and Jennie stayed.

He wondered why he was so concerned. His Scots Calvinistic background, presumably. So he had a mistress, perhaps. He hardly knew a man of his age and position who didn't have a mistress. Yet it bothered him, as that business in Mesopotamia had bothered him. And now, as then, he longed for action to relieve his internal tension.

But there was no action. On 1 November the Dutch Government pronounced a 'state of siege' which merely gave the military and the police increased powers but indicated no alteration in the strict policy of neutrality. However, ten days later the army was mobilized and moved to its frontier positions, and Murdoch was taken on a tour of the dykes and sluices and shown how the various dams were ready to be blown on a single command issued from military headquarters.

'We feel,' said his guide, 'that if we make it perfectly plain to Hitler that we intend to fight for our neutrality, he will think several times about infringing that neutrality.'

Murdoch had to presume they were right. The western front remained in a state of total quiescence which the Americans were calling the Phoney War; it was not until 9 December that the first British soldier died in action, Corporal Thomas Priday of the King's Shropshire Light Infantry being shot while leading a patrol.

'By 9 December 1914 we had already suffered fifty thousand casualties,' Murdoch reminded Lee. 'This is the damndest war I have ever heard of.'

'And long may it remain so,' she said. 'Are we going to get home for Christmas?'

'I don't see any reason why not.'

Only a few days later there came the cheering news of the Battle of the River Plate, but England was none the less a gloomy place, with bacon and butter as well as petrol rationed. They spent the holiday with Philippa and Annaliese at Broad Acres, where they were joined by Helen, whose husband was at sea, and baby Murdoch, and also by Rosemary and Helen Phillips; Geoffrey had to remain in London. It was quite a jolly party, despite the restrictions and the blackout, because both Helen and Anna were able to announce that they were pregnant; Helen, indeed, was five months on the way. Lee was delighted. Rosemary was less so, as Harriet, much older than Helen, was not yet married.

'A whole clutch of grandchildren, all at once,' Lee said. 'Oh, Murdoch, do you still love me now I'm a grandmother?'

'I will still love you when you're a great-grandmother,' he promised her, and meant it, although he wished he could stop thinking of Jennie, who had elected to spend Christmas in the village with her father and young Joe. They came up for Boxing Day drinks and kisses.

'Jennie looks kind of sad,' Lee remarked. 'I guess Christmas is a time when you really do need a man.'

367

'Yes,' Murdoch agreed. 'Maybe she'll find one.' And he hoped so too.

He got up to London for a day or two, saw Ironside, who wanted him to remain in Holland for another few months.

'If anything is going to happen it'll be in the spring,' Ironside said.

'And if nothing happens?'

'We'll have to see about launching an offensive. Or settling down to another hundred years' war.'

It became apparent to Murdoch that there were no offensive plans; had there been, he might have been more usefully employed. He went off to the Admiralty to see Churchill, and congratulate him on the victory at the Plate.

'One enemy pocket battleship,' Churchill said. 'Good for propaganda. But they've sunk more of our navy than that. Things are not going well, Murdoch. I can tell you that in confidence. And you're absolutely right, they have no offensive plans at all. Not even any to limit Hitler's prospects. Do you realize that, just for example, all of Germany's iron ore comes from Scandinavia? And it comes by sea, down the Norwegian coast, inside Norwegian territorial waters. I suppose the Norwegians don't really feel they can object. Now Germany can't fight without steel. I have been badgering my Cabinet colleagues to mine those waters. But they won't do it. It'd be infringing Norwegian neutrality, they say.'

'I imagine the Norwegians *would* complain,' Murdoch suggested.

'Well, of course they would. But we are fighting a war, Murdoch. A war of survival, although too many people can't see that. If Hitler is sitting tight right now, it's because he's getting ready for something big. It can only be here in the west. And we are doing absolutely nothing but waiting to be hit, where and when and how he chooses.'

Churchill was obviously a very worried man; at the end of January he made a speech in Manchester in which he warned the nation that they were drifting into peril, but no one seemed to take much notice. The country, like

Holland, was gripped by the coldest winter since 1894 – even the Thames froze – and the idea of campaigning in such conditions was impossible.

But there were others concerned. A week later General Reynders, Commander-in-Chief of the Dutch army, resigned, claiming that for all the Government's proud words the Dutch military forces were totally inadequate to resist any German invasion. This caused a furore, and the Government attempted to counter it by announcing that they had ordered three new battlecruisers – but these were to defend the East Indies. However, with improved weather in April, everyone, Murdoch included, was taken by surprise by the German invasion of Denmark and Norway, and the shift of emphasis to the Baltic.

Immediately there were plans to send British and French troops to aid the Norwegians – the Danes had already surrendered – and names began to be canvassed. Murdoch as usual volunteered, and as usual was rejected on the grounds of age.

'I may as well retire and take up gardening,' he grumbled.

Lee was as usual well pleased, and even more by the removal of the war to a safe distance. Helen was now in her last month of pregnancy, and Lee decided to go back and be with her; she would also be able to see how Annaliese was getting on. Murdoch and Jennie drove her to the dock, where she had secured passage on a destroyer.

'Look after him,' Lee told Jennie. 'Don't let him make himself ill with frustration.'

'I think she knows,' Jennie said as they drove back to the flat. 'About us.'

'Perhaps she does.'

She parked the car, opened the door for him. 'Does that bother you?'

'Not if it doesn't bother her, Jennie. Or you.'

Jennie followed him up the stairs, as she was in uniform. He unlocked the door, went in. She stood in the doorway. 'Will there be anything else, sir?'

'Yes. I would like you to dine with me, tonight. Here.'

369

She hesitated.

'Or have you a previous engagement?'

'Of course I have not.' She came into the flat, closed the door. 'But . . . we have to stop it, Murdoch.'

'Not today.' He unbuttoned her uniform blouse. It was absurd the way she could make him a randy young man all over again, just by being alone with him.

'When Lee comes back,' she said. 'Promise me, Murdoch. You'll send me away when Lee comes back.'

He kissed her, gazed into her eyes. 'Yes,' he agreed. 'I'm not any good for you. You should be married.'

'I don't want to be married. Do you think I could ever be happy with anyone else, after having known you? And Ralph?'

'So you are opting for being unhappy for the rest of your life?'

'I'm being very lucky,' she said. 'I'm having maybe a month with you, now. Then I must go. It's not fair to Lee.'

He nodded. 'One month. A honeymoon. Then we'll call it quits.'

He didn't know if he was going to be able to do that. He didn't know what to do about the situation he had got himself into. He did not love Jennie the way he loved Lee. And he still enjoyed making love with Lee. But Jennie appealed to the romantic side of his nature, and perhaps to the lecherous side which also lurks in every man; a woman, unusually dressed, a woman in uniform, who was now taking off that drab khaki to reveal the sexuality that lay beneath. It was the same allure that had been fascinating about Chand Bibi. Perhaps, had he taken Chand Bibi to bed, he would have exorcized it.

Perhaps he should buy Lee a uniform.

But for this month he must sate himself, utterly, and then cast her aside. He knew she was right. Lee probably did know all about it, and was prepared to accept it – but she could not be happy about it. And she was accepting it because she loved him. Making Lee unhappy by taking advantage of her love would be the greatest crime in the world, for him.

370

A month, to sate himself. There was not a lot else to do, save burn himself up watching the incompetence revealed in the Norwegian campaign, and read in the newspapers of the gradual tightening of belts in England, and the growing feeling that the Chamberlain Government was making a mess of the war. A debate in Parliament was fixed for Tuesday, 7 May, and as Churchill wrote, 'We are determined to get things sorted out, and start fighting a war instead of sitting on our backsides.'

Murdoch looked forward to reading about it, but he and Jennie were still in bed on the Tuesday morning when there was a knock on the door.

He got up, pulled on his dressing gown, released the latch, and gazed at Margriet von Reger.

14
HOLLAND 1940

Murdoch could only goggle at her in amazement. She was wearing a fur coat and was very well dressed, carried a small suitcase . . . and looked at once agitated and relieved. 'Won't you let me in?' she asked.

He stepped back, and closed the door behind her. 'God,' she said. 'I have been so afraid. Murdoch . . . ' she turned to face him, and then looked at the bedroom door, and Jennie, who like Murdoch had dragged on a dressing gown. Margriet looked at Murdoch again, her mouth making an O.

'You chose an inopportune moment, Margriet,' he said. 'I hope you haven't run away from Reger?'

'And if I have? Who is this woman?'

'I don't think that is any concern of yours. Perhaps you had better get dressed, Jennie. And make us some breakfast.'

Jennie nodded, and closed the bedroom door.

'You are impossible,' Margriet said. 'Yes. I have left Reger. I have come to you. I had not expected . . . ' her shoulders sagged, and she sat down.

'What did you expect, Margriet? I am a married man.'

'Ha,' she remarked. 'Does Lee know about that woman?'

'That, too, is none of your business.'

'So you are going to throw me out. You took Annaliese in.'

'Annaliese wanted shelter.'

'And what do you think I want? I *have* run away from Reger.'

'Why?'

'You have to ask that, after all these years?'

'It is because of all these years that I have to ask that, Margriet.'

372

She sighed. 'I could stand it no longer. I can stand the Nazis no longer. My own children have turned against me. Paul has turned against me. Your son, Murdoch.'

'He ceased being my son a long time ago, Margriet.'

'You cannot send me back, Murdoch. Reger would kill me.'

'Of course I will not send you back, Margriet. But you cannot stay here, either. I will arrange for you to be sent to England.'

Margriet glared at Jennie, who had reappeared. 'Breakfast is served, Sir Murdoch,' Jennie said formally.

'You are sending me away because of her,' Margriet snapped.

'I am sending you away because if you have left Reger you will be safer in England. Now come and have some breakfast.'

'Suppose I told you I have information?' Margriet asked.

'What information?'

'So now you are interested. Well, listen. In two days' time Hitler is going to attack the west. The orders have been given, the men are just awaiting the hour. They are going to attack through Luxembourg into the Ardennes, through Belgium, and through Holland.'

Murdoch stared at her, while he felt his pulse quicken. 'Are you telling the truth?'

'Of course I am telling you the truth. I only left Reger's headquarters yesterday. He is just across the border, Murdoch. He is commanding the force which will take Holland.'

'And you have just left him? Does he know where you have gone?'

'Not yet. I spent the weekend with him, and then I left, to return home. But I simply got off the train at the next station east, and then took one for Holland. I have my passport, and I am the wife of a German general. No one stopped me. Murdoch, listen to me. They are going to cross the Meuse just north of München-Gladbach, and then swing up for Rotterdam and the Hague. They will be preceded by a wave of parachute troops. Do you know what

373

gave them the idea for that? Your own exploit in India. They are going to smash through Holland in the south. They are not going to touch Fortress Holland in the north, or get entangled in the Zuider Zee. They know that if the south falls, so will the north.'

She paused for breath, while Murdoch realized that what she had said was far too detailed for her to have made up.

'Get me Dutch HQ,' he told Jennie. 'Tell them I'll be over there in fifteen minutes. Call Standing as well and tell him to get dressed and meet me there.' He ran into the bedroom and began to dress.

Margriet followed him. 'What are you going to do with me?'

'You had better stay here. General Weenink may wish to see you personally.'

'Is that woman going to be here?'

'She'll be driving me. Mind you stay put.' He ran down the stairs, Jennie at his heels.

'Do you believe her?' she asked.

'Yes.'

But General Weenink, in charge of Intelligence, didn't. 'Really, General Mackinder,' he protested, 'We have had so many reports this winter of imminent German moves to the west, and none of them have materialized.'

'Have any of them presented such a plan, the only way in which Holland can be smashed in quick time?'

'Perhaps not, but I do assure you that Holland is not going to be "smashed in quick time", as you put it. We are prepared to meet the Germans wherever they move. As for this particular information, you must agree it comes from a suspect source. A woman, running away from her husband. Naturally she is trying to buy the best terms for herself. Would you like me to lock her up?'

'On what grounds?' Murdoch asked. 'You are not at war with Germany. Yet.'

'I am sure we can think of something.'

'I would prefer you to allow her to go free. I will have her sent to England just as soon as a passage can be arranged.'

'As you wish,' Weenink agreed.

Jennie drove Murdoch and Standing to their office, and Murdoch got on the scrambler to London.

'Yes,' Ironside said. 'We have been hearing similar things from several sources. The Pope has just warned King Leopold that the Germans intend to invade his country. He didn't name the date, mind you . . .'

'Well, now you have the date,' Murdoch told him. 'May ninth. I hope you are going to do something about it.'

'There is damn all we can do about it,' Ironside said. 'King Leopold refuses to believe it, or to allow our troops to advance into his country in anticipation of such an invasion. Unless we can move through Belgium, there is no way we can help Holland, even supposing they'd allow us to. We have plans all ready for that. But the situation remains unchanged, from our point of view. We wait for Hitler to fire the first shot.'

'God Almighty! What a way to fight a war. So what are my orders?'

'They are also unchanged. If Hitler does move against Holland, you may be able to give them some advice. You're the only one up there who's actually seen action. But Murdoch, we'd prefer it if you didn't get either killed or captured. If the Germans can't be stopped, get out. We'll have an aircraft sent over tomorrow, and it will stand by at your disposal. Understood?'

'Yes,' Murdoch said.

He telephoned Broad Acres. 'How're things?'

'Any day now,' Lee said. 'How're things with you?'

'They could be hotting up. No matter what happens, Lee, I want you to stay put until you hear from me again. Understood?'

'Oh,' she said. 'You mean . . .'

'I mean nothing I can say over the phone. Will you do as I say?'

'Of course. Murdoch . . . you aren't going to do anything foolish?'

'I'm not being given the chance.'

'Murdoch,' she said. 'When you come out, I mean, if you have to, bring Jennie with you.'

'I have every intention of doing that,' he said. 'But I'll be sending you someone in advance.'

'Come again?'

'Margriet von Reger has turned up in Holland, seeking asylum,' he explained. 'She's run away from Reger.'

'Oh, my God!'

'Quite. I'm sure you can see I don't want her hanging about here. As soon as I can get her clearance I'm sending her over to you. Is that all right?'

'Well, of course it is, honey. I'll keep her under wraps.'

'I love you.'

'Snap. Take care.'

He replaced the phone, looked at Jennie. 'I think she does know,' he said. 'And care, about us both.'

'Are we leaving?'

'Not right away.'

'What about Frau von Reger?'

'Oh, she is.' He telephoned the Home Office to ask for clearance for Margriet to enter England, and they told him it would be processed in due course. He kept his temper and reminded them it was urgent, then booked her into an hotel.

'Can't I stay with you?' she asked. 'You have a spare room.' She had explored the flat. 'I won't interfere with you and your "chauffeur".'

'It's a nice hotel,' he assured her.

There was nothing left to do but wait. 'You really think this is it?' Jennie said at dinner.

'Yes. Scared?'

She smiled. 'Yes. But not with you about.'

'I feel so God damned helpless,' he confessed.

They listened on the wireless to news of the 'Norway debate' in the Commons. It had apparently been lively, with even the Conservative back benchers demanding Chamberlain's resignation.

'Who'll be PM if he goes?' Jennie asked.

'God knows. Probably Kingsley Wood. I know who I would *like* to be Prime Minister.'

376

'Mr Churchill?'

'Yes. With him as boss I might even be given some worthwhile employment.'

They slept fitfully, and Murdoch was up at dawn. 'Today's the day,' he said, standing at the window to look at the sky. Jennie put her arms round him.

'They're late,' she said.

They went to the office. Everyone was on edge.

Murdoch took Margriet to lunch. 'I ought to break your neck,' he told her. 'I am going to be the laughing stock of Holland.'

'Hitler has postponed it, that is all,' she said.

'Because of your defection?'

She smiled. 'I am not that important. Besides, no one can possibly know as yet that I have not merely returned home. It is just that Hitler changes his mind, regularly. He has done so before, often. Do you know the original date was last November?'

'So why should he have postponed it this time?'

'I don't know. There could be any one of a hundred reasons. It could even be a bad astrological forecast. He is like that.'

'You mean he's mad.'

'He is very superstitious,' she said seriously.

That afternoon a Lysander reconnaissance aircraft landed at the small airfield outside the city, and Flying Officer Grant reported for duty.

'Stand by,' Murdoch said. 'I may have something for you to do very shortly.'

His optimism was justified. That evening London rang through to say that Frau von Reger had been given clearance.

'Thank God for that,' Murdoch said, and telephoned the hotel.

'My plane will take you over at dawn tomorrow,' he told her.

'Will you be coming with me?'

'Of course not. You'll be landed at Croydon airport, and I have arranged transport for you. I have also arranged an

377

hotel for you to stay in tomorrow night. Next day you will go down to Broad Acres and stay there.'

'Your home,' she said. 'I have always wanted to visit your home. But you will not be there.'

'No,' he said. 'Lee is.'

There was a moment's silence. 'I suppose you want me to keep my mouth shut, about . . . well, things.'

'You are under orders to keep your mouth shut about everything,' he told her. 'Or I am going to have you locked up as a spy.'

'Do you think she will?' Jennie asked when he hung up. 'She strikes me as being a vicious woman.'

'Oh, she is. Or she can be. But I don't think what she says is going to make a lot of difference. I just wish to God I knew how much of what she's told us is the truth. But I've been wondering that about her all my life.'

She poured wine, brushed her glass against his. 'I have the strangest feeling this is the last night we shall ever spend together.'

'Don't come over all psychic on me,' he begged. 'You have a lot of nights left, Jennie.' He squeezed her fingers. 'You'll be just lucky if you can spend most of them with some other fellow.'

'I won't, you know,' she said.

She was more than usually passionate, that night, and they did not fall asleep until well after midnight. To awake it seemed only moments later to the drone of aircraft, the thud of bombs, the wail of sirens, and the screams of people.

'Holy hell!' Murdoch leapt out of bed and ran for his clothes. 'It's happening.' He dragged on his uniform as the entire house shook and the lights went out. Now the drone of planes was very close.

'Murdoch!' Jennie stood at the window, having raised the curtain. She wore only brassiere and pants. 'Paratroops?'

Murdoch stood behind her, saw the dark figures drifting down at the far end of the promenade, spitting fire as they neared the ground. He buckled on his revolver. 'Get

378

dressed,' he told her, 'and then contact Standing. Don't get involved in any shooting, but go downstairs in case the building is hit.'

'But Murdoch . . . '

'That's an order, Private Manly-Smith.' He ran down the stairs. The other tenants in the building, who were mainly military attachés and their wives, were gathering in the corridors, shouting and arguing in a variety of languages. Murdoch pushed through them, reached the street. The noise of the planes and the bombs was enormous, but none were being aimed at the front – no doubt to give their paratroopers a chance; the one which had shaken the house must have been a mistake, but he could see the crater, a huge hole in the esplanade.

There were people on the street, staring at the sky, shouting and screaming. The paratroopers had descended some distance away, and Murdoch guessed they were making for the royal palace. He ran along the street, pushing people aside, and was suddenly halted by a policeman.

'No further,' the man said in Dutch.

Murdoch had enough of the language by now to make himself understood. 'Your Queen is in danger,' he said. 'Are you armed?'

'I am armed, sir,' the policeman said. 'But . . . the Queen?'

'Follow me,' Murdoch told him, and continued on his way, the policeman at his heels. Now there was firing from in front of them, the crack of rifles being smothered in the chatter of very light automatic weapons; the paratroopers were using Thomson sub machine-guns.

In the palace gardens they encountered a platoon of Dutch infantrymen under a nervous lieutenant. 'There are so many of them, sir,' he said, recognizing Murdoch's uniform in the first dawn light. 'There are at least twenty of them holding that gate into the palace kitchens. And I have no orders.'

'Well, they can't be allowed to establish themselves,' Murdoch said. 'You're at war now, boy. Are you prepared to fight?'

'Oh, yes, sir.' The lieutenant stood to attention.

'And to take orders from me?'

'Yes, sir.'

'Then we take that gate by assault, and work our way into the kitchen. Use whatever cover is available, but keep advancing.'

Before they could hesitate he moved forward himself, followed, to his surprise, by the policeman. Immediately fire was opened by the Germans on the gate, but their tommy-guns had a limited range. Murdoch took shelter behind a tree, and waved his men up. The Dutch soldiers were now returning fire, and he could hear bullets clanging amongst the ironwork and shattering windows in the palace beyond. They were also hitting Germans, from the cries in front of them.

He advanced again, surrounded by a swarm of angry bees. The policeman coughed and collapsed. Murdoch sheltered behind another tree, now only twenty yards from the gate. 'Fix bayonets,' he called, and listened to the rasp of steel. Now the firing from inside the palace was very loud, but then it died away. He was about to give the order to charge when a Dutch voice called out from beyond the gate, 'Cease firing. You are surrounded.'

Murdoch signalled his men to wait, and a moment later the Germans threw down their arms. Murdoch waved at his men to move up and himself went forward.

'General Mackinder,' said the Colonel in charge of the palace guard. 'It is a pleasure to fight beside you, sir. These men . . . he looked at the Germans. 'They were after Queen Wilhelmina.'

'I guessed that,' Murdoch said.

'But we beat them,' the Colonel said proudly.

'Yes,' Murdoch said. 'Let's hope we can beat the rest of them.'

He went back to the flat to make sure Jennie was all right. She had been joined by Standing, and both were very anxious.

'I've got to get up to the border and see what's going on,'

Murdoch said. 'Paul, will you take Frau von Reger to the airport, and tell Flying Officer Grant to deliver her to Croydon and then return here. Jennie, you'll drive them.'

'Yes, sir,' She held his arm. 'Murdoch . . . no risks.'

'We're all at risk, right now. You take care.' He ignored Standing's presence, kissed her and left again. The bombing did not appear to have been very severe, but reports coming in from the south indicated that the Germans had already driven deep into Dutch territory, and were advancing due west, exactly as Margriet had predicted.

General Weenink agreed that this seemed to indicate that Margriet's information had been correct, if a day out, but he was continuing with his set plan, giving orders to flood the country further north, and maintaining garrisons there to resist any attack. When Murdoch pointed out that there weren't going to be any attacks up there and that it would be better to concentrate all his men in the south, Weenink said, 'There are paratroopers everywhere, General Mackinder. We must defend our people.'

The good news was that the British and French were moving forward very rapidly to assist in the defence, and the French General Giraud's Seventh Army was expected to be at the border in twenty-four hours.

Murdoch doubted they were going to be in time, as he took a train east towards the front with a Dutch liaison officer. The line had been blasted in several places, and they wound up riding borrowed horses, and taking shelter every few minutes as German planes swooped from the sky with chattering machine-guns. In several places paratroopers had indeed landed to disrupt communications, and the Dutch were falling back everywhere, confounded by these novel tactics.

They were also obeying orders and opening the dykes in every direction, allowing brown water to sweep across the flat countryside, which did not make communications any the easier. Murdoch went down to the border where the Belgians were equally bemused by events, staring to the east and the south, listening to the roar of the guns, and gazing apprehensively at the sky. But there were no Germans to be seen; their main thrust into Belgium was far to the south.

'If you were to move your people into Belgium,' Murdoch suggested to the Dutch Major-General in command of the division guarding the frontier, 'and then swing up the line of the Meuse back into Holland, you might take them in the flank.'

'How can I take my men into Belgium?' the officer asked. 'We are not at war with Belgium.'

'You're fighting on the same side, surely.'

'I cannot cross the frontier without express orders,' he said stubbornly.

Murdoch gave up and decided to return to The Hague, wondering where the British were, and Ian and Fergus and their tanks. Had they been in the vicinity the counter-stroke might have been possible. But returning to The Hague was easier decided than accomplished. All communications were by now disrupted, all railway lines out of action. He and his Dutch Captain got back as far as Breda, and were there forced to spend another night, while planes roared overhead and they could hear the crump of bombs. Next morning, Sunday, Murdoch was enormously relieved to see French troops entering the town. General Giraud had made a most remarkable advance.

'Ah, we are fighting the Boches, Sir Murdoch,' Giraud said. 'I am advancing to Tilburg, and we will check them there. You are welcome to accompany me, sir.'

Murdoch was tempted, but he did not think the French were going to get to Tilburg; he could hear the sound of heavy firing to the north to suggest that the Germans had already advanced too far. In any event, he had been out of touch with his own people for too long. 'I'll come back next week,' he said, 'and see if you're still here.'

'We will be here,' Giraud said. 'My men are veterans. How can those Boches be veterans? Have you heard the news from England?'

'What news?'

'Mr Chamberlain has been forced to resign.'

'That was bound to happen. Who is Prime Minister?'

Giraud grinned. 'Why . . . Mr Churchill.'

'Churchill?' Murdoch shouted. 'Are you sure?'

'Oh, yes. It is in all the newspapers. They are saying that now Britain will really fight.'

'You bet.'

Murdoch was more anxious than ever to get back to The Hague. With Churchill in charge surely he would be offered a fighting command. But travelling proved just as difficult today as yesterday, as Germans swooped overhead, apparently unchallenged by any Allied force, bombing and strafing. Most of the civilians he encountered seemed dazed by the whole thing, unable to grasp that their country, which had not been subjected to war for a hundred years, was being destroyed. Murdoch begged, borrowed, and even stole transport wherever possible, but it was midnight before he regained The Hague and stumbled up the stairs to his flat, his uniform torn and dusty, and extremely hungry.

'Murdoch!' Jennie threw herself into his arms. 'Thank God you're back. I've been so worried.'

He looked past her at Margriet. 'What the hell . . . you should be in England.'

She shrugged.

'The plane was hit in the bombing,' Jennie explained. 'It's a write-off.'

'Grant?'

'He's all right. He and Mr Standing went off to find another plane. They haven't come back.'

'Damnation. Any calls?'

'Yes. Lee called. I told her you were all right, but we were cut off before we could say much else. Then the War Office called. They wanted you to get in touch as soon as you returned.'

He looked at his watch. 'I'll try them now. Jennie, I am starving.'

'Food coming up.' She hustled into the kitchen.

'How is it going?' Margriet asked.

'I would say not very well.' He told the exchange what he wanted, gave his high-priority rating, waited.

'You mean you are not going to stop them?'

'Oh, we will, I suppose. The question is where.'

'I am sorry, sir,' the operator said. 'There is a breakdown in the line. It will be repaired as soon as possible.'

'How soon will that be?' Murdoch asked.

'I cannot say, sir. There is a war on.'

Murdoch replaced the phone, toyed with the idea of getting his staff up and using the radio equipment in the office, decided against it; he was too tired and everyone who mattered in England would probably be sleeping as well. 'I might as well get some sleep.'

'What is going to happen to me, Murdoch?'

'We'll get you out, Margriet. Just don't worry.'

Jennie had hot soup and bacon and eggs on the table. Nothing had ever tasted so good.

She sat beside him. 'There's not a lot left, and the shops are just about empty. Yesterday everyone just rushed out and bought everything in sight, despite broadcasts not to hoard.'

'I wouldn't lose any sleep over it. I have an idea we may be pulled out of here tomorrow. You've heard about Churchill?'

'Oh, yes,' she said.

'He'll be in touch,' Murdoch promised her.

Sleep was difficult with the recurring air raids, but these seemed in the distance and The Hague was not again attacked. Jennie and Murdoch made love, because they were both tensed up. For Murdoch this was a unique situation, a war going on and himself quite without a command or even orders. He was at the office at dawn, working with sleepy telegraphers, trying to get through to London, chafing at the delays, walking up and down. It was late afternoon when he finally spoke with Ironside.

'God, it's catastrophic,' the CIGS said. 'They're at the Meuse.'

'At it? They're across it,' Murdoch told him.

'I meant the Meuse in France,' Ironside said. 'They have established bridgeheads on the west bank. They're virtually in Sedan, God dammit.'

'Sedan,' Murdoch couldn't credit that. 'You mean they've crossed half Belgium and fought their way through the Ardennes in two days? Has nobody tried to stop them?'

'It just doesn't seem possible. You have no idea of the chaos down there, Murdoch. The Germans are using armour the way we used to use cavalry, huge squadrons of the damned stuff being hurled against infantry positions.'

'But the French have more tanks than the Germans.'

'Oh, they do. But not concentrated. And not being handled with any determination either. And then behind the lines the planes are bombing and strafing continuously, causing major disruption.'

'We've had some of that. Where the hell are the RAF and the French Air Force?'

'Being shot to ribbons. Do you know, yesterday an entire squadron of Blenheims, thirty aircraft, Murdoch, was just wiped out? We sent eight Battles to disrupt German infantry advancing through Luxembourg, and seven of them were shot down. If this keeps up we won't *have* an air force in a couple of weeks.'

'Well, at least Giraud and his Seventh Army are in Breda. They should stop the advance here.'

'They won't, you know. Giraud is retreating on Antwerp.'

'Already? In the name of God, why?'

'His troops are being strafed so heavily they can't fight.'

'What are you saying is that we are heading for a major catastrophe.'

'Confidentially, yes, unless the Germans run out of steam. Murdoch, we want you out of there. Again, confidentially, the Dutch command is making "we are beaten" noises, and I wouldn't like to say how long they'll hold out. Have yourself flown across to London immediately.'

'Bill, I don't have a plane. It got blown up.'

'Oh, hell. All right, I'll send you another. It'll be with you . . . I'll let you know. Have your staff ready to leave at a moment's notice.'

'Yes, sir,' Murdoch said.

He tried to call Lee but couldn't get through. That didn't

matter, he'd be in England either tomorrow or the day after.

'How many can a Lysander take?' he asked Grant when the two young officers returned from their fruitless search for an aircraft.

'Depends on the amount of gear, sir. But at least six.'

'So, no gear at all,' Murdoch decided. 'But there are a dozen of us, all told.'

'Oh, don't worry about me, sir,' Grant said. 'I'll find my own way out.'

Murdoch chewed his lip. He didn't like leaving anyone behind. 'You'll stay put,' he said. 'The moment we land, I'll turn that plane around and send her back for the rest of you. Understood?'

'You are going to take me in the first load, Murdoch,' Margriet begged. 'If I am captured I will be shot.'

'I'll take you, Margriet,' he promised.

'I can wait for the second load,' Jennie volunteered.

'You are coming with me,' he said, and grinned at her. 'Orders from Lee.'

He felt exhilarated, for the first time since the German attack had begun, even when one of Ironside's aides called back to say no plane would be available until Wednesday morning, but one would be there at seven a.m. He had at last been given definite orders, and he had no doubt at all that there was an important job waiting for him in England. Certainly he was accomplishing absolutely nothing here.

He went along to see his friend Weenink and say goodbye.

'I did not expect you to stay,' the Dutchman said sadly. 'Here, all is lost.'

'Surely not,' Murdoch protested. 'They caught us on the hop, that's all. Their advance will slacken any day now, as lines of communication lengthen, and we will have the opportunity for a counter-attack.'

He was preaching conventional military thinking, but he did not believe it. There was something irresistible about this German advance, and the little experience he had of the effect of strafing on defending troops – during the German onslaught of March 1918 – told him that they were entering a new dimension of warfare. Indeed news was just coming in that in the Sedan theatre the French Ninth Army had been 'destroyed' by the combination of tanks and aircraft, and that the Germans were across the river and moving on.

Weenink knew that too. But he had other things on his mind. 'This is not war as you or I know it, General Mackinder,' he said. 'It is war between peoples, not armies. We have just been informed from Berlin that unless our troops surrender they will "liquidate our cities", starting with Rotterdam. That is the word they used, liquidate.'

'Good God. That is unheard of.'

'So was Nazism, until a few years ago.'

'And are you going to accept such blackmail?'

'The matter is being discussed now.' Weenink held out his hand. 'I do not think I will see you again, General. But it has been a pleasure to know you and work with you.'

Murdoch shook hands, and returned to the office to oversee the destruction of all files and equipment that could not be taken. But why was he so shocked? Hadn't he used the threat of air power against the Mahsuds? Somehow that was different. Why? Only because the Germans were supposed to be civilized, men who would not torture or murder their captives. But he could no longer be sure of that either.

No one slept that night. They ate the last of the food in the flat, some sausages and baked beans, drank the last of the coffee. Murdoch had assembled his entire staff, ten strong, including Jennie, Standing and himself, to brief them about what was going to happen, and they drank a toast to each other.

'We *are* going to win, Sir Murdoch?', asked Sergeant Withie.

'No question about that,' he told her. 'If not this battle, then the war.'

But it was difficult to believe even that, at the minute.

The final list he made up was himself and Standing, Jennie and Margriet, Sergeant Withie and Sergeant

387

Upjohn, the chief telegrapher, for the first load. He felt like a heel to be taking the first plane himself, but he was under definite orders, and the others were the most important, after him. 'But the plane will be back for you,' he promised the rest. 'Flying Officer Grant will be in command.' He shook hands all round, and then they left for the airport at first light. There were craters on the runway and some fires burning, while the control tower had been knocked out, but it was still operational, and some of the few Dutch planes left were using it. The British party waited in the shelter of a half-destroyed hangar, watched enviously by the soldiers on guard duty, and at seven ack emma promptly the Lysander dropped out of the sky.

'Flying Officer Nolan, Sir Murdoch.' The young man saluted. 'This your group?' He looked them over. 'It'll be a bit of a squash, but we'll manage.' He arranged them according to weight: Jennie was in the very rear, Sergeant Withie and Sergeant Upjohn immediately in front of her, Standing and Margriet in front of them, and Murdoch in the co-pilot's seat. Grant, who had driven them to the airport, saluted, and Nolan, who had not actually stopped his engine at all, taxied down the runway.

'I have never flown,' Margriet announced.

'Neither have I,' said Sergeant Withie as the plane bounced over the ground. 'Wheee!'

They were in the air, climbing sharply, and then banking steeply. 'Oh, God!' she said. 'I'm going to be sick.'

Sergeant Upjohn gave her a paper bag.

At no more than six hundred feet the Lysander turned out over the grey waters of the North Sea, taking the shortest route to England.

'How long?' Murdoch asked.

'Couple of hours, sir. Piece of cake, really. So long as we don't run into Jerry.'

'Hm,' Murdoch said, and pointed away to the right, where, high above them, he could see six aircraft. 'Like those?'

Nolan craned his neck. 'Oh, shit,' he said. 'I do beg your pardon, sir.'

388

'Granted,' Murdoch said. 'They've seen us.'

The planes were peeling off and starting to descend.

'Can we really stand losing another aircraft?' Murdoch asked, wondering what it would feel like to fall six hundred feet – none of them had parachutes.

'Not this one,' Nolan agreed. 'I think I had better turn back, sir, and wait for them to go away.'

'You're the boss,' Murdoch agreed.

'They are going to kill us,' Margriet said.

'Not if we can help it,' Murdoch promised her.

The Lysander banked steeply and descended until it was only a hundred feet above the waves. The coastline of Holland came in sight a moment later, but Murdoch didn't recognize it; there was nothing but sea and beach and sand.

'A shade south, I think,' Nolan said. 'That must be one of the islands.' He banked again, and as he did so there was a sudden whoosh and a ripping sound. Murdoch saw the shadow of the Messerschmitt whipping past them in the same instant as he heard a choking gasp from behind him.

'Oh, Christ,' he said. 'Nolan . . .'

There was another whoosh, and some more ripping. Murdoch gazed at blood drifting away from Nolan's tunic, seeming to take ages before it settled, partly on him. Behind him now there were screams and moans, but he was concerned with the plane, which was plunging nose down towards the sea. He grabbed the co-pilot's wheel and pulled it back, and the aircraft responded, hanging there for a few seconds before going straight down rather gently, not more than twenty feet, into the water.

It caused an enormous splash, and seemed to settle for a moment, then remained stable.

'Everybody out,' Murdoch shouted, opening the upper window and climbing out himself; there was no other exit, and he was terribly aware that Jennie was at the very back. And that he had no idea of how long the machine would float.

A hand came up, and he grasped Margriet and pulled her out. 'God!' she screamed, 'God! They're all dead.'

Her mink coat was covered in blood, but he didn't

believe she was hit herself. Or what she had said.

'Come on,' he yelled. 'Come on.' The plane was starting to sink.

Standing crawled out, and pulled Sergeant Withie behind him. But Sergeant Withie was also covered in blood, and she was breathing it out in little frothy bubbles.

Murdoch laid her on the wing. 'Jennie,' he shouted. 'Jennie, are you all right?'

'Yes,' she called back. 'But Sergeant Upjohn is dead.'

He could see now, from on top, that the bullets had ripped through the roof of the machine, immediately in front of where she had been sitting. It was horrible of him to feel relief, but he wanted to shout for joy. 'Get out,' he shouted. 'This thing is going to go any minute.'

'Half a mo,' she gasped, and he knew she was moving the dead man's body from in front of her. He dropped his legs through the window to help her, and as he did so, the plane gave a lurch and sank. Margriet screamed as she floated off. Standing grabbed her. Murdoch's leg was caught for a moment, and he went down with the plane, his eyes open, staring at Jennie, capless, straddling Upjohn's dead body.

He had no breath left, kicked instinctively, and rose through the window, broke the surface, saw that she was not there, took a long breath, and dived again. The plane had struck the bottom; they were only in about fifteen feet of water. But it was fifteen feet too many. He gained the window, upside down, looked inside, saw her unmoved, her face expressionless, only the traces of green mucous around her mouth and nose revealing where she had reached for breath.

Her hand drifted towards him, and he caught it and pulled. Her leg had also caught, but now it came free, and she floated out of the window with him. Lungs bursting, he gained the surface, turned to her. She lay on her face in the water, motionless, and she was starting to sink again. He grabbed her hair and her arm and twisted her on her back, looked around. The beach was not far away, and Standing was nearly there, towing Margriet. Sergeant Withie's body had floated away. The two men inside the plane were there for ever.

390

Murdoch swam, on his back, using his feet, his hands tucked into Jennie's armpits. His uniform felt like lead and his boots seemed filled with water. But he forced himself onwards, and after a surprisingly short time his feet touched sand. He stood up, took Jennie in his arms, and carried her ashore. Margriet, water dripping from her clothes and her hair, sat on the sand and watched him. Standing stood beside him.

He laid Jennie on the sand, knelt beside her.

'I'm sorry, sir,' Standing said.

'Yes,' Murdoch said. 'So am I.'

A Dutch patrol found them half an hour later, told them they were on the island of Walcheren. They were taken across the island, through windswept trees and empty countryside, to the company headquarters and given blankets to wrap themselves in while their clothes dried. The soldiers also brought in Jennie's body, and that afternoon she was buried. There was no marker on the grave. The soldiers were solemn, but their thoughts were far away. Jennie was just a statistic. News had been received of the German raid on Rotterdam. A hundred Heinkel one-elevens had been dispatched to blast the city out of existence. Apparently the High Command had immediately offered to surrender, but it had been too late to recall all of the planes.

'They say the city has been devastated,' the Captain told Murdoch. 'That there are more than thirty thousand dead. It is not war. It is mass destruction.'

Which is another word for war, Murdoch thought. He went outside and looked to the north. Rotterdam was less than fifty miles away, and it was possible to see the smoke pall. As if it mattered. He had never felt to crushed in his life before. Jennie had been so unassuming, so giving without thought of reward, and so loving. And like Ralph, she was now dead.

While he was alive. And he was Murdoch Mackinder. He was not a man who could give up and weep; his reputation would not allow him to do that. He could only fight with

391

hatred in his heart, as he had done against the Mahsuds. And he was determined to do just that.

'I must get to the south, to the British army,' he told the Captain.

'It would be best for you to go to Middelburg,' the Captain said. 'There you will get a train, or a boat, down the canal to Vlissengen. Belgium is just across the Scheldt.'

He gave them his own car, first thing on Thursday morning, and they drove into the city. The three of them had hardly spoken since the crash, although Margriet had wept a lot. She was suffering from shock, Murdoch supposed. Well, they all were. And he was suffering from guilt as well. Jennie had wanted to stay behind, and he had forced her to come. Oh, Jennie!

Middelburg, all of Walcheren, indeed, seemed untouched by the war, save for the anxious faces of both civilians and soldiers, as they looked across the canal at South Beveland, and that pall of smoke on the northern horizon. They were taken to army headquarters, where a Colonel met them.

'We have surrendered,' he told Murdoch, his face ashen. 'It was announced yesterday evening.'

'Oh, God damn,' Murdoch said.

'We are under orders to disarm and arrest all British and French troops on Dutch soil.'

'Are you going to do that?' Murdoch asked.

'*I* have not surrendered, General,' the Colonel said proudly. 'My orders were to hold Middelburg, and I will do that as long as possible. But you must leave immediately, for Vlissengen. I will telephone the commander there, and tell him to have a boat ready for you to cross the river into Belgium.'

'Thank you,' Murdoch said.

They were given breakfast. Margriet could not eat, she was so terrified at learning the news of the Dutch surrender. She just stared at Murdoch with huge eyes. After the meal they were given the use of a military car, and Murdoch and Standing were supplied with Dutch greatcoats to conceal their English uniforms.

392

'Does this make us into spies, sir?' Standing asked.

He was joking, but Murdoch thought about it. 'Given the calibre of the enemy,' he said, 'if we spot any Germans we had better take these off.'

'We are going to be shot,' Margriet said. 'Oh, we are going to be shot. I wish I had gone home. I came to you, Murdoch. To you. To be spurned. I risked my life, for you. To be spurned.' She began to weep, while Standing stared at her in amazement.

'She *will* be in trouble, if we are caught,' Murdoch told him.

They reached Vlissengen just on noon, bumped over the cabled streets, and looked at the Scheldt. It was still Holland on the other side, but the Belgian border was only a few miles further on.

'I never saw a better sight,' Standing said.

The car took them to the military headquarters.

'Lieutenant-General Mackinder and party,' Murdoch told the Captain who greeted them. 'Colonel Hulder is expecting us.'

'Ah, yes, General.' The Captain looked unhappy. 'The Colonel is waiting for you.'

They were taken upstairs and into an office, where a short, somewhat stout man stood behind his desk. He saluted as Murdoch entered. 'General Mackinder! It is a great pleasure to meet you.'

'I'm quite pleased to be here myself,' Murdoch agreed. 'Have you a boat waiting?'

'I'm afraid that will not be possible, General.'

Murdoch gazed at him.

'I am under specific instructions to place you under arrest, sir.'

Margriet uttered a moan.

'We had been given to understand that you would not implement those orders,' Murdoch said, as quietly as he could.

'Unfortunately, sir, I have no choice. Upon receipt of the message saying you were on your way here, I telephoned my superior, and he told me that under no circumstances were

393

you to be allowed to escape. It appears that the German general commanding the troops in this area has specifically said that you are not to be allowed to leave the country. He has threatened reprisals if that is done, sir. I have no choice.'

Margriet turned and ran for the door, but it was filled with soldiers. Murdoch and Standing looked at each other.

'I would beg you to do nothing rash, gentlemen,' the Colonel requested. 'I would be obliged if you would lay your sidearms on the table.'

'I think we had better,' Murdoch said. He released his holster flap, placed the revolver on the table. Standing did likewise.

'Why don't you fight them?' Margriet shrieked, shaking herself against the hands holding her arms. 'Don't you realize that they are going to shoot us?'

Murdoch could understand her fear. But actually she was lucky in that she was being taken to her own husband – it could only be Reger who had given such an order. No doubt it would earn her a beating, but nothing more than that. While he . . . a prison camp in Germany. That was a deadening thought. Save that surely Churchill would have him exchanged? Far more deadening was the smile which would be on Reger's face, because he would have won, after all, this round. And who could tell it would not be the final round? At least between them.

Standing was taken away. Murdoch and Margriet were also separated, and Murdoch was placed in a car, with an armed Dutch lieutenant beside him, and driven across to the island of Beveland and thence on to the mainland. Everywhere was evidence of the Dutch surrender, soldiers standing around in groups, waiting to be disarmed by the Germans, civilians standing around in no less anxious groups, wondering what was going to happen to them. Equally, everywhere was evidence of the Dutch defeat, shattered railways and bridges, while there were German troops everywhere, always advancing. The journey took a long time, although it was not much more than fifty kilometres, and it was dusk before they reached Breda, which was apparently their destination. The car had been stopped several times, and the Lieutenant had had to show his papers. Now, on the outskirts of the city Murdoch was formally handed over to a German Lieutenant. The young man was very formal and polite, and entertained him to a good dinner. When he asked after Margriet, however, as he had not seen her since leaving Vlissengen, the young man shrugged.

'I do not know, Herr General,' he said. 'No doubt you will discover Frau von Reger's whereabouts in due course.'

After the meal Murdoch was driven into Breda itself. The houses were mostly shuttered, and there had been considerable damage. Only German soldiers were to be seen, their bicycles and motorbikes parked everywhere; the swastika drooped lazily from the town hall. Here the occupying regiment had established its headquarters, and Murdoch was taken upstairs to meet the commanding officer. He entered the office and checked, as he found himself gazing at his son.

'General Mackinder,' Paul von Reger threw out his arm in a Nazi salute. 'Heil Hitler.'

Murdoch gave a conventional British salute. Paul looked very smart in his olive-green uniform, his Iron Cross at his neck; Murdoch realized that he had to be very nearly forty, but was the same tall, spare figure he remembered from 1933.

'The fortunes of war,' Paul said.

'Yes,' Murdoch said.

'Won't you sit down?'

Murdoch said down.

'Cigarette?' Paul asked.

'I don't, thank you.'

Paul lit one himself, sat behind his desk. 'I don't know why you have been brought here, General. It is the command of my father, you understand. He will be joining us later tonight.'

'Ah,' Murdoch said.

'No doubt he wishes to ensure that you are being properly treated,' Paul suggested. 'It is sad when old friends have to fight each other.'

395

'Quite,' Murdoch agreed.

'Especially when . . . ' Paul hesitated, glanced at him. 'It is not like 1918.'

'No,' Murdoch said.

'I mean, there is no resistance, anywhere. It is incredible to us. We have advanced so far, so fast . . . in the south it is even worse. Always we expect a counter-attack, as at the Marne in 1914. But there has been no counter-attack. We cannot understand this.' He smiled. 'It makes us nervous.'

'There will be a counter-attack,' Murdoch promised him.

Paul shrugged. 'If it does not happen soon, it will be too late. Perhaps they need you in command, General.'

He was clearly serious rather than poking fun. 'I wish I was,' Murdoch agreed.

There was a knock on the door and a Lieutenant appeared, to tell Paul something in German. Paul frowned, stood up, replied.

'It is very odd,' he said in English. 'But . . . my mother is here. In Holland. It is very odd.'

Murdoch also stood up, gazed at Margriet as she was brought in.

'Mother?' Paul asked. Margriet's normally immaculate clothes had been ruined by their immersion and drying, and still showed traces of blood. Equally her normally immaculate coiffeur was a matted mess. There was no calmness left in her features.

'Paul,' she cried, and ran forward to throw herself into his arms. 'Oh, Paul, I had expected your father.'

'He will be here, Mother. But . . . did he know you were coming?'

Margriet looked over Paul's shoulder at Murdoch, who gave a hasty shake of his head. The situation was too complicated at that moment for the best course of action to be decided – in which case it was best to keep as quiet as possible until they discovered how much the other side already knew.

'Why, your father knows all things,' Margriet said, disengaging herself and gazingly openly at Murdoch.

'Please sit down,' Paul said. He spoke to the waiting Lieutenant, and the boy saluted and hurried off. 'I have ordered coffee. Now, Mother, do sit down. You look dreadful.'

Margriet lowered herself into a chair. 'Is your father here?'

'Not at the moment. He is on his way. I expect him any minute. In fact . . . ' They could hear the sound of a car engine.

Margriet clutched the arm of her chair and stared at Murdoch. Who could only again attempt to use his eyes to urge cautious patience for as long as possible.

They stood up together to face the door, which was opened by Paul himself. 'Herr Count General!' He stood to attention, saluted.

Reger's return salute was perfunctory. He stepped into the room, looked at Murdoch, and then at Margriet. 'Close the door,' he told his son.

Paul obeyed, looking mystified.

'Adultress,' Reger said to his wife. 'Not satisfied with betraying me before our marriage, you do so afterwards as well.'

Margriet's nostrils dilated.

'You are taken, in flagrante delicto. But, stupid woman, you would have been found out anyway,' Reger said. 'Did you suppose you could escape so easily? Someone who knows you saw you on the train, going towards Holland. Three days before the invasion. Did I not know better, I could accuse you of treachery.'

Paul was looking from one to the other, more mystified than ever.

'Have you nothing to say?' Reger shouted, and suddenly slapped her face, with such force that she fell. Paul caught her just in time to stop her hitting the floor, set her back on her feet. Blood dripped from her cut lips.

'Father?' Paul asked in alarm.

'That was uncalled for,' Murdoch said.

'And you,' Reger snarled, turning to face him. 'You call yourself an officer and a gentleman.'

Murdoch had had to make a quick decision. Margriet was obviously going to have to suffer, but the important thing was to steer Reger away from the treachery issue. 'Your wife came to me, Reger,' he said evenly, 'because she had nowhere else to go. She was sickened by you and your Nazis, and she took the opportunity of being close to the Dutch frontier to leave you. I was flying her to England and political asylum when we were shot down. I can give you my word, as an officer and a gentleman, that we have not committed adultery.'

'Your word,' Reger sneered. 'I do not give a damn for your word. You are a liar, and a man who takes other men's wives to bed. So, now you will give me satisfaction.' He slapped Murdoch's face in turn.

'No!' Margriet screamed.

Paul looked more astounded than ever.

'Well?' Reger demanded. 'Will you meet me? Or will you prove yourself a coward after all, for all those pretty ribbons you wear?'

'Father,' Paul protested. 'General Mackinder is a prisoner of war. You cannot challenge him to a duel.'

'Bah,', Reger said. 'No one as yet knows he has been taken prisoner. No one who matters. I will have satisfaction. This man has plagued my bed for too long. I will have satisfaction.'

'Well,' Murdoch said, licking blood from his lips and deciding to allow his simmering anger to take over. 'If that is what you wish . . . '

'No,' Margriet screamed again. 'He will kill you, Murdoch. He is a practised swordsman.'

'Be quiet, woman,' Reger growled. 'I will deal with you, after you have seen your paramour die. I will take every inch of skin from your ass. That is what I am going to do.'

'We did not sleep together,' Margriet shouted. 'I wanted to. But he already had a mistress.'

'You are lying. And it does not matter. You have confessed your guilty intent.'

'My intent,' she cried. 'Not his. I am the guilty one. Do you want to know the real reason I fled to him?'

'Margriet!' Murdoch snapped. 'Shut up.'

'I took your plans with me,' Margriet said. 'I betrayed you, Reger. I betrayed you, and I betrayed Germany. It was my pleasure to do so, for all the hurt and humiliation you have made me suffer for forty years.'

Reger stared at her with his mouth open. So did Paul. 'You did that, Mother?' the boy said at last.

'Yes,' she shouted. 'Yes.' And gave a bitter laugh. 'No one believed me.'

Murdoch said nothing. It was too evident that her menfolk *did* believe her.

'Then you will be shot.' Reger said. 'I command you to be shot. Now. Now!' he screamed at her.

'Father!' Paul protested.

'Now,' Reger shouted again.

'There has been no trial . . .'

'Trial? I do not need a trial. I am commanding general of this area. I am her husband. I am her accuser and her judge, and her jury, and I condemn her to death. Take her into that courtyard and fill her with bullets. Now. I want to see her die.' Murdoch realized that the man was not quite sane, at this moment. Then he turned on Murdoch. 'I will deal with you afterwards, adulterer.'

399

15

Dunkirk 1940

For a moment there was silence in the room. The three Regers stared at each other, and Murdoch gazed at them in a mixture of horror and consternation.

Then Reger spoke again, in a lower voice. 'I have given you an order, Colonel von Reger. This woman is a traitor to our family. She has betrayed me, and she has betrayed you, and she has betrayed your brothers and sisters. She is no better than that despicable girl Annaliese. But far worse than that, she has betrayed the Reich. She has betrayed the Fuehrer.'

'But if the enemy did not listen to her . . .'

'That is immaterial. Will she not betray us again? If I do not shoot her I must hand her over to the Gestapo. They will interrogate her, and, if she survives, place her in Ravensbrueck Concentration Camp. Either way, she is lost to us. But she was lost to us from the moment she took that train into Holland. What is more, if she is handed over to the Gestapo, the taint of her crime will affect every one of us. Do you wish that?'

Margriet gave a moan and sank back into her chair, blood still staining her chin.

'So,' Reger said, 'it is a choice of having her die now, with some dignity and privacy, or in agony in a Gestapo cell, or of starvation and beatings in a camp. I have made that decision, and given you an order, both as your father and as your commanding officer.'

Paul gazed at him for a few seconds longer, then he went to the door, opened it, and snapped an order in German.

'You cannot do it,' Murdoch said. 'Reger, you cannot execute your own wife.'

'I have that right more than anyone else,' Reger said.

'You have interfered sufficiently in my life. This is the result of that interference. Now be quiet.'

Murdoch drew a long breath. 'I will accept your challenge.'

Margriet groaned.

Reger stared at him, then laughed. 'In the hopes of saving Margriet's life? How romantic. But it is too late. She will be shot.'

The room was filling with soldiers, and they were dragging Margriet to her feet. She seemed to have gone into some kind of a coma as she realized what she had done, what was going to happen. There was only one hope of saving her now.

'Paul,' Murdoch said in English. 'You cannot murder your mother.'

'I must obey orders, Herr General. As given me by both my superior and my father.'

Margriet was being dragged to the door.

'That man is not your father,' Murdoch said.

Paul frowned at him.

'He is a liar as well as a coward,' Reger snapped.

'I am your father, Paul,' Murdoch said.

Paul's frown deepened, then he looked at his mother; but she was already through the door and being taken downstairs.

'Ask her,' Murdoch said. 'Quickly, before it is too late. Or better yet, look in a mirror.'

'You are a swine,' Reger remarked. 'Trying to disrupt my family to the last. It will not work, Mackinder. But you will see your paramour die.' He gave orders in German, and Murdoch was seized by two of the soldiers and marched downstairs behind Paul, who was following Margriet. They emerged into the courtyard, where a firing squad was already assembling in the gloom of the night – the men were obviously unaware of the domestic drama upstairs, and were only concerned with carrying out their duty and executing a traitor. It was obviously a duty they had carried out before, despite having been in Breda only about forty-eight hours; there was a heavy wooden stake erected on the far side of the yard, against a blank wall – both the stake and the wall had been chipped by bullets.

Margriet was marched across the paving stones to the stake, and her wrists bound behind her back and to the wood. She stared in front of her at the men facing her, and past them, at Paul, Reger and Murdoch just emerging into the courtyard. Murdoch felt a hundred years old. But there was nothing he could do, if Paul would not believe him. Instead he remembered that sunlit day on the veldt, when he and this woman had hidden from their Boer pursuers in the waterhole, and she had gone into the water to bathe . . . and the tragedy of her life had begun.

The Captain in charge of the execution was waiting, bandage in hand, looking at Reger for confirmation of the sentence.

'Proceed,' Reger said.

The Captain stepped up to her.

'Margriet,' Murdoch called. 'You have nothing to lose.'

'Take that man inside,' Reger snapped.

But Margriet had heard. Her head jerked as she stared at him, and the Captain hesitated. 'General Mackinder is your father, Paul,' she said, not shouting, but speaking in a strong, clear voice. 'General Mackinder . . . '

Murdoch was forced into the building, and the door closed. He was taken upstairs, but before he had gained the office from which he would have been able to see the yard he heard the ripple of gunfire. He reached the window in time to see the Captain putting his revolver to Margriet's head and squeezing the trigger. But the once beautiful woman was already an unrecognizable mass of bones and blood.

Reger and Paul had both watched the execution. Two men so steeped in the savage duality of Prussian militarism and Nazi fervour they had no spark of humanity left. They were no different to Chand Bibi – perhaps they were worse. Thus he had to combat them with the same white-cold hatred he had known eleven years ago.

The door opened and Reger came in, followed by his son. Paul had given no sign of believing his mother. Nor did he show any remorse for what had just happened.

'Take this man out,' Reger said. 'Have him sent to Germany.'

'I beg your pardon,' Murdoch said. 'You and I have some unfinished business.'

Reger stared at him.

'I have accepted your challenge, Herr General,' Murdoch said formally.

Reger looked at Paul, who said nothing. Then he laughed. 'You are mad. I will kill you.'

'Then you will have avenged the wrong I have done you,' Murdoch said quietly.

Reger gazed at him for several seconds longer, then he looked at Paul. 'You will attend?'

'Yes,' Paul said. 'But General Mackinder has no second.'

'I will do without a second,' Murdoch said.

'You will fight with swords?'

'I will fight the general with any weapons he chooses,' Murdoch said,

'Very well,' Paul looked at Reger.

'We will find a place,' Reger said. 'There is no need to bring anyone else.'

'General Mackinder may try to escape.'

'And will you let him?'

Paul opened the door. Murdoch followed him down the stairs. Reger came behind, led him on to the street, gestured towards the command car. His driver stood to attention, opened the door for him; it was, Murdoch noted, the same driver who had acted as chauffeur for them on their last visit to Germany. Murdoch sat down and Reger sat beside him; he had drawn his revolver and kept it pointed at Murdoch. Paul emerged from the building a moment later, carrying a military greatcoat under his arm; the coat was stiff and clearly wrapped around the two swords. He sat in the front seat beside the driver, the engine was started, and they moved off behind dimmed headlamps.

'Any convenient place,' Reger said.

They drove out of the city and along the bank of the canal. As earlier in the evening, there were only German troops to be seen, only German planes flew overhead.

403

'Your armies are being defeated, one after the other,' Reger said. 'You have nothing to live for, Murdoch.'

Murdoch made no reply. He only really wanted to live for another few minutes, anyway.

Paul was pointing, and the car was pulling off the road into the shade of a stand of trees next to the canal. Here they were reasonably concealed, and yet the night was light enough for them to see each other. The chauffeur opened the doors for them, and Murdoch stepped out. He might have wished he was not quite so exhausted from his ordeal of yesterday and the all-day drive, but he did not think it was going to affect the outcome. Reger, as Margriet had said, was undoubtedly the more practised swordsman. But Murdoch knew he was the younger, fitter man – even if he was considered too old for combat by the British army. And far the more deadly, when he meant to kill. He knew this of himself now, and had no regrets for it.

Reger removed his belts and tunic, pulled his gloves back on. Murdoch did likewise. Paul presented him with a choice of swords, and he took the one nearest him. Paul looked into his eyes. 'May the best man win, General Mackinder.'

'Thank you,' Murdoch said, wondering just what thoughts were going on behind those cold blue eyes.

Paul gave the other sword to Reger, and said something in German. No doubt he was wishing him good fortune as well. Then he stepped aside and stood by the chauffeur, who was watching the scene with impassivity.

Reger advanced, testing the ground with his boot. Murdoch presented the heavy cavalry sword. Reger's blade touched his, and then moved forward rapidly. Murdoch jumped backwards, moving to his right. Reger followed him, face set with determination, but also still flushed with anger, and perhaps, Murdoch thought, with anxiety – he must know that both he and Paul were going to suffer a reaction when they realized what they had done.

Murdoch let him come on, circling to left and then right, while Reger chased him, the sword flailing in the darkness, but seldom making contact. Sweat poured out of Reger's hair and soaked his tunic. Murdoch was also wet with sweat, but his breathing was in much better shape, and he knew that every second brought his victory closer.

After several futile exchanges, Reger stopped, panting. 'Stand and fight, damn you,' he shouted. 'Paul, make him fight.'

Paul made no reply, and after a moment, while the two adversaries faced each other, chests heaving, Reger gave a shout and came on again. But Murdoch calculated that he was nearly out of strength as well as breath, and this time stood his ground. Reger's skill was undoubted. The blades clashed and Reger disengaged in time for another thrust, far more quickly than Murdoch. But the lunge lacked strength: the arm wielding the sword was too tired. Murdoch swayed out of the way and allowed their bodies to cannon together. The impact left him winded, and Reger bereft of defence. Murdoch stepped back, and brought up his blade. Reger stared at him, and for a moment Murdoch hesitated. RSM Yeald was the only man still alive whom Murdoch had known longer than Reger. Then he remembered that only yesterday he had watched Yeald's daughter die.

And that Reger had just killed his son's mother.

Reger stared at him, and realized his fate. His lips twisted in a snarl. 'Damn you,' he said. 'Damn you!' he shouted, and lunged for a last time. But Murdoch easily swept the blade aside, and drove his own point deep into Reger's chest.

Reger hit the ground with a thump, carrying Murdoch's sword with him. Murdoch stepped back; blood had spurted over his glove and shirt sleeve.

He stared at the dead man, and heard a click. He turned his head to gaze at the revolver in Paul's hand. 'German honour?' he inquired.

Paul's face twisted. 'Having just murdered my mother,' he said, 'I do not wish to have to kill my father.'

Murdoch stared at him. 'You mean you knew?'

'I know, now.' He pointed at Reger's body. 'The truth of what you have said is confirmed.'

Murdoch could not resist a bitter laugh. 'Trial by combat? Isn't that a little pagan?'

'Nazism is more than a little pagan, Father,' Paul said. 'Do not misunderstand me. It is my life. Adolf Hitler is my leader. His victory, and Germany's, far transcends personal feelings. But,' he added, watching Murdoch's expression, 'I believe my . . . foster father wronged you, as he wronged my mother. Having just found you, I would like to start with a clean slate, as it were. Do you wish to return to the British?'

'Can I?'

He nodded. 'I will arrange it. You have parachuted before?'

'No,' Murdoch said.

'Are you afraid to do so for the first time?'

'No,' Murdoch said.

Paul nodded. 'Then we will drive to the airfield.' He gestured towards the car, and Murdoch got in. Paul sat beside him, and the chauffeur took his place behind the wheel. It occurred to Murdoch that the young man had shown no more emotion towards the death of his father than that of his mother.

'Are you just going to leave him there?' Murdoch asked.

'It is best.'

'But . . . won't there be repercussions?'

'Of course. But none I cannot answer. My father insisted on personally escorting you from Breda. This will have been observed by my people there. Where he was taking you, I do not know. But, having reached this spot, he commanded me to let you out, with him, and return in two hours' time. I did not know his purpose. I was doubtful of it. But he was at once my father and my commanding officer, so I obeyed.'

'My God,' Murdoch said.

'When I returned, as instructed, I found my father dead. And you had disappeared. I will ask you to support this story when you regain the British lines.'

'And the chauffeur?'

'Will not betray us. He works for Count von Reger. I am now he.'

406

'Ah,' Murdoch said. He had never known such a cold-blooded man. But . . . there was warm blood in there, somewhere. His own. 'Yet you are taking a great risk,' he remarked.

'You are my father,' Paul von Reger told him.

Murdoch had no answer to that. A few minutes later they reached the airfield. By then Paul had given Murdoch his father's greatcoat to wear, and his father's cap.

'I often fly,' Paul explained. 'It is something I would do, to pass the hours until it is time to return to my father.'

His total confidence was almost frightening. He left Murdoch in the car with the chauffeur while he went off to speak to operations. Neither man said anything – they both had too much to think about – and a few minutes later Paul returned, got into the car, and they drove across the strip towards a waiting plane.

'This is called a Stuka,' Paul said. 'It is slow, but sure. We use them as dive bombers. Give the mechanic the proper salute, and then get into the rear seat, and strap yourself into the parachute.'

Murdoch obeyed, threw his arm out in front of himself and barked, 'Heil Hitler!' then climbed into the rear of the cockpit, sat down and thrust his arms through the straps of the parachute, carrying the centre one between his legs to buckle on to the belt. Paul got into the front, and the mechanic closed the Perspex hood. The chauffeur saluted and then drove away, back to the parking apron; he was apparently going to wait for his new master's return. Murdoch found the morality of this new Germany almost as frightening as their confidence in their destiny. But he would be a fool not to take advantage of it, and it was time to concentrate on the ordeal which was rushing at him.

The engine roared, and Paul taxied across the field. Seconds later they were airborne, flying south. Murdoch wondered what would happen if they were intercepted by British or French aircraft, but he presumed there was little chance of that in the darkness. Paul did not fly high, and even at night it was easy to make out the country beneath them, and what was going on. Murdoch's breath was taken away by the huge masses of armour moving along the roads to the west. His information before leaving The Hague had been that the main battles were taking place on the French border, but beneath him was more armour than he had ever seen before.

He recognized the line of the Albert Canal, and realized they were in Belgium, south of Antwerp. Antwerp was burning. And so was Brussels, judging by the glow to the south. Paul turned west, and a few minutes later they could make out the flashes of guns firing beneath them.

'That is the Dyle River,' Paul said on the intercom. 'That was the line your troops were holding. But they are pulling back.' He flew on a few minutes more, and beneath them was darkness. 'Prepare to jump,' Paul said. 'Undo your safety belt. I will do a roll and release the hood. We are two thousand feet up. Count to seven before pulling your cord. Do you understand?'

'Yes,' Murdoch said. 'May I say thank you?'

'It is my duty,' Paul said. 'We will not meet again, except in combat. I will wish you good fortune, Father.'

Before Murdoch could reply, the plane was rolling and the hood sliding back. Paul was hanging in his harness. Murdoch instinctively grabbed at the dashboard as he started to fall, then took his hands away, and counted instead. The feeling of floating through the air was mesmeric, and he discovered he had reached seven before he was really aware of it. Then he pulled the cord. For a moment nothing happened, and he wondered if he was about to die in this most bizarre of situations. Then there was a jerk on his shoulders, and he was truly floating, looking down into the darkness. He had no idea what was beneath him. The rumble of gunfire was still audible, but far to the east now.

The ground came upon him far sooner than he had expected. He saw a tree, looming out of the darkness, and tensed himself. He missed it, but then there was another tree, and he realized he was travelling to the east at quite a speed – there was a fresh westerly breeze. A cow lowed and his feet actually kicked the poor animal in the back. This helped to break his momentum, and a moment later his feet struck the ground. He ran for several yards, dragged on by the parachute, then tripped and fell. Still he was dragged, until he came up against a stile, where he was covered by the still inflated chute.

He caught his breath, feeling as if every bone in his body had been broken, and painfully began reeling in the parachute, hand over hand, taking advantage of every lull in the breeze. Fifty bloody nine, he thought, is a bit old to be taking up new pastimes as vigorous as this. But at last he got it all down, and packed against the stile, and could start taking off the belts.

Now he heard voices, speaking Walloon, he guessed, and a few minutes later two men stood over him, one armed with a shotgun and the other with a pitchfork. They looked distinctly hostile, so he struggled to his feet and took off Reger's coat.

'I am an English officer,' he said in his best French. 'Where are the nearest British troops?'

Fifteen minutes later he was having a cup of tea with the Captain of a tank squadron.

'General Mackinder!' Captain Lucas clearly could not believe his eyes. But he had been one of those, as a young second-lieutenant in the hussars, whom Murdoch had helped to retrain for armoured combat. 'By all that's holy, sir.'

'Thought I'd drop in,' Murdoch said. 'Actually, I'm on my way out of Holland.'

'Ah,' Lucas said. 'But . . .' he looked up.

'I had a friend. I'm afraid things are a little nasty up there.'

'Things are a little nasty down here too, sir. We just don't seem able to stop them. We're just pulling back all along the lines. We're told we must go back to the Scheldt tomorrow. The Belgian Government is abandoning Brussels. Well, I'll get on the radio to brigade, and arrange for you to be taken out, sir.'

409

'Wait a moment,' Murdoch said. 'You're part of the Light Brigade, aren't you?'

'Well, I suppose you could say that, sir.'

'Concentrated?'

'Well, no, sir. We've been split up into regiments to give support to the infantry as they fall back.'

Bloody fools, Murdoch thought; the only effective way to use armour was in concentrated masses, as Napoleon had taught the world how to use artillery. But he was here, and he was going to stay here, until the battle was won. If Lee would be alarmed when his plane did not reach England, she would not know he had been shot down, would presume he was at worst still in Holland. As for Ironside or Gort . . . they just did not know where he was. 'Do you know where the Royal Westerns are?'

'Yes, sir. They are about twelve miles to our south. South of Brussels.'

'Can you supply me with transport to get over there?'

'Yes, sir. But . . . don't you want to regain your command?'

'They are my command,' Murdoch told him.

'Oh. Brigadier Destry . . . '

'Is expecting me,' Murdoch said. 'My pilot just dropped me in the wrong place, that's all.'

'Ah,' Lucas said, clearly totally mystified, but not wishing to appear so before a lieutenant-general.

'My arrival should be kept secret.' Murdoch said.

'Oh, quite, sir.' Lucas was disappointed.

'So, if you can provide that transport . . . '

'It'll be a tank,' Lucas pointed out.

'Why not?'

Half an hour later he was sitting behind the driver, beside a very anxious Lieutenant, who had clearly never been so close to top brass in his life before. 'Do you know,' Murdoch confided, 'this is the first time I have ever actually driven in one of these contraptions?'

He was riding a high of exhilaration, a mixture of excitement and despair, battle fury and blood-lusting vigour such as he had not known since he had seen Chand Bibi's Mahsud army arrayed before him. He wanted to take on the whole world, and especially the whole German army, and he wanted to do so with the Westerns. That done, they could retire him. He would have fought his last battle.

He was also exhausted, and fell asleep a few minutes after the tank moved off. It bumped and rattled and stank, and every so often he half woke up, then nodded off again. He was surprised when it finally came to a halt. The hatch was opened, and he painfully climbed out, to find himself surrounded by more beret-wearing soldiers. He looked over his shoulder, saw that the glow of Brussels was now to the north.

'Good God,' he remarked. 'How long did that journey take?'

'Four hours, sir,' said the Lieutenant.

Murdoch realized that there was actually a hint of dawn fringing the darkness. He shook hands. 'Thanks. Your name?'

'Prettilove, sir.

'I'll remember it.' He faced another officer. 'Take me to Brigadier Destry.'

The young man peered at the bareheaded, dishevelled figure with the unshaven chin. 'Who the hell . . . my God!'

'Quite,' Murdoch said. 'But we'll keep Him out of it, Captain Mackinder. I want Brigadier Destry.'

Fergus looked about to faint, but he gave orders, and a few minutes later Murdoch was in a command car bouncing over what might have been a ploughed field. 'Are you all right?' Fergus asked anxiously. 'You look quite done in.'

'Nothing a few hours' sleep and a square meal won't fix,' Murdoch said.

'But . . . where on earth did you come from?'

'The Hague,' Murdoch said.

Fergus scratched his head. 'Must have been tricky. The enemy aren't all that far away. We don't seem able to stop them.'

'Well, we're going to try,' Murdoch said. 'That's why I'm here.'

411

'Sir Murdoch!' Brigadier Colin Destry shook his hand. 'By all that's holy, but it is good to see you.'

Billy Rostron was there too, and a few minutes later Major Ian Mackinder also appeared.

'And to see you, gentlemen,' Murdoch said. 'I'll have to borrow a razor and a cap, I'm afraid.'

'I'm afraid we have nothing with quite the right amount of scrambled egg on it, sir,' Rostron said.

'That's all to the good. I don't want anyone to know I'm here. Yet.'

'But . . . you mean you weren't sent to take command of the army, sir?'

Murdoch grinned at them. 'I'm a volunteer on this one, gentlemen. But . . . if you'll have me . . . '

'By God,' Destry said. 'Just show us where to go and who to fight, Sir Murdoch. We've done nothing but retreat. We have orders to pull out of here tomorrow morning and establish ourselves behind the Scheldt.'

'I heard that from the hussars. Let's have a look at the situation,' Murdoch said.

Maps were spread in front of him, with the latest German positions marked. 'But it's changing all the time,' Ian said gloomily. 'Every hour they advance still further.'

'Thus every hour they are getting more exhausted, and their machines are getting more worn out,' Murdoch reminded them. 'Show me the latest information that you have.'

Destry pointed. 'We know that Guderian's tanks are already some ninety kilometres west of Sedan. That is, actually, west of our position here at this minute. The real point is that he's ignoring Paris, and continuing to drive west. He's making for the Channel, to cut the Allied armies in two.'

'Therefore he's leaving exposed flanks,' Murdoch argued.

'You would suppose so,' Destry agreed. 'But things aren't quite what they were in 1914. These are the old Hutier tactics on a grand scale, save that they are being supported by aircraft on a grand scale too. The speed of Guderian's advance is what has taken everyone by surprise, and quite frankly, not all the French generals seem to want to fight. You heard about the Ninth Army? It just disintegrated.'

'I heard about it,' Murdoch said. 'Corap should have been cashiered.'

'He has been sacked, anyway. Giraud has taken over the command there. But it's a patchwork affair. Add to that the Stukas. They are playing merry hell behind the lines, dive bombing or shooting up everything that moves. They're letting the civilians have it too, and this of course is causing a massive panic, which hampers troop movements; every road is clogged with refugees.'

'But it doesn't hamper the Germans.'

'No,' Destry said. 'They just shoot them out of the way.'

'And the situation up here?'

'Well, we have been holding them at the Dyle. But we've been ordered to retreat to the line of the Scheldt, as you know.'

'Why, if we're holding them? Why this constant preoccupation with defence and retreat?'

Destry shrugged. 'It's a combination of several things. Tactically, I suppose HQ is anxious about Guderian getting round behind us . . .'

'One armoured column?' Murdoch snorted.

'Strategically, I believe they may be having some trouble with King Leopold, who is apparently stunned by the whole thing.'

'For God's sake, his father fought the Germans for four years, with just a scrap of Belgium unoccupied.'

'Unfortunately, this is the son,' Destry pointed out. 'But I think most important of all, psychologically, everyone seems to have the idea that the Germans are just unstoppable.'

'That is something that has to be changed, and right now. *They* know they're not unstoppable. They can't understand why they haven't been counter-attacked already. Colin, can you get me to Gort's headquarters?'

413

'Well, I should think so.' He looked at his watch. 'When it's daylight.'

Murdoch nodded. 'I could do with a few hours' sleep. And that razor.'

'You realize I am pulling out today.'

'Get me to Gort,' Murdoch said. 'But first, I would like to have a word with Private Albert Manly-Smith.'

'He's Corporal Manly-Smith, now,' Ian said.

'His mother would be proud of that,' Murdoch said.

The boy listened to the story of his mother's death with a stony expression, not overawed by the presence of a lieutenant-general; he had known Murdoch since his birth.

'We are going to beat them, sir?' he asked when Murdoch finished.

Murdoch squeezed his hand. 'We are going to beat them out of sight, Bert.'

Because he had no doubt that they would, given the chance. He slept heavily, awoke to the sound of the guns, and columns of weary and despondent infantrymen, mostly in trucks but some on foot, wending their way to the rear.

'The Germans are in Brussels,' Destry told him over coffee. 'And they've blown Middelburg in Holland flat. I thought the Dutch had surrendered.'

'Not Middelburg,' Murdoch said. Those gallant men, he thought. 'When do you leave?'

'As soon as the last of the infantry are through. We're to cover their retreat. There is some evidence that the German advance is slowing up, at least here.'

'Then now's our chance. Let's go, Colin.'

Rostron was left in command of the brigade, and Destry and Murdoch drove off to find the BEF headquarters. It took them all day, and then they discovered that Gort wasn't there, having been called to a high-level conference with the French Command. They were given beds for the night, awoke on Saturday morning to be told that Guderian had reached the Somme at Peronne, and that Antwerp had fallen. Everyone seemed in a state of shock at the continuous disasters which poured upon them.

'I don't think we're doing any good here,' Destry muttered; Murdoch was wearing an ordinary greatcoat and cap and no one had recognized him. 'I'd like to get back to brigade.'

'Hold on another ten minutes,' Murdoch said. He had seen a command car bouncing down the road, and a few minutes later Gort entered the building, looking anxious, but also pleased.

'Well, gentlemen,' he told his staff. 'One positive step has been taken, at least: General Gamelin is going to be dismissed. It will be announced tomorrow. General Weygand will take command. We have a fighting soldier at our head at last. And a fighting French cabinet; M. Reynaud is himself taking over defence. Now, let's look at these maps.'

He took in the latest situation, then one of his aides mentioned the presence of Brigadier Destry. 'Ah, Destry, he said. Murdoch remained at the back of the room. 'All going well?'

'So far as I know sir. Permission for a private interview, sir.'

Gort raised his eyebrows. Now was not the time for personal matters. 'Five minutes. Gentlemen.'

The office was cleared. The ADC looked at Murdoch closely for the first time, gulped, and turned towards the Commander-in-Chief. But Gort was already concerned with Destry. 'Speak.'

'I . . . ah . . . ' Destry also turned to look at Murdoch, who closed the door.

Gort stared at him. 'My God! You're dead.'

'Am I?' Murdoch asked, coming into the centre of the room.

'I have a report that the Lysander taking you from Holland was shot down over the North Sea, and that there were no survivors.'

'That was inaccurate. We were shot down over the Scheldt estuary, and there were three survivors. Now there are only two. Or possibly, only one. Johnnie, we have got to counter-attack these fellows.'

415

'Now, Murdoch, this isn't 1918.'

'That is exactly it. It is a totally fluid instead of a totally static situation. The Germans are almost out of control, they are advancing so fast. And I can tell you that they are scared of their own success. One check, and they will start pulling back.'

'You would like to attack with the armoured brigade.'

'Yes, I would. I believe that will end this myth of German invincibility once and for all, and completely alter the situation.'

'Are you aware that such a counter-attack was carried out yesterday by French armour, led by a colonel name de Gaulle? He tried to stop Guderian at Moncornet, but was beaten off.'

'That is no reason why we shouldn't have a go.'

'Yes.' Gort was suddenly thoughtful, as he picked up a report which had been lying on his desk. 'Yes,' he said again. 'I see that two panzer corps are being reported as moving south, behind the German lines.'

Murdoch snapped his fingers. 'To reinforce Guderian. After one, unsuccessful, counter-attack. That's how nervous they are. So that's weakened their armour here. If we now counter-attacked. they'd either crumble or send for that armour back again. We'd have them reeling.'

'Yes. Hm.' Gort stroked his chin, looked at the map. 'I'll put the idea before Weygand.'

Murdoch pounded the table. 'It has to be done now, Johnnie. Can't you give the orders?'

'We're supposed to be working with the French,' Gort pointed out. 'Give me twenty-four hours. Very good, Brigadier. Return to your command and stand by. I'll get you some action if it's humanly possible. Now, Murdoch, we must see about getting you home.'

'I'll stay with Colin,' Murdoch said.

'My dear fellow, we can't have you up in the line. You're a lieutenant-general.'

'I'm dead,' Murdoch pointed out.

'Yes, but . . .'

'Just let's leave it that way for a few more days.'

416

'But . . . your wife . . . '

Murdoch hesitated. But if Lee had been told he was dead, then the shock of discovering he was still alive would be as great in a week's time as today. And to tell her that he was alive now, and then that he had been killed in battle in a week's time – as could easily happen – would cause far greater distress. 'No one,' he said. 'Until we've sorted this out.'

Gort sighed, and pointed. 'You have no command, and no officer will take any orders from you, Murdoch.' He looked at Colin Destry. 'Understood?'

'Yes, sir.'

'And no action is to be undertaken without specific orders from me,' Gort said. 'Understood?'

'Yes, sir.'

'Then I'll pretend you didn't come here today, Murdoch.' Gort shook hands. 'For God's sake don't get yourself killed twice. If I am allowing you to stay, it's as an observer, nothing more.'

Murdoch grinned at him. 'It's the best way to get killed, twice.'

He sat beside Destry in the back of the command car. 'He didn't say anything about advice, now did he, Colin?'

The brigade, consisting of the Westerns, the hussars, and the lancers, had by now re-established itself, with the rest of the army, behind the Scheldt, which left them really a very small corner of Belgium to hold, together with the Belgian army and the French First. But the position looked defensible, and as Murdoch told Ian and Fergus, after a tour of the brigade, 'We're better off than in 1915, at least.'

Yet the news continued to be bad. While Weygand's appointment was made public, that same day the French Ninth Army was again scattered, and its commander, General Giraud, taken prisoner. That was on the British right, and the Germans stormed through St Quentin. Murdoch hardly slept that night, fretting and waiting for orders to attack, but there were none, and next day news came that Guderian's panzers were in Abbeville, at the mouth of the Somme, and the Allied armies had indeed been cut in two.

At last that night the orders came for the brigade to move south as rapidly as possible and link up with the French armour in an attempt to cut Guderian's now very long lines of communication. This had apparently been decided at a conference between Weygand, King Leopold and General Billotte, the new French commander in the north; Gort had been unable to get to the meeting in time, but he had accepted the plan, which had been in any event partly based on Murdoch's recommendations, although it was not in the direction he had suggested, against the weakened northern wing of the German panzers – the real urgency was now to reopen communication between the severed halves of the Allied command.

Murdoch was just happy to be attacking, in any direction. The three tank regiments moved south under cover of darkness, passing retreating Belgian troops as they did so; the Belgian officers told them they had been ordered to take up new positions on the line of the Yser, behind the Scheldt. As the Yser was the very last river position before the beaches of the North Sea, it seemed to reveal that the Belgians had very little hope of an Allied success in the coming counter-stroke.

'We'll have to show them different,' Murdoch said to Ian, with whom he was sharing a tank. It was the oddest form of warfare he had ever known, the clanking, grinding noise of the machines, the stench of petrol, the constant chatter of the low-range VHF radio sets with which each vehicle was equipped – and yet the feeling of immense power with which one was surrounded.

'It gets to you,' Ian agreed. 'But do you know, Dad, we have never actually taken these things into action? I mean, properly?'

'Tomorrow,' Murdoch said.

At dawn they reached the village north of Lille which had been appointed as their rendezvous. This was very familiar territory to Murdoch; he had retreated through these coalfields with the regiment in 1914, desperately fighting off the masses of Germans coming down from the north. Now he was going to try to fight off masses of Germans coming up from the south!

At the village there was a freshly constructed fuel dump, guarded by a company of French poilus under an anxious captain, and they were able to fill their tanks. Here too there should have been, according to the schedule they had been given, those elements of the French First Army which were to carry out the northern attack, while the rest came up from the south. But they found no one at all, save for a guard and a few frightened civilians – and there weren't many of them, as the majority had fled before the German advance.

'I wish I knew what the devil is going on,' Colin Destry complained. The two hundred and fifty-odd tanks were halted beneath a large stand of trees, and thus somewhat sheltered from the air, but enemy planes had flown overhead just on dawn, and although they had not stopped to strafe – they were clearly hurrying back to base to refuel – the brigade could not doubt they had been spotted. Now the feeling of being abandoned was very strong. Destry sent Ian down into Lille itself to try to raise GHQ, but all telephone communication was out, and they could not make radio contact; although the Germans had by-passed Lille in their charge for the sea, Ian reported that the infantry battalion holding the town seemed to be just waiting to surrender to the appropriate authority.

'Total defeatism,' Destry grumbled. 'We don't have a hope in hell with allies like that.'

'They'll get some guts back when we win a victory,' Murdoch promised him. 'Where the hell is the rest of the armour?'

The hour for the attack came and went, with no sign of any support, and no sound of firing from the south to suggest that the other half of the counter-stroke had commenced action. Although they were sure they could hear the sound of a large number of engines to the east of them, which was not reassuring. Destry dispatched four tanks on reconnaissance, but before they returned, just after lunch, a motorcycle dispatch rider arrived, covered in mud and dust.

Destry took the envelope, opened it, read it, and looked at the corporal. 'When were you given this?'

'Dawn, sir. But I had a breakdown, and then there was a Stuka raid . . . ' he stood to attention.

Destry looked at Murdoch. 'The attack was cancelled last night,' he said.

'Cancelled? In the name of God, why?' Murdoch demanded.

'In the name of that bloody awful luck which is hounding us,' Destry said miserably. 'It seems that Weygand, Billotte and Gort met yesterday afternoon to coordinate their plans. After they split up, Billotte was driving to his headquarters when his car skidded, went off the road and rolled over. The General is in hospital in a coma as a result of head injuries.'

'Holy Christ! But doesn't he have a second-in-command?'

'General Blanchard. But Blanchard had been told nothing of the offensive, and the French armour has not moved. Lord Gort only found out this morning. Weygand suggested he carry out the attack on his own, but we just don't have the machines.'

'So?' Murdoch demanded.

'So we are ordered to withdraw as quickly as possible, before we are cut off. Those planes we saw this morning definitely reported our movements, and there is German armour to the east of us, moving north-west.'

They both turned to look east. The noise was, if anything, north of east now.

'God damn,' Murdoch said. 'But it looks as if we had better obey, Colin.'

Destry gave the orders immediately. The other two regiments pulled out first, with half an hour between each one. The Westerns formed the rearguard, as they had formed the advance guard of the southern movement, and they allowed the hussars a half hour start too. While they were waiting they saw the reconnaissance tanks hurrying

420

back towards them, rolling across the fields and ditches in great haste.

Their hatches were open, and Fergus was leaning out of one. 'German armour,' he shouted as the machines ground to a halt. 'Maybe a division. Huge bloody things. They're not more than three miles away, moving along the road parallel to ours.'

Certainly the noise from the east was tremendous.

'Did they see you?'

'I'm damned sure they did, but they ignored us.'

Destry and Murdoch looked at the map. 'There,' Murdoch said. 'They're making for that crossroads.'

'If they get there first . . . '

'We'll have to shoot our way through.'

'A regiment? Against a division?'

Murdoch grinned. 'We don't have any choice. You weren't thinking of surrendering, I hope, Colin?'

Destry swallowed. 'Dispositions?'

Murdoch raised his eyebrows. 'Or advice?'

'I would be very happy for you to take command, General. After all, you are our Colonel-in-Chief.'

Murdoch gave another savage grin. 'All right. Those bastards are no different to the Turks or the Mahsuds.' Or the Somalis, he thought. 'Survival. That is the name of the game. Fergus, fuel your machines, and then fire that dump; no point in concealing our presence now. Colin, we head north. But we turn off and cut through them when the enemy approach.'

'Yes, sir!'

The orders were given, the tanks manned. The French Captain hurried across to Murdoch. 'You cannot fire that dump, mon Général,' he protested. 'I have no orders permitting that.'

'You do,' Murdoch told him. 'I have just given them to you.'

The officer stood to attention. 'I must have orders from General Billotte.'

'General Billotte isn't giving any orders today. And we haven't the time to waste. Take your people and stand clear,

Captain, or go up with it. Lieutenant Mackinder, when you are ready.'

'Yes, sir,' Fergus said. The four reconnaissance vehicles were refuelled, and while the French soldiers watched in consternation shells were pumped into the fuel dump, which exploded with a huge whumpff! sending a pillar of black smoke high into the sky.

'That'll bring them on,' Murdoch said, standing in the turret of the command tank, and surveying the regiment as it swung on to the road. His regiment, he thought proudly. His men.

He sent twelve tanks out as an advance guard under Captain Soames, left twelve as a rearguard under Fergus. The remainder formed column on the road and opened their throttles, bouncing over the rutted surface. His own tank was in the lead, followed by Destry's, then Rostron's, then Ian's; the rest were under the command of their squadron commanders. They had travelled about four miles when they heard shots from in front of them, and Soames broke radio silence to report that he was approaching the crossroads and in sight of about twenty enemy tanks. This was obviously the German advance guard.

'Maintain contact,' Murdoch commanded. 'But move away to the west, gradually. Major Mackinder,' he said into his mike, 'take the remainder of C Squadron, and pull out of the column to the west. Move north and link up with Captain Soames, then turn east again and engage the German advanced units. Fight your way through them and then rejoin our main body. Understood?'

'Yes, sir!' Ian's voice was excited.

'Colonel Rostron, form your remaining squadrons into two lines, and follow me. Our objective is to smash through the neck of the enemy forces, disrupt him, and gain open country beyond. Understood?'

'Yes, sir,' Rostron replied.

'Captain Mackinder, bring your rearguard across country to the east of the column as rapidly as possible. Understood?'

'Yes, sir!' Fergus's voice was more faint.

422

'Brigadier Destry, you will remain at my shoulder,' Murdoch said. 'You will take command should it prove necessary. You know my intention. It is to suggest to the enemy that we are retreating to the west, as he will expect us to do, but to break through his column with maximum effect. We cannot destroy such a large force, but we can damage his morale. And escape ourselves. Understood?'

'Yes, sir,' Colin replied.

Murdoch ducked down into the interior of the tank, next to Lieutenant Munro. 'I want you to alter course to the right,' he said. 'Leave the road and advance across country.' He looked at the compass. 'Steer oh two oh.'

'Oh two oh. But sir . . . ' he gulped. 'That'll take us through the enemy main body.'

'That,' Murdoch told him, 'is the idea.'

He stood in the hatch again, as the tank swing off the road, lumbered through the ditch and then moved on to the meadow bordering the highway. This stretched for perhaps half a mile, before there was one of the low ridges which are so typical of the Flanders countryside. To one side of the ridge was the slag heap of a recently abandoned coal mine. Surrounded as he was by tank engines he could hear no other vehicles, but he could hear cannon fire as Soames withdrew to the north-west.

He looked over his shoulder; Ian's tanks were rolling across the fields on the left-hand side of the road, making directly towards the engagement. Behind him, the sixty tanks of the main body had formed two lines and were also leaving the road. Behind them again he could see Fergus's twelve machines racing up to take their places. He looked forward, at the ridge, as they began to climb.

The tank topped the rise, and he could see into the next valley, and a sight he had never expected to witness in person. Below him the main body of the German division, some five hundred tanks, were hurrying to gain the crossroads, but still on the road, in single file; they stretched back as far as the eye could see. To the left, some fifty of them had deployed across the fields in hot pursuit of Soames' advance guard, which was conducting a fighting withdrawal; there were three fiercely burning vehicles, but Murdoch could not immediately tell whether or not they were British.

The tank was descending, and with a roar the first squadron of the Westerns gained the ridge behind it. Murdoch looked down at the handset he still held, and grinned. This was modern warfare, mechanized, grim, unromantic and horrifying. But he was Murdoch Mackinder, and this was his regiment. He flicked the switch.

'Dragoons,' he said. 'This is your Colonel-in-Chief speaking. I wish you to join me in prayer.' He waited a moment, then continued: 'May the great God of battle, who has guided the fate of this famous regiment on many a hard-fought field, and never failed to lead it to distinction, grant that on this day, faced as we are with a host of enemies of our King and our Country, every man will do his duty, so that should we fail in our ordained task, it will yet be said of us, they were the Royal Western Dragoon Guards, who fought and died according to the ancient valour of their regiment and their blood.' He raised his arm. 'Gentlemen, there is your enemy.'

He had no idea what the Germans thought of it, but the radio trembled and the dragoons cheered. Murdoch dropped through the hatch and closed it above him. 'She's all yours,' he told Munro. 'Just keep her on course.'

The Germans had seen them and were swinging off the road to face the threat to their flanks, but they had been caught napping in their supposition that obviously the British regiment would attempt to withdraw to the west, round the head of their column, rather than engage so superior a force.

'Fire as you bear, Mr Munro,' Murdoch said.

Munro was already lost in his rangefinder. 'Shoot,' he said, and the thirty-seven-millimetre gun roared. Murdoch had never been inside a tank when the gun had been fired and for a moment he supposed he had gone deaf, while the stench was suffocating.

Munro seemed unaffected. 'High,' he muttered, fiddling with his instrument. 'Shoot!'

Murdoch got his eyes adjusted and peered through the narrow slit in front of him. He could see about a dozen of the German tanks, and watched their gun muzzles flame as they fired, but equally as he watched one of them developed a much larger flame and half slewed to the right, one track shot off and smoke issuing from inside.

'Brewed the bugger,' Munro said with some satisfaction.

Murdoch felt vaguely sick as he watched a man emerge from the hatch, his clothes on fire, and fall heavily to the ground, while flames were now issuing from inside the tank as well. None of the crew had had a chance. And it could happen to them. Anything less like the glorious impetus of a cavalry charge could hardly be imagined.

But Munro was shooting again and again, as was the entire regiment, while to the left Ian's troop had swung in to join Soames and was taking on the German advance guard on almost equal terms, crumpling it up with the fury of their assault.

And suddenly, in front of him, was open country. He threw up the hatch and looked back. Only a third of the Germans had deployed in time, and they had been smashed through by the Westerns. Most of the Westerns. He watched the British ranks rolling behind him, and counted desperately. There were about fifty of them. This meant at least ten had been knocked out. He didn't dare allow himself to wonder which ones.

The Germans were turning in pursuit, but they would know that they were now closing the rest of the British brigade, and indeed Murdoch suddenly saw in front of him a body of tanks topping the next rise. For a moment his heart stopped, then he recognized the hussars, who had heard the sound of firing and turned back.

'Munro,' he said. 'Turn this machine. Let's have another whack. Brigadier Destry! Brigadier Destry!' There was no reply. 'Colonel Rostron!'

'Yes, sir.'

'We have support. Let's have another go.'

'Yes, sir.'

All the Westerns were now turning, and Ian and Soames

425

were bringing their forces down as rapidly as possible. The enemy had also gained the north side of the road by now, and for a few minutes there was a furious mêlée, but the Germans, as Murdoch had estimated, had had it too easy on their drive through France. The vigour and determination of the British attack, as well as the accuracy of their shooting, was too daunting, and soon those enemy tanks actually engaged, began to pull out of the battle and withdraw towards their main force, which was still hurrying up from the east.

'Do we pursue, sir?' Rostron asked.

'How's your fuel?'

'Not too good. But . . . '

'These God damned things aren't horses,' Murdoch said. We've proved our point, Colonel. And the rest of that division is coming up fast. Brigade will continue its withdrawal to the north west.'

Now at last he could ask for the casualty list.

The ADC looked at the card and gulped. 'Acting Brigadier Lieutenant-General Sir Murdoch Mackinder, sir,' he read.

'For God's sake, Murdoch,' Gort hurried forward to shake his hand. 'That was an utterly brilliant action.'

'If I had had a full division . . . '

'You'd be in Berlin. I don't doubt it for a moment. Casualties?'

'Twelve lost in battle. Brewed up, the lads call it. Makes one shiver. Four lost to the air attack we had to take on just before dusk. But I estimate we knocked out nineteen Germans. Oh, and two Messerschmitts.'

'That'll make good reading for the papers. God knows they are going to need it. Destry?'

'Didn't make it.'

'Rostron?'

'All right.'

'Ian Mackinder?'

'All right.'

'Very good. Promote Rostron to Brigadier, Ian Mackinder to Colonel.'

Murdoch nodded.

'I suppose Fergus is all right?' Gort asked.

'Yes.'

'Quite something, three members of one family in one battle. You realize that, as I intend to give this to the newspapers, your survival will now become known.'

Murdoch nodded. 'Lee'll forgive me.'

'I'm sure she will. And my aim is to get you back to her as soon as possible. Make those depositions and then return here. I'll have a plane standing by to fly you to England.'

'Now, Johnnie, if you don't mind, I'll stay here. As an observer, dammit.'

Gort's face was sombre. 'You are going to have nothing to observe, Murdoch, except disaster. King Leopold has informed GHQ that he intends to surrender Belgium.'

'To do what?' Murdoch shouted. 'But he can't do that.'

'Unfortunately, he can. I know it is against the wishes of his own government, but he is Commander-in-Chief.'

'And where does that leave us?'

'Up the proverbial creek without a paddle. We're cut off from the south, and we have no support here, except for the French First. Oh, the navy is saying they'll try to evacuate as many men as they can, and I've orders from home to form a perimeter around Dunkirk – it's the only usable port still in our hands – to enable an evacuation to begin. But I don't think we have a hope in hell.'

'And you expect me to leave the regiment now?'

'Murdoch, there is nothing to stay for.'

'Oh, yes there is,' Murdoch said. 'Jerry might just give us another crack at his armour.'

'So there it is,' he told Rostron and his officers. 'We make a slow, fighting retreat to the south-west, allowing the infantry to move ahead of us and reach the port.'

'Bloody Belgians,' someone muttered.

'I think the Belgian army is as disgusted as we are,' Murdoch said. 'But there's damn all they can do about it, either. Billy, you're in command.'

Rostron didn't look all that happy. 'And you, sir?'

427

'I'm an observer.'

He brightened. 'Then you'll give the orders, sir.'

'Very good. Have your vehicles fuelled and re-armed. If any armoured column shows its nose on that river bank, we are going to shoot the shit out of it.'

But amazingly, while there were certainly Germans in strength on the east bank of the river, there was no armour. Murdoch knew he could probably cross and drive the infantry away, but that would be to expose himself to a counter-attack, and to an air strike – there were sufficient of those as it was. He wanted to preserve his strength for when the panzers tried to break through.

They withdrew to the Lys, as ordered, followed at a cautious distance by the Germans. When they reached their new position they found only half rations waiting for them. 'Jerry struck our dump,' said the RASC Brigadier.

'God damn,' Murdoch commented.

'Doesn't look too good,' Ian said as he shared their meagre dinner.

'Seems there's quite a show going on in Dunkirk,' Murdoch said. Indeed they could see and hear the constant air battles over the port, now only a few miles distant, as the Luftwaffe tried to destroy the navy ships coming in to the harbour. 'But they're getting men off.'

'Not the rearguard,' Ian said. He was thinking of Annaliese – and the son he had never seen: Ian Mackinder the Third.

'Well . . .' but Murdoch had little cheer to offer. He was going to be a prisoner of war after all. Paul would shrug and think: Damned fool.

But until then, he would fight, and fight. It was the only thing he did really well, he thought ruefully. And it would help to avenge Jennie. He could not understand why the full weight of the German armour was not being thrown against them; for all the feeling that machine for machine, and man for man, his people had proved they were as good as the Germans, he knew that the enemy could now bring an immense superiority to bear. But the only attacks were by infantry units, easily driven off, and designed, he felt sure, just to keep them moving back rather than to destroy them. That was apparently being left to the Luftwaffe.

He lost track of days. It had been Thursday, 23 May, when he had seen Gort. The Belgian surrender was actually not announced until the following Tuesday, and was immediately repudiated by the Government, but it took effect just the same. The following day Lord Gort came up to see them for the last time.

'How's it going?' Murdoch asked.

'Touch and go. We've got more than sixty thousand men out, but it's costing. Three destroyers, and fifteen other vessels, so far. Mind you, they're coming from all over the place. I have never seen so many ships. You name it, yachts, trawlers, anything that floats. Murdoch, I've been ordered to leave.'

'Well, of course. We can't risk the commanding general being taken prisoner.'

'Quite. I have orders to take you with me.'

'Forget it.'

'Murdoch, you are senior to me, in terms of service. You are also our most famous fighting soldier. More famous than ever now. The Government can't risk you, either, being taken prisoner.'

'Are you going to arrest me?'

'I'm tempted, believe me. But I am instructed to inform you that if you do not leave now, as of this moment you are retired and are a civilian.'

Murdoch grinned at him. 'Well, that's that. You certainly can't offer an itinerant civilian a place on your plane.' He held out his hand. 'Godspeed.'

Gort squeezed the fingers. 'Murdoch! Why? You have a wife and family. And enough fame to last five men five lifetimes.'

'This is my regiment, Johnnie. You don't really expect me to walk away from them when they're up against it.'

'No,' Gort said. He saluted. 'Godspeed, General.'

That night they were instructed to fall back again. They had now crossed the Lys, and the thunder of the guns from

429

Dunkirk were continuous. The Germans were now in Ostend, as well as Lille and Ypres; news came that Calais had fallen. But still there was no all-out assault on the British rearguards. The brigade held their positions for another twenty-four hours, but early on Friday morning they were visited by Major-General Harold Alexander, who had taken command of the evacuation.

'You have done your duty, gentlemen,' he told Brigadier Rostron. 'Now it's time for you to get to the beaches. Make sure every tank and every piece of equipment is destroyed, and then pull out. The route is marked by MPs.'

They stared at him. 'Destroy our tanks?' Murdoch asked.

'Yes, General Mackinder, sir. They cannot be taken off, only men can be saved. And your equipment must not be left in any shape which can be utilized by the Germans. I will expect the brigade to be on the beach by tomorrow morning.'

His command car bounced away, and Murdoch stared at his officers in consternation.

'That's it, then,' Ian said. 'We are licked. We no longer exist as a unit.'

'They'll give us new tanks, in England,' Fergus said.

'When we get there,' Rostron commented.

'If,' Ian growled.

'We have orders,' Murdoch told them. 'So we carry them out.'

They couldn't take any of the ammunition either, so they destroyed their own tanks by gunfire, taking turns at shooting into the abandoned vehicles. It was good, heartbreaking practice. The German infantry joined in, no doubt supposing that a battle had mysteriously broken out amongst the retreating Allies, and a few shells were sent off in their direction. But by evening every tank in the brigade was a burned-out ruin. Murdoch could only reflect that it was a saving grace they were not still horse cavalry: to have had to destroy the entire brigade's mounts would have been just about psychologically impossible.

430

They set off for the beach, a long column of dispirited men. Rostron led, with Murdoch at his shoulder, and Ian behind him. The squadron commanders each marched with their men. They followed the road, first marching for an hour then stopping for ten minutes. Each man carried only a rifle and haversack – there was precious little food in the haversack.

By dawn they were within sight of the sea, and a sight which none of them could ever have envisaged in their wildest nightmares. The surface of the water, fortunately calm, was covered with boats of, as Gort had said, every size and description, some lying off, others close to the shore. Towards the boats columns of khaki-clad men were wading, up to as deep as their shoulders, to be hauled on board. Other columns waited patiently on the beach. To the left the rooftops and spires of Dunkirk could be seen, surrounded by smoke and flames; larger ships were constantly entering and leaving through the breakwaters.

Overhead was a continuous swirl of planes and vapour trails, both German and British. But the battle wasn't only going on overhead. Whenever allowed to do so, the Germans were swooping over the beaches and strafing or bombing the waiting troops. The scattered corpses and the occasional burned-out trawler or yacht testified to their accuracy. Yet the men on the beach and the small boats on the sea gave no sign of being under attack, proceeded about their work with a massive calm.

There was a military police sergeant waiting for them. 'You'll keep your people in the dunes, sir, if you will,' he said. 'Until we're ready for them. Beach is a little restricted at the moment.' He grinned. 'Don't want to make it easy for Jerry, do we?'

Murdoch looked up at the Messerschmitts, some of them hardly a hundred feet up, it seemed. 'Can we pot those fellows?' he asked. 'Just to pass the time.'

'Why not, sir. Sir?' The man saw Murdoch's shoulder straps. 'Sir!'

'Forget it,' Murdoch told him. 'I'm a civilian.'

★

431

They crouched amongst the dunes, but still presented a target, several hundred men. The Messerschmitts swooped low over them, and the dragoons opened up with their rifles. It was like 1918 all over again, only worse. The Messerschmitts were far faster and more heavily armed than the old Fokkers, and while none were hit their screaming cannon tore great holes in the sand and grass, and in men.

'It's sheer bloody murder,' Rostron growled. 'We might as well be on the beach.'

The officers and medical staff crawled around the men, keeping up morale as best they could, tending the wounded, praying for either darkness or orders. It was a bitter business, being shot at and not being able effectively to reply, and Murdoch could understand some of the panic which had set in amongst the French troops earlier in the campaign. The morale of even the Westerns suffered, their misery exacerbated by the scream of the Stukas and their shortage of rations. By midday they were out of water and soon after that of food as well.

Murdoch found Corporal Manly-Smith. 'We showed them what we could do, sir,' the boy said.

'We did, Bert. And we'll show them again. Your mother would be proud.'

'What a bloody way to end a war,' Ian remarked as he and his father and Fergus sat together, waiting to be hit: there was no further shelter to be had.

'This isn't the end,' Murdoch told him. 'This is just the beginning.'

At last, at four thirty, the MP returned. 'Time to move off, sir,' he said cheerfully. The lines of men on the beach didn't look any the less, but the numbers sprawled on the sand had grown.

'Let's go,' Rostron said, waving his arm. The dragoons got to their feet, carrying their wounded. Some thirty remained lying amidst the dunes.

They made their way down the beach, grateful for a temporary lull in the air attack; the Germans seemed to be refuelling. But if the dunes had been bad, the beach was worse. There was no wind, and the evacuation had now been going on for some four days, with no time to bury the dead or dig latrines.

'God,' Fergus remarked. 'Have you ever smelt anything like it?'

'Yes,' Murdoch told him. 'In the trenches, in 1915.'

The MP was marching in front of them, down the slope towards the sea, where they were to join an already existing line of men. They took their places behind these, the officers moving back to the rear of their own column, to urge the men on and make sure there were no stragglers.

'You really should go first, Sir Murdoch,' Rostron said, and grinned. 'You don't want to forget you're a civilian.'

'That means I'm doubly expendable,' Murdoch said.

He stood between Ian and Fergus, watched General Alexander stamping across the sand towards them. 'Won't be long now, Sir Murdoch,' he said. 'I imagine you'll be glad to get home.'

'Why, yes,' Murdoch said. 'I'll see you there, I hope.'

'So do I,' Alexander said debonairly, and marched off to speak with the next column. Poor devil, Murdoch thought; as commander of the evacuation he would have to be the last man on the beach.

They listened to the drone of the planes returning. The men looked up, and one or two left the ranks.

'Steady there, lads,' Rostron called. 'This is your only way out.'

Murdoch felt an odd sensation, looked down, and realized he was up to his ankles in gentle surf. The column actually was moving, although it hardly seemed obvious.

'Oh, Christ,' Fegus muttered, and he looked along the beach. A Messerschmitt was flying low, strafing. The sand erupted to either side of the bullets, as if a giant drill was coming towards them. The dragoons watched it, and the plane passed not more than fifty feet over their heads. Its cannon had cut a neat swathe through the column, and five men were lying in the shallow water. One was alternately screaming and choking.

433

Stretcher bearers hurried forward; two of the casualties were only wounded.

'Sheer bloody murder,' Ian growled, echoing Rostron. They were up to their knees, and then another aircraft was swooping low. Now the water itself was leaping as though under the impact of heavy rain. Murdoch watched it coming closer. One never hears the bullet which kills one. The oldest essential piece of knowledge in the business. But one can watch it coming. He felt no pain, just a sudden deadness in one of his legs, and then a shortness of breath and he was under the water.

Hands grabbed him and brought him back to the surface, and he realized he was in Ian's arms. 'Okay, Dad, okay,' Ian said.

Murdoch rested on his son's shoulder, put his legs down. One had no feeling and he nearly fell again, and Fergus caught his other arm. He watched the water around him discolouring with blood. But now they were nearly up to one of the boats, and hands were helping the men in front of them on board. 'Get on,' he told Fergus. 'I'll be all right.'

'Yes,' Ian told his younger brother. 'Get on.'

'We'll get on together,' Fergus said. They were against the boat now, and he was being drawn up. He turned to reach down. 'Give me your hands, Dad.'

'Sorry, soldier,' said the fisherman. 'We're full.' There were men lying or sitting on every inch of deck.

'But . . . that man is wounded,' Fergus shouted.

'So are a lot of the chaps on board,' the fisherman said. 'There'll be another boat along in a minute.'

The engine was already growling and the propeller turning. Murdoch saw Fergus making ready to jump back into the sea. 'Don't be a chump,' he shouted. 'I'll be all right. Stay with your men.'

Fergus hesitated, and the trawler drew away.

'Let's hope he's quick,' Ian said. 'The next bloke.'

Murdoch agreed; there was an awful lot of blood in the water. Talk about stuck pigs, he thought.

There were more men behind them now, waiting patiently. 'Looks like you're hurt, mate,' one of them said.

'Yes,' Ian and Murdoch said together.

'Here he comes,' said another, and they saw a once sleek fifty-foot motor cruiser approaching. A Messerschmitt saw it too, and came screaming down, but its bullets missed on this occasion and then the yacht was up to them.

'Let's hurry,' said the man in a blue jacket and white yachting cap. 'That chappie may come back.'

'Take the General,' Ian gasped.

There were three men on board the yacht. Two of them grasped Murdoch's arms, while Ian and another man pushed from underneath, and they got him on deck.

'Bandages,' said the skipper. 'He's hurt.'

'So's this one,' said the soldier, and Ian was passed up. Murdoch sat up, to look from the rent in his trousers through which blood was seeping to the mass of blood that was Ian's tunic. His heart constricted, and he reached for his son's hand.

'Bloody cold, once you're out of the water,' Ian said, and died.

'Oh, Murdoch,' Lee said. 'Oh, Murdoch!'

He smiled at her from the hospital bed. 'I made a right cock-up of everything, didn't I?'

She wore black, and even her make-up couldn't hide the tear stains or the dark shadows. 'You fought like Murdoch Mackinder. All the papers are full of how you defeated that German armoured column.' She sighed. 'And Ian fought like your son.'

'Fergus?'

'Fergus is fine. But feeling so guilty at having left you.'

'Neither of us realized Ian had been shot too,' Murdoch said. 'I am so proud of those boys. How is Annaliese taking it?'

'Remarkably well. She keeps looking at young Ian, as though she can see his father. The odd thing is, he looks just like you. I have a suspicion she's actually suffering from shock. But I guess she'll get over it.'

I wonder, Murdoch thought. Problems ahead. But when

were there no problems ahead? 'We'll have to tell her both her parents are dead.'

'Both?' Lee frowned at him.

Murdoch told her.

'Holy Jesus,' she said. 'When that gets in the papers . . . British general kills German general in duel . . . '

'It's not going to get into the papers,' Murdoch told her. 'That would be a betrayal of young Paul.'

'Um. He stood by and watched his mother shot.'

'I know. I think he was confused, and dominated by his father. And he's a Nazi. But he's courageous, and he's honest. And he saved my life.'

'And for that, I'll always love him. I guess you have reason to be proud of all your sons. I've heard from Harry.'

'Brother or son?'

'Son.'

'Oh, yes.'

'Murdoch, he's joined the United States Army.'

Murdoch turned his head.

'Fact,' she said, and squeezed his hand. 'He is a Mackinder, after all.'

'A doughboy,' Murdoch said. But he grinned. 'I'll write him.'

'Oh, Murdoch, will you? I'd be so happy.'

Sister came in. 'I'm afraid your husband will really have to rest now, Lady Mackinder.'

'Oh. Yes.' Lee got up, hesitated, flushed. 'I saw young Bert,' she said. 'He's on leave down in the village. I'm terribly sorry about Jennie.'

'So am I. About everything.'

She gazed at him. 'I loved that girl, Murdoch. Did you?'

He looked into her eyes. 'I think I probably did.' He found her fingers again. 'An old man's madness. Can you forgive me?'

She kissed him. 'I wanted it to happen, I think. For both your sakes. I . . . I didn't want her to die.'

'Neither did I,' Murdoch said. Neither of them, he thought.

★

436

It was not every day the Prime Minister visited a hospital; Sister was in a panic of straightening sheets, and patients.

'Are you comfortable?' Churchill asked.

'I was, until it was learned you were coming,' Murdoch said.

'How long are you going to be here?'

'Another week.'

'And then there'll be convalescence,' Churchill remarked.

'Yes. But not too long. The thigh was really only gashed by the bullet.'

'Good. We need you, Murdoch.'

'Don't tell me you're giving me a command?'

'Of what?' Churchill asked. 'Oh, everyone is calling Dunkirk a miracle. So it was, a miracle of guts and hard work. But it was also one of the most resounding defeats ever suffered by the British army. We got off more than three hundred thousand men, two thirds of them British, the rest French and Belgian. But we left all our equipment behind.'

'Don't remind me,' Murdoch said. 'But those men are battle hardened, Winston. They know we can lick the Nazis, given the equipment.'

'So do I. But we have to gather the equipment. That's going to take a long time. Meanwhile, Hitler is master of Europe. You'll have heard France has surrendered?'

'I heard,' Murdoch said. 'It's us against the field now, is it?'

'It was like that against Bonaparte, and we won. We have our ideas. We can't let that man sleep easy, Murdoch. I can't put an army into the field against him, right now, but I can certainly prick him as often as possible. And there are sufficient people in the occupied countries who want to help us to do that. Will you take command of that operation?'

'Secret service, Winston? Not my style.'

'Not secret service, Murdoch. We have one of those already. Secret *warfare*, against the enemy. I would have thought it was just your style. Nothing but the offensive.'

437

'Well . . . ' But it was a command. A fighting command. 'Sounds as if it could be. I'll have to learn.'

'I have the men to teach you. So get well, fairly quickly.' He stood up. 'Oh, by the way, we're giving Ian a posthumous VC.'

'Thank you,' Murdoch said.

'He deserved it. He must have known he was dying, all the time he was supporting you in the water. You have sons to be proud of, Murdoch.'

Yes, Murdoch thought. All of them.